Immortal Wounds

A Doctor Nora Kelly Mystery

Kate Scannell

The Staff at Mountain View —
thank you,
from a real fan.

Kate Scannell

WORD HAVEN MEDIA, INC

ALSO BY KATE SCANNELL

NONFICTION
Death of the Good Doctor—
Lessons from the Heart of the AIDS Epidemic

FICTION
Flood Stage–A Novel

First Edition, 2018. Word Haven Media, INC

Cover and interior design by Maureen Forys
Cover photo by MRaust/iStockphoto

Library of Congress-In-Publication Data available on request

ISBN: 978-1-7325714-0-2 (print)
ISBN: 978-1-7325714-1-9 (epub)

For Diane

The instruments of darkness tell us truths.

WILLIAM SHAKESPEARE

A man that studieth revenge, keeps his own wounds green.

FRANCIS BACON

ACKNOWLEDGMENTS

THIS BOOK would not have come into being without the steady encouragement and vital support of Diane Buczek. I am deeply grateful to many beloved friends who offered important suggestions and criticisms. Many thanks to close readers who good-naturedly read through multiple drafts of this book: Susan Riter, Leslie Larson, Leslie Lopato, and Ruth Palmer. My heartfelt gratitude to friends who commented on earlier drafts: Michelle Paymar, Jean Kaufman, Véronique Martinaud, and Andrée Abecassis. And for her unfailing patience and thoughtful editing, I am grateful to Elizabeth Campbell.

All the characters, institutions, commercial entities, and events portrayed in this book are entirely fictional, and any mistakes are entirely my own.

And yet ...

While the events and conversations in this book are entirely fictional, they are not entirely implausible—at least not to me, both as a physician and a patient. So, in writing this mystery, I also wish to acknowledge healthcare workers and patients who heroically participate in ethically complex life-and-death interactions that occur in hospitals every day, often behind the curtain, and often without neat resolutions. They are the inspiration for this book, at the heart of this mystery.

CONTENTS

Part I

Two Deaths,
One Funeral

FEBRUARY 6

CFO Richard Pulaski's Office

10ᵗʰ Floor, Oakland City Hospital

8:55 A.M.

THE PHONE KEPT RINGING, but the hospital's chief financial officer wasn't answering. The call went to voicemail, and an angry message blared: "Pulaski, where are the numbers you were supposed to give me before the goddamn meeting in *five minutes*?"

Three minutes later, there was a second call. "Where the fuck are you, Pulaski? You got a lot of gall for someone facing fraud and embezzlement."

Richard Pulaski's head rested on a stack of spreadsheets, facing an office window that offered a panoramic view of the East Bay hills. It was breathtaking—while he'd been alive. Lingering raindrops shimmered on the window's aluminum frame.

The phone rang again.

But, as of yesterday, CFO Richard Pulaski no longer answered to bullying lawyers or snarky members of the hospital board. He was forever freed from his daily battles with grim state regulators as he tried to restore his once-stellar reputation.

His fraught quest for redemption had ended with thudding finality.

ER

Such a glorious morning!

At least that's what Dr. Nora Kelly willed herself to believe as she stepped into the ER to begin her workday—her knee-length white coat crisply pressed, her sensible black pumps shining.

I am ready for work! To heal, to cure, to raise the dead!

(One can always hope.)

She then dutifully submitted to the therapeutic routine prescribed by her frustrated psychotherapist. Scanning the ER, she attempted to generate a self-revitalizing charge before her shift started. She instructed her flagging spirit to *buck up!* and become attuned to the resuscitating rhythms of life that surrounded her—the cacophony of the cardiac monitors, sirens screaming in the ambulance bay, and the head nurse barking commands to her aides. *Yes, take it all in!* The rattling crash carts, LVNs sprinting with gurneys, trundling doctors shouting, wheelchairs clanking, patients moaning . . . *This is your life's enlivening soundtrack!*

Now she inhaled deeply and grounded herself in the ER entryway by practicing "mindful presence," taking inventory of her back and neck, arms and shoulders, and her heart. *My heart.* It was gratifying to register the warmth suffusing her calves—to feel *anything* pleasurable from her new jogging routine around Lake Merritt. (*Nora, we cannot continue therapy if you do not start exercising your body. Comprends tu? Body-mind, mind-body—the same.*) All the while, she invoked her psychotherapist's advice: *Like a whiff of smelling salts, Nora! Inhale l'essence de l'humanité!*

For added measure, she drew a second fortifying breath, taking in the complex fragrances that emanated from patients of every shape, color, and age who colonized this urban ER and infused its airspace. Their exhalations of gum and tobacco . . . clothes scented by dogs and cats, sex and urine . . . bodies radiating musky colognes, herbal soaps, and hair products screaming coconut or kiwi.

Finally, though wrestling with doubt, she internally chanted: *Today is another opportunity to relieve the suffering of patients who've come here— trusting me with their lives, generating the very air I breathe.*

Cellblock 47, San Sebastian State Prison

Marin County

8:55 A.M.

Prison guard Glen Baldwin approached Dr. Jack Griffin—*the* sole heir apparent to *the* Griffin's Garden and Hardware Stores family dynasty. He gleefully announced, "Sorry, Doc. But the warden nixed your request to make that 'important' call."

Jack sat on his bunk and tried to conceal his disappointment.

Baldwin taunted, "What? Not going to complain, big man? Not going to do any more fancy whining?"

Although it required Herculean effort, Jack resisted the bait. But in the not-too-distant past, he would have returned barbed retorts worthy of the Algonquin Round Table, drowning Baldwin in devastating streams of 50-dollar words spewing forth in impeccable grammar. However, after months of incarceration, he could envision the punishing cost. Protesting the warden's denial of his request to phone Richard would merely risk another "accident" in the cafeteria or "incident" in the showers. Or perhaps there would be another dead rat under his pillow. Still, he urgently needed to contact Richard, because something had to be seriously wrong to prevent him from showing up for their regular Sunday visit yesterday.

Baldwin puckered up and whispered, "Want a kiss for being such a good boy?"

Jack stared dimly back while focusing inward on the calming mental exercises he had honed over time to defend against Baldwin's provocations. Sometimes it sufficed to conjure up his life prior to incarceration—to call up his identity as a renowned oncologist at

Oakland City Hospital, his meaningful ministrations on the cancer ward, and the affirming embrace of his tailored white coat around his broad shoulders and chest.

If that initial strategy failed, he would begin meditative recitations of the elements of the periodic table or the inventory in his grandfather's store that he had long ago helped to maintain. Each arrangement, through a sensible ordering of elementary chaos, offered organizing principles that deeply reassured him.

Baldwin's flinty eyes squinted, and his meaty hips rotated while he spoke. But Jack heard nothing of what he said.

. . . hydrogen, helium, lithium, beryllium . . .

Baldwin grimaced while Jack looked impassively back.

. . . iridium, platinum, gold . . .

He didn't flinch while Baldwin ground his sizable backside against the iron bars.

. . . seeds, bark, mulch, rakes, trowels, spades . . .

He was taking inventory in aisle 3 while Baldwin laughed.

. . . wheelbarrows, sprayers, fencing, trellises . . .

And when Baldwin finally turned away, Jack jumped to aisle 7.

. . . pickaxes, machetes, scythes . . .

ER

Oakland City Hospital

8:59 A.M.

"Hey, Dr. Kelly!"

Nora turned to find Fergie—good friend and nurse extraordinaire—standing in the corridor. Of course she was there, working a double or even triple shift. Her steady presence in this decrepit ER had established her as one of its most dependable fixtures. Attired as usual in pristine blue scrubs, her compact figure popped against a drab backdrop of beige walls.

"Fergie!" Nora said. "You were just starting a shift when I left yesterday. So now you're on, what?"

"My second. I'm working a double."

"It's not fair that you always look fresh after working such long hours. I'm envious."

Fergie half smiled. "It's probably my positive attitude toward life that keeps me renewed."

Still, Nora heard Fergie's Midwestern accent sneaking into her speech—the bleating and flattening of her As—which was a sure tell of her deep fatigue. As always, it transported Nora to the South Side of Chicago where she had attended medical school, bringing back memories of McKinley Park barbecues, shopping at Marshall Field's, and wild times in Bridgeport on St. Pat's. She teased, "But I *know* you're tired, Fergie. Because I'm hearing it now! I'm in the bleachers at Comiskey Park! Grabbing a cold one on Rush Street—"

"Stop."

"I'm eating a slice from Gino's. And Jim Croce's singing, *'Bad, bad Leroy Brown*—'"

"Okay! I give. I *am* tired. Just don't start with that song. It'll be stuck in my head all day." She cocked her head and shot Nora the notorious hard-boiled look that some nurses had mastered to put doctors—anyone, really—on notice.

"Fine," Nora conceded, "but on one condition. Promise to look tired occasionally, like the rest of us mortals."

"Deal," Fergie said. "But let's get started on the whiteboard—the ER's been crazy-times-ten. We got weekend spillover from yesterday's Super Bowl—the usual accidents and injuries, brawls and booze, and guys with chest pain who waited for the game to end before coming in."

Nora followed Fergie to the whiteboard that had been densely scribbled over with red, blue, green, and black Magic Markers. Colorful arrows linked patients' names to provisional diagnoses or pending orders. MRI and CT scanner appointment times had been erased and changed so often that they showed hazily through inky smudges. Nora felt the cache of serenity she had banked from her morning's work-entry ritual deplete precipitously.

"Here's the scorecard," Fergie began, pointing to various board entries while she spoke. "Right now, we got these four exam rooms and this procedure suite free. These three patients are waiting on X-ray, and these two are psych holds. Here's a preeclamptic, waiting on OB. This guy has a fishhook in his butt—*don't ask*—and he's with the surgical resident. Here's a COPDer we tubed, and she's on her way to ICU now. These two patients are heading to telemetry, and these three to OR— just waiting on transport. These five—on launch for dispo. Ortho's reducing a shoulder in 7. We're giving clot busters to this CVA in 16. And neuro's in 18, supervising an LP by one of the interns—*god help them all*. And, of course, the waiting room's full."

"Piece of cake," Nora said, feigning optimism. (*You must stay positive, Nora. And if you cannot, puis juste faire semblant—then just pretend to be so.*) She tried to boost her morale by reminding herself of her profession's high calling and capacity for great goodness. Still, she knew this attempted self-inoculation of passion was unlikely to kick in. Certainly, not in time to immunize her against apathy and distraction today. Certainly, not in time to benefit all the patients waiting on her service this shift—all the coughing, bleeding, crying, despairing, sick people who not only waited on the white board; they also waited in corridors, exam rooms, pharmacy lines, laboratory queues, and the ER waiting room itself. They waited for medical attention, a splint, a cup of water, or a translator to convey their predicament to an overextended nurse. They awaited an ER doctor to diagnose their troubled breathing, their sudden blindness, or their bloody urine. To explain why they could no longer walk, eat, sleep, or raise an arm. To inform them whether the baby was delivered safely, the suicide attempt succeeded, or a loved one survived CPR. Trying not to sound disheartened, Nora said, "Give me a minute to put my purse in the office and grab a cup of—"

But a naked patient escaped from a psych-hold room and bumped against her. Then he sprinted down the hallway, yelling, "Freedom! Yip! Freedom!" Seconds later, the shamefaced security guard emerged from the room and said, "Sorry, Fergie. But I swear, I wasn't asleep this time. That patient is a regular Houdini!"

"I'll give you two minutes to do *your* magic," she replied. "Bring him back before I call real security."

Nora and Fergie watched the stout guard waddle down the corridor in laborious pursuit of his escaped charge. Then they faced each other and the game began—who would be first to laugh at this workplace absurdity? Fergie usually won this old contest. With her close-shaved head, impossibly large bifocals, and tattoos covering her neck and arms, all she usually had to do was hold an expressionless stare at Nora who was incapable of masking her delight in all things wondrous and mind-boggling about Fergie. Today, Fergie gratuitously provoked Nora's capitulation by deadpanning, "That guard is so slow, he couldn't catch a cold in this ER."

Nora groaned; game over. "How many beers do I owe you now?"

"A couple million," Fergie said, as her cell chimed a text. "But gotta go—they need me for that LP. *What a surprise.*"

Watching Fergie dash down the corridor, Nora felt grateful to be working with such a wonderful colleague. These last couple of years, after losing her family, she rarely experienced any semblance of joy on her job—at least in any genuine, nonprescriptive way. She made a mental note to report this spontaneous delight to her therapist, who she knew would interpret it as a sign of progress. But almost immediately the idea sounded desperate and pathetic. She issued a new note to herself: *Delete prior note to therapist.*

After rounding the nurses station, she arrived at her office. Hand on the doorknob, she ritually recited, *I'm opening to a new day and—*

It happened so fast. A forceful blow struck her from behind and slammed her against the door. The door shuddered, and she lost footing and fell. Her skull clunked once, perhaps twice, against the floor. She lost consciousness for a moment or two. Then, searing pain surged down her arms. When she turned her neck, the pain intensified, and she spotted the naked psych patient sprinting away.

Her professionally honed reflexes were triggered, and she began to assess her injuries. But roiling confusion intruded. Her head pounded, her ears rang, and she felt dizzy. Still, the diagnosis was obvious—*a concussion, at a minimum.* Staring up at the popcorn ceiling, she lamented, "I've got a fuckin' TBI."

Still, how bland and remote that diagnosis sounded considering all that she was experiencing. How insufficiently *TBI* expressed the loopy shifts of her wobbly mind and her whirling subjective state. *How many times have I taught medical students about traumatic brain injury? Or diagnosed TBI in high school football and soccer players? And now, knowing how a TBI actually feels . . . my god. I never knew what I was talking about!*

She cautiously sat up and resumed her self-assessment. She tested her vision one eye at a time. She moved each limb and checked sensation in her fingers and toes. Then her diagnostic sights jumped to the future, and she worried about potential long-term consequences—prolonged neurological recovery, and post-concussion headaches and seizures. Already, pushing 60 and distracted by grief, she'd been struggling with insecurity about her memory and capacity to absorb new medical information. *I don't need a TBI to make matters worse.*

After retrieving her purse from the floor, she stood up and noted the strange detritus that clung to her clothing. (*Don't even speculate what it could be.*) Instinctively, she began to self-administer the mental status exam that she routinely gave her TBI patients. But it was instantly apparent—she could not legitimately assess her own brain function. *How do I determine whether I'm correctly answering my own questions? How can I judge whether I'm recalling the words and numbers that I challenge myself to remember?* "Just fuckin' fine," she complained to no one in particular. Already, there was a *second* workplace absurdity and so early in the day. *I'll have to tell Fergie about this—if I can remember it.*

Entering her office and donning a clean white coat, she deliberated about obtaining a head CT and reporting her TBI to Employee Health. But in this dazed moment, with her busy shift just beginning, she decided to forgo both. A delayed start could bottleneck the ER for the entire afternoon.

Still, she wished she had a personal physician who could help her with this troubling injury. But having worked in varied capacities at Oakland City since 1987, she knew a little too much about all her colleagues: who wasn't up to snuff, who drank and/or inhaled, and who was too burnt-out, depressed, or longing to retire. She knew several who would fail cognitive testing themselves. And, after attending 30 years of holiday parties and social events at the hospital, she had observed nearly everyone in an unsettling or compromised state that constricted her comfort zone around them. She'd developed reservations about the character or clinical expertise of most every physician on staff. Everyone except for Jack—currently imprisoned—and Rosalie, whom she regarded too much like a daughter.

Finally, she resignedly self-counseled, *Physician, heal thyself.* She exchanged her pumps for a sturdy pair of rust-colored Keens and stored her purse inside a locked desk drawer—the same locked drawer from which her purse had been stolen twice before. With her skull pounding from the fall, she began to feel increasingly vulnerable. She darkly recalled recent reports about escalating workplace injuries and violence within ERs. At Oakland City, her own colleagues had been voicing concerns about unsafe worksite conditions, especially after an active shooter incident last year. And despite all the security guards and metal detectors here, she knew of patients and staff who'd been threatened by people who had carried knives or guns into the ER.

Putting aside her distress, Nora switched on her work cell and stepped into the hallway. She invoked a quick supplemental ritual to gird herself for the hours ahead. Closing her eyes, taking a steadying breath, she internally chanted: *One day at a time; one breath at a time.* But when she opened her eyes on the out-breath, she found herself staring at an overhead security camera that stared dispassionately back. Though it was suspended from the ceiling just a few feet outside her office, she hadn't noticed it before. It was just one of the surveillance fixtures so ubiquitous throughout the ER that it had remained inconspicuous. But with acute relief, she thought—*it must have witnessed my injury a couple minutes ago! They—whoever "they" are behind the camera—were watching over me!*

And yet . . . *No one has come to help me or to check whether I need medical attention. No one is here registering any concern whatsoever about me. No one seems to be pursuing the dangerous—and endangered—"Yip!"ing patient.*

Nora stared curiously back at the so-called security camera and readjusted her position to stand within the imagined crosshairs of its vacant gaze. She watched the camera's metal eyelid open and close, and its glassy eyeball shift side to side. Its steel-plated throat emitted tinny churning noises that communicated no decipherable message. Its metallic casing ticked like a mechanical heart. She moved testily within the camera's range, but nothing seemed to affect its programmed gaze or nerveless eye.

Scanning the empty ER corridor, Nora was flooded with Twilight Zone angst. Meanwhile, the red phones rang with distressing urgency. Patients buzzed frantically for assistance. Cardiac alarms beeped dire warnings. And still, she observed no human response. In this 21st-century techno void, nobody was alerted by alerts or alarmed by alarms.

"Damn," Nora whispered, turning back to face the security cam. "Someone could commit murder here in broad daylight, and no one would even notice."

CFO Richard Pulaski's Office

10th Floor, Oakland City Hospital

12:20 P.M.

Code Blue, 10th floor, room 10-82!
Code Blue, 10th floor, room 10-82!

The urgent pronouncement blared through the hospital's public-address system, summoning all available medical personnel to the chiefs' suite. A tsunami of attending staff and medical residents surged up the stairwells toward the administrative offices on the hospital's uppermost floor. And moments later, just as swiftly, the tsunami reversed course after the operator announced: *Cancel Code Blue, 10th floor.*

A few retreating residents voiced regret about a lost opportunity to hone their emergency resuscitation skills. One lamented, "Why don't they at least let us *practice* on the dead guys?" But most of the staff doctors looked relieved—they knew how much time could be consumed by working a code, at the expense of their clinic schedules. They would have to apologize to every irritated patient made to absorb the delay—a delay that only lengthened with each serial apology.

Meanwhile, in Room 10-82, CFO Richard Pulaski's bloated, blue body lay lifeless on the orange carpet inside his C-suite office. Kneeling alongside it, Dr. Rosalie Karlov—who discovered Pulaski's body and triggered the hospital operator's call for a Code Blue—looked despondent. She tried to stem the tide of her tears, barely managing to say, "He . . . he had an appointment with me this morning." She lowered her head, and her long black hair draped across her face like a lush veil.

"I'm sorry, Rosalie," said Dr. Fred Williams, chief of Oakland City's medical staff and the second person to arrive on scene. Sitting in Pulaski's chair, he placed a comforting hand on her shoulder. "I know how shocking it must've been to find Richard like this."

Several feet away, nurse Edna Atkinson was fixated on her iPad, into which she irritably entered copious data to comply with mandatory reporting requirements for this exceptionally brief code. Her earnest nursing student, Lizbeth Tanner, observed each keystroke and duly recorded into her spiral-bound notebook all the computerized checklists that Edna begrudgingly completed. Tonight, she would transcribe those notes—appended with personal reflections—into "My Nursing Student Years," an ever-lengthening journal on her home laptop.

Hearing Edna mumble something ("*So much damn nonsense to document on these computers, and for no good clinical reason!*"), Lizbeth whispered, "I'm sorry, Edna—I didn't hear what you just said."

Realizing the need to cool down, Edna stalled for time by fussing with the bobby pins that secured her nurse's cap to her graying red hair. She knew her cap was anachronistic and even amusing to some colleagues. But she didn't care one bit. For her, it signified professional nobility and the ideals of competence and service—aspirations, she felt, that were in dire need of resurrection within nursing. Besides, on a practical level, she had come to appreciate her cap's many useful applications—such as now when it provided a convenient pretext for stalling. Its multi-folded brim could also hold a narcotics cabinet key and a couple of pens. More recently, it served to conceal her expanding bald spot. "Lizbeth," she finally responded, "I believe what I said was . . . you must press *this* button on *this* keyboard on *this* screen, or *all* the data you so *painfully* entered into the computer will disappear *forever*."

Though doubting the fidelity of Edna's response, Lizbeth nodded respectfully and said, "Thank you."

Rosalie looked up at Fred, her chestnut-brown eyes swollen, and said, "He was two hours late. I knew how stressed out he was. But he never missed his appointments. And, god, he was so sick! So, I came here during lunch hour, and . . . this . . ."

"All right now, take a deep breath," Fred said, feeling paternal toward the young doctor. He cringingly recalled his own first time arriving at a dead patient's bedside and reflexively initiating an adrenaline-laced code. He remembered the dead woman's dentures floating in her regurgitation, which he unwittingly ingested while performing mouth-to-mouth resuscitation. Only after the experienced code team arrived and interrupted his panic did the debacle end. Now he sagely counseled, "I've been a doctor for three decades, and still I find these situations traumatic and—"

"Richard was not returning my calls," Rosalie interrupted. "And when I knocked, he did not answer the door . . ."

"You're in shock. Try to—"

"I panicked and called a code! But I *knew* he was dead. I even dragged him out of his chair and laid him on the floor and started CPR, but . . ."

"Rosalie, you did what any of us would've done."

Edna looked askance at the two of them, her fleeting judgmental expression escaping their notice. But Lizbeth registered it and then watched Edna return her attention to the iPad while grumbling something in Gaelic—a cue to Lizbeth to leave Edna alone. Finally, Edna huffily instructed, "You must mark *every* checkbox on this Code Summary Checklist screen. It's a *master* checklist to verify that you've addressed each of the *individual* checklists you're required to complete."

Rosalie wept loudly, drowning out Edna's complaints. Fred patted her shoulder several times, repeating, "Hush, now." But all the while, his anxiety intensified as he recalled his skirmish with Richard just three days earlier. They had run into one another in the C-suite breakroom and, immediately, Fred began lobbing harsh complaints at Richard. Though they ostensibly concerned next year's hospital budget for physicians' salaries and bonuses, he had hurled them with a decidedly personal spin. Even at the time, he knew his rancor was misplaced and his behavior was unprofessional. Still, despite this heightened self-awareness, he could not redirect his rage to its more deserving targets outside the hospital. Taking aim at Richard—already enfeebled—was just too expedient at the time.

Fred looked at the crumpled notepaper that Rosalie clutched. With searing apprehension, he wondered whether his blistering attack could have nudged Richard over the proverbial edge to commit suicide. And he worried that colleagues in adjacent C-suite offices might have overheard his bullying tirade that Friday night. Still, he reasoned, Richard had to have endured comparable—even worse—attacks as the hospital's CFO. He had to have possessed tremendous resiliency to stay the course at a job that reliably disappointed both the medical and administrative halves of the hospital staff.

Rapidly approaching footsteps sounded from the hallway. Fred, Rosalie, Edna, and Lizbeth looked to the doorway to see Nora who exclaimed, "My god, it's true!"

Fred motioned for her to enter, despite Edna's contrary advice: "You shouldn't be here, Dr. Kelly. Not with us waiting on the police and coroner."

Taken aback, Nora said, "The police?"

Still, Fred cast her a beckoning look. Then he cleared his throat and told Rosalie, "You'll have to give Richard's note to the police when they arrive."

Responding to his cues, Nora approached, progressively absorbing a fuller view of Richard's body, feeling as if she were stepping deeper into a fevered dream. The scene looked surreal, perhaps generated by bruised neural circuitry from her TBI. *Here is Richard, Jack's partner, blue against the orange carpet. Rosalie and Fred are arguing over a sheet of paper. Edna and her student are staring at an iPad, absorbed in virtual reality. A flock of sparrows flies by the window, casting shadows on Richard's body.*

When Nora heard her name called, she snapped back to attention. She found Rosalie looking at her with an anguished expression and stammering, "Nora, I . . . I found him."

Nora stooped to hug Rosalie whom she'd long regarded as a daughterly protégé. But she was shocked to experience intense personal discomfort when she wrapped her arms around the young doctor. Stymied and off-guard, she instantly withdrew from the embrace and scrambled to reconcile her reaction. Realizing that she had never fully embraced Rosalie before, she wondered, *How can that be? Especially given all the life-and-death experiences we've shared?* But then the answer arrived like a thunderbolt—with the memory of her own daughter reaching out for her, moments before being swept into the ocean, and her powerlessness to reach her daughter and keep her safe. Yes; it felt fraudulent to reach for Rosalie now.

Nora's abrupt disengagement jolted Rosalie. In bewilderment, she cried out, "This is my fault! I was Richard's doctor, and I failed him."

"Stop that, Rosalie," Fred insisted. "You should—"

Richard's office phone rang, providing a welcome—if awkward—interruption of the emotional tension in the room. Everyone fell silent and listened to the caller's message: "Hey, Pulaski. I'm still waiting on your pharmacy budget. And, ha! Maybe on winning the lottery, too?"

While she listened to the message, Nora stared intently at Richard's body, the fierce fact of his death hitting her now as violently as the yipping ER patient earlier today. Her stunned brain labored to absorb the vivid details of Richard's mottled face, frozen in a lax expression. She took in his puffy bloodless lips and dimmed emerald eyes. Her eyes scanned over the IV line that had been inserted into a venous port inside his left forearm. She noted the indigo hue of his body, suggesting that death had occurred many hours ago. And, finally, her eyes rested on his desk, which held an empty syringe sitting alongside a photograph of his partner Jack.

After the phone fell silent, Rosalie's moaning resumed. Fred glanced at Nora and silently mouthed, "Help!"

Nora nodded, then turned to Rosalie and said, "You can't blame yourself for Richard's death."

Fred had to refrain from rolling his eyes. But he was disappointed by Nora's lame assistance in limiting Rosalie's continued lamentation. Desperately trying to shift the group's emotional gears, he said, "Nora, do you realize how long you and I have worked alongside Richard?"

As if emerging from a trance, Nora dully replied, "A long time."

"Yes, since our last day of residency in 1990," he said. "Can you believe it?" Picking up the photo of Jack, he continued, "And this head-shot of Jack was cropped out from the group photo that Richard took of us that day in the ER."

"Of course," Nora said, her attention revived. "From our gang-of-six photo: July 2, 1990."

Fred recalled Richard's presence behind the camera as the reason for Jack's Olympic smile in the photo. He turned the picture over and read its dedication aloud: "To Richard—The first time ever I saw your face. Love always, Jack."

Nora said, "Yeah. That was also Richard's first day of work at the hospital—in some entry-level admin position. I was in the ER, struggling to save my last patient. Then our whole gang showed up, trying to get me to leave so we could celebrate the end of residency. Poor Richard—tasked with prying us out of that patient's room."

Edna slammed shut the crash cart door. After Fred shot her a disapproving look, she said, "Excuse me!" though with no discernible remorse.

Lizbeth was surprised by Edna's seeming insensitivity. Then again, she also saw that Edna's action had served to shore up the voluble emotional tides inside the room. Even Rosalie calmed and handed over the rumpled note to Nora.

Nora took out her reading glasses—regrettably noting that a lens must have popped out during her ER mishap. But then she immediately realized their irrelevance—the note contained a single word written across the paper. Perplexed, she looked at Fred and said, "Sorry."

"For what?" he asked.

"No," she said, handing the note to Fred. "That's what this says. It's all that it says."

Rosalie protested, "But Richard had nothing to be sorry for! I am, I *was*, his doctor. I *know* he did not steal from this hospital. I *know* he did not cause its financial troubles. And now . . . now he is dead, and everyone will think him guilty of all those things!"

Rosalie's passionate defense of Richard rekindled the emotional temperature in the room. Nora's head pain intensified. Edna discharged her renewed agitation by banging louder on her keyboard, while Lizbeth turned visibly anxious. Trying again to manage the escalating distress, Fred donned his administrative mantle and spoke in his practiced authoritarian tone: "Well, it's possible that the pressure might've gotten to Richard. Lots of people were at his throat." He thought but did not say, *Regrettably, I was one of them.* "But we should wait for the independent financial audit to speak to culpability."

Rosalie cried, "But with this suicide note, everyone will believe he was guilty! No one will be motivated to prove otherwise. But his *life*—it should be worth the effort."

"Excuse me," Lizbeth interrupted, pointing to the doorway. "The coroner is here."

Lydia's Office

Pathology Department, Oakland City Hospital

8:00 P.M.

"You like my Cupid?" Lydia asked.

Nora—splayed across the couch and holding an ice pack to her skull—smiled at her best friend, Dr. Lydia Chandler, the hospital's chief of pathology. Pointing to the faded cardboard Cupid that dangled from the ceiling, she said, "You've hung up that same old thing for the last hundred Valentine's Days."

"Yeah," said Lydia, spinning in her swivel chair. "It's durable, like Velveeta cheese. Like us!"

Nora laughed. "Speaking of oldies but goodies, are we still having Saint Pat's at your house next month?"

"Sure. We can handle any serpent who shows up. You do recall that I invited my sister?"

"Yes, Carrie—your 'evil twin.' I haven't seen her in—what?—20-some years?"

"It's been 15 for me—in person, at least. But we started Skyping last year after her husband died. Funny—but I'm actually looking forward to seeing her again."

"I'm happy to hear that, especially after the troubles between you two. I'm looking forward to her visit, too."

"Yeah?" said Lydia, grinning. "Well, I mostly invited her because I saw she wasn't dying her hair. It's stone cold white! She was born two minutes before me—something she's always lorded over me. But now she's gonna have to sit at my table and actually *look* like an older sister."

"Well, at least I'll be able to tell you apart."

"If you have any doubt, remember our secret handshake."

"Will do," Nora said. Then, taking in her friend's customary enthusiasm for the holidays demonstrated by the exuberant decorations throughout the office, she said, "It's so ironic that your department—brimming with death and body parts—is always the most festive place to be during holidays."

"Especially on Halloween!"

"Yeah. No place better'n a morgue for Halloween spirits."

"And the best part? I usually get to keep all the candy."

Nora groaned. "Only because you wear those disgusting gloves soaked in fake blood when you hand it out."

"Guilty," Lydia said. "And smart."

Repositioning the ice pack to her neck, Nora said, "Remember our first Halloween here a few months after we started residency? 1987? You and Fred were ghosted out on the autopsy tables, and I paged Jack and the Klufts to a Code Blue here."

"That was priceless! Though I don't think the Klufts ever forgave us. Cheryl nearly needed a pacemaker, and Carl peed in his pants." Lydia sighed and continued, "God, I miss having pagers."

"Still, *my* favorite times in this department were when the six of us would just meet up for spontaneous get-togethers. And, well, other stuff, too."

"Expressing our youthful impulses? Having sex? Getting high to rock-n-roll?"

"Yikes! I hope your office isn't bugged."

"It's a miracle none of us ever got caught—or struck by lightning."

"Lydia, do you think the residents and medical students still sneak around here at night to . . . *do stuff*?"

Lydia created a clearing on her cluttered desk through which she could better view Nora and said, "Well, with all the security cameras around here now, the current crop of residents couldn't follow our bad examples even if they wanted to. And all the locks and passcodes . . ."

"Don't get me started on hospital security! Those damn cameras in our ER—they're dummies, Lydia! They see nothing and do nothing! They're a colossal waste of taxpayer dollars for a false sense of security. Clearly, someone is profiting off them. But it's not patients or staff."

Feigning a contemplative pose, Lydia said, "Then perhaps we should call them *scam*eras."

"Ugh! Perhaps you should stop *pun*ishing me. My head hurts enough already."

Lydia reached into a desk drawer and withdrew a pill that she held out to Nora. After Nora declined, Lydia said, "Fine—one more for me." She popped the oxy into her mouth and swallowed.

Nora cringed, reminded of patients coming into the ER with pills stuck in their throats. Of patients overdosed with opioids who were blown out of their minds, their lives, their families, their careers. Of patients injured or killed by drugged drivers. She thought, *How can Lydia—any doctor, really—use narcotics so casually?* She felt prompted—*yet again*—to question Lydia about her oxy intake, which seemed to be escalating since her breakup with Fred two years ago. But Lydia quickly resumed their conversation: "Still, I'm grateful there weren't *scam*eras around in our days. It's creepy now how everything is being recorded and stored for eternity."

"Well, to your point," Nora said, "let's release your old Cupid to its eternal rest and hang up a new one. We could hit the Fruitvale CVS? Or the fancy aisles at Hallmark? I'll even go to Michaels with you."

"Such a tempting offer! But no—I'm loyal to my buddy here." She gazed affectionately at Nora and said, "Still, it's good to hear *you* talk about a break with the past. Even if it only involves a cardboard Cupid."

Nora turned self-consciously away, defending against Lydia's prodding for deeper conversation. But her energy bank was depleted, and her brain still felt muzzy after the TBI. She said, "I think I've been doing better overall."

"Does your Dr. Frenchie agree?"

"She does. I saw her after my shift ended today. But seriously, Lydia, you've got to stop calling her that."

"*Oui.*"

"You're incorrigible. Anyway, truth is, half the time I'm not sure what she thinks. Or means, actually. Still, she somehow succeeds in getting me to run around the lake most days, meditate, and practice mindful medicine. I even psychobabble with her inside my head all day."

"God! Being you is so much work."

"Then a day like today literally whacks me on the side of the head . . . and Richard dies." Nora shook her head. "Being in his office today and looking at his photo of Jack, I couldn't help but feel guilty about abandoning both of them. And then, when I hugged Rosalie, I was transported right back to Stinson Beach, looking over Jack's shoulder and watching that rogue wave grab my daughter and husband."

"So sorry, pal," Lydia said, joining Nora on the couch. "Everything is always so damn connected for you. But that's what also makes you such a great diagnostician—putting patients' signs and symptoms together, and figuring out the whole picture."

Dabbing her eyes, Nora said, "I've been trying to stay optimistic— engaged. But setbacks keep coming out of nowhere. And now, my therapist is leaving *tomorrow* for an entire month in France!"

Aiming for healing levity, Lydia said, "Does Frenchie ever just advise: '*Que será, será*'? Maybe she even sings it with you?"

"No," Nora laughed. "Besides, I think that's Spanish."

"Really? Still, it's great advice in any language." Lydia pointed to her cardboard Cupid and said, "I'm debating whether to show you something I came across while looking for Timmy the other day."

"Timmy? I never knew your Cupid had a name or a gender."

"You're right. These days, I should allow that Timmy might be trans or queer-questioning. Or gender nonconforming. Actually, yeah . . . look at all the rainbow colors in his wings."

"God, Lydia—you're such a cornball."

"Thanks! But, back to you seeing Jack's photo today?"

"Yeah?"

"You'll see," Lydia said, heading to a file cabinet. Returning moments later, she tossed an old photograph onto Nora's lap.

Nora's eyes widened. "It's our gang-of-six photo! My god—I remember Jack distributing copies of this decades ago. Mine's in storage at home."

"So, when you told me what happened in Richard's office this afternoon, I thought . . . what a coincidence."

Together they stared at the photo labeled "Gang-of-Six—July 2, 1990." Nora remarked, "Wow! We were all so young! And that picture of Jack on Richard's desk was cropped out from this picture and blown up. It was grainy, but . . . that smile . . ."

"Yeah, Jack could really smile. He has—what?—two hundred perfect teeth?"

"He was looking straight through the camera at Richard when this photo was taken," Nora said. "They were smitten with one another the moment they met. I remember Jack nearly fainting when Richard walked into the ER, and how he kept telling Richard to 'relax' in . . . well, a *suggestive* manner. Then handing his clunky old Pentax to Richard and asking him to take our picture—pure chutzpah!"

"Ironic, too, that everyone in this photo *except* Jack looks like they're facing a death sentence."

Nora grimaced, but Lydia continued, "C'mon—it's true. We were hoping for a group photo in a more celebratory environment—at Trader Vic's, remember? But we ended up with *this* photo—in the *ER*. And with you refusing to leave your last patient!"

"But I couldn't leave him, Lydia. You know that. It was . . . awful. It felt wrong to hand him over to some rookie intern on his first day out of med school. And then . . . well, then he died anyway."

"I shouldn't have brought this photo out. But, seriously? You got to give yourself a break. Over a quarter century has passed since then. Besides, don't you think patients should know better than to get sick on the *one day* of the *year* that new residents take over? They should know to steer clear of a teaching hospital on rookie roulette day!"

"I don't know," Nora said. "Right now, it's just strange to think that Richard's dead. Remember him walking into the ER that day? His first day on the job and he's assigned the task of throwing us old guard out of the hospital on our last day of residency. He barges into my patient's room and tells us to—what was it?"

"To 'skedaddle,'" Lydia howled. "*Skedaddle!* I thought it was some new dance craze."

Nora rolled her eyes while Lydia laughed uncontrollably. Finally, she said, "You're your own best audience, Lydia."

Lydia rested her head on Nora's shoulder and tried to reprise Richard's Oklahoma drawl. "Listen, y'all. Yer glory days here are over. Skedaddle! Step aside for the new kids on the block."

"That was an impeccable accent. Meryl Streep would be envious."

After catching her breath, Lydia said, "Sorry—you're right. It's strange to realize Richard is dead. Even if we weren't close, he's a part of our history."

After a restful pause, Lydia tapped the photo and said, "Look at how handsome we were back then. You, with your long brown hair and those gorgeous waves. You were so tall and thin."

"Hey, I'm hearing too much *past* tense."

"Nah, you're still a looker, Nora. And me—see? I'm a Clairol blonde, same then as now! Although never 'nice' and never 'easy.'"

"I'll attest to that."

"Say, don't you think I looked a lot like Amy Schumer back in the day?"

"Hmm . . . I'm thinking more Amy Poehler."

"I'll happily take that! And Fred—we agree he looked fabulous, yeah? I sometimes forget that he used to have hair. He's been bald so long."

"Do you think his hair loss could have something to do with being the only African-American in our residency group?" Nora gazed knowingly at Lydia and added, "And because of a certain someone I'm looking at now."

"Ouch! I'm changing the subject. Look at the Klufts—Tweedledee and Tweedledum! It's so eerie—they look exactly the same today. Thus, proving my theory about them being zombie doctors."

"Carl's actually a very decent guy, Lydia."

"How can you tell? His alpha-Über wife controls him. You know she's his ventriloquist."

"That's cold! Carl has Asperger's, or whatever we're calling it nowadays."

"Stop. You're just making me feel bad for not liking the Klufts."

"No, it's just that Carl really struggles with 'being on the autism spectrum.' Besides, you have to admit, he and Cheryl seem to have accommodated each other for a very long time. They've uniquely survived as a couple since our residency."

"Still, I don't like Cheryl using Carl as her minion."

"Well, it seems to work for them," Nora said, tossing aside the photo. "And that's remarkable, given how close the six of us were, even deciding to stay together after residency and work on hospital staff. But then ... our friendships fell apart pretty fast."

Lydia scoffed. "No surprise to *me*. You know I hate people—*live* people, anyway."

"Still, we six were pretty tight during residency."

"But that was trench comradery back then. And after any battle, things always change—borders are redrawn and alliances shift. As your shrink might say, '*C'est la vie*.'"

"God, I hope she never says that to me. I pay her too much for clichés."

"Still, our group broke up for reasons—some good, some bad, some neither. We were like any family, really. The Klufts spun off in their own orbit. We both know what happened between Fred and me. And—I've always felt bad about *this*—but when Jack came out after hooking up with Richard? Well, I had had no idea he was gay, so the news made me feel like I hadn't known him before. He felt like a stranger. So, lucky you, Nora—you're the only friend I've kept from the group."

Nora and Lydia rested silently on the sofa and stared up at Timmy. Finally, Nora said, "This morning in the ER, I sang 'Bad, Bad Leroy Brown'."

"Were you trying to clear out the patients?"

"Funny—not."

Cold air burst from the ceiling vent and made Timmy gyrate. "Hey," said Lydia, "Timmy's dancing the 'skedaddle' now! Richard's spirit remains with us!"

"Stop. That gives me the chills."

"You're not seriously spooked, are you?"

"No. But ... I'm haunted by Richard's death. I can't believe he'd kill himself. In fact, I don't."

"Oh? So, you think Richard is here now, trying to tell us ... *SOMETHING!*"

"Honestly, Lydia! You're like a three-year-old."

"Thanks! Then I've matured some."

After a capacious yawn, Nora said, "So, let's just aim for symmetry and end this sorry day with another song."

"Okay. How about that *Que será, será*? Whatever that means, it means."

"Perfect."

"In any language we choose?"

"Sure."

"Wanna hold hands?"

"Yeah."

"Okay. On the count of three . . ."

FEBRUARY 7

El Gourmet Burger

Downtown Oakland

8:15 A.M.

Nora and Fred sat at their usual table, eating their usual breakfasts at El Gourmet Burger. Except for the chalkboard's daily specials, little had changed throughout the years they'd been meeting here weekly. And that was more than fine with them.

"Who's informing Jack about Richard?" Nora asked.

"His lawyer," Fred said. "In fact, he told Jack last night."

"Good. I mean . . ."

"I know. There's no 'good' in any of it."

Nora mindlessly prodded her scrambled eggs with a fork. She broke an over-long silence with, "How horrible—to learn that your partner died. And while you're in prison. And then, hearing about that from a *lawyer.*"

Their server arrived and poured more coffee. "Thanks, Amelia," they chimed in unison. It pleased Nora to see that Amelia finally had the basal cell on her nose excised.

Fred asked Nora, "Jack and Richard were never legally married, right?"

"Right. In the past, Jack said they were waiting for federal law to change on same-sex marriage. After it did in 2013, they set the date for July, 2015—the 25th anniversary of when they met in the ER. But that's when Jack's legal troubles began, and the court dates started piling up—not optimal timing for a wedding or honeymoon. So, they postponed. Still, it's interesting you ask, because just a few weeks ago, Edna told me she expected them to marry soon."

"Edna Atkinson from the ER? She stays in contact with Jack? Didn't know they were friends."

"Apparently, they grew close after Jack helped Edna with . . . well, her husband's death."

Fred pushed aside his plate. "I'm still sickened by all that. Still don't know what actually happened. It's always seemed fishy to me."

"I wish I knew more, too. But I was in a major fog back when Jack's legal troubles started. And losing Michael and Caitlin, I was traumatized every time I saw Jack. So, I dropped our friendship."

Placing his hand on Nora's, Fred said, "I remember. I can't imagine much worse than what happened to you—losing your husband and daughter like that. God, it's unthinkable."

Nora winced. "Even now, when I merely think of Jack, I relive that horrible moment all over." She took a deep breath. "And how odd—to come across a photo of him *twice* within the last 24 hours."

"Oh? His photo on Richard's desk yesterday and . . . ?"

"The second time was last night, while visiting Lydia in her office. After I told her what had happened with Richard, she brought out our old group photo—the one from which Jack's picture had been cropped."

Fred nodded. "Yeah, I keep a copy in my wallet." He did not explain that it was the only photo of Lydia he felt he could carry with impunity. "And, just so you know, I'm driving up to San Sebastian on Thursday to convey staff condolences to Jack."

"Could you say 'Hi' for me?"

"I could. But, if you're ready, and, under the circumstances . . . why not do that in person? Come with me. I could serve as a buffer between you two. It'd be a win-win, all around."

"Thanks, but no. The timing still feels wrong. And regardless, Richard's death seems like a terrible occasion for reconnecting with Jack."

"Or it might be the *best* occasion for that."

"I don't think so. Because I keep thinking about Richard's 'suicide,' and it seems . . . suspicious. 'Fishy,' as you'd say. Yesterday, when I walked into his office, I felt like I was stepping into a Salvador Dali canvas. I worried that my TBI was messing with my mind. But as my head cleared later, I became increasingly convinced that Richard did not commit suicide. So, I know that if Jack saw me, he'd immediately detect my doubts and pull me into a passionate Q&A about Richard's death. Fred, I'm sorry, but I'm not ready for that much intensity with Jack."

Fred shook his head. "Hold on. *Please* don't tell me that our master diagnostician thinks Richard's death is suspicious."

Nora licked the jam off her butter knife. "Yeah, well . . . Maybe it's just my TBI talking."

"Look: I want to know what you're actually thinking, TBI or not. Besides, maybe that ER patient knocked *more* sense into you yesterday."

"I forget how funny you are—not."

After clearing his throat, Fred said, "You're making me anxious. So, let's think this through. Richard had metastatic melanoma. And with Jack in prison, no family, his career in ruins, lawyers beating him down . . . Well, I'm not saying suicide was a 'good' answer for Richard, or an inevitable one. But I am saying I think it's *understandable*."

Nora wondered whether Fred's long-standing discomfort with Richard and Jack's sexuality was coloring his perspective. "Do you think suicide is more 'understandable' if a person is gay?"

"Nora, c'mon! Not fair! Don't go there again. Besides"—he pulled out a journal article—"you know about rising death rates in middle-aged whites. Listen to this—'because of an epidemic of suicides and afflictions stemming from substance abuse.' There's an *epidemic* of suicides, Nora, *especially* in Richard's demographic."

"Sorry, Fred. But we're talking about a man we actually knew. Richard was an individual, not some statistic or demographic. And as the chief, if you aren't *open* to other possibilities about his death, that creates obstacles to finding the truth."

"Cut to the chase, Nora. What's your concern?"

"I have *concerns*. Plural."

"All right then. I'm listening. I'm *open*."

After they exchanged conciliatory looks, Nora said, "Okay, first off, as Edna suggested, there was some expectation of Jack and Richard marrying soon. Why would Richard kill himself now?"

"Because he was seriously ill? Maybe he thought he wouldn't survive until Jack's release. Or maybe he didn't think Jack's release was ever going to happen."

"But you should've heard Edna—cynical, curmudgeonly Edna. She sounded certain of Jack's exoneration any day now. But we were doing a thoracentesis at the time, and, frankly, I didn't think I had any right to ask her more about him. But . . . maybe she knows something about his next appeal? Last year, the physician-assisted suicide law went into effect here. That might help Jack's case—whether he actually did what they accused him of doing."

Fred sighed. "Look—Edna can't be certain about Jack's release. She's probably just trying to stay upbeat for him. Maybe her optimism helps Jack get by."

Nora raised her brow. Fred laughed and said, "You're right. Edna? *Optimistic?*"

"Thanks. I couldn't keep a straight face much longer. But, let's get back to Richard. He'd never traumatize Jack by committing suicide. Especially since he knew about Jack's abandonment issues."

"But desperate people sometimes do desperate things."

"Sure. But *Richard*—the *individual*—was never prone to desperation. You've said as much yourself—how positive and levelheaded he always was, even during your epic fights with him. And, with his dismal prognosis, he was still undertaking difficult and hopeless cancer treatments."

"Even so, optimism always has a shelf life."

"Besides," Nora said, "Richard was intensely private. He was never one for public display. So, tell me why he'd *kill* himself at his *very public workplace?*"

"Don't know. Maybe it was a hostile act—trying to upset his tormentors by committing suicide right up in their faces?"

Nora disagreeably shook her head. "And one word—'Sorry'—for a suicide note? No way. Did you ever receive an email from Richard containing fewer than a bazillion words?"

"Well, no. Still, what evidence they've gathered since yesterday supports a very convincing story for suicide. It looks like Richard injected potassium directly into his chemo port. I mean, what a convenient setup. And it certainly would've been easy for him to obtain potassium chloride in the hospital. Besides, they detected no other substances in the syringe. And, hell—his blood potassium level was record-breaking lethal! I'd never seen such severe hyperkalemia before."

"Still, it's unconvincing to me," Nora said as Amelia swung by with the bill. "And Fred, I was fond of Richard, but . . . he was a bit dull. Reserved, I mean. He'd never kill himself in such a melodramatic fashion. Dropping dead over stacks of spreadsheets during an investigation of his work? No, it's not in his character."

"You going all Agatha Christie on me, Nora?"

She smiled. "It's *DCI Jane Tennison*, please."

"All right, you know how much I appreciate your brilliant analytic mind, but . . ."

"And a final point. Besides being a devout Catholic, Richard was what my mother would've called a *Goody Two-shoes*. He never would— or *could*—have committed suicide."

"No, no, no! You're *not* insinuating that Richard was *murdered!*"

Looking into Fred's copper eyes, Nora said, "You're right. I'm not insinuating it. I'm seriously proposing it."

Fred turned away and stared through the window at the morning commuters who passed by. Ruefully, thinking again about his recent clash with Richard, he had to agree with Nora. That Richard—though beleaguered by hefty accusations of fiscal wrongdoing—had thoughtfully, even politely, responded to each of his barbed complaints. Richard had calmly explained the standard process by which physicians' salaries and bonuses were budgeted within the broader context of budgeting for all of Oakland City Hospital and its clinics. He had invoked values of fairness and justice while explaining how "one finite pot of money" had to cover expenses for the nonphysician staff as well—the nurses, social workers, physical therapists, mailroom clerks, phlebotomists, and maintenance workers. How it also had to cover hospital operations, like pharmacy, lab, radiology, *and* hospital equipment—purchases, upgrades, repairs. Then, there were utilities, building maintenance, and janitorial upkeep. There were the ICU and ER renovations. There was the costly hospital earthquake retrofitting mandated by the state of California. *And, and, and* . . .

And, Fred privately admitted now, *even during our altercation, Richard seemed neither desperate nor upset. Certainly, he didn't seem suicidal— not like a man slouching toward oblivion.* He turned back to Nora and conceded, "Well, I suppose a hospital CFO is in a fit position to make a few enemies."

Nora said, "Yeah—sorry. Murder has to be included in the differential diagnosis of Richard's death."

"All right now. I promise to stay *open* to your hypothesis. But *you* have to stay open, too. I still think it's plausible that a beaten-down guy with a terminal disease and a partner in prison . . . It's conceivable someone like that might rationally choose to leave the world."

"But again, knowing *Richard*, that's inconceivable. I'm not buying it—or this breakfast." She tossed the bill to Fred.

"Fine. Regardless, though, you should see a doctor about your TBI."

"I don't trust doctors."

"Me neither," Fred said, plopping a twenty on the table.

Nora smiled at her old friend. "Sorry if I'm a little off. I didn't sleep last night. Well, actually, I intentionally stayed awake. I was nervous about my head injury."

"What? You were monitoring your own level of consciousness? And during the *night*? You can't do that!"

"Stop with the lecture! And, speaking of . . . I used those dark hours to brush up on hyperkalemia for the talk I'm giving today."

Throwing up his hands, Fred said, "Of course! Because, like Dickinson, you 'could not stop for death.' Why read the poets or philosophers in troubling times when you have medical textbooks and journals? Why not immerse your mind in potassium disorders?"

"Well, make fun all you want, but now I feel confident about giving my lecture. Besides, it feels good to do a favor for Rosalie after all she's done for me these last two years. Especially after she stepped up to run the residency teaching program."

"So, you're giving grand rounds to the residents today?"

Nora nodded. "Rosalie's scheduled speaker called yesterday and canceled—some family emergency, I think. And, as you saw yesterday, she was in no shape to substitute, so I volunteered. 'The Diagnosis and Management of Hyperkalemia'—sounds like a real thriller, yeah?"

Fred smiled, debating whether to applaud Nora on her return to teaching—stimulated, it seemed, by her suspicions over Richard's death.

She's been so withdrawn since she lost her family, dare I mention the glimmer of her old passion for medicine that I'm seeing? But, afraid to jinx things, he only said, "Glad to hear it."

"Don't get too excited," Nora cautioned. "I'm also doing this because my therapist made me promise to give teaching another go." She took a final swig of coffee. "And maybe my TBI has something to do with my decision."

ER Exam Room

Oakland City Hospital

10:15 A.M.

Dr. Carl Kluft—intellectually gifted and technically skilled Obstetrician-Gynecologist—snapped off his nitrile exam gloves and stated, "Your bleeding has stopped." He rose from a chair at the foot of the exam table and told the patient who lay before him with her knees spread apart, "It won't happen again." Just before his swift exit, the patient lifted her sweaty head in time to catch a glimpse of his expressionless face.

"But I wanted to thank him," she told her husband.

Her husband said, "Really? I dunno, honey. I mean, was the guy even human? He acted like a robot."

She glanced knowingly at Fergie and said, "Yeah, he's no Prince Charming. But he's the best doctor I ever had."

Fergie was prepping the room for the next patient—securing bloodied gauze in red biohazard bins and collecting surgical instruments for the autoclave. "Your wife is correct," she said. "He's the best."

Recognition flickered in the husband's eyes. "Was *that* the doc who found your tumor last year?"

"Hello? Yes!" his wife said. "And after all those 'Prince Charming' doctors told me my bleeding was just early menopause and that I was only being hysterical."

"Sorry, honey! Wow, I'd like to thank him, too." He asked Fergie, "Any chance of that, nurse?"

"Maybe," Fergie said. "I'll see if I can catch him. But, as you saw, he's lightning quick. He could be back to clinic by now."

Fergie left in search of Carl, heading first for the doctors' workstation where she hoped to find him typing notes into the patient's electronic health record. But, though the workstation was vacant, a dozen computer screens were aglow with EHRs, displaying "private" health information about patients. One screen projected a patient's chest x-ray, and another held a Pap smear report. There were blood test results for patients attending the diabetes clinic, and insurance and billing records associated with social security numbers. One screen advertised crockpots for sale on the Amazon website. "Damn!" she cursed. "This is so freakin' wrong!"

"Excuse me, sir," someone interrupted.

Fergie turned to find a housekeeping employee entering the workstation.

"Oh, sorry," he said after he saw Fergie from the front. "Excuse me, *ma'am*." His coworker arrived seconds later, followed by a mailroom clerk who began distributing envelopes to various desktop stations.

"Un-freakin'-believable," Fergie muttered. "It's Grand Central Station here." She started logging off the computers until someone yelled, "Stop!"

Fergie recognized that adenoidal voice and its condescending tone. No big surprise—Carl's wife, Dr. Cheryl Kluft, was standing in the doorway.

Cheryl said, "Just what do you think you're doing?"

"These EHRs are supposed to be kept private," Fergie insisted.

"Please," Cheryl chided. "When you log off those computers, it takes forever to get back into the system. Doctors don't have time for such nonsense, Nurse Ferguson."

"It's unethical, unlawful, and against regulations to expose patients' health information like this. It's plain *indecent*."

"Fergie, are you campaigning to become the HIPAA queen of the hospital?"

Despite the heat of the moment, Fergie fleetingly entertained the possibility. Becoming "HIPAA queen" might not be such a bad idea—even if it was Cheryl who suggested it. After all, she deeply valued privacy—medical and personal. And holding a hospital leadership role protecting patients' health information might provide an effective means to put Cheryl in her place. Even the ER docs often complained about Cheryl commandeering computers for her self-serving research projects.

"Look," Fergie said. "You can't leave these computers on, exposing intimate details of patients' lives for anyone to see—or even manipulate! Staff with no right or need to know this stuff come in here all the time—patients and families wander in. It's an *unlocked* room! But, you find it *inconvenient* to turn a computer off and on?"

Cheryl sighed. "Nurse Ferguson, you fail to understand the real time-suck involved in opening and closing EHRs or logging back into the system. We can thank our fevered—and uniquely overfunded—IT department for the burdensome, Rube Goldberg security protocols they keep churning out inside their IT dungeons. Protocols that have, in fact, made these computers *less* secure and *less* private by acting as disincentives for busy doctors to use them."

A housekeeper chimed in, "In the hospital, on the wards and in the clinics, they leave the computers on all the time, too."

Fergie's face turned crimson. "But that doesn't make it right."

Releasing a loud, extravagant sigh, Cheryl said, "Okay, look. See this ugly security badge I have to wear around my neck?" She sauntered over to a computer and continued, "So . . . first we swipe this badge through the card reader like *this*. Then we wait for the internal server to recognize it. And we wait . . . do you feel hell freezing over? Okay, there. Now, I type in my user name. And we wait for the next screen . . . now, my password . . . next screen . . . we enter a randomized six-digit code that changes every 10 seconds on this separate security token attached to my keychain. There. And now we wait for the system to recognize us and . . . now it needs to relaunch." She crossed her arms and warned, "In other words, Nurse Ferguson, don't *ever* turn off one of my computers again!"

The housekeepers exchanged nervous looks and departed, lugging bags stuffed with medical documents ostensibly headed for secure disposal.

Fergie said to Cheryl, "How can you be so cavalier? How—?"

Someone tapped Fergie's shoulder. She turned to find her patient's husband standing behind her, smiling. "Hey," he said, "did you ever find my wife's doctor?"

Teaching Conference Room

Oakland City Hospital

NOON

Nora stood behind the podium, scanning her noontime audience. Its three dozen residents sat classroom-style, lunching on standard fare—bulk-purchased sandwiches, single-serve packets of veggies, and mealy apples. Having reminisced last night with Lydia about their own residency, she was pleased to observe the contrasting diversity—nearly half the residents were women, and whites comprised a minority. She also knew of two gay residents who were advocating for an LGBTQ clinic at Oakland City. *What a tectonic demographic shift in our profession.*

She worried about being unfamiliar to the two-thirds of attendees who had begun residency during her two-year retreat from the teaching program. She hoped they would not equate any rustiness in her presentation with ineptitude.

At five past the hour, she convened the lecture with, "Hello, everyone." After the chatter and crackling cellophane silenced, she introduced herself, double-clicked on her PowerPoint file and said, "Today, we're talking about hyperkalemia."

Her lecture proceeded smoothly for the first half hour. *Too* smoothly, perhaps. While she had found it unnerving to look out intermittently to a roomful of dead-eyed faces, at least no one had fallen asleep or walked out. Now she guardedly smiled and said, "So, now that we understand how a healthy body regulates blood potassium levels, we can better understand the underlying diseases that might be responsible for high blood levels."

But no one smiled back. She acutely regretted dismissing Lydia's advice last night to include a few *New Yorker* cartoons in her presentation today. After taking a gulp of water, she advanced her slides to "Part-II—Hyperkalemia" and said, "So, let's construct a differential diagnosis of hyperkalemia. Clearly, we need to identify and treat the medical problem causing hyperkalemia if we also hope to normalize potassium levels. Among other examples, it could be kidney disease, a genetic condition, an adrenal gland disorder, or a medication side effect."

Her next slide displayed a bulleted list of 20 medical disorders. She said, "We'll focus on these most common disorders responsible for hyperkalemia. But, of course, a much more extensive differential exists. The key point is that your investigation of hyperkalemia always begins with a detailed history and physical examination of the patient. Your evaluation should also include an assessment of the patient for signs and symptoms of hyperkalemia itself—like muscle weakness and distinctive EKG changes."

Nora recognized a resident who thrust his hand into the air, a shiny iPhone in his grasp. "Yes, Aditya?" she said.

Aditya Singh—an amiable third-year resident who had spent his ER rotation under Nora's tutelage—pointed to his cellphone and said, "Dr. Kelly, we all have this software program. It provides a very thorough list of all the causes of hyperkalemia you are talking about."

Quincy Naubert, a first-year intern unfamiliar to Nora, said, "And, actually, we don't read EKGs anymore. They just send an automated digital report directly to the patient's EHR. Then we read the report—not the EKG itself."

Nora felt the smile on her face sag.

Aditya added, "And this software program has many algorithms, also. So, if the patient has hyperkalemia, it tells us next steps to take and what tests to order—that kind of thing."

Nora replied unguardedly, "By 'that kind of thing,' you can't possibly be referring to *clinical reasoning* and *medical decision-making*?"

A prickly silence ensued. Nora winced, noticing that even Aditya recoiled, an injured expression on his face. She quickly offered, "What I mean is, when a patient's test result indicates elevated potassium, do you . . . well, do you *think* about that? Are you *curious* about it? Or do you just . . . do what a software program tells you to do?"

Again, her inquiry was met with blanket disengagement—bored or offended expressions, averted or rolling eyes. *My god*, she rued, *I've joined the ranks of the curmudgeonly old docs I once suffered. I'm sounding like a wounded dinosaur, wallowing in medicine's past glory days.* "Sorry," she said. "I'm just trying to understand what 'being a doctor' *means* anymore."

Lena Grabowski, a wiry intern in the back row, replied, "Dr. Kelly, with all due respect, you sound condescending and critical. That makes it hard to respond to you."

Aditya said to Lena, "I think Dr. Kelly is only trying to explain that she has a different experience of practicing medicine." He said to Nora, "And maybe you're demonstrating how fast medicine is changing. Many of those 'things' you consider important for doctoring and patient assessment are automated now. Or they're made obsolete by newer technologies."

Nora took a deep breath. "Okay. Anyone else? Please—let's talk."

A hand clutching a sandwich raised. Nora acknowledged Darique Pointer, a second-year resident with a prior doctorate in mechanical engineering who often worked with Cheryl on medical device research. He said, "I don't think doctors should waste time *speculating* why someone's potassium is elevated. Or entertaining themselves intellectually with extensive differential diagnoses. I mean, hyperkalemia can be lethal. It's more important to *do* something about it."

The residents sounded a concurring chorus. Lena said, "Besides, what's so wrong with software algorithms or clinical practice guidelines? You could argue that they facilitate fairness because everyone gets treated the *same*—women, racial and ethnic minorities, the poor, LGBTQ's. And that's good for reducing healthcare disparities and injustice."

Darique said, "Besides, it's time-efficient to use CPGs and algorithms. And as the bean counters here always remind us, saving time means saving money that could be spent on things the hospital needs." He held up his sandwich and said, "Like better lunches for interns and residents! The kind *your* generation enjoyed."

Waiting for the laughter to subside, Nora counseled herself against becoming defensive. She said, "Well, you're right. In *my day*, the pharmaceutical companies paid for our lunches. They also paid for our stethoscopes and doctors' bags. We attended their free medical conferences and read their free journals that they filled with biased, self-serving 'research', enriching their stockholders. They gave us pens, coffee mugs, and t-shirts—all emblazoned with pharma logos and drug names. And we ate it all up. But if you believe that Big Pharma's owning us was a *healthy* arrangement for patients and—"

"Okay!" Darique conceded, hands held up in surrender.

Nora softened her tone. "I'm just saying, we doctors should always question what we *think* we know and *where* we get our information. Patients' lives depend on it. And you have to be able to tell when your patient is not a statistical norm in some algorithm or CPG. You have to know when to be disruptive and step in as a *doctor* to rescue an *individual* patient from some population-averaged script. But you can only do that by thinking *critically*. You can only recognize an individual by recognizing uniqueness—which means unearthing a patient's unique history and detecting what a patient's unique body is trying to tell you through the physical exam." Her heart thumped against her chest.

Aditya gleefully proclaimed, "Dr. Kelly! You sound like my grandfather! He was a doctor in Mumbai. When I used to visit him, he took me to his hospitals and played this game. He'd say, 'Take my stethoscope, Aditya, and go listen to that patient. Tell me why he has a heart murmur.' Or, 'Palpate that belly, and tell me the patient's problem.' Unfortunately, I often disappointed him, and that made him sad. But I tried to explain how different it was for me in America, where no one paid such attention to histories and physicals."

Darique said, "It's way more important for doctors to possess computer skills. You need them to manage the EHR. And the EHR is *everything* now."

Lena said, "That's true. We definitely spend more time with virtual patients inside our computers than the actual patients they represent."

Nora steeled herself and put aside her lecture notes. Darique said, "Seriously, if you want *anything* done for your patients, you got to master the keyboard! You order tests, x-rays, and medications on the computer. You communicate with patients and consultants by email. When you want to look something up, you connect with a virtual medical library. You maintain your clinic schedule on your electronic device. You receive text reminders about meetings and lectures, and automated alerts about abnormal lab results. Dr. Kelly, these days, you have to be a computer whiz to be a physician whiz."

"Look," Nora said, "I know medicine keeps evolving, still—"

Lena interrupted, "It's different for subspecialists or docs like you in the ER, compared to us in primary care. You don't manage a couple thousand patients at a time—and for *long* periods of time. So, you don't have to type up a billion notes, or document *every* little thing you do just to generate insurance billings for the hospital. You don't have to document compliance with so-called 'quality goals' every time you see a patient! You just have your simple templates and checkboxes to fill in."

"And you ER guys don't have to respond to *never-ending* emails from patients," said Quincy.

Nora stepped in front of the podium, hyperaware of her seeming irrelevance to this budding future of the medical profession. She said, "I understand things are different. But, still, as a *doctor*—doesn't it feel strange to be . . . *programmed*? To have what you do, in the name of doctoring, be so automated? To deliver patient care that's directed by algorithms and CPGs and software? I mean, at what point do you become an automaton yourself—an actual cog in the machine? And then, who or what is programming you?"

A violent silence erupted. Finally, Quincy suggested in an ostensibly therapeutic tone, "Most doctoring has transitioned from the bedside to the mobile desktop. And frankly, no one sees that trend reversing course any time soon. So, Dr. Kelly, it would be more helpful to us if you understood the skills required to negotiate the complexity of patient care *using* newer technologies—without *them* using *you*. It would be more relevant to hear from you how to practice good medicine given current reality."

"Thank you," Nora said, imaging reporting to Lydia tonight that not even a million cartoons could have saved her from this fiasco.

Lena delicately added, "If we're talking honestly about doctoring, well, a lot of us think that your generation was self-centered and self-referential. It acted as if it *owned* medicine. As if only doctors should—and *could*—have knowledge and skills to heal people or keep them healthy. But under your watch, millions of people couldn't access doctors or afford adequate healthcare. And that wasn't right."

"It's more of a healthcare democracy now," Darique said. "Patients can use the internet to access the same information we have, and for free. They can become experts on their own medical conditions."

Aditya gave a thumbs-up to Darique and said, "Besides, Dr. Kelly, like I used to tell my grandfather: even if you are most masterful at histories and physical exams and making bedside diagnoses, still, the patient's official diagnosis will be whatever the x-ray or the blood test says it is."

"Amen," Quincy said. "It's always a drag when a CT or MRI trumps your clinical judgment by suggesting a different diagnosis to your patient—*and* to your patient's lawyer!"

An intern who'd been thumbing texts said, "You know the only time I do a physical exam? When a patient—usually someone old, over 50—asks like, 'Aren't you going to examine me?' And they look at me like, *Because you really should.* So, I do something—place my stethoscope on her chest or take her pulse. But, honestly, the physical exam doesn't make much difference. Dr. Karlov agrees, and it's what a lot of current research suggests."

Nora felt like an alien in this strange new world of medical practice. *How did this happen so fast and decisively? Have I been so immersed in grief and so insulated in the ER that I didn't see how far I had drifted from the medical mainland?* Desperately wanting to cast an anchor to the present reality of these young doctors, she tried again. "But it matters to patients—being touched and examined by their doctors. That builds trust and strengthens the doctor-patient relationship. And the therapeutic value of that is impossible to quantify."

Darique said, "Hold on. You can't have it both ways—claiming that the value is 'impossible to quantify' while, at the same time, *insinuating* that value exists."

"And the broken doctor-patient relationship you're so worried about?" said Lena. "We inherited that from *your* generation. So maybe all that therapeutic touch you practiced doesn't really work."

Aditya pointed to the wall clock, conveying that the hour had expired. Nora nodded, feeling Time's big hands tossing her to the wayside of modern medical practice. She managed, "Thank you all for coming."

While the audience gathered their things and headed for the exit, she took out her phone and texted Lydia: *911—the Tavern at 6?* In the background, she overheard the residents talking and laughing, and tossing trash and recyclables into bins. They were leaving her lecture and heading toward the future of medicine on paths that emphatically excluded her.

A hand alighted on her shoulder. She turned to see Aditya's smiling face.

"Dr. Kelly," he said, his eyes shimmering. "My grandfather would have loved you so much."

OakTown Tavern

Downtown Oakland

EVENING

Rosalie popped her head into Nora's office doorway and said, "Glad I caught you! Are you up for a drink?"

Nora was buttoning her jacket, preparing to meet Lydia at the Tavern across the street. "Did you hear I might need one?"

"Well . . . yes."

Nora cringed. "So, who told you about my teaching fiasco?"

"Lena Grabowski—she is shadowing me in clinic this month."

"My lecture was total disaster, Rosalie. No, actually, *I* was the disaster."

"Come on, Nora. Everyone has bad days teaching. You are probably just a little rusty, and, well, a little didactic? Maybe the PowerPoints are a bit old-fashioned? But I am sure it was not so terrible."

"It was an epochal catastrophe. And I behaved like a cranky old geezer doc, railing against medical modernity."

"My bad—I should have warned you about the residents. This group is very vocal and challenging. They work and learn so differently, even compared to just a couple years ago when my residency ended. But that is when they had to deal with the hospital transitioning to digital records.

The EHR learning curve—what chaos! A 'curve'... like a roller coaster, really! And you were not engaged much during those transitions."

"Yeah. I feel like an ancient fossil around them."

"It sounds like you could really use a drink! Frankly, I could use one myself. I did not sleep last night because I was feeling so guilty about Richard's death."

"I'm sorry," Nora said, snapping out of her self-pity and resolving to be more supportive of Rosalie. "Let's have that drink. I've already arranged to meet Lydia at the Tavern at six, okay?"

They exited the hospital and stepped into hazy streetlight. Despite the rain, people strolled along Broadway, visiting trendy galleries, pop-up eateries, and artisanal cocktail bars. A crowd stood under the lofty Tribune Tower—the once regal home of the city's historic newspaper. Nearby, customers sat at covered tables outside the OakTown Tavern, appearing not to notice the gaunt old man who was sleeping against the curb on a bed of cardboard.

When Nora entered the Tavern, its jovial host Bill greeted her above the din: "Doctor K!"

"Hey, Bill," she returned. "We'll just grab a table."

"Your pals are here already," he said, pointing. "That table, under the mirror."

Nora froze when she saw Fred and Lydia sitting at the table, sharing a bottle of wine and a dessert. They looked so happy and intimate—like the couple they were no longer supposed to be. She turned away and headed in the opposite direction.

Rosalie caught Nora's sleeve and asked, "But why not join them? Is something wrong?"

"No," Nora whispered. "I just prefer ... a quieter, more private conversation tonight."

Rosalie craned her neck to get a better view of them. "They look intense. Are they ... ?"

"Come on," Nora said, leading Rosalie to a faraway table.

But within minutes after they were seated, Lydia approached with a perturbed expression on her face. "What's up?" she asked. "You think I have cooties? Ebola? You *do* realize that I can see people?"

"Yes," Nora said, preparing for Lydia's continued reproach.

Lydia pointed to Rosalie's huge, yellow purse occupying the third chair at the table and complained, "This requires its own seat?"

Rosalie frowned and placed her purse under the table.

"I'm concerned," Lydia said. "What do you carry in that? A portable dialysis machine? An oxygen tank?"

Looking sympathetically at Rosalie and then wearily at Lydia, Nora said, "Please. We just didn't want to intrude."

Lydia glanced skeptically at Nora. "Yeah? Well, Fred's *gone*, if *that's* what turned you away."

Rosalie said, "Dr. Chandler, it is just that . . . Nora had a tough day. She—I mean, *we*—thought we could talk more privately here."

Bill tossed menus on the table and left. Nora extended a hand to Lydia and said, "Please join us."

Lydia sat down and said, "And FYI, Nora? He's been gone in *that* way for a *long* time—as I've *told* you many times." She glanced coolly at Rosalie and said, "So here *we* are, meeting 911 at the Tavern."

Well, this is uncomfortable, Nora thought. *How does this day just keep getting worse?*

Rosalie said, "We have not ordered drinks yet, Dr. Chandler."

Lydia bristled, hearing Rosalie say *we* for the third time tonight. *When did this punk doctor earn the right to claim such intimacy with Nora? And why is Nora so clueless as to how off-putting that might sound to me? In fact, why is Rosalie even here with "us" tonight?* She replied, "Then let's take care of that." She motioned for Bill who cheerily approached and asked, "Ready to order?"

"Just an old-fashioned for me," Lydia said.

Nora handed her menu to Bill and said, "I don't know why I even look at this anymore. I'll have my usual, please."

Lydia heard Nora's request with some relief, hoping it conveyed a private—if subconscious—preference for all things "usual," including their longstanding friendship. But this heartening reprieve instantly vanished when Rosalie told Bill, "I will have what Nora is having."

"Of course, you will," Lydia muttered.

Although not hearing Lydia's remark, Rosalie registered its acidic tone. And while the Tavern was loud now because of happy hour, the cryptic silence at their table grew deafening. Rosalie anxiously watched as Lydia, with an imperfect sleight of hand, withdrew a pill from her purse and popped it into her mouth. Meanwhile, Nora appeared haggard and oblivious to the communal tension. Feeling like an outsider, and powerless to influence the cryptic discord, she dropped into a familiar despair. She fantasized about taking a hammer-swing of truth to this most *un*happy hour at their table, shattering silences and smashing veneers. Instead, she blurted out another topic sure to cause distress: "Did you see that old man sleeping on cardboard in front of this place?"

Nora emerged from withdrawal and said, "No. But so close to the ER—maybe he's one of our patients?"

"Will be—sooner or later," Lydia said. "'Cause, come street-sweeping day, push comes to shove, he'll be at our doorstep."

Rosalie looked to Nora, hoping to witness any expression of shared outrage. But all she saw was Nora's weariness.

A staff worker arrived with a basket of warm sourdough. "Excuse me," he said, his accent so potent that it automatically transported Rosalie hundreds of miles away.

"Thank you," Rosalie said, watching him limp back toward the kitchen, witnessing his seeming invisibility to the Tavern diners and the revelers at the bar. But how excruciatingly visible he was to her. How dignified and unapologetic and insistently present he was, regardless—perhaps because of—this menial job, and whatever fate had bent his spine and bowed his legs and caused him to lurch and waddle. He maneuvered his way through the boisterous crowd, indifferent to anyone's perception or judgment of him. His presence was brave; audacious. It was important.

Nora said, "Rosalie—you look lost in thought. What are you thinking about?"

"Nothing," she responded flatly. *Absolutely everything*, she thought.

FEBRUARY 8

ER Exam Room

Oakland City Hospital

7:15 A.M.

The patient writhed in bed. His anguished mother entreated, "Ayúdanos, por favor!"

Exasperated, Fergie shouted to Cheryl, "Dr. Kluft!"

The interpreter pleaded, "Doctor, the mother asks to help her son. *Please.*"

Cheryl stood in a corner, her back to everyone. She muted her phone's mouthpiece and replied, "In a minute." Returning to her conversation, she whispered, "I *will* get the data to you before Monday."

"Dios mío!" the patient screamed. "Mi estómago!"

"I'm summoning the on-call doctor," Fergie said, texting for ER backup.

Cheryl ended her call, sighed theatrically, and turned to the interpreter. "This time, I believe our patient asked for 'God'?"

"Doctor," the interpreter said, "this patient is hurting."

"And you think I need an interpreter to tell me that?"

Fergie, struggling to harness her rage, said, "This patient needs morphine and an ultrasound. And we should notify the OR now!"

A patently false smile stretched across Cheryl's alabaster face, forming a thin red crescent under her aquiline nose. "Now you're a doctor, *Nurse* Ferguson?" She winked at the patient and said, "Don't worry. I'm an *actual* doctor."

The interpreter asked Fergie, "Vas a conseguir otro médico?"

"Sí," said Fergie.

"Aye, gracias," said the mother.

"Excuse me?" said Cheryl. "What are we all saying now?" Then, without warning, she placed a hand on the patient's belly and pressed it into his right upper quadrant. He wailed in pain, his mother recoiled, and the interpreter pushed Cheryl from the bedside.

Outraged by the interpreter's boldness, Cheryl shouted, "How dare you!" Simultaneously, Fergie yelled at her, "What's wrong with you?"

Edna rushed in, accompanied by Lizbeth, and said, "What's going on?"

Rosalie arrived, responding to Fergie's summoning text. "I came as fast as I could. I was upstairs, getting ready for clinic . . ." Then, registering Cheryl's presence, she looked inquisitively at Fergie and said, "But you texted that you needed a doctor here."

The interpreter insisted, "We do!"

Edna looked disapprovingly at Rosalie, and Lizbeth took hold of the patient's hand. Fergie walked out while Cheryl exclaimed, "Edna, your nurse Ferguson is a loose cannon!"

Rosalie followed Fergie into the hallway and demanded, "What is this about?"

Fergie seethed, "I would've killed Kluft if I stayed one more second in that room!"

"Calm down," Rosalie said. "I need to understand what is happening before I go back in there."

Fergie clenched her jaw. "Kluft doesn't give a damn about patients! All she cares about is making money off her stupid medical device research."

Rosalie saw tears form behind Fergie's bifocals that expanded when they trailed past the bottom lenses. "But what did she do that was so terrible?"

"The patient in that room has an acute abdomen. But *we're* all waiting on her freakin' conference call with some freakin' device company. She just jabbed her freakin' hand into his abdomen like . . . like a cattle prod!"

"Okay," Rosalie said, placing a comforting hand on Fergie's back. "I got this."

"And she's working *extra* ER shifts this week just to finish more of her freakin' research before her freakin' surgery on Monday! She's been making my life hell!"

"I told you—I got this," Rosalie said, heading back to the patient's room.

Nurse Sarah June Ferguson paced the hallway, trying to discharge her anger. She checked the time—it was 7:15 a.m., and Kluft's night shift would end soon. Nora would clock in at nine, and work would become tolerable again. It would become good again.

Conference Room, Paradox Hotel

Berkeley Marina

8:20 A.M.

Carl Kluft entered the Sadie Lopato Conference Room in the Paradox Hotel on the Berkeley marina. As usual, the registered attendees for this perennial seminar on physician communication were devouring bagels and morning refreshments at side tables, while the centrally located precision-cut fruit cubes remained untouched. SoShanna, the seminar moderator, greeted Carl. As usual, she hyper-smiled and was "so very happy" to see him here—*yet again*. She offered him a seminar tote bag emblazoned with "Better Communication, Better Care!" that contained (they both knew) a similarly inscribed pen and study binder.

"No, thanks," he said. "I have several."

SoShanna said, "Of course. Then just help yourself to the refreshments. We start in—wow!—*two* minutes! Excuse me!"

Carl took a back-row seat, aware that conference staff would try to convince him to move to the front. They would say, "Come on up—we don't bite," not realizing the inanity of this purported inducement. He knew that his chance of being bitten by seminar staff was virtually nil. He also knew that the miniscule risk was distributed equally throughout the room. Still, it had never done any good in the past to explain that to the staff.

And yet, today could prove a statistical outlier on another front. It might mark the day he finally said "no" to these tedious seminars. It might become the day he spoke up for himself and his "communication-impaired" colleagues who'd been forced to attend this banal training as punishment for their low scores on "patient satisfaction surveys" (soon to be renamed, "consumer satisfaction scorecards").

From his vantage point in the back of the room, he recognized many doctors who, like him, were repeat attendees at this remedial communication seminar. Many spoke English as a second—sometimes third—language, or they belonged to cultures in which regarding patients as "consumers" or "customers" was a foreign concept. Like him, they tended to be baffled by the "teachings" and "learnings" they were supposed to "take home" from these dreary lectures. They felt embarrassment and dread when forced to take part in SoShanna's role-playing workshops.

Carl spotted one of the regulars—urologist Huan Kim—and they exchanged a look of commiseration. It pained him to remember how demoralized Huan had looked during their last shared role-play—Huan becoming a Nordstrom's shoe clerk, and Carl acting as his customer. The exercise was supposed to help them understand how to better serve and satisfy their "healthcare consumers." But the only "learning" Carl "took home" that day was a newly realized gratitude for his ability to order shoes online without any human intermediary.

As usual, precisely at 8:30 a.m., SoShanna opened the meeting. She acknowledged "many familiar faces" in the crowd and applauded their "eagerness in returning for more learnings!" Then, as customary, she invited Fred Williams to the stage for his opening remarks. Following a minute of their rote banter, Fred began: "These seminars are offered to help us understand how to create a better care experience for patients at Oakland City Hospital." On cue, SoShanna popped up alongside him, pointing to the logo on the tote bag: "Better Communication, Better Care!" Fred cleared his throat and said, "Surely, we can all get behind that?"

An awkward silence ensued. Fred said, "Look, I know some of you find these seminars . . . *difficult* to attend. We're all busy clinicians, right? You don't need me to tell *you* that."

Carl knew that Fred was attempting to bond with attendees. But no one laughed, nodded, or responded "Amen" today. Perhaps, Carl thought, this group's workshop fatigue had reached its tipping point. Besides, it felt Groundhog-Day surreal, listening *yet again* to the same motivational messages from the same moderator and her staff of so-called "communication experts." If the staff genuinely possessed such expertise, why did it consistently fail to convey its "teachings" to this group? Why did it fail to understand what was being communicated by the repeated appearance of these attendees, providing damning proof that these seminars were a colossal waste of time?

Smiling guardedly, Fred said, "All right now. Say, isn't it nice, finally, to have a day without rain?"

How desperate that sounded to Carl. Still, it was the first agreeable thing anyone said all morning. He looked through the window and watched muted sun glimmer on the bay, the San Francisco skyline beckoning a short distance away. *Yes*, he thought, *'nice' except for having to spend the day here. Here in this aggressively air-conditioned room, listening to another eight-hour replay of nonsensical, mind-numbing corp-speak. Here for a day of slow death by bullet points on PowerPoint slides.*

"We're excited," Fred continued, "to reach out to our community. Especially to those people who are newly insured and looking for doctors. So, learning today how to gratify our very diverse East Bay population ..."

Carl knew by heart every behavioral and communication script that this consulting group had devised to "help" a physician increase patient satisfaction ratings from each and every demographic group of consumers/customers (previously known as *patients*). And he understood those scripts beyond their univariate considerations. He did not know them merely based on whether the patient was white, black, Asian or Pacific Islander, Native American, Hispanic, or Other. He did not know them merely by consideration of sex, gender, religion, age, or economic status. Rather, he could integrate multiple demographics in any permutation and compute a composite gratification strategy. He could deduce a multivariate script designed to gratify a young, biracial, transsexual, impoverished Methodist; or an elderly, Asian, heterosexual agnostic.

Fred asked, "Now who has ever consulted Yelp or Angie's List to find a plumber or electrician?"

Several hands limply rose.

"Excellent. Then you understand the importance of internet rating sites and public report cards. So, people looking for *doctors* are also consulting online ratings!"

It pained Carl to watch his old, if somewhat estranged, colleague spouting such superficialities about doctors and healthcare. *What ever happened to turn Fred so corp? At least Cheryl doesn't disavow her loyalty to device companies. Does Fred even remember how passionate our gang of six used to be about genuine healthcare reform?*

Fred extended his hands as if lifting a weighty truth. "That's why we need your team spirit! Your *personal* patient satisfaction ratings contribute to the hospital's collective score, which is publicly reported."

Carl saw Huan's head lower, his eyes close, and his lips move as if in prayer. He wondered if Huan was praying for release from this bewildering circle of hell, or, perhaps, the strength to endure another role-play as a shoe clerk or short-order cook. Regardless, it felt wrong to idly witness Huan's humiliation. And any further complicity with it through having to "share" another role-play today seemed unconscionable. Yes, there existed ample justification for walking out of this seminar today.

And yet . . .

Carl also knew he would upset his wife by ditching this seminar. Not only would he forfeit the $5,000 compensation he received for his attendance, he'd also lose points on his year-end evaluation that, in turn, would translate into diminished prospects for an annual bonus and salary increase. Indeed, his Cheryl satisfaction score would drop precipitously.

"So," Fred concluded, "that's why we call this workshop 'Better Communication, Better Care!' And we hope you'll take today's learnings home—and to heart."

A newbie in the group—a tall, Brazilian cardiologist of regal bearing—raised her hand. After Fred acknowledged her, she said, "But we all deeply care about our patients and the medicine we practice, Dr. Williams, even if we communicate that in our different ways. We are here today only because our chiefs forced us to come. And, well, just a comment—I don't believe *learnings* is a legitimate English word."

Oh, boy, Carl thought. *A newbie making a classic newbie comment. She'll be returning here for sure.*

The Lakeside Grill

Oakland

NOON

"Dammit," Lydia grumbled, walking into the Lakeside Grill. "Rosalie's like Waldo and herpes—she's everywhere and won't go away."

Nora looked in the direction of Lydia's gaze and saw Rosalie lunching at a window table with Lena and Aditya. The three young doctors were animated and conversing feverishly, looking out to a view of the restaurant's dining piers—long wooden fingers stretching over Lake Merritt. Crystal wineglasses hanging from ceiling racks reflected sunlight that bounced merrily around them. They seemed distant; a world of difference away.

"Do we have to join them?" Nora asked.

"Hell, no!" said Lydia. "I'm not sitting at the kiddies' table."

The host said, "Welcome to Lakeside Grill, ladies. Have you been . . . ?"

Lydia pointed to a faraway table and said, "We'll sit there."

"But I could seat you with a lake view!"

Nora and Lydia shook their heads.

The host shrugged and smiled in a rehearsed way. "Of course." She handed menus to a waiter with instructions to, "Seat these ladies in the dark corner."

The waiter ushered Nora and Lydia to a somber back room. Nora told him, "We already know our orders. And, sorry, but we're in a hurry to get back to work within the hour." After taking their orders, he asked whether they would like waters: "Since the drought began, we don't serve it automatically."

Lydia said, "Sure. In fact, bring a pitcher so I can take some home. I'm doing laundry tonight."

The waiter looked muddled until Nora advised, "Ignore her. And, yes—waters, please." After he left, Nora said, "Really, Lydia? That routine's so old."

"Well, so is his. Like it actually matters if a restaurant saves a glass or two of water?"

"They say every drop counts, although we've had a bit of rain recently."

"It's just absurd dining theater. First, it was about pepper. Why pepper? Why did they start rationing it, carrying it around in sacred vessels, and asking people if they desired a dash of the precious commodity? And the ceremonial pepper grinding! Well, now it's all about water. Salt will be next, mark my—"

"Thank god!" Nora interrupted, waving to Edna and Lizbeth in the entryway. She whispered to Lydia, "Now you'll have to behave like you're at the adults' table."

Lydia groaned. "But I wanted to talk, just you and me—about our lives, Fred and me, your suspicions about Richard's death . . ."

"Hello," Edna said. "Well, you two being here is probably a healthy endorsement of the food."

Nora said, "You know that we doctors know nothing about nutrition."

"That I know," Edna laughed. "May we join you? It was so loud in the main dining room."

Nora made a welcoming gesture, and Lydia offered a synthetic smile.

Edna said, "Drs. Nora Kelly and Lydia Chandler, this is Lizbeth Tanner, a nursing student from the Palmer Institute. She's shadowing me in the hospital."

"You have a great teacher," Nora told Lizbeth. "And, I'm sorry, but haven't we met?"

"Yes and yes," Lizbeth replied. "I'm learning a lot from Edna, especially hands-on clinical care. And, well, we didn't officially meet. But I was with Edna the other day, when Mr. Pulaski's body was found."

"Yes, I remember," Nora said, an added measure of sobriety weighting her spirits.

Intending to shift the discussion, Lydia said to Lizbeth, "But Nora keeps telling me that nobody's interested in hands-on care anymore—well, doctors, at least."

"That's a shame," Lizbeth said. "I love learning the physical exam. This morning I heard rales in a patient's chest. And, well, it felt . . . *sacred* to get that close to another human being and hear him inside out. To understand what his lungs were saying so we could help him breathe."

"What a refreshing point of view," Nora said. "My medical residents insist that the physical exam is almost worthless, and that the art of auscultation or palpation is quaint."

Edna said, "Isn't that the truth now? Nora, down in the ER, some of your residents don't even touch the patients. They just whip out their iPads, order tons of tests and x-rays, and then they leave. They become ghost doctors. Later, from some faraway place, they text their medication and discharge orders to us nurses. And I can't tell you how often we nurses are preparing patients for discharge from the ER, and we have to convince them that, at some point, they had actually been seen by a doctor."

Lydia said, "Modern patient care: where every body part is tested, but no body and *nobody* is touched."

Noting the pained reaction on Lizbeth's face, Nora offered an antidote. "So, it's heartening to hear that nursing is keeping the clinical arts alive." Still, she was surprised by the effort it required to sound buoyant for Lizbeth. She recalled that last week a resident tried to rationalize his inability to identify a patient's heart murmur: "What difference does it make what I hear—or don't—through a stethoscope if we're going to order an echo on the guy anyway?"

The waiter arrived with waters and—to Lydia's dismay—Rosalie trailed behind him. "Hello, everybody," she said, pulling up a chair. "Good to see we *still* have appetites."

Edna shrugged and looked away.

"Meaning what?" Lydia said, her ears scorching from Rosalie's repeated and presumptuous utterance of *we* in present company.

"Well," Rosalie said, looking sheepishly at Lydia, "it has been a hard few days for many of us. I lost a patient—Richard—on Monday. Everyone at this table—except you—witnessed him dead. And this morning in the ER, Fergie and Cheryl fought over a patient. I got involved, and Nora took over for me when she started her shift. Everyone here—except you—was involved in that, too."

A prickly silence ensued. It ended when Lizbeth said, "It sounds stressful, all around."

"Yes," Rosalie said. "And, poor Nora! Yesterday, you had such a traumatic experience teaching the residents."

"Oh?" said Lydia, unhappily blindsided by the news. She glanced at Nora, her expression conveying, *Why didn't you mention that to me before?*

Nora's face flushed. "It was nothing, Lydia. I was hoping to talk about it last night at the Tavern. It just . . . just didn't come up."

Winking at Nora, Rosalie said in a conspiratorial tone, "Do not worry. I just finished lunch here with two residents who attended your lecture yesterday, and I convinced them how great you really were."

Nora froze upon hearing Rosalie say "were." She couldn't tell whether Rosalie intended that to be past or present tense. And when she tried to check her insecurity against the reactions of others at the table, she found no edifying clues in their expressions.

Cellblock 47, San Sebastian State Prison

Marin County

EVENING

Jack waited for the "Lights out" command to bring shielding darkness to cellblock 47. He waited for the nightly cell check to end before allowing himself to dwell freely on Richard.

Only after the guards retreated did he finally let down his own internal guard.

And the agony was instant; the rage primal.

A harsh phrase looped cruelly inside his head: *I should have been with Richard.* It was so loud and insistent that he didn't hear the usual nocturnal howling from nearby cells.

Through the small boxy window in his 10×10 cell, the watchtower light flickered.

I know you didn't leave me, Richard.
I know you didn't kill yourself.

FEBRUARY 9

Lake Merritt

Oakland

8:00 A.M.

Nora sat under a stone portico, staring at the rippling waters of Lake Merritt as another welcome rainfall pummeled Oakland. Dark clouds were reflected in the massive windows of the nearby Cathedral of Light.

She recognized several familiar faces among the stalwart lakeside crowd: two joggers in rain gear who appeared unhappy today; the nun and her labradoodle, strolling under an umbrella marked with AARP logos; and the techies, clutching their tablets and Starbucks, gathered under a canvas canopy.

Today, she simply could not do any of "it" to prepare for work—not the jog, the self-awareness ritual, or the mindfulness practice. Instead, she sat here idly with her black coffee and bad attitude. *My therapist will be disappointed to hear of this—if I tell her. But she vacations an entire month in France? Well, then, she risks missing some of the show.*

Glancing toward Oakland City Hospital, she wondered how she was going to survive her morning shift. The dowdy building appeared so outdated in relief against the fashionable new condominium complexes surrounding it. It looked uninspired, like a child's simple drawing—all straight lines that rigidly intersected at 90-degree angles—no suppleness anywhere. Its leaden industrial color suggested anemia, fatigue, and essential nutrient deficiencies. In too many ways, it reminded Nora of herself.

She was also reminded of the photograph of her residents group, oddly resurrected twice this week. It companionably paralleled this view of the hospital, projecting its timeworn landscape of past-generation doctors.

It's probably time to retire, Nora thought. The clues were stacking up: waning passion about healthcare reform, no energy for admin or policy battles, and fading trust in "the system." Add to that the diminishing comradery in the trenches, her irrelevance to the teaching program, and a threadbare sense of belonging to the profession. *Yes, time to retire—period!*

It was a mistake two years ago—clear only now in retrospect—to return to work after losing her husband and daughter. She should have opted instead for early retirement which would have allowed her to exit the profession with her reputation and clinical legacy intact, and her love of medicine preserved. *I'm going to blame that bad decision on my therapist—at least while she's away.*

"Hey, Nora!" someone shouted.

Winston Wang, Fergie's statuesque husband, was fast approaching. Nora happily made space on the bench and asked, "Where are you rushing off to?"

After catching his breath—and the eye of a stylish jogger in signature REI rainwear—he said, "Well, Fergs is getting off at 8:30 and—"

"No! I thought she was working a double!"

He grimaced.

"Sorry," she said. "It's totally selfish, I know. But working with her was the only bright spot in my shift ahead."

"Well, she phoned just an hour ago. Said she got a colleague to sub for her, and that if I didn't come to rescue her *at 8:30 sharp*, she was going to murder *someone*."

Nora laughed. "If she does, it wouldn't be much of a mystery to guess her victim."

"Yeah, boy—that Cheryl Kluft sounds like a real pain."

"She is. Still, I admit, in her own dark way, she does some good for the hospital. Her device research generates tons of money for Oakland City. And it attracts choice research-minded candidates to our residency programs."

"Still, I haven't seen Fergs this angry in a while. People rarely get under her skin."

"Well, fortunately, it'll just be a few more days that she'll have to put up with Cheryl's ER overtime."

"Yeah?"

Nora nodded. "Cheryl's having cardiac stent surgery on Monday—and, yes, she actually *has* a heart. So, she's trying to finish some data collection for a grant beforehand. Unfortunately, a lot of the data she needs is tucked inside old paper charts in the ER."

"Well, I wish that was the all of it for Fergs. But Cheryl also filed a disciplinary action against her over some 'incident' yesterday. Then Edna reprimanded her for breaking protocol by calling in a backup doc. And last night, *another* meth-head (or K-head?) took a swing at my girl."

"That's awful! Is Fergie all right?"

"She's okay. But, man—she desperately needs a break."

Two male passersby glanced overlong at Winston, reminding Nora of Fergie's complaint about her husband's pansexual appeal and the intrusions on their privacy that it often invited. Shaking off the distraction herself, Nora continued, "Things are really stressful at work. Everything's changing so fast. Don't even get me started on the electronic health records! Our patient loads keep increasing, and compliance requirements are proliferating like weeds. The money's always drying up while the government's playing politics with everyone's health insurance. And the hospital's getting so top-heavy with managers and admins . . ." She winced. "Sorry, that was indelicate of me, after Richard's death."

He reassuringly patted her hand and said, "We're attending his memorial service on Saturday. Fergs said they were strong-arming all staff to attend in a show of support for the hospital. Are you going?"

"Yes. Though I'm feeling guilty because I'm one of the few people at work who knew Richard, and I'm afraid no one else will speak up. But I'd feel phony offering a tribute after dropping contact with him and Jack—my fault, entirely. And then, there's the forced turnout because of admin's delusion that robust attendance will boost public trust in the hospital."

Winston said, "Well, even if it doesn't, maybe it'll boost some feeling of community among the staff."

Nora studied Winston's profile—his smooth, chiseled face and tousled black hair. *How lucky he and Fergie are to have found each other.* She said, "That's an uplifting view."

"For me, it's a choice—and often a chore—to maintain optimism. Still, that's what I consciously choose every day." He pointed to the sky and said, "Besides, look; we're finally getting respite from the drought. And the Warriors trounced the Bulls last night. Fergs and I got a lead on an apartment we're checking out tomorrow." He stood, assumed a superhero posture—arms akimbo, chest expanded—and declared, "And now I'm going to rescue a beautiful damsel in distress."

"You'd better hurry! It's almost 8:30. *Sharp.*"

Exaggerating his deep baritone, he proclaimed, "Do not fear! The damsel will experience a magnificent day." He relaxed his pose and said, "We're having breakfast at Saul's, and then catching an afternoon matinee. Tonight, I'm surprising her with karaoke at the Mel-O-Dee Lounge. I'm going to serenade her with 'My Funny Valentine.'"

"Fergie's going to die laughing."

"Well, not a bad a way to go, right?"

Nora gave a thumbs-up and waved goodbye. She watched in awe as Winston proceeded so damn optimistically toward the old hospital.

Lydia's Office

Pathology Department, Oakland City Hospital

Noonish

Lydia pleaded over the phone, "C'mon, Nora! You gotta eat."

"I can't," Nora said. "All hell's broken loose here. And Fergie took the day off! Besides, I already had a . . . what? A protein bar, maybe. But it might've been a cardboard sandwich."

"What a shame. 'Cause here I got us two garden salads, sides of basmati rice and organic greens, and strawberries for dessert."

"Really?"

Lydia tossed another handful of microwaved popcorn into her mouth. "Well, no," she confessed. "But I could—"

"Sorry, Lydia. I got to go."

Lydia hung up the phone and brokenheartedly scanned her exuberantly decorated office, adorned with Valentine's Day paraphernalia everywhere. But instead of the festivity it should have evoked, a dispiriting note prevailed. The ornamentations oppressed and exerted a tyrannical message that made her feel contrary.

She lobbed a popcorn kernel at Timmy, which caused him to dance. But not even his skedaddling could make her laugh.

A knock sounded, and she called out hopefully, "Nora?" But when she opened her office door, Edna answered: "No, just me." She handed over a paper bag.

Lydia peered into the bag and said, "Okay. Thanks."

"Nora's at lunch with Rosalie. Or, at least, she was."

"Oh?" said Lydia, her heart constricting.

Before turning away, Edna appraised the office decorations and said, "Very festive."

Visiting Room,
San Sebastian State Prison

Marin County

2:50 P.M.

"I knew something terrible had happened," Jack said, tears clinging to his jaw. "When Richard didn't show on Sunday and didn't call . . ."

Edna said, "I'm so very sorry, Jack."

"These last few days . . . just agony."

Shifting uncomfortably in her chair, Edna said, "Everyone at the hospital sends their condolences on your loss."

Jack took a deep breath. "Richard is no 'loss.' He is . . . was . . . my *life*."

"Of course," Edna said. "I do understand about that, as you well know."

"So, did you draw the short straw? Did Nora, Fred, and the others fight you for the opportunity to come here and convey everyone's condolences?"

"Don't waste time talking such nonsense."

"Or did you come because you *owe* me?"

She looked harshly at him. "There's no disagreement between us about me owing you." She glanced at her watch, dreading the unbearable eternity of their remaining 10 minutes together.

"You're right. Sorry, Edna. Still, I'm calling in a favor from you now."

Edna winced. It was painful seeing Jack in such distress, especially knowing she was to blame for most of it. "What favor, Jack?"

"To repeat, in detail, everything you saw and heard in Richard's office on Monday."

"Please, not again. Why keep torturing yourself? Richard left a note! His death was clearly suicide."

"Impossible. Something's being overlooked."

"You're feeling doubtful only because you hadn't known the details of his cancer. But he was terminal, and surely he just wanted to spare you. You already had your share of troubles. Besides, he was getting *aggressive* medical care."

Jack shook his head—part disagreement, part bewilderment. "Richard visited here every Sunday. And through this fucking glass, I watched him being worn down by false accusations at work. So, it kills me to imagine him withholding . . . that he was dying. *Dying*, Edna! It breaks my heart, wondering if he didn't believe we were close enough, strong enough . . . wondering if he couldn't trust me to suffer the ordeal with him."

"No. It's just the opposite of what you're saying. He said so little because he knew how much you cared. Look, he even took that Hail Mary chance with experimental chemo, trying to stay alive for *you*. Well, at least until he literally couldn't."

"You don't understand. I knew him. He was constitutionally, philosophically, and spiritually incapable of suicide. He'd never take his own life."

Edna sighed. "Well, by all the doctors' accounts, his death—his *suicide*—was painless. The potassium went straight into his chemo port.

And he went by his own hand, on *his* terms. We both know how important that is."

"But Richard's death is unreal to *me*. And it makes no sense. So, just . . . convince me. Make it *real* to me. Describe everything again in vivid detail so I can see it and feel it."

Edna steeled herself, aware of her immeasurable debt to Jack. She knew she'd never be able to repay him for his unwitting self-sacrifice on her behalf. Or worse still, for being kept in the dark about the fuller extent of her betrayal. Finally, she submitted, "I'll always be grateful for what you did for Benny and me."

She was relieved when Jack placed a finger across his lips to suggest silence about Benny. She already agonized daily over Benny's final tortured days and Jack's selfless actions to alleviate his suffering. She despised her role in the sordid debacle and her responsibility for Jack's imprisonment. "From the beginning?" she said.

"Yes; from the moment you stepped into Richard's office. Exactly where and who—"

"I understand. But remember: I didn't see everything. And you know how distracted I get by those horrid computers. I had a student with me, too."

"Just do your best."

"All right," she began. "It was Monday, February 6. I was lead nurse on the code team. The operator called a Code Blue to the 10th floor . . ."

FEBRUARY 10

Jack London Square

Oakland Estuary

EVENING

It was dusk at Jack London Square, and trendy restaurants along the Oakland estuary brimmed with patrons. Winston and Fergie walked the shoreline bordering the vibrant plaza.

"Nothing beats a night like this," said Winston.

Fergie looked into his tobacco-brown eyes and sighed. "You've made your point."

"Sorry. I just miss you, Fergs. I miss us. I miss our weekends, and nights out together, like this."

She handed a dollar to a stranger who was requesting 10. "Yeah, but my extra shifts pay our rent."

Winston cringed. Moving to Oakland from their more affordable Hayward rental had been his idea. And the one-bedroom they checked out today (at $2,900 per month) was even more decrepit than the last prospect. "I wish I'd known what was going to happen with East Bay rents."

"Who could've predicted that Oakland would become the fifth most expensive rental market in the country? And I never expected afford-ability problems on an RN's salary."

They strolled along the waterfront, watching boats rock in their berths and passengers piling into ferries headed for San Francisco. They took the Bay Trail back to the central square where people held signs soliciting money, food, jobs, or a home for a beloved pet.

"Look," said Winston, pulling Fergie close. "I'm expecting a check for my piece on homelessness in *The Register*. And I've almost finished my first draft—"

"Stop, Win! I know you're trying. And I don't want you to give up on writing. You write about things that are important to me and lots of other people. Besides, I love my work . . . well, most of the time. And it makes me happy when I can make a difference in a patient's life."

"Sarah June Ferguson, let's make a deal: one more year in Oakland, and if I can't make it, we leave. We can move someplace affordable where we don't have to sacrifice our lives for a house, a location, a *thing*. Someplace where we live and work for each other, not some landlord."

"I'm wooed," Fergie said, laughing. "Just don't start singing 'My Funny Valentine' again! Man, I couldn't believe you did that last night!"

"Even I didn't know I could sing that badly," he said. "But I'm serious about moving. Besides, Oakland is changing so fast. It's losing its diversity, and artists can't afford to live here anymore. The moneyed class is buying up everything and branding the entire city, treating it like some damn commodity—"

"Stop!"

"Sorry. I was on my soapbox again, huh?"

"Yes, but . . . over there? It's Lydia and Fred."

"Wow, they look real angry with one another."

"Don't stare!"

"Okay. But, man, are they fierce! Still, I'd place my money on Lydia."

"Let's go, Win. I can't be around any more angry doctors this week."

He raised his Warriors jacket to obstruct her view of them. Then he buried his face in her neck and tried to make her laugh.

"Stop," she begged as they stole away.

"Ain't never gonna happen, Fergs."

Fred's Home
Berkeley

LATE EVENING

Fred dimmed the headlights of his silver Lexus before stealthily maneuvering it up the driveway of his Grizzly Peak home in the Berkeley hills. Trying not to alert his family to his arrival, he stared wearily up at the illuminated windows of their tri-level home and braced against the darkness he saw.

But within minutes, he felt as if the oxygen inside the car was diminishing, and the steering wheel was pressing against his chest.

He grabbed his inhaler from the glove compartment. *One puff, two puffs.* Gradually, his shortness of breath abated. Still, he could not forget Lydia's wounded expression, and his breathtaking foolishness in mistakenly confronting her an hour ago.

Shadows flickered across the living room windows—silhouettes of his wife and children pulsed by the light from their giant TV screen. He took an extra puff off his inhaler, fantasizing about its ability to fortify him against another sleep-deprived night of hang-ups from an anonymous caller that provoked such damning glares from his suspicious wife.

Nora's Home

Oakland

EVENING

Nora lay in the zero-gravity chair on her back deck, wishing it could actually free her from her earth-bound sorrow. She stared at the night sky above Oakland's scintillating cityscape, while Bix, her tuxedo cat, rubbed his velvety head against her forearm. Reviewing her dispiriting workweek, topped by her disastrous lecture to the residents, she said, "Bix, I'm not irrelevant to *you*, am I?"

He mewed and placed a paw—so white, practically luminous—on her chest.

"I definitely prefer you to my therapist," she said. "You're easier to talk to. I understand you. And you *always* make me feel better. God knows, you're less expensive."

Her cellphone chimed, predictably disturbing Bix. His ears pricked up—two perfect triangles—and he jumped off her lap.

"Come on, Bix!" she beckoned. "We've tried every sound option on this phone."

But he crouched under a chair, only the white ruff on his chest visible.

"You're so sensitive," she admonished, typing in her cell's security code. A new text from Lydia appeared: *Sorry. Can't make 2night.*

"Argh! Can you believe this, Bix? Lydia keeps complaining about not having enough *quality time* together. She insists we need to talk tonight, and then she stands me up!"

Bix started toward Nora, but suddenly stopped to assume a balletic pose—one hind leg up behind his head, the other stretching forward.

Nora sighed and texted to Lydia: *Sorry, 2. R U OK?*

Lydia replied: *No. But 2 complicated 4 text. C U 2morrow at memorial.*

"Great," Nora complained. "I'm spending Saturday at Richard's memorial, and now I have a vexed friend to boot. Bix, you're damn lucky to be a cat."

Nora signed off: *OK. C U 2morrow.* After she put aside her phone, Bix returned to her lap. She told him, "I know. I'm damn lucky you're a cat, too."

Cradling Bix, Nora shut her eyes and sunk into her chair. She prayed to someone, anyone listening, for a dream tonight in which her family appeared. She just wanted to see them again, in any conceivable form.

FEBRUARY 11

Mountain View Cemetery

Oakland

AFTERNOON

Lydia scanned the rolling grounds of Mountain View Cemetery, imagining all the buried bodies here. As chief of pathology, she had "met" many of them. She had excised and examined their organs—livers, lungs, spleens—trying to determine a cause of death. She had scrutinized biopsies of their breasts or prostates or skin, searching for malignancy or infection.

But here at the cemetery, miles from the path lab and morgue, she could be tenderly present with them, with her hands freed of knives, scalpels, and all mutilating instruments of her profession. She could keep gentle company with these beautiful bodies that rested in a consummate peace that reliably grounded her as well.

On countless occasions, she had walked meditatively through this cemetery or driven its meandering roads. Wherever she looked, sage stone angels and benevolent saints perched atop old tombs and gazed meaningfully at her. Some pointed their fingers to the sky and others pointed to the ground, profoundly reassuring her with their collective uncertainty.

And it soothed her to see the gravesites so lovingly attended— evidence of the living in caring communication with the dead. The bent old women clearing tombstones of weedy overgrowth. The small toys, worn photographs, and sacks of oranges that were left for lost loved ones. The families laying floral wreaths or pine boughs at burial sites. Ubiquitous metal cones that contained offerings of remembrance—daisies, roses, ferns, flags, colorful pinwheels. Here, the dead were identified in terms of human relationship—as grandfather, grandmother, spouse, child, parent, friend—connections writ in stone.

But today's visit to Mountain View was not a routine solitary sojourn. Instead, she was present for the very public occasion of Richard's memorial, joining many coworkers, who, like her, attended halfheartedly under pressure of admin's strong-armed "request."

Still, she closed her eyes to the assembling crowd to steal a private moment and feel her connection to this reliable place of solace. *My paradox*, she thought. *My sanctuary and my—*

A hand landed clumsily on her shoulder. She gasped, her fiercely private moment of deep serenity ending, and she turned to discover Carl Kluft, the source of the ham-fisted greeting. Big-boned, doe-eyed Carl, who—despite his enormous hands and predictable obtuseness—had long sustained a successful OB-GYN practice at Oakland City.

"Dammit, Carl! You scared me!" she scolded.

"Sorry," he said, giving her a whiplash hug.

Lydia glared at him, infuriated by his intrusion and the overly rehearsed expression of sympathy on his face—a byproduct, she knew, of his seminar trainings in empathy mirroring. She took a moment to cool down, recalling Nora's sympathetic words about him. She also gave thanks that, as a pathologist, she had never needed to worry about patient satisfaction scores from corpses, and she'd never been forced to endure all the patient-physician relationship workshops that were routinely foisted upon Carl. She said, "Didn't they ever teach you not to sneak up on people?"

"Actually, no. But it is sensible advice."

My god, Lydia thought, *this poor guy* ... He was always struggling to overcome his social inadequacies, yet with meager evidence of success throughout the *decades* she'd known him since residency. But Nora was right; at least he *tried* to attune to other people. Still, how much easier it would be to deal with him if his face didn't always look like an emoticon. Attempting a conciliatory tone, she said, "Sorry. I'm a little over-caffeinated."

But Carl compulsively proceeded with his goal of connecting with her. He leaned closer and whispered, "We'll all miss Richard." Then he pulled back, frowned, and gave her a knowing, sympathetic wink.

His response stripped Lydia of any remnant of tranquility. And for the first time, she felt herself incapable of experiencing the deep peace that she had always been able to find here. She felt the urge to retaliate against his witless intrusion. But before she could speak, he said, "Lydia, you look upset, and that's understandable. It's difficult when someone dies—"

"You moron!" shouted Lydia, her tears evaporating in the heat of her anger. "I'm not upset over Richard!" Pushing him away, she yelled, "Leave me alone! Comfort someone else!"

Carl was stymied by the hostility that his good intentions seemed to have provoked—*yet again*. But what had he done that was so off-putting? What was so wrong about trying to comfort someone who was (A), standing alone in a crowd, (B), looking somber, and—for heaven's sake!—(C), attending a *funeral*.

And yet, he was not completely surprised by Lydia's rebuff. It sadly reaffirmed his tortured self-awareness about his universal failure to relate, and his innate inadequacies as a friend and colleague . . . a human being . . . a doctor incapable of improving his patient satisfaction scores.

He decided to brave a final attempt to connect with Lydia, reviewing purportedly useful communication strategies recommended by seminars past. There were abundant tips and mnemonics to consider (a burdensome consequence of his photographic memory). And sundry communication "maps" and templates to guide one through "critical" or "courageous" conversations with patients and colleagues. The basic *ABCDs of Communicating Well* (which, as Carl had argued with its teacher, improperly suggested the plural for a single, non-repeating set of four letters). Or, he could try one of the *Five Fab Tips for Tackling Difficult Subjects* (each tip worded in 1960s cool). Perhaps he might use *Talk to Me, Talk to Thee* (a nonsensical directive, impossible for any rational person to implement).

He decided upon *Three Big Steps for Crossing a Long Bridge*. He understood that the "bridge" was metaphorical, representing both a divide *and* a connection between two parties. Accordingly, he would (1), *acknowledge*, (2), *validate*, and, (3), *respond to* Lydia's emotions. He began, "Lydia, I acknowledge that you're upset, and I validate your—"

But before he could take the final *Big Step*, Lydia stepped away. He watched her heading toward the mausoleum, her back turned to him, the bridge between them lengthening (metaphorically).

Post-Op Recovery Room

Oakland City Hospital

AFTERNOON

"Sorry, Mr. Holtzman, but I need to leave," said Nora, eyeing the exit from the surgical recovery ward. "I can't be late for a funeral."

Her patient, an ER frequent flyer in his late forties, replied, "Not mine you're planning on, I hope."

"No," she said. "It's for a man who worked here almost as long as me."

"Oh—that guy in the papers who killed himself? Was he the one who maybe fleeced the hospital?"

Nora shrugged. "Investigations of both are still underway."

"Wait!" he said, pointing to his freshly amputated leg. "I heard that guy didn't have a leg to stand on in court."

Nora groaned.

"Look, Doc, it's your fault! If you hadn't taken such good care of me in the ER and sent me off to surgery, *this* never would've happened."

"Yeah, because otherwise you'd be dead from infection and gangrene. Seriously, you're going to lose your other leg if you don't start taking your diabetes meds. You have MediCal now, and there's no excuse anymore."

An impish smile spread across his face. "But if I stayed healthy, I'd miss our ER liaisons. I can't let my new health insurance keep us apart. How would I ever see you again?"

"In your dreams," Nora said, waving goodbye.

Minutes later, she was driving along Piedmont Avenue en route to Richard's service. Her sage-colored Prius passed a world of restaurants she hadn't frequented for two years: Baja Taqueria ... Ninna's Thai ...

Cesar's tapas bar . . . Little Shin Shin . . . Lo Coco Italian. *But I've so little appetite for the world anymore.*

Despite what her therapist claimed, she knew it was unrealistic—impossible, even—to "rejoin the world" and return to "normal life." What did that even mean for someone in her situation? What legitimate "normal" could exist for how a person should live, think, and feel after witnessing her family being swept away by a rogue ocean wave? No one experiencing that would ever be "normal" again.

Nora drove through the cemetery's massive metal gate that was flung, disconcertingly, wide open. Driving by so many tombstones and mausoleums en route to Richard's service, she thought: *How comforting it must be to have a physical gravesite or urn to locate the people you've lost. But having only the ocean to look to . . . the loss feels so vast and boundless.*

When she arrived at the hillside lot where funeral-goers were congregating, she took a moment to recall her therapist's parting advice on Monday: *Take a few deep breaths to center yourself before the service begins so you're not thrown off balance by the weight of another death.*

But when drawing her first meditative breath, she was shocked to realize that it was Jack's absence that generated any destabilizing force. He should be here to mourn Richard, and to defend him against the banal corporate narratives that will doubtlessly ritualize his internment. Yes, it was Jack's figurative death—without Richard, his freedom, and his career—throwing her off balance now. And, she also realized that his losses were as oceanic as hers.

ER Nurses Station

Oakland City Hospital

AFTERNOON

"Glad I could help," said Fergie, secretly grateful for any excuse to bow out of Richard's service.

Edna said, "Thanks all the same for switching with me. I'll be back for overnight shift." She removed the doctor's coat she had borrowed from the residents' on-call room to protect her black pantsuit from occupational exposures.

Fergie recognized that pantsuit. It was Edna's perennial outfit for every hospital occasion. "No need to hurry back," she said, hoping to clock as many hours as possible today.

"Don't forget: hourly dressing changes for the GSW in 3, and saline for the overdose in 7."

Fergie saluted.

Lizbeth said, "Have a good time, Edna!"

Edna rolled her eyes and left.

Shamefacedly, Lizbeth asked Fergie, "I said something wrong *again*?"

"No," Fergie said. "It's just . . . well, Edna's going to a *memorial service*. It's for that CFO, Mr. Pulaski. The code you both attended on Monday?"

Lizbeth slapped her forehead. "I might've figured as much. I just always get so nervous and . . . stupid around her."

"You act like lots of people around their bosses. Besides, Edna could've told you where she was going."

But this fresh gaffe left Lizbeth feeling even more insecure. "She doesn't tell me personal stuff. Still, I watch her like a hawk, and I had no clue she was even close to Mr. Pulaski. In fact, during his code I thought Edna acted . . . businesslike. Even annoyed sometimes."

"Lizbeth, you gotta cut yourself some slack if you hope to survive as a nurse. You need to realize you can't—and *shouldn't*—take responsibility for what other people do and say. That goes for colleagues as well as patients." Sensing that Lizbeth only half-heartedly concurred, she added, "And, by the way? Edna wasn't close to Pulaski."

"Well, then I'm really thickheaded, because, to me, Edna looked upset heading to his service."

Fergie shrugged. "All I know is she called me last night to ask if I could sub for her today. So, something must've happened pretty recently to change her mind about going."

Lizbeth was not surprised to hear about Edna abruptly changing plans. Lately, she'd done it so often that it had been difficult to rely on her for predictable teaching hours. And her moods had become erratic, too, tending, unfortunately, toward edgy and combative. Last night, outside the breakroom, Lizbeth overheard Edna arguing with Rosalie about something. The day before, in the parking lot, she saw Edna alone and crying in her car.

Looking probingly at Fergie, Lizbeth debated whether to mention these observations. But her insecurity lent too much self-doubt to her judgment. Besides, disclosing such vague observations about her mentor might be disrespectful, intemperate, and even risky. Better to reflect on these concerns in her journal tonight. Instead, she asked, "Do *you* think Pulaski committed suicide? I heard that Dr. Kelly doesn't."

"I have no idea," Fergie said. "People are so indecipherable."

"That's for sure," Lizbeth concurred, thinking of Edna.

"You see so much life, working in the ER," Fergie said. "Some of it is incredibly beautiful, but there's also lots of ugly and sad. Still, you never know what your colleagues and patients are thinking, or how they suffer, or whether they're even telling you the truth. However, there's *one* thing a *good* nurse *always* knows: how to care for wounds and the wounded. In my book, that's a huge freakin' deal." Fergie motioned for Lizbeth to follow. "Come on. I'll show you."

Mountain View Cemetery

Oakland

AFTERNOON

It had been years since Cheryl Kluft last routinely cringed over her husband's incessant social gaffes and alien-like behavior. Now she watched him retreat after Lydia's public brush-off, dispassionately noting: *Well, that was bound to happen.*

She had not appreciated the severity of his social impairment when they met in 1987 as residents at Oakland City and, months later, impulsively married. And subsequently, throughout their three all-consuming years of residency, she had remained oblivious to his awkward social interactions simply because they could so rarely spend time outside the hospital setting where his behavior and habits were tolerated—rewarded, even. Then, with each of them on staggered overnight call at the hospital every second or third day, they rarely shared a wakeful hour between them.

Still, she knew that meeting Carl had saved her soul. Beforehand, her four years spent in medical school had been little more than a tortuous attempt to satisfy her parents' demand that she become an MD. Carl's kinetic energy had provided an immediate antidote to her numbing despair. His exuberant companionship uplifted her sails throughout their exhausting 80-hour workweeks.

But after residency ended and they joined the hospital staff, everything changed. With their work schedules suddenly relaxed, they faced ample opportunity for unbuffered time together. She began to wear down in the near-constant exposure to Carl's racing mind and whirlwind ways. His incessant, rapid-fire speech made her anxious and irritable. His need to stay close to her, at work and home, felt aggressive and intrusive. Soon, she felt just as imprisoned by his day-to-day compulsions as she had by her parents' obsessive control over her life. And she became solidly reacquainted with her old despair.

Those early post-residency years also proved lonely. Her parents withdrew, having accomplished their mission to see their doctor-daughter marry. And, after realizing they would not be provided the grandchildren they expected, they vacated her life completely and moved to the family villa on the Amalfi Coast. More significantly, no one from their gang of six made themselves available for friendship, or even seemed to notice her entrapment and misery. Jack promptly disappeared into the closet with Richard. Lydia took off for a pathology fellowship in Michigan, returning even more antisocial than she'd been. Fred began climbing the admin ladder and never looked back for her or Carl. Nora single-mindedly focused on establishing her clinical reputation and family.

Attempts to socialize or share a public life with Carl were always wincing endeavors. And privately, his physical awkwardness and fixation with scripted technique made lovemaking depressing, devoid of spontaneity and attunement to her desires.

And yet, he had always "been there" for her. He was, to this day, the only person who hadn't abandoned her. Without complaint, he helped carry her through residency and into a phenomenal career. And, unlike her parents, he never demanded she relinquish her vocational aspirations or bear him children.

Feeling deeply indebted to Carl, she was determined to return his loyalty. She worked hard to devise work and life strategies to adapt to his idiosyncrasies—strategies that could accommodate his closeness while protecting her sanity and allow mutual activities to compensate for their lack of social and family lives.

And she succeeded finally in this regard. By happenstance, five years after joining the medical staff, she attended a healthcare conference where she was recruited by the medical device industry. Its glittery parallel universe offered her a bright refuge from loneliness and the humdrum of daily clinical practice. The device companies provided her with generous research grants and stock options, sent her on lecture tours, and gave her prospects for lucrative patents on devices she would help to market.

Most importantly, she could companionably coexist with Carl in that parallel universe. His indefatigable energy propelled her research productivity. His photographic memory, always impeccable regarding fine detail, helped her to track complex projects. His compulsiveness facilitated grant applications, data collection and analysis, budget oversight, and publication submissions. In fact, *with* Carl, she soared in ever-expanding orbits of this parallel career. *Because* of him, she survived the broken world she inherited from her parents, and she thrived in a new world of her own making.

Presently, taking stock of the assembling crowd for Richard's service, she thought: *How radically life has changed for our old group.* Jack was in prison and now forever without Richard. Lydia had become a pill-popping spinster. Fred was the beleaguered captain of a sinking hospital. And Nora no longer had a family or unassailable reputation. Among the gang of six, she alone (with Carl's help) could claim a self-made fortune and national reputation.

She prayed that today's service would sustain Carl's attention throughout the next hour while she participated in a teleconference. VivoZeel Devices, Inc, was going to report quarterly revenues for one of her patented "million-dollar babies." Hopefully, the numbers would earn her ranking as the company's Top Physician Entrepreneur of the year.

She leaned against a giant redwood, her Bluetooth on, and waited for VivoZeel's CEO to initiate the teleconference. Meanwhile, it occurred to her that, with Richard's death, she might have to renegotiate all her device contracts and grants with the hospital's next CFO.

Employee Parking Lot

Oakland City Hospital

AFTERNOON

Edna waited in her old, blue Acura, repeatedly checking her watch, anxious about being late for Richard's service after promising Jack that she'd attend. Surely, he was going to grill her about it during their visit tomorrow.

Finally, Rosalie arrived. Edna let down the window, handed her a paper bag, and then keyed the ignition.

"Wait!" Rosalie protested.

"Can't—I'm late. And remember: you've now got the last of it. I've none left whatsoever."

"I want to know why you changed your mind."

Though her resolve began to crumble under the weight of Rosalie's suspicion, Edna said, "I just did. Is there a law against that?"

"I was waiting for you in the ER like we planned. So, I am wondering why, just minutes ago, you chose to meet here instead. And why you decided to go to Richard's service."

Fearing an unwitting revelation of her actual plans under Rosalie's haunting gaze, Edna forged a smile and said, "I was ambivalent at first. But then I decided it was my duty to attend and represent my nurses. That's all."

Edna drove toward the exit, all the while tracking Rosalie in the rearview mirror.

Mountain View Cemetery

Oakland

AFTERNOON

Carl studied his wife from a distance. She leaned against a redwood, tethered to her cellphone, undoubtedly engaged in a *very important* business call, because *all* her business calls were *always* that important. Still, it seemed to him that a funeral service should be her priority and that paying attention was a minimal requirement for showing respect.

Ceremonial bells chimed, and the priest began the opening prayer. But Cheryl heard nothing of that with her headset's volume cranked up to hear VivoZeel's report. Though she nodded intermittently while facing the crowd, her vision was turned inward—an old, practiced strategy allowing her to appear attentive should anyone look her way.

Now the priest invited attendees to greet one another "in peace and loving kindness"—a dreadful directive for Carl. Nonetheless, he tried to comply by shaking hands with Nora and Fred. But the experience proved anything but peaceful. Instead, he began to worry obsessively about the potential for such contact to disseminate infections throughout the crowd, particularly this crowd of healthcare workers, who were likely to be colonized with nosocomial microorganisms. He indelicately wiped his palms against his jacket and opted instead to wave at fellow congregants.

He glanced desperately at Cheryl. How peaceful she looked, standing apart from everyone! How could it be right that he was the one to suffer isolation while longing for connection? How could it be fair, when it was he who labored to relate to people and endured all the psychotropic meds and psychoanalyses, the behavioral classes and empathy trainings, and the interminable seminars in communication skills?

And how hurtful that she maintained distance from *him* now, oblivious to—though fully aware of—his social insecurities and phobic compulsions. *She should be standing supportively beside me now. Haven't*

I always been loyal and attentive? Haven't I always been willing to take a backseat to her driving ambition?

His anger toward Cheryl took him by surprise. But he was vexed by her audacity—listening to financial news concerning yet another of *her* "million-dollar babies." *How is she always so insensitive to my grief about our own childlessness?*

With relief, although with irony, his attention was redirected to children from the Norma Benson Performing Arts School who earnestly began to sing, "You'll Never Walk Alone." After their performance, the priest announced, "Now it's time to hear from anyone wishing to speak to the memory of our dearly departed, Richard Pulaski."

But a long awkward silence ensued, followed by a longer, more awkward silence.

Fred prayed for someone to speak up. Otherwise, as chief of the medical staff, he'd be obligated to fill the void. Though he'd expected Richard's boss on the admin staff to offer tribute on behalf of the entire C-suite, she was nowhere in sight, likely a political (and cowardly) decision to maintain distance from the damning financial allegations against her CFO. And, as Fred well knew, his predicament was doubly fraught, because so many attendees were aware of his troubled relationship with Richard.

The priest beckoned, "Anyone?"

Carl knew that Fred would feel obligated to speak. And, already, Fred was clearing his throat and fidgeting with suitcoat buttons—telltale signs of his distress. Carl thought, *It would be easy for me to help him out. To say something with appropriate (A), empathic content, and (B), emotional tonality.* Indeed, various communication templates for addressing "bad, sad, and glad news" effortlessly sprang to mind, courtesy of the interminable seminars Fred had forced him to attend. But the spectacle of Fred's communication distress was too gratifying.

Finally, Fred walked toward the front of the crowd, internally rehearsing the generic tribute he had plucked this morning from What-ToSayAtFunerals.com. But before he could speak, the priest relievedly exclaimed, "Yes! You, over there!"

Unfortunately, Fred's reprieve proved fleeting. Because when he looked in the direction of the priest's gaze, he saw Cheryl nodding robotically in her familiar charade of attentiveness.

The naïve priest called out again, "You, by the tree?" And though Cheryl appeared to be looking responsively back, her eyes were fixed on VivoZeel's financial horizon.

Fred cursed under his breath, then said, "Good afternoon, everyone. It's good to see so many of Richard's coworkers here paying their respects . . ."

But little of that was actually transpiring while he spoke. Instead, Nora grappled with doubts about Richard's suicide and a reconnection with Jack. Lydia popped another oxy and, her heart aching after last night's dispiriting encounter with Fred, she walked away. Watching Lydia exit, Carl hoped in vain for her to cast a conciliatory look his way.

OakTown Tavern

Downtown Oakland

EVENING

"Lydia, we were supposed to meet up at the cemetery," Nora countered. "But you left before Richard's service ended, and I couldn't find you. So, some of us just decided to stop here afterwards."

Lydia sipped her old-fashioned and said, "Well, I couldn't tolerate any more of Fred."

"And you stood me up last night, too. So, I'm sorry if you don't think I've been available. But you—"

"Okay! Guilty as charged."

"Don't get defensive," Nora said, motioning for the waiter to bring a second round. "And why not take advantage of this time to talk before Fergie and Rosalie show up?"

Sighing dramatically, Lydia took an oxy from her purse and said, "A vitamin for my aching back." She swallowed the pill with her last bit of drink.

"How much of that stuff are you taking now?"

"Don't get started on that, Nora. Not tonight."

"I'm concerned—"

"Yeah? Well, I have a concern, too—about Fred's new psycho ways." Nora scoffed. "What?"

"Dammit, Nora! That's what I've been wanting to talk about—Fred losing his marbles."

"That's absurd. He seems awfully sane to me. Except . . . well . . ."

Lydia testily asked, "Except what?"

"Well . . . I saw you both here Tuesday night, and things looked old-time cozy between you two. It looked like maybe you had *both* lost your marbles?"

Lydia's face brimmed with injury. "Really, Nora? Tuesday night was our second annual 'same time, next year' meet-up for a drink. That's all it was!"

Nora winced, suddenly recalling this anniversary arrangement between her two old friends. "I'm sorry, Lydia. I forgot."

Lydia stalled, agitatedly rearranging the long, green scarf around her neck while trying to manage her fresh disappointment in Nora. "Boy, first Fred, now you."

"Forgive me. Can't we start over?"

After waiting a moment to underscore her grievance, Lydia said, "Truce."

Nora reached for Lydia's hand. "So, back to square one. How was your second breakup anniversary with Fred?"

Lydia's eyes welled.

"Of course," Nora said. "It's still painful. You two go back decades."

Lydia blurted out, "Nora! Again: *not it*." She withdrew her hand. "Look, we had a nice time Tuesday. It felt, as you said, 'cozy.' But we felt good about how we've handled ourselves since our breakup. It wasn't easy to end what we'd had for 28 years."

"That, I remember. I've got scars on my eardrums from listening to each of you wail."

Lydia half-smiled. "Now just listen, okay? My concern is about what's been happening *after* Tuesday night. Fred's been acting weird; even paranoid. He made crazy insinuations about me calling his house at night and hanging up."

"You? That's so . . . high school. Besides, you'd never be so indirect."

"Precisely! And *that's* what's upsetting. You'd think he'd know me better! At first, I thought he was joking. When he called on Wednesday and asked if I was having trouble accepting our separation, I thought he was just trying to be cute, and expressing a little nostalgia."

"Did he misconstrue something you told him Tuesday night?"

"No way! I mean, I love the guy, but I checked myself into Hotel Reality two years ago, and I've suffered no illusions about us getting back together."

After the waiter served their drinks, Lydia continued, "But then, over the next couple days, I realized he was serious. He told me someone was phoning his house—at 3:00, 4:00, 5:00 in the morning—and hanging up. It made Vickie suspicious that he was seeing someone. Then that reignited her resentment about our relationship, which he still claims only began *after* our breakup. Go figure. You know, last night, he even demanded I meet him at Jack London Square so he could look me *in the eye* and ask if I was the caller!"

Nora's brow furrowed. "That's really troubling."

"You think?" Lydia said sarcastically. "Sorry. But *that's* what I've been wanting to talk with you about. It's been difficult since you started spending so much time with your new BFF."

"What, you mean Rosalie? You can't possibly be jealous of her."

"Well, I am."

"Now *you're* sounding paranoid. Maybe you've been taking too many 'vitamins'?"

Lydia tried to rein in her irritation with Nora and distinguish it from unrelated mood-altering influences—from the oxy, the Xanax, the bourbon, her anger toward Fred, Carl's ruinous intrusion on her solitude at Mountain View. Finally, she said, "I've politely requested we not talk about that. It would be nice, Nora, *really nice*, if tonight you could just act like a supportive friend."

"I don't have to *act*. I *am* your friend." Nora held up her merlot, a hopeful look on her face, and toasted, "To my BFF, Lydia."

Lydia hesitantly tapped Nora's glass. "Now I feel like I'm stuck in some sappy after-school special with you. BFF competitions! Boyfriend troubles! Just say 'no' to drugs!"

Nora laughed. "Well, no one ever really leaves high school."

"Yeah? Now you got me worried about pimples before the big dance."

"God, please don't let my period start during gym!"

After heartily toasting one another, Nora said, "Okay, about that nonsense with Fred . . . I'm really sorry, pal."

Lydia whispered, "Still, you know, Vickie might be right about Fred having an affair."

"Nonsense! Fred wouldn't. You and he . . . that was different. Unique. It was a once-in-a-lifetime relationship that defies categories. Besides, it makes more sense that an actual high schooler is calling them. It's probably someone from their kids' school."

"I doubt it. Because it seems more than some high-school prank. I think the caller has to be the same person who left a creepy package on Fred's doorstep the other day. Otherwise, it would be too weird a coincidence."

"What creepy package?"

"Well, technically, it was an envelope. Fred wouldn't say what was inside because—get this—last night he expected *me* to tell him! I was supposed to fess up to his face, if you can believe it."

"Wow. That's hard to believe."

"Clearly, w*hatever* was inside, it somehow incriminated me. Or Fred and me."

"But why would something of that nature surface two years *after* your relationship ended and—"

"Hey!" Fergie interrupted, sitting down, looking annoyingly fresh in her blue scrubs. She signaled the waiter and requested "a Heineken, please."

"Just getting off?" Nora asked.

"Yeah. I finished a shift for Edna. The ER was crazy-times-eight today, so thanks for the invite. How was Pulaski's service?"

"Sad," Nora replied. "And I kept thinking about Jack."

"And you, Lydia?"

"It was deadly," Lydia said. "And I left early."

Fergie grimaced. "Well, ladies, in a related matter, the decision about the hospital should be on the news about now."

"Go for it," Lydia said, pointing to the TV. "Besides, Nora and I need a break from each other."

Nora rolled her eyes, and Fergie turned on the TV. Minutes later, they heard:

"Tara King at KTVY, where Oakland turns for breaking news! It now appears that Oakland City Hospital will receive at least three more years of life support. The beleaguered public hospital has been struggling to stay alive amid chronic funding shortfalls and allegations of fiscal mismanagement. In a statement released late yesterday, Alameda County supervisors proclaimed, 'The city's safe harbor for all citizens—especially the region's poor—will continue to stand as a testimony to healthcare justice in our community.'

"They also announced that the independent audit of the hospital's finances revealed no evidence of fiscal impropriety, exonerating its chief financial officer, Richard Pulaski, who died earlier this week.

"And, speaking about being in the clear; Mark, are we finally getting a break from the rain?"

"That's right, Tara. And—"

Fergie muted the TV and said, "What a relief! I was afraid they were going to close us down."

"Yeah," Nora said, "some good news, finally." Privately, however, she'd been looking for the hospital's closure to resolve her uncertainty about retiring.

Lydia said, "Oakland City is indestructible. Like Velveeta. Like Timmy. Like Nora and me."

"Timmy?" Fergie asked.

"It's a goofy Cupid," Nora explained; "a cardboard relic from Valentines past."

"Okay," Fergie companionably replied. "Still, it's too bad Pulaski died without hearing this news."

"Yeah, so ironic," Lydia said. "The hospital is resurrected on the day of his funeral."

Rosalie appeared. "Hello, everyone," she said, trying to stuff her yellow purse under the table. "I heard the news. Do you think Richard would not have killed himself if he knew he would be cleared?"

Lydia pointed to Rosalie's purse and said, "You brought Big Bird again? Do you mind moving it? It's pecking my leg."

"Sorry," Rosalie said, repositioning her purse. Nora frowned at Lydia and then answered Rosalie, "Unfortunately, we'll never know."

Rosalie said, "I think the official confirmation of his innocence would have made a difference to him."

A member of the kitchen staff arrived and, despite his pronounced limp, deftly served Fergie her beer. Smiling at Rosalie, he also placed a chardonnay on the table and said, "For you. I saw you coming in."

"Thank you, Victor!" she said. "You are so sweet to me."

After he left, Rosalie asked Fergie, "So, what do you think about Richard?"

"I don't know. Then again, I'm just a nurse on a low rung of the ladder in hospital admin. I don't see the darkness at the top—all the money and politics and power."

"Right," Nora scoffed. "You're just majorly responsible for holding the ER together."

"Any holding I do is at the bottom of that ladder."

Lydia dismissively waved at Fergie. "But, Nora, you *should* have an opinion about Richard. You were friendly with him and Jack for 30 years . . . since *our* residency" she added, in a territorial slight to Rosalie.

"I don't feel like talking about it," said Nora.

"C'mon," Lydia persisted. "Besides, you've already told everyone you don't think Richard fleeced the hospital or committed suicide."

Rosalie said, "But, Nora, if you were sure of his innocence, why did you not speak up to support him?"

A long, pervasive silence ensued.

Finally, Nora took a deep breath and said, "Maybe you're right. I could have—probably *should* have—been more vocal about that. I did tell Fred I didn't believe the allegations against Richard. But, of course, I had no way of really knowing. I mean, I didn't have access to the actual financials. And even if I did, I wouldn't have known how to interpret them."

Lydia said, "Because the bean counters have secret codes and language. *They* decide what actually goes on at Oakland City. And despite what you say, Fergie, every person at this table stands on a low rung of the ladder when it comes to actual power at the hospital."

"Still," said Rosalie, "it might have helped Richard if friends like you had said—"

"Excuse me, Dr. Phil," Lydia interrupted. "Richard wasn't a *friend*. He was just some bigwig admin who'd been around since the Stone Age with us old guard: me, Nora, Fred, Jack, and the Klufts."

"I do not mean to be confrontational," Rosalie said. "But, perhaps even just out of loyalty to Jack, you could have—"

"I'm shifting the gears!" Fergie proclaimed, raising her glass. "Besides, we should be toasting Richard Pulaski. May he rest in peace."

Everyone clinked glasses. After another thorny pause, Nora said, "The *Stone Age*, Lydia? Really?"

Lydia shrugged. "It's true. We met him in 1990. We were just reminiscing about that in my office the other night. Remember?"

Nora nodded. "Still, it's weird to hear you mention the actual year—so 'other century-ish.'"

Lydia said, "Fergie, you probably weren't even born then."

"That's true," Fergie said.

After signaling the waiter for a third old-fashioned, Lydia looked at Rosalie and said, "And you ... you're, what? Early 30s maybe?"

"As you say: 'maybe.'"

Lydia persevered. "Thirty-one? Thirty-two?"

Nora intervened, "Rosalie didn't have a straight shot through school or training." Then, worried she may have leaked a confidence, apologized. "I'm sorry, Rosalie. Your story isn't mine to tell."

"No!" Lydia protested, pounding the table. "You can't just end a story at its beginning!"

"It is okay, Nora," said Rosalie. Then, looking to Lydia, she explained, "I graduated from high school when I was 23 because of family issues." Responding to Lydia's wry grin, she added, "No, Dr. Chandler, I did not go to prom."

Nora tried to kick Lydia under the table but instead knocked over Rosalie's purse. Lydia continued undeterred, "So, adding four years of college and four for med school, you were ... 31 when you started residency. Then add three years for residency—"

"Lydia, give it a rest," Fergie said.

Looking fleetingly to Nora for support, Rosalie said, "I was 34 when I finished residency and was hired on staff."

"Whoa!" said Lydia. "So, you're *36* and kinda just *beginning* your career?"

"Yes," Rosalie said, retrieving her purse and standing up. "Look, they are busy here tonight, and I need to stretch my legs anyway. Should I bring back your drink from the bar, Dr. Chandler?"

"Sure; but no need for your mega-purse. We're running a tab. Besides, you'll get a hernia carrying that thing."

Ignoring the advice, Rosalie asked, "Anyone else want something?"

Nora shook her head. Fergie said, "I'll go with you. I could use a break myself."

When Fergie and Rosalie were beyond earshot, Nora said, "Damn it, Lydia! You're harassing Rosalie! It's been hard enough on her. She had to drop out of school so many times to care for family—"

"How was I supposed to know her hallowed past? And tell me, why does she keep calling me 'Dr. Chandler'? It's offensive."

"Lydia, really?"

"Well, it's ageist for sure. And off-putting. And, clearly, she's not *that* young. Besides, she's been on staff with us a couple years already."

"It's just an old habit. It's out of respect. She's spent more years under staff supervision than being a staff member herself."

"Well, she doesn't call you 'Dr. Kelly,' and we know she respects you."

Lydia's escalating inebriation was wearing Nora down. She cringed when Lydia lifted her glass yet again and unhappily registered its emptiness. "Just stop picking on her," Nora demanded.

"Whatever. What's she gonna do about it anyway? Clobber me with her purse?"

"I wouldn't blame her."

Lydia smiled mischievously. "Seriously, though. What's in it? A house? An SUV?"

Nora rolled her eyes.

"I know! It's a clown purse! A dozen clowns pop out when she opens it."

"Well, you'd definitely fit in with them."

"That's good," Lydia said, laughing loud—louder than normal.

Minutes passed, during which Nora and Lydia inched back into the rhythm of their old comradery. They debriefed about Richard's service, and Lydia described her fraught interlude with Carl. They wondered about Jack in light of Richard's death. They speculated more about Fred.

They talked about the Safeway sale on avocados, the Oroville flood, and impending healthcare reforms. Increasingly, Nora was reminded how much she missed private time with Lydia. She was about to suggest they have an old-time sleepover tonight, but Fergie reappeared.

"We got snacks," Fergie announced. "Anyone for these cheesy things, or chips or pretzels?"

Rosalie followed with Lydia's drink.

"What took you so long?" Lydia asked. "Fifteen minutes to get a simple drink?"

"They were busy at the bar," Rosalie said, sitting down and shoving her purse under the table.

"Hey," Lydia complained, "your purse is attacking my leg again!"

"Sorry, there is so little room," Rosalie said.

Ignoring Nora's vexed expression, Lydia said to Fergie, "If you and Winston can't find an apartment, maybe Rosalie will rent you room inside her purse."

Rosalie said, "You seem to be obsessed with my purse, Dr. Chandler."

"Not really," Lydia said. "But I'm intrigued about something else: what it was like to find Richard's body. Because, like I said, Nora here suspects he didn't kill himself."

Lydia's bullying interrogation stunned Nora. "Lydia, that's so inappropriate!"

"C'mon," Lydia objected. "I'm a pathologist, and you're our master diagnostician. Besides, everyone here's an adult, and a healthcare worker to boot!"

Fergie said, "Dr. C, you're going too far."

Nora debated whether to admonish Lydia for sounding cruel and ridiculous, and for her words slurring. But she refrained, fearing that would make Lydia feel shamed in front of her purported nemesis, Rosalie.

Rosalie eyes glistened. She stammered, "Well, it was . . . shocking to find Richard. And to know I was responsible. He would not be dead, Nora, if you had been his doctor."

"That's preposterous!" Nora said.

"No," Rosalie countered. "He had advanced melanoma. I thought we were getting it under control. And with no permanent replacement for Dr. Griffin yet, I was helping oncology to supervise Richard's home infusion protocol. But Richard . . . he was always at work, trying to disprove all those false allegations. So, I helped him take chemo infusions in his office."

Lydia scowled. "And you're responsible for his death *because* . . . ?"

"Because," Rosalie began, searching in her purse for a tissue, and wiping her tears. "Because all I ended up doing was make him sicker with that toxic chemo. Sometimes he said he could not take it any longer, but I kept encouraging him, and giving him hope. Or maybe I did not give him enough hope to want to continue, so he killed himself. Nora, you would have figured it out. You would have done something different."

"Stop!" Nora said. "I'm sure I would've seen things exactly as you did and done the same."

"I think he would be alive if you—"

"My god," Lydia groaned. "Listen to you two! You're gonna be the death of *me*."

"Dr. C," Fergie said, "take a breather, please."

"Don't you see?" said Lydia. "This is precisely why I, and most medical school graduates now, steer clear of . . . what's it called? Yeah, 'whole patient care.' *Especially* primary care." Pointing at Nora and Rosalie, she continued, "You two are guilt-ridden, die-hard daughters of Sisyphus! You keep trudging up a steep hill, pushing against a healthcare system that's only going to roll back down over you and crush your spirit."

"This discussion is depressing," Fergie said.

Lydia countered, "But Dr. Karlov is just getting what it's like to practice medicine in the real world. She's understanding that healthcare is unjust; that it's not in doctors' or patients' control. And she's just now getting that patients *hurt* you and make your life miserable! They *die* on you, lie to you, and don't take care of themselves. And then you're left feeling responsible for all of it—even *blamed* for it. Sued for it! Patients suck the life out of you, your family, and your creativity. It's no wonder we doctors have such high suicide rates."

"And substance abuse rates," Nora said pointedly.

Fergie sighed, tossed a twenty on the table and said, "Okay, I'm outta here. I've got work in the morning." Turning to Rosalie, she said, "Sorry you're feeling bad about Richard, but I hope you'll listen to the good doctor Nora here." To Nora, she said, "See you tomorrow." And to Lydia, she offered, "Can I drive you home?"

Lydia laughed. "Well, I suppose you *could*. There's just no good reason for it."

Fergie resignedly threw up her hands and left.

Nora signaled for the check. Infuriated, she said to Lydia, "Let's call it a night."

Accommodating Nora's firm directive, Lydia began preparing for departure. But when she pushed away from the table, she discovered that her center of gravity had shifted to some mysterious location. She felt unsteady in the chair and uncertain about her ability to thread her arms through her overcoat's sleeves. Trying to readjust the scarf around her neck—*How did it become so uneven?*—she said, mystified, "I can't find my purse."

"Don't worry," Nora said, pulling out a credit card. "I'll pay the tab."

"Thank you, Nora," Rosalie said.

"Yes, thanks," said Lydia, smiling broadly at Nora. "And the next tab's on me! Well . . . if I ever find my purse." Groping blindly under the table, she joked, "Probably wouldn't have such trouble if my purse was as big as Rosalie's."

Rosalie pointed to the floor and said, "It is under your chair, Dr. Chandler."

Lydia almost fell off the chair while retrieving her purse. Task finally accomplished, she looked up hazily to see Rosalie and Nora standing alongside the table, conversing vigorously, their voices muffled. The waiter arrived and looked concernedly at her. Then Rosalie was shaking her head, Nora was signing the tab, the waiter shrugged and walked away. Blackness descended for a moment or two. Then Lydia's pixilating vision returned. Now she saw only Nora at the table—*Thank god, Rosalie is gone.* But . . . Nora looked upset, maybe angry even. And she was earnestly trying to convey something—*but what?* She heard such loud ringing in her ears now. She felt thunderous thumping inside her chest. The ceiling quivered; fog permeated. Now, somehow, Lydia was upright. And when she took her first step away from the table, she could be walking on air, or walking on a bad dream. Her feet sensed no contact with the floor, and her legs felt separated from her intentions to direct them.

The next thing Lydia realized—she was behind the wheel of her black BMW. Its engine was running, and its headlights were beaming. Somehow, she had exited the hospital parking lot across the street from the Tavern.

While driving on automatic pilot along Harrison, she was blinded by an oncoming car's headlamps, its stupefying light flooding her mind. Still, her hands reflexively steered, negotiating the route home, which she had driven for decades.

Now she was on Oakland Avenue, and her cellphone rang. "Private caller" flashed on the dashboard screen. It rang again while she drove down Highland, and again when she turned onto Moraga. She struggled to mute the obnoxious audio, fumbling with buttons on the steering wheel, and trying to locate her phone to switch *everything off*.

The ringing finally ceased when she reached Mountain, and her rattled nerves began to calm. She waited at a red light two blocks away, and, when it signaled green, she turned onto Snake Road—a thin, meandering coil of roadway that unfurled skyward through the Oakland Hills. It was so dark. Short segments of the serpentine road were irregularly made visible when her car triggered motion-detection lights from the occasional home along the way.

Her cellphone rang, incessantly rang. She clutched the steering wheel on another hairpin turn. A vehicle suddenly appeared in the rear-view mirror—a menacing presence at her bumper, its horn blaring, its blinking, blinding headlights obscuring everything.

Part II

Private Investigations

FEBRUARY 12

Somewhere along Snake Road

The Oakland Hills

4:42 A.M.

"OUR ETA? Um, maybe 10 minutes. Just waiting for clearance. . . .

No, no vitals still. . . . Three shocks, so far. Nothing. . . .

Are you serious? . . .

Well, it took forever to find the car, man. These creepy hills—there's no streetlights up here! And, 'A car off a bend on Snake Road'—what kind of clue was *that*? . . . Hey, pal, if *you* never took a night call up here, you got no business giving me advice. . . . Nah, we couldn't even get our truck up this skinny corkscrew road. . . . The car? It's a BMW—black, *of course*. It's just demolished, man. It took a 150–160 foot drop down the hill. With all the brush in this canyon, it's a miracle anyone spotted the car. . . . Yeah, the fire crew chained it to some trees, but it was still unstable. Man, it rolled right back down the hill again. . . . Hey, I agree. These rich folks living up here on these crazy roads! There are no street lights, and the cell reception for emergencies is bad. . . . Yeah, that's right, 'dying to live in the hills.' . . . Okay, just got my signal. Gotta go. 10-4."

After signing off with ER receiving, OakCity paramedic Albert Mohalani told the police that his crew was ready for escort to Oakland City Hospital. Turning on his emergency lights, he looked idly through the cab's front window into the predawn, waiting for the police convoy to assemble. And suddenly, in this happenstance perspective, his mind registered the distant view. Beyond the immediate rolling landscape, from this high, hillside vista, he saw shimmering strings of light—luminous thrumming strands of electric diamonds draping across Oakland's hardscrabble flatlands. The city's nocturnal beauty shocked him. From here, he could see nothing of the poverty or crime in his neighborhood—no run-down houses, no boarded-up stores, no desperate people pushing carts in the streets.

In the morning, he would tell his family how he had tried to locate their flatlands house from atop this hill in the middle of the night. He would even suggest that they drive up here one evening to see how different their city could look in this light, from this distance.

ER

Oakland City Hospital

8:40 A.M.

There'd be no jogging around the lake this morning. There'd been too much alcohol last night—first at the Tavern, later at home—and so much vexation with Lydia. This hangover made Nora's brain feel like a sack of wet concrete, and every heel strike rattled her skull.

And, obviously, there'd be no ritual of gratitude to initiate this workday. There was no time for a lovefest kumbaya with patients waiting in the ER. Her only entry ceremony would entail self-administering a liter of saline in the privacy of her office. And her only mission: surviving her shift without killing any patients.

Nora snuck through the ER's back entry and headed straight to her office, gastric acid wicking up her throat. She walked by patients who waited in the corridors on gurneys, in wheelchairs, and even languid on the floor.

But midway to her office, she halted abruptly, stunned to discover that she'd felt no connection to all the patients she'd passed by. She had experienced nothing compelling about them, and nothing drawing her to them, even in some vague, impersonal way.

Resuming her trek and passing even more of them, she became increasingly convinced of her capacity to remain unaffected by them. She was astounded to experience this newfound immunity to their tattered predicaments and their perpetual neediness. And the most amazing shock of all was to discover how good this detachment felt.

Lydia's cynical comments about doctoring surfaced to Nora's consciousness. They rang so true now, and even resonated throughout her body. Her stride lightened, her neck muscles unclenched, and fatigue lifted from her bones. There was such sweet unburdening in adopting Lydia's view, and in relinquishing the uphill battle of practicing medicine.

When Nora came upon the scamera that had turned its blind eye to her injury on Monday, she paused again. Now, it exerted a chilling, magnetic hold on her. And while staring curiously at it, she felt a growing sense of uneasy kinship with it. She thought, *I can be equally capable of viewing patients with a blind eye of my own.*

Indeed, as a confirmatory test, she looked back at the patient-lined corridor and felt no psychic or emotional stirrings. She marveled, *How much easier it is to be present here when you can detach from all those people and their problems.*

Those people.

In the moment, they were imperceptible as individuals to her; they collectively formed a backdrop to a steady stream of her coworkers who also walked by, undeterred and unscathed. She saw an intern step over a patient who was sprawled across the floor. She watched a cardiologist on his cell blithely pass someone begging for a blanket. Doctors and nurses weaved through the corridor, insulated against the pervasive sting of human suffering. No one seemed to notice the dull-eyed child who clutched an empty bottle and sat too limply on his sleeping mother's lap, or the wiry woman who paced and moaned, her track marks oozing. They ignored the incoherent man screaming at a broom.

Those people.

Yes, you had to defend against *those people* in order to do your job. The trick was to see them as medical conditions, stripped of subjective concerns. You had to see them as "cases," really—the DVT, the heart failure, the GSW, the ankle fracture, or the failed pregnancy. You had to see them as their diseases.

She already felt radically displaced by the time she reached her office. And stepping into it now, all its furnishings seemed unpossessed, belonging to someone else. Posters on the walls created a museum-like retrospective of discarded passions: *Healthcare for People, Not Profit!* ... *AIDS: Silence = Death* ... *Women's Bodies, Women's Rights* ... She tried to recall the last time she'd rallied with colleagues around something other than their salaries and bonuses.

And how obsolete her textbooks were; especially her extensive collection on the art of the physical exam, which belonged to antiquity now.

You'll know the right time to leave medicine, her therapist kept advising. And finally, in this moment, for a handful of insistent reasons, Nora knew that time had arrived.

Scanning her office in stunning remove, she viewed it now as a memory of her prior self. She felt her career shift into past tense. *Tomorrow, I'll tell Fred about my decision to—*

A rattling knock sounded, and Fergie stood breathless in the doorway. "Nora," she said, her voice quavering. "There's been an accident. Lydia is dead."

C-Suite Conference Room

Oakland City Hospital

11:00 A.M.

Nora and Fergie were the last to arrive for the emergency meeting in the C-suite conference room. Fred sat at the head of a table where Rosalie, Edna, and the Klufts were assembled. Two male lawyers from the hospital's legal department were also there. Each sported a ponytail, one wispy and gray, the other thick and black.

Fred said, "All right now. Everyone's here." The tightness in his throat diminished his voice, and he worried about breaking down during the meeting. He looked to Nora for support, but she appeared lost in her own grief. Bracing himself, he continued, "We all know that . . . that Dr. Lydia Chandler died early this morning."

Carl registered the assembly's collective distress. He knew that, in the midst of such misery, one should (A), name the feelings in the room and (B), offer an empathic statement. Accordingly, he said, "Lydia's death is sad and shocking." Though Cheryl derisively rolled her eyes, he continued: "And her death occurs with Richard's fresh on our minds. This is a difficult time for everyone."

"Thank you," said Fred, genuinely grateful for the cushioning intervention. "I wanted to speak with you all before you spoke with the police."

"The *police*?" Edna exclaimed. "Why would we need to talk with them about Lydia's accident?"

The announcement also surprised Nora. But before she could gather herself to speak, Cheryl replied, "You really need to ask?"

A disparaging look from Fred alerted Cheryl to her indecorum. But, fact was, she had had it! Up *all night* in the ER with Carl, *trying* to collect patient data buried in old paper medical charts . . . she was *exhausted*. And it didn't help knowing that Nora, Rosalie, and Fergie were out drinking last night with Lydia after Richard's service, and *no invitation extended to her or Carl, thank you very much*. Still, she would have held her tongue had Fred not admonished, "Cheryl, let's be civil." But his flinty reprimand ignited her foreshortened fuse and she scoffed, "Civil?" Pointing sequentially at Rosalie, Fergie, and Nora, she charged, "How 'civil' is it that *they* allowed Lydia to drive home in her condition last night?"

Nora just wanted to retreat under the covers and mourn Lydia's death. But Cheryl's insinuation that she was blameworthy for it could not stand. And how inappropriate it was for Cheryl to be re-airing her old bitterness about feeling excluded now! Haltingly, Nora said, "Don't you think we tried to stop her?"

Rosalie added, "Each of us offered to drive Dr. Chandler home. We even called a Lyft. But she refused everything."

Fergie looked reproachfully at Cheryl. "And she had three drinks, which, you may know, was not excessive for her."

Cheryl said, "Yeah, well, Carl and I were working in the ER when they brought Lydia in. *We* saw her mangled body. *We* saw her bloodied face. *We* witnessed her death pronouncement. So, Nora, while you all were sleeping it off last night, *we* were watching the nightmare unfold!"

Nora paled while listening to Cheryl's account. It provided a brutal dose of unbidden reality; it confirmed that Lydia was actually gone. When she looked to Fred, hoping to commiserate, he looked away, and a troubling thought crossed her mind: that he, like Cheryl, might hold her accountable for Lydia's death. She privately panicked. *I should have grabbed Lydia's keys! Dragged her into my car! Called the police! How stupid to worry more about shaming her in front of Rosalie.*

Cheryl continued, "And it interrupted everything! The entire ER came to a standstill. I couldn't complete my data collection."

Fergie shouted, "How untimely for you that Lydia died!"

At this woeful juncture, Fred harbored no pretensions about controlling the meeting. In fact, he didn't care. Lydia was dead. Nothing else mattered.

Cheryl returned, "Your insolence is uncalled for, Nurse Ferguson!"

The black-haired lawyer pleaded, "Stop!"

"Good Lord," Edna whispered, praying as much for group civility as for private spiritual counsel.

The gray-haired lawyer warned, "This divisiveness is risky. I seriously advise everyone against finger-pointing. That's how we lose money for the hospital."

Nora looked probingly at Cheryl and said, "Your insinuations are cruel. Lydia was my dearest friend. How could you be so . . . cold?"

"So *bitchy*," Fergie whispered, only loud enough for Nora to hear.

"That's right," Cheryl said. "You two were friends. You *always* made that clear. So, let's be frank: as Lydia's close friend, you knew more than anyone about her 'problem.' Still, last night you let her drink and drive and take *whatever* she's always taking."

Edna looked crossly at Rosalie and said, "I agree with Dr. Kluft. It was unconscionable to allow her to drive home like that."

Fred threw up his hands. "People! We don't yet have all the facts about Lydia's accident. The tox report isn't—"

Carl interrupted, "The emotional temperature in the room is too high. We should turn it down so everyone feels comfortable to participate in this difficult conversation."

"God, Carl, turn it down yourself," said Cheryl.

Uncharacteristically ignoring her, Carl said, "Cheryl is stressed because she's undergoing surgery tomorrow morning. She's having a cardiac stent implanted for an occluded artery. Last night, she was just trying to finish ER data collection on deadline for one of her device grants."

Cheryl said, "But when the entire ER went slack after they brought in Lydia's body—"

"You've already told us how Lydia's death inconvenienced your freakin' research!" Fergie seethed.

Cheryl asked Fred, "Why are you tolerating this nurse's snark?"

"Enough!" Fred said. "This is painful enough—"

Rosalie cried out, "Cheryl and Edna . . . you are right. We *are* to blame for Lydia's accident." She caught her breath and, turning to Nora and Fergie, apologized, "Sorry, I should speak only for myself."

The ensuing tense silence finally broke when the dark-haired lawyer said, "So-o-o . . . the police are interested because they found evidence—a *lot* of evidence, actually—inside Dr. Chandler's car. Evidence suggesting she might've been involved in trafficking prescription drugs."

The gray-haired lawyer clarified, "Narcotics and sedatives; and, as my colleague said, they found *lots* of them."

Nora couldn't believe what she heard. *Overly cautious Lydia never transported drugs in her car. Maybe a few pills in her purse, but . . .*

Fred whispered, "Dear god, Lydia." This lament was rendered inaudible by Rosalie's distraught questioning: "Does that mean *another* narcotics investigation of the hospital?"

The black-haired lawyer tapped his pen against the table. "Yes," he said. "And the police, the state department, the DEA—they'll want to know what each of you knew about Dr. Chandler's drug activities. And they'll ask whether you were involved in any kind of system with her."

The gray-haired lawyer added, "Specifically, they'll be curious about a system of drug trafficking involving the hospital. Unfortunately, as you folks know, there's a serious opioid drug crisis in the country. More than 15,000 Americans died from overdoses involving prescription opioids the last year they checked. And doctors and nurses, sadly, are big players in that tragedy. And Oakland . . . well, it's a big marketplace."

Fred summoned his leadership mantle and said, "The police already spoke with the crew who brought in Dr. Chandler. But Nora, Rosalie, and Fergie—you were the last to see her alive as far as anyone knows. And Carl, Cheryl, Edna—since you were in the ER and variously involved with . . . with the proceedings, the police are interested in talking with you, too."

The black-haired lawyer said, "Remember that our hospital is still under heightened scrutiny regarding narcotic prescribing because of Dr. Griffin's felony conviction for 'enabling'—is that the term we're using?—for enabling patients' deaths."

Edna's stomach churned. *What in God's name have I gotten myself into?*

The gray-haired lawyer said, "That's why we, your crack legal team, are going to guide you through this new investigation."

"Listen," Cheryl said, "I'm not worried about talking to *anybody* about Lydia's death. But I need to finish my data collection and get *some* sleep before my surgery tomorrow. So, anybody wanting to talk with me needs to do it soon. Or they wait until I'm post-op—"

"Well, lucky you!" the dark-haired lawyer interrupted, pointing to his cellphone. "According to this text, the detectives are downstairs. They just arrived."

Visiting Room, San Sebastian State Prison

Marin County

MIDAFTERNOON

Before leaving, Baldwin looked impassively at Jack and said, "Fifteen minutes. That's it. It's not my fault she came late."

Overhearing his comment, Edna thought: *It's not my fault, either! How was I supposed to know Lydia was going to die this morning, and that an emergency meeting and senseless police interview were going to follow?* She took a deep breath and decided, given what constricted time remained for the visit, to withhold the news of Lydia until Jack was satisfied with her report on Richard's service. She said, "Jack, I'm sorry about being late. Traffic was terrible on the Richmond Bridge."

Jack said, "I'm just grateful you came, especially after working midnight shift. I hope you got some rest in-between?"

But of course, she did not. She was bone tired and wouldn't have had to work such a uniquely dreadful shift had she not needed to switch schedules in order to attend Richard's memorial yesterday. Even after this visit with Jack, she had to return to the ER to complete the work she had promised Cheryl last night. "Yes, thanks," she said.

"So, then . . . Richard's service?"

She knew the truth would wound him—the coerced attendance, dearth of tributes, Fred's rote eulogy. Instead, she said, "It was lovely. There were so many people there. Fred gave a tribute worthy of Hallmark." Jack's eyes welled while she unfaithfully recounted the priest's words. He was surprised to hear that the Klufts attended, and he smiled when Edna mentioned Nora.

Edna glanced at her watch, debating how to cover everything else warranting discussion. She began, "And it's been confirmed: Richard died of potassium toxicity. They're certain he injected the potassium himself."

His face flushed, camouflaging fresh bruises, and he insisted, "Richard did not commit suicide."

"Jack, nothing suggests otherwise. They've searched diligently and—"

"*Diligently?* No. They didn't talk to *me*."

"I'm sorry. But it does make dark, terrible sense."

"What does Nora think?"

"Well . . . I don't know, but—"

A buzzer sounded, signaling three remaining minutes for the visit. Edna looked fretfully at Jack and said, "Look, we can keep circling around this same conversation. But . . . the real reason I was late today was that I had to attend an emergency meeting that didn't end until noon. And I should tell you about that, Jack. I should tell you what happened to Lydia Chandler."

Pathology Department

Basement, Oakland City Hospital

LATE AFTERNOON

Fred hesitated at the entrance to the pathology department, scanning its dungeon-like environs. This basement enclave had both haunted and captivated him since he and Lydia first set foot inside it in 1987 and proceeded to make love on every surface that would hold them—the exam tables, metal countertops, cement floor. "My god," he said to no one in particular, remembering how exhilarating it had been. He closed his eyes and envisioned their younger selves, bodies flushed with lovemaking, each of them oblivious to, and animated by, death's hovering presence here.

Looking to the autopsy theater, he saw organs suspended in glass jars, freezers that stored body parts, and vaults containing corpses. But only now, with Lydia gone, did this place feel lifeless.

He walked into Lydia's office and saw the IKEA pullout on which they last made love two years ago. The same old cardboard Cupid hung above it, cruelly bidding "Happy Valentine's!" He took in a familiar ground-level window view of the hospital's entryway—the perennially tired camellias, the constant traffic on Broadway. A foghorn sounded from the Oakland estuary. *How does all this normal go on without Lydia?*

He sat in her chair, hoping to feel any lingering contour of her body. He surveyed her desktop . . . its coffee mugs, pathology journals, and the hollowed-out bone she used for a pencil cup. Her calendar was opened to the week ahead, revealing a schedule now rendered moot. And Dr. Fred Williams—chief of Oakland City's medical staff—cried like a child.

Sometime later, his phone alarm sounded, reminding him that Vickie would expect him home within the hour for Sunday dinner. To be late, especially for a reason involving Lydia, would only exacerbate their titanic marital discord. Since informing Vickie two years ago about ending his relationship with Lydia, he had daily weathered her threats of divorce, homicide, lawyering-up, hanging him in the public square, and making his life forever miserable.

He dried his face and hurriedly searched Lydia's office for any potentially incriminating evidence—pill bottles, drug samples, narcotic tabs lingering in drawers. Though finding none (typical of her caution) he did discover an incriminating item of another sort. Concealed under a desk drawer lining was the late-80s Polaroid he had always suspected her of keeping, despite her assurances otherwise. And in it, he saw the two of them together as they'd been—naked and happy, their youthful bodies pressed together, luminous, and brimming with life.

ER Exam Room

Oakland City Hospital

LATE AFTERNOON

Family members surrounded the patient, declining to leave the cramped exam room. Nora, failing to find a colleague to take over her shift, struggled to focus on her work. But she kept dropping into grief, and Cheryl's accusations clawed at her heart. Her struggle intensified while the family argued in a language she didn't understand, and the interpreter's words were often unheard through the faltering Language Line speakerphone.

Attempting to raise her voice above the din, Nora asked the interpreter, "How long has he had trouble swallowing?"

The interpreter's translation of Nora's question sparked heated debate among family members. Throughout, the patient remained silent.

Suddenly, the interpreter shouted something to which the family vigorously objected. Fergie stood up on a chair, pleading, "Quiet, please!"

The commotion drew Aditya and Darique into the room. They were eager for experience and a chance to exercise authority. But noting Nora's presence, they immediately resigned themselves to observer status.

When silence finally prevailed, Nora asked the interpreter: "What's the problem here?"

His voice sputtered through the speakerphone: "The family . . . problem . . . don't speak . . . language."

Now on her last nerve, Nora fumed, "This connection is useless!"

Darique gingerly interjected, "Dr. Kelly, why not just get routine lab panels and a chest CT on the guy?" Aditya conveyed "why not?" with a shoulder shrug.

Nora drew sufficient strength from Fergie's steadying look to try once more. With hammering enunciation, she said, "Just . . . tell . . . me . . . how long . . . the patient—"

"Stop!" the interpreter said. "The problem . . . I . . . Zulu but they . . . only . . ."

A young girl timidly stepped forward, encouraged by family elders to speak. She smiled sweetly at Nora and said, "Doctor, we are South Africa. But we do no speak Zulu. We speak Xhosa."

ER Doctors' Workstation

Oakland City Hospital

4:30 P.M.

Nora knew she was spending thousands of dollars on diagnostic testing to bypass communication gridlock with her patient and his family. By ordering a chest x-ray and CT scan, an abdominal ultrasound and EKG, and an extensive battery of lab tests, she was blindly casting a ridiculously wide net, hoping to snare any telling clues about an available diagnosis.

It was such an expedient solution—keystroke, click, repeat on the computer keyboard—to simply tick off checkboxes on the Physician Orders screen. Within hours, test results would accumulate, speaking not only for themselves, but, literally, for the patient as well.

Now, typing her clinical note into the patient's EHR, Nora marveled at the ease of this blind-net approach to diagnosing patients. It was so much less stressful and time-consuming than having to listen to a patient's complaint, to think through a differential diagnosis, and to tailor appropriate testing. To *care*, really.

Still, she knew she was doctoring in a manner she had always disdained. Like a cowboy MD with sloppy diagnostic aim, who needed too many bullets to hit some target. And she felt guilty about exposing her bewildered patient to so much bloodletting and radiation, all for the lack of a few clarifying sentences that might have elucidated his diagnosis.

But what choice did I have? It's been hell just surviving this shift, and waiting to collapse at home and let down about Lydia—

Rosalie unexpectedly appeared and, casting a sympathetic look, said, "How are you doing, Nora?"

The penetrating inquiry pierced Nora's fragile self-composure, and tears streamed down her face. "I honestly don't know," she managed. "I'm having trouble accepting . . . believing Lydia is . . . gone."

"I am sorry," Rosalie said, taking Nora's hand. "My god, how did you even work today?"

"I couldn't find backup. Fred helped out where he could, and Fergie was great as usual. I put my feelings on ice. But this shift . . . it's been an eternity."

"I wish I had known! I would have taken over for you. I just assumed you would not be here working after what happened. Now I feel terrible, because I was here all day. And instead of helping you . . ." She adopted a pained expression. "But why did you not just ask me during the meeting this morning?"

Her question sounded so glaringly reasonable that, in retrospect, it took Nora by surprise. And yet, when she searched for an answer, she found only this: it felt disloyal to Lydia to turn to Rosalie for help or comfort now. She said, "My mind was blown during that awful meeting. I wasn't even thinking about work."

"That is understandable. I, too, cannot believe Lydia is dead. We were with her just last night!"

Nora steadied herself. "You were here all day?"

Rosalie yawned. "After Fred called us in for that meeting, I did not feel like going home. Besides, I had to wait around to talk with the police. So, I borrowed these scrubs from the ER call room and took a nap in my office. Then, I decided to catch up on my EHR documentation—I do that most Sundays, anyway. Well, ever since they doubled our workload by forcing us to email with patients."

"Excuse me," Nora said, heading to the sink. "My cheeks itch—all the salt." She splashed water on her face and continued, "Well, this workday's almost over. And I got shifts covered every day this week except Wednesday." Then she blew her nose into a hospital-supply tissue, inadvertently creating a gaping hole through its gossamer center. "Damn!" she cursed. "With so many people *coughing* and *sneezing* and *crying* here—it's a *fuckin' ER*, for god's sake—you'd think a *hospital* with any concern for public health would stock decent tissue! It's shocking we haven't all died of TB, bird flu, Ebola . . ."

Rosalie waited for Nora to settle down. Truth was, she'd known that Nora was working today. Why else would she have been wearing her white coat and Keens during this morning's meeting? But subbing for Nora in the ER would have risked more unnerving encounters with Cheryl and Edna. Finally, she said, "I am troubled by something Lydia said last night about being 'the death' of her."

"No, Rosalie, you can't believe you jinxed her. Besides, she wasn't just talking about you. She was referring to you *and* me—to *any* doctor who allowed herself to be affected by patients."

Looking doubtful, Rosalie said, "But how could any good doctor *not* be affected?"

Nora felt defensive again, wondering whether Rosalie intended her remark as a judgment against Lydia. "Well," she said, "Lydia thinks . . . or, she thought . . . " She dried her eyes and continued, "Lydia thought that doctors who did were foolishly following unhealthy trends in medicine—like, healthcare becoming too 'Yelp-y' and touchy-feely at the expense of medical science. She thought the patient-as-consumer and doctor-as-service-provider trends were *literally* killing doctors *and* patients." She reached into her wallet and handed a yellowed scrap of paper to Rosalie. "It's an old *New Yorker* cartoon," she explained. "Lydia gave it to me to remind me of the dangers."

Rosalie studied the cartoon. "Is this supposed to be funny?"

"Funny-painful. But keep it. You'll understand at some point. I certainly don't need it anymore."

Stuffing the cartoon into a pocket of her white coat, Rosalie said, "Well, what I do understand is that I should have taken Dr. Chandler's keys from her last night."

Nora shook her head. "No. It should've been me watching her back."

After a momentary silence, Rosalie asked, "Did you know about her drug problem?"

Nora fell mute.

"Forgive me," Rosalie said. "It was insensitive to ask."

Nora knew it was futile to deny knowing about Lydia's prescription narcotic use. In fact, lately, anyone who'd spent even a couple hours in Lydia's company would have witnessed her pill-popping. "Lydia had a back problem," she feebly offered.

"You never reported her to the DEA, or the medical board, or to admin even?"

Nora shook her head.

"Well, it is disappointing," Rosalie said, "that we doctors tend to protect each other at all cost. Cost to ourselves, but also to patients and society. And we keep silent about our alcohol or drug problems, and our mental illnesses. Our mistakes."

Overcome with shame, Nora admitted, "You're right. Protective self-regulation is embedded within our profession's culture."

Rosalie sighed. "Well, did you ever talk personally with Dr. Chandler about her addiction?"

"Not seriously enough," Nora answered. But the last two years had been such a blur—one long dark moment of losing her family, and, for Lydia, of losing Fred. Given their intense parallel griefs, it was a miracle, she thought, that she and Lydia had stayed in any meaningful contact whatsoever. Still, it pained her to acknowledge that she had possessed neither the courage nor wherewithal to intervene in Lydia's escalating opioid use. And she also had to admit how much she had secretly envied Lydia for having something, *anything*, that helped her to endure grief.

Rosalie thought: *How pathetic. How disillusioning. Where are Nora's ethics? Where is her concern about impaired physicians and patient safety?*

And how oblivious she chooses to remain about Lydia's character and drug use! The revered Dr. Nora Kelly—you were handed such telling clues, and, again, chose not to act. She said, "Nora, I had my interview with the police an hour ago. You should know they will be asking you about Lydia and drugs."

"I expect so."

Nora's seemingly lax reply accelerated the momentum of Rosalie's outrage. She said, "They are going to turn the hospital upside down and inside out looking for systems breaches involving prescription narcotic trafficking! And they are going to review all of Lydia's work in the path department! So, if her drug problem was so obvious . . . well, I wish someone had said something to someone, or at least talked with Lydia so she could have gotten help. And then all of this—even her death— might not have happened."

Nora felt sick and lightheaded. And, looking into Rosalie's eyes, she wondered what lurked behind the aggressive questioning. Did Rosalie intend to be hurtful? Why were they discussing anything other than the devastating loss of her closest friend? She said, "Lydia was completely dedicated to Oakland City for decades. Whatever they find, the bottom line is that she always did her job extremely well. She was loyal to her 'dead patients.' She considered pathology a sacred calling. And . . . I can't continue this discussion with you."

Rosalie responded with a wounded expression. "Of course. What is wrong with me? It is just that everything is so . . . upsetting. And I am questioning *everything.*"

"Don't worry about it," Nora said half-heartedly, wondering how their conversation relentlessly bent back to focus on Rosalie.

"Thanks," Rosalie said, smiling wanly. "Anyway, I am meeting Fred in his office in a few minutes. Wow, some 'day off' this has been for me! But that meeting should be over by the time you finish your police interview. Maybe we can grab something at the Tavern afterward?"

"No, thanks," Nora said. Food and socializing were unthinkable. "I just want to go home and break down."

"A raincheck then?"

Nora nodded. Then she watched Rosalie walk away, an obscure distance increasing with each of her exiting steps.

C-Suite Conference Room

Oakland City Hospital

4:30 P.M.

Exasperated, Fergie repeated, "Like I said, because Lydia *refused* my offer—my *strong recommendation*—that I drive her home."

Detective Darinda Johnson nodded at her partner, Tom Burka. In her low throaty voice, she said, "So, you're all out drinking, medical professionals every one of you, and you let your friend drive home . . . alone. A friend who was also popping pills, according to everyone. And because she says 'no thanks' to a ride, you—"

The black-haired hospital lawyer objected, "She's already answered that."

Burka persisted, "Dr. Chandler, inebriated, driving up those twisty roads in the dark . . . You knew she lived high up in the hills, right? No pun intended."

Fergie looked stonily at him. "I've never been to her house, and she's never visited mine. And I mean no disrespect, but we've all seen her drink lots more than she did last night. And far as I know, she never had a problem driving."

Johnson said, "Okay. Then tell what you knew about your friend's oxy habit."

"Nothing specific, and she wasn't really a friend."

"Yeah? You just hang out at bars together?"

"Some of us at the hospital meet after work sometimes, and that was the extent of my relationship with Lydia."

"Well, you two not being 'real' friends—was that because of some power imbalance? A doctors-not-mixing-with-nurses kinda thing? Did you feel *excluded*?"

"That's nuts."

"Okay," Burka said unconvincingly. "And you'd say the same about the two other doctors with you last night: Rosalie Karlov and Nora Kelly?"

"Nora and I are friends. I am *friendly* with Rosalie—but not *friends*."

"Sure," Burka said. "So, the bartender said you and Dr. Karlov brought Dr. Chandler a third drink from the bar. Is that correct?"

"Yeah, but Lydia had already ordered it. We offered to go pick it up at the bar because we both wanted a break from the table."

"Why was that?"

Fergie removed her bifocals and rubbed her tired eyes. "We needed to stretch our legs."

Burka said, "So, then you and Dr. Karlov just sat at the bar, taking a breather?"

Fergie sighed. "I was texting at the bar. She was in the restroom, I think."

Johnson looked probingly at Fergie. "What did you do after leaving the Tavern last night?"

"I went straight home and slept. Then I showed up for work this morning. Why?"

"Just routine inquiry," Burka said. "But can anyone verify you being home all night?"

"My husband," Fergie said.

Neither the lawyers nor the detectives could conceal their surprise. After an edgy silence, Johnson managed, "Your *husband?*"

Typical, Fergie thought. Annoyed by their collective dimwittedness, she provocatively removed her jacket to expose more of the copious tattoos across her muscular arms and neck. On her right shoulder, she had a V and an E in Cerulean lettering. On her left shoulder, she had one half of a broken heart. She slid a slow hand over her close-shaved head and said, "That's correct. My *husband.*"

Fred's Office

Oakland City Hospital

4:45 P.M.

Rosalie argued, "But I *can* do it, Fred! I am sorry Cheryl felt disrespected by me. But I only ran into that patient's room because I was ER backup, and *they* called *me* in!"

Fred countered, "Actually, 'they' was only Fergie—not Cheryl, not Edna, not the standard chain of command that should've been followed. And then, when you saw Cheryl in the room, you should've backed off if *she* didn't want your help."

"But Cheryl was making a mistake! They all said so! The patient, his mother, the nurse—"

"Careful. *Mistake* is a highly charged word inside a hospital. If you are alleging a doctor made one, you better be fully prepared to make your case."

"I am! Cheryl was *mistaking* a patient—*a human being*—for an *object!*"

Fred crossed his arms, leaned back in his chair and thought—*How incredible it must be to feel so certain about everything. What is it like to see right from wrong in black and white?* Though he barely remembered Rosalie as a resident here, he'd been responsible for monitoring her performance since she joined his staff two years ago. Initially, he thought she just sounded passionate and idealistic about medicine, like many newly-minted doctors (like himself in the distant past). Lately, though, he had wondered whether she was sounding unduly critical, and pontificating from a private moral high ground. Indeed, she had impugned administrative personnel for harassing Richard, questioned Nora's clinical competence and teaching, and criticized Cheryl for *being* Cheryl. And now she was calling him unfair and punitive for deciding to limit her work schedule.

"Rosalie," he said, "I've known Cheryl Kluft and her husband for years—decades, actually. She's smart as a whip, and she worked hard to earn a national reputation for device research. Granted, she may not have the best bedside manner—"

"She did not even *have* a bedside manner, because she was not even *at* the patient's bedside! She was away, in a corner of the room, making deals on her phone with a device company while the patient—"

"All right now. You've had a rough week, with losing Richard as a patient, and even being the one to find him dead—"

"What? So, you are penalizing me for getting upset over a patient's death?"

"No. But I am saying you're working too much. You've taken on too many responsibilities after being on staff just two years! Besides clinic, you're working hospitalist shifts, taking ER backup, picking up slack in the teaching program since Nora withdrew—"

"It is not too much for *me*! And I need the money. Do you have any idea what medical school debt is nowadays? I still owe over $200,000."

"I'm sorry, but—"

"I have no family or spouse to support me. Your wife, she is working and successful. I do not have millions like the Klufts."

"Stop," he commanded, and then silently counted to 10. "Look, I'll make an offer. You can keep all your extracurricular activities for now, except ER backup. Besides, that pays the least of them all."

"My god! All because Cheryl complained about me calling her out for abusing a patient?"

"No," he said, trying to contain his frustration on such an emotionally fraught day. Against his better judgment, he blurted out, "It was Edna, not Cheryl, who complained about you disrupting patient care in the ER. It was Edna, not Cheryl, who requested—no, *demanded*, actually—your removal from backup call. It was—" His cellphone rang, and, grateful for the interruption, he told Rosalie, "I need to take this." He then stepped into the hallway to speak privately with Vickie.

"It's me," Vickie answered. "Can you pick up some half-and-half on the way home?"

"Sure," he said, and the call abruptly ended. But its jolting termination triggered his realization that he would never again be able to speak with Lydia. Hoping to have archived a recorded message of her voice, he frantically scrolled through his phone log. But then he heard a door open and saw Fergie and the lawyers emerging into the hallway. Wanting to avoid them, he reentered his office. Rosalie was there, sitting behind his desk.

"I was just wondering," she said, "what fairness and justice look like from where *you* sit."

Her startling comment and insolent presence at his desk had the power to distract him momentarily from grief. *What in God's name just happened? How did we get to this high drama from a discussion about a minor schedule change?* He stared back at Rosalie with mounting incredulity, struck by her unflinching glare, stymied by her audacity. *How can she so freely make such egregious charges against my character?* Something alarming and ambiguous about this conflict was creeping under his skin. He said, "Your behavior confirms my concern about you being overly stressed. I'm not changing my mind."

Rosalie buried her face in her hands and sobbed so violently that her body shook. "I am sorry," she said. "So much is going on."

Fred waited a respectful minute, all the while regretting the mistake he'd made in wedging this meeting with Rosalie into his schedule now. Among all other attempts to distract himself with work today, this one uniquely backfired. He glanced at his watch, estimating the time required to stop by the 7-11. Then he opened his office door and declared, "It's time for you to go."

ER Breakroom

Oakland City Hospital

4:45 P.M.

With just 15 minutes remaining in her shift, Nora could finally trust that this workday would end. There was a meeting ahead with police and lawyers, which would be undoubtedly grim. But the end was definitely in sight, and a caffeine boost could help her across the finish line. But when she entered the breakroom, her heart sank—Cheryl and Carl were there, and, salt to the wound, emptying the coffee pot into their mugs. She lamely said, "I thought you'd be home by now."

"We just finished our work here," Carl said. "We're going to drop it off at Cheryl's research office and then head home. Hopefully, she'll rest a few hours before having her surgery in the morning."

"Well, good luck with all that," Nora said, turning away.

"Wait," Cheryl said. "I want to apologize for what I said earlier today. Carl is right. I was stressed about my research and surgery."

Nora nodded.

Cheryl continued, "See, I had to submit my data by a deadline today. So, last night, when they brought Lydia in, and everyone in the

ER just stopped doing their jobs ... well, any help I'd been counting on also stopped."

"You bitch!" Nora said.

"Excuse me? I was *apologizing!* And, look: sorry you lost your friend, but Lydia was no friend to me. I may have known you both since residency, but neither of you ever gave Carl or me the time of day."

"Oh, fuck off, Cheryl! If you think I'm going to have *that* old discussion with you *today*, you're insane."

"Yeah, well, I'm no longer convinced of your diagnostic acumen. No one is."

"Calm down," Carl said. "Let's try to—"

"Shut up, Carl!" Cheryl snapped. To Nora, she said, "Did you use your vaunted medical judgment in deciding to let your pill-popping friend drive home?"

Nora invoked her therapist's advisement: *When a person is full of poison, do not stand within spitting distance.* She accordingly stepped back and said, "You've made your views known."

Carl pleaded, "Cheryl, Nora ... imagine walking in each other's shoes."

"I wouldn't be caught dead in those clunky Keens," said Cheryl.

As Nora headed for the door, Cheryl shouted, "You've held court in this hospital since our residency. But your reign is over! You've outlived your reputation."

Fergie appeared in the breakroom with Lizbeth at her side. "What's going on? We can hear you out to the waiting room!"

Emboldened by Fergie's presence, Nora charged back at Cheryl, "All you care about is making 'million-dollar babies' that just keep bankrupting the healthcare system! You treat patients like guinea pigs to test your stupid medical devices—"

Cheryl scoffed. "Stupid medical devices? Like *stupid* stents or *stupid* pacemakers? Innovations that actually *save* lives and advance medical technology?"

"You're delusional! What you mostly advance is your bank account. I'm on the institutional review board, Cheryl. So, I've reviewed all your grant applications and research. I know—hell, the entire IRB knows—you're mostly just tweaking old devices so you can file new patents on them and charge higher prices!"

Lizbeth whispered to Fergie, "I'm getting Edna. She just got back from San Sebastian."

Cheryl yelled at Nora, "My research attracts millions of dollars to Alameda County and this Podunk teaching hospital!"

Carl was astonished to witness two highly educated colleagues proving themselves so incapable of speaking civilly with one another, and so unable to reconcile a disagreement. And these two intelligent people, unlike him, weren't saddled with social handicaps. Worse, it was excruciating to hear someone so disdainfully regard Cheryl's "million-dollar babies." Painfully reminded of his childlessness with Cheryl, he walked away.

His abrupt departure stunned Cheryl. How unprecedented for him to leave her at a time like this—at any time, really. Starting after him, she told Nora, "Maybe now you'll see what it's like when a friend leaves you."

Nora followed her into the corridor, shouting, "How many millions in kickbacks do you get from your device companies?"

Cheryl stopped and turned to Nora. "Look at you. You're still here at this pathetic little hospital wasting time putting tiny bandages on enormous social problems you'll never fix. Here you are, still peddling your ancient ideas about being a doctor and relating to patients. About differential diagnoses and the physical exam. About things no one cares about anymore. It's pitiable! Still, you're somehow convinced that makes you noble. But, hey . . . I think it just makes you sad. And tragic, actually."

Nora watched Cheryl dash down the hallway and catch up to Carl. But then she saw Carl recoil, push Cheryl away, and leave her standing there alone.

"Let's go," Fergie said, coaxing Nora away from rubbernecking coworkers. But when they reentered the breakroom, Edna was standing at the sink, furiously scrubbing the coffee pot, complaining to Lizbeth: "No, doctors just *drink* coffee. You'll never see one of them *making* a new pot."

"Excuse me?" Lizbeth said, trying to get Edna's attention.

"What now?" Edna grumbled, turning to Lizbeth but startled to see Nora and Fergie. "Nora," she said, "I'm sorry for what I said."

Nora had zero energy for additional conflict, so she only said, "But you're right. I drink coffee and never—"

"No," Edna interrupted. "I'm sorry for what I said at that horrid meeting this morning. My judgment was off. It's no good excuse, but I was ... exhausted after working night shift, worrying how I was going to get through an interview with police, and then a visit with Jack. And after all that, I had to return here to complete work I'd promised Cheryl yesterday. This stupid coffee pot was just the last straw."

"It's okay," Nora said, feeling it was not. She wanted to ask how Jack was faring, but the timing seemed wrong. Besides, finally, it was 5:00. "Good night," is all she said, turning away, and leaving Edna bent over the sink, holding the coffee pot filled with sudsy brown water.

Fred's Home

Berkeley

EVENING

Charlie Williams swallowed a forkful of mashed potatoes, wondering how much longer he was expected to remain at the table. The tension between his parents made time move slowly and achingly.

His sister, Ella, took small, deliberate bites of corn salad, deciding what refinements she'd make to the recipe. She could not imagine serving the so-called food on her plate—the processed, precooked, mass-produced "specials" from Universal Foods—to the family she would one day raise.

Their mother, Vickie, poured opaque brown gravy over everything—the beef, potatoes, Brussels sprouts, corn salad—creating a monochromatic scorched landscape on her plate. She ate quietly, all the while wondering what her husband was feeling about Lydia's death. But did he think he was fooling her, sitting stoically at the table, acting as if nothing happened?

Fred dutifully ate his supper despite a profound lack of appetite. It was important that everything look normal to his family. He needed to appear convincingly present with them. He spooned something green into his mouth, then something white, then something yellow—it all tasted the same.

He prayed for someone to talk about something, anything, to drown out the voices of the police, the lawyers, and the colleagues who referred all day to Lydia as a *thing*—as "the body," "the case," or "the deceased."

He glanced at his wife and children, seeking evidence of genuine connection to them. He didn't know what was safe to say; there were so many potential landmines buried in the silences. His comment a moment ago about the "delicious meal," a banal but distressed attempt to jumpstart conversation, merely elicited "whatever" looks from his family. To interrupt the painful disconnect now, he asked Charlie to pass the butter.

Like a forklift, Charlie maneuvered the butter plate over the salad bowl and delivered it to his father's hand.

"Thanks," Fred said, proceeding mechanically to spread butter (which he didn't actually want) on his bread, his potatoes, and his beef. Still, it gave him something to do while privately struggling with his grief over Lydia. Lydia whose name he dare not mention, and whose death he dare not mourn. Not here at this table, in this house, in front of these people.

Finally, he asked Vickie to "Pass the salt, please," covertly testing the waters with her. He observed her guarded reaction—tight mouth, questioning eyes—as she nudged the saltshaker toward him.

Now hoping to have bought some time before next needing to exert his presence, he mindlessly rearranged food on his plate while dwelling freely on Lydia. But horrifying images rushed into mind: the paramedics' descriptions of her mangled body, the ER accounts of her crushed skull and bloodied face, and the police reports of her crumpled BMW. They were such hideously different pictures of her than the one he had most cherished for years: of riding beside her in her BMW, zooming up Snake Road toward her house, negotiating the final steep ascent to her hilltop home like a NASCAR pro. "Come away with me, Lydia," he'd routinely say at the end of the drive.

And now, recalling their final drive two years ago, he closed his eyes, fearful they might otherwise reveal his agony. That final drive, on such a seemingly ordinary day, when Lydia surprised him by answering "yes" to his routine proposal. When she made the mistake of believing him and finally gave herself to the life they had long imagined together *if only*. That final drive, when she flipped everything upside down and said, "Yes, Fred, I'm ready for us now."

Nora's Living Room

Oakland

EVENING

Nora lay on the sofa, wrapped in a fleece throw, and stared out through the glass doors leading to her redwood deck. The San Francisco skyline appeared ghostlike through night fog, and pinpoint lights flickered along the Bay Bridge. She poured more merlot and braced herself against another crying jag that would surely upset Bix again. She rubbed the soft underside of his throat and felt the trill of his masterful purring. "I'm glad *you* feel something good," she said.

She glanced at pictures on the mantle of her husband and daughter, her parents and grandparents—all dead. She told Bix, "Our living room's become The Museum of Great Loss. And today we're adding . . ." But she couldn't say Lydia's name. She reached for the phone to call Lydia's number and hear her voice on the so-called greeting that she knew by heart: *Don't leave any unsolicited message that a highly private and litigious person would not want to receive.* But the prospect of hearing it now forever disembodied was too brutal a confirmation of her death.

Instead, Nora pulled up Lydia's photo on her cellphone and propped it against the armrest. There she was, bright as life, smiling, beside her on the couch again.

You're smiling at me, Lydia. But, you know, some people are saying that I could've saved you.

Bix began grooming in a fussy way, sending Nora a cautionary signal to chill out. "Okay," she said, taking a steadying breath, looking back to Lydia's photo.

After all the wine I had last night, I started today with a hangover from hell. And when Fergie told me that you died, my mind short-circuited. My heart collapsed . . .

Bix freed himself and took refuge under the coffee table, concealed but for his tail sticking out and moving conspicuously.

Then Cheryl attacked me during a meeting, and, still, I had to finish my shift. All day long, I couldn't get her accusations out of my head. So, pal, I gotta know if you think I'm responsible for your . . . ?"

She downed her glass of merlot and stared at Lydia's photo. *Lydia, I'll regret to the day I die that I let you drive home last night. I'm sorry I let my fear of shaming you in front of Rosalie trump my better judgment. And still, I'm confused. You always knew your limit, and I've seen you drink way more than you did. So, really, how did we let this happen to you?*

Nora stared at the ceiling and let the day's events unfurl in her mind. Fergie announcing Lydia's death . . . *unthinkable.* Claims of drug stashes inside Lydia's car . . . *implausible.* Carl pushing Cheryl away . . . *unprecedented.* Finally, as she drifted asleep, it occurred to her that she'd been conducting her deepest conversations today with a cat, an absentee therapist, and, now, a dead friend. She wondered whether she was going a little nuts.

Fergie and Winston's Apartment

East Oakland

LATE EVENING

Reclining in bed, Fergie and Winston listened to Dorothy Donegan play "My Funny Valentine." Fergie supplied the lyrics, and Winston joined in the refrain. When the music ended, he said, "I'm so sorry about Lydia."

"Yeah," Fergie said. "We weren't close, you know. But, wow, she was fierce . . . and funny. So unique."

"You always called her a 'tough old broad.' You rarely give that prop to anyone."

Fergie weakly smiled. "Lydia never suffered fools, that's for sure. And she was one of the women who 'came before' and made it easier for other women to follow in medicine. And, god, she was good for Nora. A good balance for her."

Winston drew her close, and she continued, "So, I'm worried about Nora. She's already suffered so much loss. With Lydia gone now . . ."

He stroked her back while she cried. Finally, she managed, "You should've seen how lost and sad Nora was at work today. It was weird to see her struggle with patients and families. And her so-called colleagues . . . not only did no one offer to cover her shift, but one of them even blamed her for Lydia's death."

"It sounds horrible," said Winston. "But why do you think she's being tested by so much fire?"

"Really? Well, Aristotle, sometimes, life just sucks."

"Well, I don't believe life operates on bleak slogans. I just think there may be reasons for some of what's happening to her. Not on a cosmic level; on ground level."

"What do you mean? That people are out to get her?"

"I don't know. But the world can be unkind. And when people are seen as vulnerable and defenseless, they can become easy prey for others who need to feel superior. Nora seemed pretty worn down when I ran into her at the lake the other day. Maybe, after her family disappeared, she lost the will to defend herself against the slings and arrows of daily life."

Fergie nuzzled against his neck. "It's been such a freakin' rocky time . . ."

In his best Barry White, he said, "Well, how about us having our own 'rocky time' right now?"

Fergie rolled atop Winston and kissed him softly. When her left arm pressed against his right arm, their tattooed half-hearts completed each other. And when her right shoulder pressed against his left, his L and O linked to her V and E.

Part III

Deadly Devices

FEBRUARY 13

Operating Room

Oakland City Hospital

8:00 A.M.

A COOL BROOK TRICKLED through deep furrows in her brain. Sweet medicinal balm abolished all trouble and sorrow. How wondrous to experience this intoxicating elixir of freedom, this grand physical unburdening! *General anesthesia for everyone!*

Her spinal cord unknotted, her tendons uncoiled. Tranquility infused her nerves.

Dr. Cheryl Kluft could not believe how progressively light she was becoming.

As the anesthetics and sedatives took further hold, she looked hazily up from the operating table at the surgical team swarming around her, which appeared as a shifting sea of blue: blue masks, blue scrubs, blue . . .

Another pulse of chemical sedation nudged her closer toward unconsciousness, though something in her resisted. *Please! Just a little more time here at this sublime edge.*

But already her limbs were limp feathers, her torso was air, and she floated inexorably toward blissful surrender.

Then a voice . . . or a memory of one? Perhaps a visiting deity welcoming her? Something . . . something beckoned her.

It happened again. She heard, or imagined hearing, her name spoken in a tone conveying urgency: "Cheryl Kluft."

And then something—a small rock?—was grinding deep into her breastbone, causing pain that summoned her last vestige of consciousness. Yanked back into a fleeting awareness, she opened her eyes and saw a surgically gloved hand knuckling hard against her sternum. Then an object was shoved in her face. After another knuckle of pain, she roused sufficiently to see that the object was an AccuStent-II—one of her million-dollar babies. Her eyes widened as she registered the horror, but she could do nothing to prevent the impending catastrophe. Then the gloved hands retreated, the pain in her sternum subsided, the anesthesia assumed total reign, and Cheryl Kluft drifted toward oblivion.

Cardiac Suite

Oakland City Hospital

1:15 P.M.

"How could you let this happen?" Fred shouted. "How could you do something so . . . *stupid?*"

Peter Yuen, the cardiologist, replied, "You can ask that same damn question another hundred times, and you'll get the same damn answer from me. But say 'stupid' once more, and I'll deck you."

"You implanted a *defective experimental stent* in one of our doctors! Explain how that is anything *but* stupid! Explain how making such a colossal mistake—"

"I've told you: that stent was *not* the stent I laid out during OR prep."

Fred kicked Peter's desk. "What about the surgical safety checklist? Did you even bother?"

"Nothing on that checklist could've prevented that error!"

Hammering each word, Fred said, "Did ... you ... use ... the ... damn ... checklist?"

"No! That checklist *is* stupid. It's a page straight out of *Surgery for Dummies.*"

"You arrogant son of a bitch!"

"It's a waste of time—mine and the OR's. Besides, I had eight other procedures scheduled this morning!"

"Pete, you even worked on the committee that developed our hospital *policy* requiring the use of that checklist!"

"Only to play defense for us lowly clinicians! To make sure that policy didn't end up as bureaucratic nonsense. Hospital policies exist for the lawyers and regulators—"

"Yeah? Well, you'll see about that now. Because you'll be meeting with those 'lawyers and regulators' over Cheryl's case. You can share your views about policy with *them.*"

"Stop talking to me like a schoolmarm, Fred."

But Fred could not amend his tone. "And since we're talking policy and standards of practice, why the hell did you put Cheryl under general anesthesia? And in the OR? You should've placed her stent in the procedure suite under conscious sedation!"

"Because we don't force treatments on patients who refuse them! And Cheryl *refused* conscious sedation. Why? Because she knew too goddamn much about everything that could go wrong and didn't want to remain aware and worrying about it."

Fred's emotionally triggered asthma began compromising his speech. "On top of everything ... once you *finally* realized your mistake ... and realized you'd probably destroyed Cheryl's brain ... *then* you initiate *CPR!* For god's sake, Pete, she had a DNR on file! And an advance directive clearly stating 'no CPR' under *any* circumstance. And didn't you, Mister Medical Ethics ... didn't you just tell me we didn't *force* treatments on patients who *refused* them?"

Peter scoffed. "We always override patients' DNRs during surgeries."

"Of course, you do! Because not only do we have hospital *policy* against that, we have California *law* requiring us to honor patients' documented wishes! But you? You're above policy . . . and law . . . and patients' rights."

Peter, his body stiffening, said, "Here's some free medical advice: take a breather. You're going to keel over." Watching Fred struggle, he tamped down his anger and continued, "We ignore DNRs during surgery for *good* reason. Patients who choose to undergo *major* operations *intend* to survive them. It's foolish to think otherwise."

"There's no asterisk around *Do Not Resuscitate* that gives you permission for that."

"I disagree. Those Advance Directives are always subject to interpretation. And today I made a clinical *judgment* about their relevance to Cheryl's best interests."

Fred shook his head. "No. What actually happened is that you didn't want Cheryl proclaimed dead on your operating table because that would count against your surgical mortality stats. You kept her technically 'alive' just long enough to get her out of the OR and into the recovery unit."

"Enough, Fred!"

"You left Cheryl suspended in a godforsaken vegetative state to protect your stupid—"

"Hey—you're the one always harping about hospital scores. And I warned you . . ." His fist slammed into Fred's face.

Cheryl's Room, ICU

Oakland City Hospital

AFTERNOON

"Thanks for coming," Carl told Nora. "I know you have the day off. And, of course, Lydia just died. But I had no one else to call."

Nora nodded (there seemed little more to say) and sat alongside Carl. They stared at Cheryl's limp body, which was tethered to machines and IVs. The ventilator sighed; monitors beeped. Calf compression stockings rhythmically hissed. A chorus of living machines worked hard to animate Cheryl.

"Shell shock" was the term that kept recurring to Nora. Her brain, already fragmented by Lydia's death, was suffering new sets of explosions in the wake of Cheryl's apparent demise. And sitting here at Carl's forlorn request, she was guiltily reminded of her fractious interactions with Cheryl yesterday. Still, one question kept emerging: *Why would this happen to Cheryl, so close to Lydia's death?*

Fred appeared, startling Nora with his disheveled appearance—bloodstains on his coat and tie, an oozing wound straining against stitches on his cheek. He held up a hand to convey, *Don't ask,* then he sat beside Carl and said, "If there's anything we can do, Carl, for you or Cheryl, trust it'll get done. We're family."

"There is something," Carl replied. "Tell me how a defective experimental stent that was securely stored in Cheryl's research office across the street got implanted in her coronary artery." Pointing to Fred's tie, he added, "Use cold saline to remove the blood."

Fred debated whether to mention his conversation with Peter Yuen or his urgent dispatch of the Situation Management and Response Team to begin a formal investigation of Cheryl's case. But what little information he currently possessed was preliminary and more likely to confuse matters than clarify them. "We'll figure that out," he said. "I've already asked the SMART team to open an investigation."

Carl said, "That AccuStent-II was lethal. It never even came close to approval for human use."

"What?" Nora exclaimed. She recalled group discussions about the AccuStent-II during meetings of the hospital's Institutional Review Board on which she sat. "I'm on the IRB, and I remember discussing that stent a *long* time ago. By now, Cheryl should've disposed of any in her possession. She's contractually and legally obligated. Why would she still be holding onto any in her office?"

Unable to mask his annoyance, Fred said, "We'll look into that, too, Nora. If you don't mind . . ."

Carl said, "It had to do with the timing of a VivoZeel shareholders' meeting. Cheryl withheld closure on the AccuStent-II because she didn't want to divulge bad news of the stent's failure beforehand."

"Of course," Nora said. "Because hearing that the AccuStent-II had no future in clinical trials, let alone the device market, would've jeopardized VivoZeel's stock value."

"Correct," Carl said.

Fred sighed. "Look, Carl. I promise to find out how this horrible accident—"

"I know everything about that stent," Carl said. "It was supposed to be one of Cheryl's million-dollar babies. I helped her with the original research."

"All right now," Fred pleaded. "Can we slow down a minute?"

All three sat silently while Cheryl's body shook with the rhythmic pulsations of the machines sustaining it. And during this oddly orchestrated moment, Nora began to feel mentally roused. In this blazing wake of Lydia's death and Cheryl's demise, she felt the good fire enter her. Its heat seeped through her skin. Its warmth wicked up her spine and began burning away the fog in her brain. Internal lights, long-dimmed, now flickered, and illumination returned to her eyes. The good fire reached the deadwood inside her heart and lent its flame. It rekindled her curiosity and intellect. She confidently asserted, "What happened to Cheryl was no 'horrible accident.' It was intentional."

Fred was shocked to hear Nora make such a provocative claim, especially while he struggled to contain Carl's reactions. "C'mon! We don't know *anything* yet. This just happened to Cheryl a few hours ago—"

Carl interrupted, "Peter Yuen told me that someone must've switched the stents. That he had personally laid out the correct one during OR prep."

"Yuen came to see you?" Fred asked.

"Yes. To say he was sorry about what happened. He said Cheryl coded on his table right after they unknowingly inserted the wrong stent. They realized the error only when they reviewed her post-op CT in the recovery room."

Fred protested, "That was inappropriate of Yuen."

"No," Carl insisted. "Apologizing was the *right* thing to do. Didn't you hear about the 'extreme honesty approach' to disclosing medical mistakes? Maybe if *you* attended some of the communication seminars you mandate for *me*, you'd learn how doctors *should* be informing patients and families about their mistakes."

It surprised Nora to hear Carl's strong voice and emotion, unfiltered through Cheryl.

Fred said, "How about we meet tomorrow and calmly discuss—"

But Nora's mind was racing. "We need to focus on how that AccuStent got into the OR in the first place. That'll help determine who was involved and why this happened."

"Hold on," Fred said. "Any official investigation should be handled by SMART and—"

Carl said, "The AccuStents were stored in a sealed box in a locked cabinet inside Cheryl's research office. You can't access her office without multiple security clearances. I only ever got inside by accompanying her."

Nora said, "So we're probably looking for someone with official clearance who is familiar with the building's security protocols."

Fred shouted, "This is no time to speculate! We should be focusing on Cheryl now."

Carl countered, "We *are* focusing on Cheryl if we're figuring out what happened to her. *She* would want that. I want that."

Fred peered through the slits of his swollen eyes, trying to read Carl's facial expression. It was hard enough under normal circumstances, but now it was physically difficult as well. The one thing he clearly saw was the futility in continuing to press for restraint. Still, as chief of the medical staff, he knew the collateral damage that could befall the hospital because of poorly coordinated and amateurish investigations of a medical mistake. And if news about this high-profile error were to leak to the media, the public's trust in Oakland City Hospital, already threadbare, could fray irreparably. The hospital's research program could lose millions in grant funds from medical device companies if charged with sloppy internal oversight of the AccuStent.

Though aware of being up against Carl's native obsessiveness and Nora's ostensibly reawakened curiosity, Fred tried one last time: "Carl, I'd like to wait on standard error protocol and the SMART team's look into this case—"

"Did you just say 'this case?'"

"Whoa! I—"

"She's no *case*, Fred. This *person*—do you see her? I'm pointing at Dr. Cheryl Kluft. This *person* is my wife of 30 years. She is a *person* who's worked alongside you for decades."

"Carl, I wasn't minimizing—"

"Let's be honest," Carl said. "The SMART team protects the *hospital*, not the hospital's patients; not Cheryl, not me. It investigates medical mistakes with the primary goal of shielding the hospital and its staff from lawsuits. SMART is not neutral. It's not objective or transparent. And right now, Cheryl and I need genuine advocacy."

"Look, you're upset with this situation—"

Carl shouted, "This is no 'situation' either! Remember: you're talking to an expert in corp-speak. I know every 'situation management' strategy in the books, thanks to all those seminars you make me attend because of my low scores on patient satisfaction surveys. Surveys on which my patients rate me 'excellent' for their *actual* medical care, and the *actual* care of their *actual* babies. Most of *them* understand my struggle with Asperger's, and *they* know I do my best. They understand that I *communicate* my care through the *actual medical care* I provide."

Fred frowned, unwittingly tensing the stitches on his face. "Carl, your medical expertise and clinical outcomes were never under question. It's just—"

"It's just that our hospital needs better ratings on Yelp ... on Angie's List ... on Facebook? On all those authoritative arbiters of medical competence and quality care?"

"That's not—"

"Let me share one of my 'learnings' with you, Fred. When you say 'case' or 'situation management,' I hear you repackaging reality with corp-speak; wrapping it up in self-protective aphorisms. I hear you manipulating truth and creating obstacles to finding out what *actually* happened to Cheryl."

Nora couldn't help but feel invigorated by Carl's electrifying passion, despite its obvious toll on Fred. It even seemed immodest, ignoble perhaps, to feel so aroused in the midst of so much mourning. Still, her intellectual reflexes continued to thaw and nudge her toward the mystery at hand. She asked Fred, "Have you examined Cheryl's office?"

"Not yet," Fred responded curtly. "And, look, we should leave. We should let Carl have private time with Cheryl."

"I'm glad Nora is interested," Carl said. "And I want her involved in figuring out what happened."

Fred looked desolately at Cheryl, sympathetically at Carl, and resignedly at Nora.

Nora's Living Room

Oakland

EVENING

The thermostat read 68 degrees, but the wine-blush in Nora's face made the house seem warmer. Bix rubbed his head against Nora's cell, which leaned against the sofa armrest, displaying Lydia's photo.

"Well, here we are—the three of us together again," Nora said. She finished her pad thai and began settling in for another night on the sofa. But when she lay down and stared up at the barren ceiling, she remembered Timmy dancing the skedaddle and regretted not liberating him from Lydia's office. She made a mental note to rescue him tomorrow after her weekly breakfast with Fred.

She held her phone and, looking at Lydia, said, "There will be hell to pay if some stupid hospital policy about dead employees' belongings tries to keep me from Timmy." When the screen dimmed, Nora said, "You weren't as durable as Velveeta after all."

Lydia—I need to talk with you about all the weird shit that's happening. And now, with this renewed stirring in my bones . . .

You and I understood the language of bodies and heard it in our different ways. And we loved puzzlements of the flesh. So, see, you should be here, helping me figure out what's happened to Cheryl. To Richard. To you.

Am I crazy to think all three are connected?

And I know you'd never be so careless with drugs in your car and body. I know Richard wouldn't commit suicide.

Now recalling the gang-of-six photo that Lydia brought out in her office last week, Nora decided to retrieve her own copy from the bedroom. There, she also printed out the photo of Lydia from her cell. She carried both photos back to the living room, propping them side by side against the armrest. And she fell asleep peaceably enough, surrounded by her old residency mates whose stories stretched across decades and anchored her in the confounding present.

FEBRUARY 14

Cheryl's Room, ICU

Oakland City Hospital

DAWN

For nearly 24 consecutive hours, Carl had been sitting at his wife's bedside. "Cheryl?" he inquired again.

Still, she didn't answer; didn't flinch.

He again tried to rouse her with a gentle shake of her shoulder, but his touch elicited no response. He sunk back into his chair, deprived of sleep, of food, and of any opportunity to ask Cheryl for forgiveness. *Of all nights for me to get angry with you . . .*

He began his ritual again: he stared at Cheryl's inert body and then proceeded to note, in rote sequence, every detail in the room. He noted every object on the walls: each waffled ceiling tile, every scuff on the floor, and each piece of medical equipment.

And then he noted them again . . . and again.

A binding loop of consciousness replayed . . . and replayed.

At fitful junctures, doubts about the sanity of his wife's predicament pierced the protective walls of his obsessive thinking. *Why are we pretending Cheryl is going to get better?* Still, cheerful nurses and optimistic doctors continuously paraded through Cheryl's room, acting as if everything were copasetic; normal. They worked earnestly to improve her blood test results, the numbers on the ventilator, the vital signs on the monitor, and the volume of urine output in the collection bag. Increasingly, to Carl, they seemed to be complicit in a charade of Cheryl's life.

Still, how could they *all* be so blind to Death's visitation here?

I am the odd one out, as always. My perception of reality must be off. Cheryl, I need your guidance—

He remembered how she had advised him that the trick to negotiating conflicting realities was to put aside subjective experience and
imagine becoming an object that fit neatly in the alternate reality. *Yes,*
he thought, *an object like my wife.* A figurine like Cheryl, placed in this
strange diorama called *The ICU* that was ornamented with imitations
of life. A cardiac monitor provided audio of a beating heart. An IV drip
simulated nutrient intake. A respirator rhythmically expanded Cheryl's
chest. The narrative created by the diorama was that his wife was alive.
And he could fit neatly within it, a typical figurine, as *the loved one at
the bedside.*

I-C-U . . . Even the letters labeling this diorama implicated a powerful observing entity of the death-denying pageantry inside this room.

Defensively, desperately, Carl began again: he stared at his motionless wife and proceeded to note every detail in the room . . .

El Gourmet Burger

Downtown Oakland

MORNING

"Where's your buddy today?" Amelia asked, removing Nora's plate from
the table.

"Good question," Nora said, handing her a ten.

Nora checked her phone—still, nothing from Fred. She texted him:
Just 8. Leaving now. U OK?

She left the restaurant, concerned about Fred's unresponsiveness.
Our first breakfast after Lydia dies, and he doesn't show? To make matters
worse, it was Valentine's Day. *Goddamn Valentine's Day. No husband, no
family, no Lydia, no Fred.*

Being a doctor, she also imagined the worst. Fred could be lying in
an alley, unconscious from a subdural that developed after his fight with
Peter. He could have been derailed by Lydia's death and out on a bender.
Or perhaps he was upset about her involvement in Cheryl's case.

She looked to the lake a short block away and tried to convince herself to take a healthful walk around it. *I should force myself to do what I routinely tell patients to do—*

A car's aggressive honking intruded, and a silver Lexus pulled up. Fred called out, "Get in!"

"This is mighty cloak-and-dagger of you," she said, taking the passenger's seat.

He parked up the road and turned off the ignition. "Sorry about breakfast. I had to pack a few things. Vickie kicked me out of the house."

"No! Oh, friend—I'm so sorry." She placed a comforting hand on his back. "Well, if it's any consolation, you've outscored me for the worst Valentine's Day."

He smiled weakly. "I suppose that's something."

"So, what happened?"

"It's . . . complicated. And it goes beyond Vickie. Because I think someone's stalking me."

Fred's dramatic claim alarmed her and called to mind Lydia's concern about him losing his marbles and becoming paranoid. She said, "You really believe you're being stalked? Look, I know you're stressed out. And with Lydia's death, if you're experiencing even a fraction of the crazy grief I'm—"

"C'mon, Nora. You're the only one I can talk to now." Frustrated, he rested his forehead on the steering wheel. Sunlight illumined his shiny scalp.

"Sorry. But Lydia was worried because you—"

"Please, no," he groaned.

"She told me you suspected her of calling your house."

"I know."

"And leaving some mysterious envelope . . ."

"Look: Vickie thought that was all Lydia's doing. Because that envelope she found on our doorstep contained my credit card receipt from last Tuesday at the Tavern, with 'Happy Anniversary' written across it. So, naturally, Vickie became suspicious of Lydia and me."

"God, how . . . awful. And creepy. I'm queasy just hearing this."

"I had to convince Vickie I hadn't gotten back with Lydia. And I kept reminding her that I'd always been honest about that relationship.

So, well, things finally calmed down after a couple days. We even started thinking together, trying to figure things out. One thing we agreed on: it made sense to think it was the same person making the calls who left the envelope. But then Vickie ..."

"Vickie what?"

"God ... I made a mistake! I told her about Lydia's oxy use and how it worsened after our breakup. That's when Vickie worked herself into a lather, imagining Lydia unhinged and all *Fatal Attraction* on me. Making those calls. Delivering that damn bar receipt."

Nora moaned—a soft, almost inaudible lament—as her heart clenched around this distorted portrayal of Lydia. She held Fred's hand, and they sat in silence a while. *Still*, she thought, *while I can forgive Vickie's paranoia about Lydia, Fred should've known better.* His poor judgment made her question whether she could depend upon him as a sage thought partner throughout this terribly confusing time. Indeed, why hasn't he questioned the ludicrous reports about Lydia's so-called accident? Why doesn't he seem to remember that Lydia never stashed drugs in her car, and never took so much oxy that it would impair her driving and put others at risk? She cautiously asked, "Fred, do *you* believe Lydia would—?"

"Of course not! I just flipped out for a moment. A moment! But Vickie was so goddamn sure about it being Lydia. And then ... then she got this idea that, if it wasn't Lydia, it had to be *another* woman. I felt desperate. Vickie was freaking out. My kids were upset. I just got worn down, and my judgment suffered. And, Nora, at the same time, something fishy was *actually* happening with the calls and the envelope. So, I made a very tired and very stupid mistake when I confronted Lydia."

Nora reached into the glove compartment and passed Fred's inhaler to him. He took a puff and continued, "That night at the Square when I confronted Lydia? God—I got hold of reality real fast. Her reaction brought me straight back to my senses. Still, as you'd imagine, she got angry. And hurt. I kept apologizing, and trying to explain. But she stormed away. I was hoping we'd talk the next day at Richard's service." He withdrew a cigarette pack from his coat pocket. "But she left early, and I didn't get the chance. And now, I'll never have another."

Nora confiscated his cigarettes and placed them in her purse. "Smoking? Are you kidding? With your asthma? Fine if you want to be self-destructive, but you're not taking me with you."

"C'mon, it's just an old pack from the last century. I found it this morning while I was packing things from my bureau."

"Well, let's keep it last century. In the current one, we doctors no longer promote tobacco."

Fred rubbed his forehead, the stitches on his cheek pulling uncomfortably. Nora asked, "Did they clear out Lydia's office yet?"

"No. They're boxing it up tomorrow. Why?"

"Just something I wanted."

"I'll ask them to put it aside for you . . . *if* you return my cigarettes."

They stared at one another until their mutual pain forced them to look away.

"I miss Lydia so much," he said.

"I know," she said, glancing at the lake and the dark clouds mirrored on its surface.

The Palmer Medical Research Center

Near Oakland City Hospital

MORNING

Edna and Lizbeth waited at the crosswalk outside the hospital, en route to the research center across the street. One of the city's free Green Buses drove by, and a passenger leaned out to snap a photograph of the Tribune Tower. Edna remarked, "There are so many tourists in Oakland now. Who would've imagined that just a few years ago?"

Uncertain how to respond, Lizbeth said, "Thanks for letting me tag along today."

Edna furrowed her brow.

"Did I say something wrong?" Lizbeth asked.

"No. It's just . . . you always sound so tentative. I'd like to trust that you'll someday develop greater self-confidence."

Upon their arrival at the Palmer Medical Research Center, Edna looked probingly into Lizbeth's eyes and said, "We're investigating a very serious medical error. What I need you to learn from this experience is . . . well, even the best nurses and doctors can make terrible mistakes. No matter how hard we try to do good, we sometimes do bad or foolish things that hurt patients or people we care about."

It stunned Lizbeth to receive this message imparted with such paralyzing solemnity. Its *momentousness* was overwhelming, and Edna's heightened intensity and fretfulness confused her. She shakily replied, "I understand."

Edna looked doubtful but persisted: "And you need to understand that some of those 'mistakes' are not completely innocent. They can happen because we are negligent, or incompetent, or greedy. And once in a great while . . . because we actually *intend* to make them."

Lizbeth felt obligated to reply, but . . . to what? *Why is Edna telling me this, and in such a dramatic manner?*

"Promise me something," Edna said. "As a nurse, you *will* speak up whenever you suspect any of those 'mistakes' have happened. No matter who prefers otherwise and no matter the doctor, lawyer, or nursing admin who stands in the way of you telling the truth or expressing concern. You *must* stand up for yourself—on behalf of your patients and all nurses. Do you understand me?"

"I think so."

"Promise you will remember what I said."

"I . . . I promise."

Edna nodded gravely. They then proceeded to the security entrance where a cheerful clerk with cobalt blue hair greeted them. "Welcome!" she said. "My name's DeeDee. You can call me Dee."

Edna said, "We're from the Situation Management and Response Team, and we're here to take a look at Dr. Kluft's office."

"Yes; from the SMART committee. We've been expecting you. If you could just show me your ID badges . . . yes, okay, great . . . thank you! . . . sign in here, please . . . fabulous! All set! I'll buzz you through."

DeeDee led them through a labyrinthine corridor, chatting along the way. "Everyone here was bummed to hear about Dr. Kluft's surgery. We all know her. Well, we know *of* her, at least. She's kinda . . . *independent?*"

Turning a corner, they ran into a young man who, upon seeing Lizbeth, removed his thick-lensed glasses and smiled.

DeeDee said, "Hi, Joel! We're headed to Dr. Kluft's office. This is . . . um . . ."

"Hello," Edna said, extending her hand. "I'm Nurse Edna Atkinson from the SMART committee, and this is my student, Lizbeth Tanner. I understand you're Dr. Kluft's research assistant?"

"Yes; I'm Joel Plawecki. And I hope she gets better soon. I'm not qualified to substitute as principal investigator on all her projects."

"Well, these ladies need to check her office," DeeDee said.

"Can I be of help?" asked Joel, his eyes fixed on Lizbeth.

Edna replied, "You can tell us whether you noticed anything or anyone unusual in her office."

"Sure," he said. "Like the person there the other night on Sunday?"

Edna reproached DeeDee, "When we spoke by phone, you said all the security codes activated at her office on Sunday belonged to Dr. Kluft herself."

"They did! I'm sure of that."

Joel said, "Sorry, Dee, but it's a factoid. I definitely saw someone in her office Sunday night."

Edna looked disapprovingly at Joel. "So, you saw someone you didn't recognize in your boss's office *and* on a weekend night. And you weren't alarmed?"

"Well, it wasn't a big deal. Dr. Kluft always had medical residents or fellows working on grants with her and earning research creds. They came and went all the time. Besides, with all the security around here, you'd have to be Penn *and* Teller to get into her office if you weren't legit."

Concerned about Edna losing patience, Lizbeth intervened. "Joel, can you say whether it was a man or a woman?"

He looked sheepishly at DeeDee and said, "A woman. I was here in the hallway, and I saw her through Dr. Kluft's doorway. She was bent over with her back to me, and she had a nice . . . body. Definitely a woman's."

"Okay," Edna said. "And she was . . . what? . . . tall, thin, white, black, green?"

"Sorry; I'm not sure. Like I said, her back was to me. I remember she was wearing blue scrubs. But, to be honest, I'd taken off my glasses in case she turned around."

DeeDee laughed. "Joel has an eye out for the ladies! But he thinks he looks ugly in his glasses, so he takes them off whenever he's around them!" She winked at Lizbeth and said, "I keep telling him they're cute."

Lizbeth blushed. Edna sighed dramatically and asked, "What time was that woman here?"

Joel said, "About 5:15. Maybe 5:25 at the latest. I remember because I was on my way to the vending machines to take my break and listen to my favorite podcast, which started at 5:30."

"What was that woman doing in the office?" Edna asked.

"Don't know. Like I said, I saw her *vaguely*. But I did ask if I could help."

"Good Lord!" Edna scowled. "You're just now telling us that you also spoke with her?"

"No! But I wish! She just threw her hands up like, 'No thanks; goodbye.'"

"How long was she there?" Lizbeth asked.

"All I can say is she was gone by the time I returned around six."

Edna shook her head disapprovingly and said, "Young man, I'd advise you to keep your glasses on at *all* times."

"See?" said DeeDee. "I told you they were cute!"

Joel smiled at Lizbeth and walked away.

DeeDee punched in the code to the door to Cheryl's office, and the three women entered. "No one bypasses our security system," she said. "I'm sure we'll identify that woman and verify she's legit."

Informed by Fred's prior instructions, Edna headed for a particular storage cabinet and located the box labeled *AccuStent*.

"There they are!" said Lizbeth. "Should I take a picture with my cellphone?"

Edna scoffed, "This isn't CSI!" She turned to DeeDee and said, "Turn up the lights, please."

The room brightened, and Edna saw that the seal on the box had been broken. Also, the thick dust layer on adjacent shelfing had been swiped. Chills rattled her spine, and time violently constricted. She internally anguished, *My god, it's true. What a monstrous thing to have done!*

She reached into her pocket and shakily withdrew a pair of surgical gloves. Putting them on, she told Lizbeth, "A prepared nurse always carries exam gloves."

Lizbeth nodded. But it was excruciating to witness how distraught and frail her mentor suddenly appeared. *Why is Edna trembling? What is she thinking?*

Edna opened the box, which contained multiple identical packets labeled *AccuStent-II—Experimental Use Only*. She rummaged through the box, feeling faint, and almost losing her nerve. But she took a steadying breath and then withdrew her hand, extending it toward Lizbeth. And when she opened her hand, there was something small and shiny in her palm.

Lizbeth looked quizzically at Edna, desperately searching her face for clues. *What is Edna trying to tell me now? Why this strange spectacle?*

But Edna only looked back with a stern, unyielding expression.

"I don't understand," Lizbeth began. "Why are you—?"

"Look," Edna commanded, further extending her palm, and glancing furtively at DeeDee.

Lizbeth felt that Edna was cuing her, urging her to enact a scene for which she'd been unprepared. But, trusting Edna's forceful direction, she obligingly leaned in for a closer view, withholding for now so many questions that burned with urgency.

"Why, it's such a pretty brooch!" DeeDee exclaimed, peering over Edna's shoulder. "Nothing too expensive, but it's pretty all the same. And two snakes, two wings—it's very unique."

"It's a caduceus," Lizbeth said, her searching eyes still unmet by Edna.

"A what?" DeeDee asked.

Edna whispered, "A caduceus. It's a symbol of the medical profession."

Lydia's Office

Pathology Department, Oakland City Hospital

AFTERNOON

It was time for Operation Timmy. Nora, having finally completed interviews with all staff involved in Cheryl's surgery, walked into Lydia's office.

Everything appeared exactly as it had when she last visited here eight days ago. She took a final look around, absorbing as much of Lydia's absence and uniquely appointed office as she could bear. Then she stood on the couch and yanked Timmy from the ceiling. "I got you," she proclaimed.

Fred's Home

Berkeley

AFTERNOON

It was a good day to call in sick and stake some solitude at home. Besides, Tuesdays were rarely busy at the art gallery, Fred was out of the house, and the kids—teenagers now, independent—were on autopilot with after-school activities. Today belonged to Vickie Williams.

But it was such a disheartening Valentine's Day. And she was so distracted, having watched Fred leave the house this morning, lugging his old suitcase, his face battered. She didn't want to think about him. And, certainly, not about Lydia, which was, unfortunately now, an automatic association.

She poured tea and looked through the kitchen window at her back garden. But no matter where she focused, Fred and Lydia came to mind.

Aren't I entitled to some solitude? And haven't I sacrificed enough of my inner life to accommodate those two?

But how could she not think about Lydia and her death, or the envelope containing Fred's tavern receipt, or the nocturnal phone calls? *They must be connected. As mom used to say, "One strange occurrence might be happenstance, and two might be a coincidence; but three always means you've got a stick in your eye."*

So, I've got a stick in my eye, and I can't see the connection.

Her frustration expanded with each attempt to connect the dots, ultimately pulling her forcefully back into her anger toward Fred and Lydia. *I always kept my end of the bargain with them! But they just decide— no consultation with me!—to end our arrangement two years ago. And to this day they've given me no explanation!*

All she had ever wanted from Fred was steady companionship, children, and the security of house and home. When they first met, it was a bonus to discover he was already involved with Lydia. Lydia rejected marriage and children, but could offer Fred sex and romance—things without appeal to her. Marrying Fred under such befitting preconditions was a godsend. And but for rare glitches over the years—most notably, the hospital's 2010 annual staff dinner—their threesome succeeded, even lasting longer than most traditional, two-person marriages.

As a loyal member of their abiding trio, she deserved to understand why Fred and Lydia had ended it. It was a matter of mutual respect; of compassion. *But with his stubborn refusal to explain and, now, with Lydia's death, I'll be forever in the dark about my divorce from them.*

And there had been misery all around since that breakup. Fred was at home more, interfering with her established routines, and trying to insert himself in their kids' lives. He moped and sighed excessively. He even once tried to have sex with her and she yelled, "I'm not goddamn Lydia, Fred!"

Glancing at her watch, she grimly noted the time she'd just wasted grappling with questions she couldn't answer. She stared out at the gnarly persimmon tree, bare of fruit; the fava bean ground cover, beginning to flower; and coppery hillocks of leaves, windswept against the redwood fence. And she felt a seasonal shift inside her bones, a decisive turning of her life away from Fred's. This deep sting of truth shook her hard, dislodging the "stick in her eye." Now she could see that she'd been fooling herself about the old arrangement. She recognized Fred's profound sadness after separating from Lydia. *My god, he must have loved her deeply. How unequal the alliances of our three hearts must have been after all. But now . . . now I'm left in the ruins with Fred, whose love for Lydia is forever fixed with her death.*

Vickie dried her tears and abandoned any hope for restful solitude today. Instead, she would keep busy and accomplish a few tasks. She'd pick Meyer lemons from the front yard and make Mediterranean chicken tonight. She'd register for the mosaics class she'd been considering for years. She'd phone her sister and agree to the Alaskan cruise together. And tomorrow, she'd inform Fred of her decision to divorce him.

But when she opened the front door to get the lemons, she found another envelope on the doormat. It looked exactly like the one left last Wednesday and containing Fred's tavern receipt.

Tectonic plates abruptly shifted inside her brain, and her thoughts rode out on shockwaves. *Clearly, Lydia isn't responsible for this delivery! So, she probably didn't deliver the other envelope or make those calls. My god! Someone else—who?—is intimidating me; haunting my home.*

Quickly scanning the front yard and seeing no one lurking, Vickie grabbed the envelope and went inside. She bolted the door, drew the living room drapes, and sat trembling on the couch. Finally, when her heart stopped thumping, she opened the envelope. This time, she found an old Polaroid inside. It showed Fred and Lydia, young and naked. They were smiling, their smooth bodies pressed together, luminous.

OakTown Tavern

Downtown Oakland

EVENING

Rosalie sat at a window table, lost in thought and sipping chardonnay. Passersby on the street occasionally looked in without grabbing her attention. With her long black hair, faultless complexion, lush crimson lips, and piercing gaze, they might have taken her for a model, an actress, or a woman of royal lineage.

But she was ruminating about how invisible she always felt. Even in the company of people who purportedly knew her, she felt seen at mere surface level—that they didn't see the depths of her heart and soul. As her mother used to caution, "It is a very superficial culture here."

Nonetheless, Rosalie wished her mother were alive to witness her success in that culture. She wished she could see that the dream of her daughter becoming a doctor had come true. She privately renewed a vow to her mother that she'd someday practice as a genuine healer and—

A hand alighted on her shoulder, and Nora appeared with an apologetic look on her face. "Sorry I'm late," she said.

"No problem," said Rosalie. "Here, I ordered this merlot for you."

"Thanks," said Nora, sitting down. "You look a little gloomy, though. Are you okay?"

Rosalie pointed out to the street. "I was wondering about the old man who was sleeping on cardboard against that curb last week."

"What old man?"

Trying to conceal her disappointment—*Of course, Nora does not remember him*—she just said, "Oh, never mind. How are *you*, Nora?"

"Hanging in—barely. But it's helped a bit, having the last two days off."

"I am glad you could join me tonight. I did not expect our raincheck so soon. I think I was not so easy to be around on Sunday."

Nora smiled wanly. "Forget it. Besides, tonight you're sparing me from another depressing evening with my cat and a bottle."

"Do you want to talk about Lydia?"

"No! I mean, thank you, but, no. I could actually use a little reprieve. It's too paralyzing to constantly think about her."

"Still, I should have been more sensitive. I had no right questioning your friendship or ethics."

Recalling their knotty interlude, Nora said, "Seriously, I'd like to forget that entire day for tonight."

"Of course. Should we talk about . . . what? Cheryl, maybe?"

"What's happened to her is so sad and shocking. And poor Carl; he called yesterday to tell me about it. Though I was an emotional wreck over Lydia—" After steadying herself, she continued, "He asked me to sit with him at Cheryl's bedside. Then he asked me to get involved in her case."

"Oh? Can you handle that? There is already so much on your plate."

"I think I can," said Nora, a trace of doubt in her reply. "Anyway, I visited them again this morning. Carl's really struggling with the likelihood of Cheryl being brain-dead. So, if I can help him make sense of how the surgical mistake—"

"I want to work with you on the case!"

Nora shook her head. "Thanks, but Fred's already upset about there being too many cooks in the kitchen—he doesn't even want me involved. And you'd need his endorsement to join SMART."

Trying to manage this fresh resentment against Fred, Rosalie shifted the conversation. "I have not yet paid condolences to Carl."

"Well, they're premature because Carl hasn't given up on Cheryl yet."

"But Cheryl is *dead*," Rosalie insisted. "Brain-dead *is* dead."

Bill arrived with a second round and told Nora, "On the house—in honor of Dr. Lydia. We're all devastated by her death."

Tears welled in Nora's eyes as he walked away. "Damn," she whispered, staring blankly at the wine. She suddenly felt foolish for having come here tonight with Rosalie. She shouldn't have come to this haunting place of missed opportunity to save Lydia's life.

Trying to gain Nora's attention, Rosalie raised her glass and said, "To Lydia."

Recalling Lydia's jealousy of Rosalie, Nora replied, "Yes—to my BFF, Lydia."

Rosalie struggled to shore up her hurt feelings. *Why must Nora remind me I am second best, even after Lydia is dead? Drug-addicted, morally defective Lydia . . .* But the injury also renewed the shame she had experienced when Nora recoiled from their embrace in Richard's office last week. And that painfully reminded her of Nora's general withdrawal over the last two years—after losing her precious family. *Yes, it was a mistake to join Nora on staff then—Nora, who was my so-called mentor and friend.* Still, aiming to sidestep another messy clash with Nora, she channeled her aggression back to an earlier conversation and said, "Cheryl must be an organ donor. I mean, she was always doing research with human tissue. And, if she is, Carl is wrong to stand in the way of her organs being transplanted and saving others' lives."

The whiplash from Rosalie's tone threw Nora off balance. She took a generous sip of merlot and replied, "But Carl's beside himself. His life and identity are shattered without Cheryl."

"But he should speak up for what is right by her, even if he is uncomfortable with her wishes."

"It's . . . complicated, Rosalie. He and Cheryl existed like a single unit. So, ending her existence with such finality is like ending his, too."

"Maybe it is simpler," Rosalie said. "Maybe he is hesitating to let her donate because he feels guilty about arguing with her the night before her surgery."

"Well, a lot of us could get in that line—"

"Do you know how many people die each day waiting on a transplant list?"

Feeling strangely protective of Carl, Nora said, "If you knew Carl . . . these last two days, he's read *everything* about brain death. And he's obsessing over the fact that the 'minimally acceptable observation period' to wait before declaring the loss of neurologic function to be de-facto *irreversible* remains categorically unknown. Carl is extremely . . . literal. He needs more absolute evidence that Cheryl is dead. He's requested an EEG and tech scan."

"All the while he delays, Cheryl's organs become less viable for transplant. For people *literally* dying for a kidney or liver."

Nora urgently suggested, "Can we talk about something else?"

"Of course," said Rosalie. "Sorry. My bad again."

What a colossal mistake to come here tonight, hoping for comfort, Nora thought. But after deciding to excuse herself and return home, Rosalie surprised her with a tender remark: "Nora, you and I each lost our family. That marks us for life, yes?"

Nora nodded, and Rosalie continued: "Sometimes I wake up and feel nothing but loss—my mother, my father, my little brother. I fall into a deep black hole, and I cannot escape. Sometimes I do not even care to."

"And I remember you saying you were only nine when your father died," said Nora. "Then, caring for your brother and mother, getting through medical school on your own . . . I don't know how you found a way through."

"But it is just two years ago that you lost your husband and daughter. And now, Lydia. Still, here you are; determined to keep going. So, you are finding 'a way through' as well."

Nora gulped more wine. "Well, I've been forcing myself through. I've been seeing a therapist, attending grief groups, and jogging around the lake. Every morning, I practice 'mindfulness meditation' and 'gratitude rituals.' It's often difficult to wake up for work."

"You should take a vacation, Nora."

"No, thanks! The cosmic irony is . . . I lost my family *during* a vacation. A *vacation* I finally took because everyone kept *insisting* I take one. Jack came with us, too."

"I am sorry! I did not know. What happened?"

Nora hesitated, afraid of not making it through the telling. "The four of us were staying at Stinson Beach," she finally began. "It was a beautiful, sunny day. No fog. A slight breeze. Anyhow, after lunch, Jack invited me on a short walk, and we were maybe five minutes away when I heard Caitlin and Michael scream. I thought at first that they were just goofing around . . . shrieking, jumping into the cold ocean maybe. But when I turned to look . . . it happened so fast. I saw a gigantic rogue wave crash down on them and sweep them away. And my life since has been pinned to that one horrible moment. I've not been able to 'move on,' as they say."

"My god, Nora. How painful that must have been. And believe me, I know what you mean. Every day, I think about my father dying. And I try to make sense of what happened to him and to my family afterwards. There has to be great meaning in their fates, beyond my small personal sorrow. Choosing to become a doctor has helped in my search for that meaning."

"Making meaning of what happened—of life and death, really—it's existential," said Nora. "More the realm of poets and philosophers, no?"

"But we doctors can use science to whittle down those big mysteries and make them more manageable questions. And we get to work at the intersection of body and mind, and of life and death—where those big mysteries reside."

Nora smiled and said, "I'm thinking again about how you remind me of my younger physician self."

Rosalie blushed. "That means a lot to me. I want—"

But Nora's cellphone chimed an interruption. "Sorry," Nora said, keying in her PIN.

"Is everything all right?" Rosalie asked.

"Yes," Nora said. "It's just a text from Fergie, suggesting we have lunch after tomorrow's SMART meeting."

"Oh? Fergie is on that committee?"

"It's funny, actually. She applied for membership on the HIPAA committee after a run-in with . . . Anyhow, HIPAA had too many members, so Edna convinced her to join SMART instead."

"I would like to join SMART, too. It is so influential and powerful. And, as I said, I would like to help investigate Cheryl's death."

"Well, again, it requires Fred endorsing your membership, because he's the committee's physician cochair. Just like Fergie needed nursing's endorsement from Edna—who must've also been happy to get someone like Fergie to serve as her replacement."

"Wait. Edna is leaving SMART?"

Nora shrugged. "Apparently; and, wow, it'll be strange when she's gone. She's been with me at Oakland City since I started residency in 1987. She's like an actual part of the hospital to me. Like a wall. A ceiling. She's something so foundational and routine, I sometimes don't even notice her."

"I know something about not being seen," said Rosalie, her jaw tightening. "But I thought Edna was waiting on her pension, which was still about a year away. You make it sound like she is leaving the *hospital*—not just that committee."

"You're right; I'm probably just projecting about my own retirement and disappearance." Then, noting Rosalie's worried expression, she asked, "Hey, what's wrong?"

"I am just . . . probably just being selfish. I do not like thinking about people leaving. And, like you, I have worked alongside Edna my entire career at the hospital."

Nora wondered—*Am I reading her correctly? That was such an impersonal and self-referential response instead of something attuned to me leaving. Still, she's suffered so much trauma; she is likely defending herself against further loss.* She charitably offered, "Don't mourn me yet. It could be a while before I retire, given the glacial pace of my decision-making lately."

Rosalie half-heartedly smiled.

Nora continued, "Besides, I'm starting something new tomorrow. And it's occurring to me . . . you want to be on the SMART committee? Well, because of Carl's insistence, I'll be on it temporarily as a 'special consultant.' But I intend to make myself indispensable to them. So, when my mission involving Cheryl's case is over, I'll ask them to enlist you as my replacement."

Rosalie said flatly, "Thank you. And maybe with your help on the case, Carl will decide sooner than later for Cheryl's organs to be transplanted."

This recurring talk of Cheryl in terms of organs made Nora's stomach knot. Cheryl: a pile of kidneys, corneas, lungs, liver, skin, and bones. A sum of body parts that did not add up to the colleague she'd known for 30 years. Trying to shake off her discomfort, she said, "I'm sure Carl will make his decision soon."

"What makes you so confident?"

Nora deliberated, feeling her reservations dissolve in two fast glasses of merlot. She was also experiencing convivial eagerness to align with Rosalie's desire to 'make sense' and 'meaning' of things. She whispered conspiratorially, "You must keep it confidential."

Rosalie nodded.

"Okay," Nora said. "So, yesterday afternoon while I was with Carl in the ICU, I noticed an intense, circular bruise on Cheryl's sternum."

"What is so remarkable about that? I would expect bruising there. I mean, she had surgery. And CPR, too."

"Well, I realize it's just my old clinical mind speaking, but that bruise is telling. It has a very unique shape. It's not from an IV or defibrillator, and it's not from a hand or the heel of a hand. It is a focal, hyper-intense bruise in a *nontherapeutic* location. It looks like the mark a doctor leaves after grinding his knuckle into a patient's sternum—you know, as a clinical test to determine whether the patient is pain-responsive and arousable—*alive*, in other words. It's very old school. Thank god we now have less barbaric ways of testing."

"What are you making of your little bruise, Nora?"

"I'm just thinking outside the box. And, frankly, thankful that I can think at all these days! But having this conversation with you . . . well, it's helping me to do that. I'm grateful to you, Rosalie."

Rosalie raised her glass. "Happy to help," she said.

Nora met the toast and said, "So, that bruise? I think it was inflicted by the same person who snuck the lethal AccuStent into the OR."

Rosalie nearly aspirated her chardonnay. "Whoa!" she said, coughing. "That is a huge leap!"

"Yes," Nora said, "because I did a lot of leg work! In fact, yesterday, I interviewed every hospital employee who had contact with Cheryl, from pre-op through post-op, and no one could account for the bruising."

"But that proves nothing, Nora. And how are you connecting that to the wrong stent?"

Nora grinned. "Maybe I shouldn't be so cocky. But I think I figured it out. So . . . the *pre-op* nurse swears there was no bruise on Cheryl's sternum when she placed EKG leads on her chest. But then, on the *intra-operative* video, we see early evidence of it—a pronounced red swelling in that location—*before* they insert the stent. So, that bruise had to be inflicted *after* pre-op prep but *before* stent insertion. And that's a *very* narrow window of time. The *same* narrow window of time during which the stent had to have been switched: *after* Peter Yuen placed the correct one on the pre-op table, and, of course, *before* the actual stent insertion procedure."

Rosalie looked concernedly at Nora. "As you say, you are thinking 'outside the box.' But . . . do you actually think someone could do those things unnoticed by everyone else in the OR?"

"Yes. It's likely this malevolent person was dressed like everyone else—scrubs, mask, and cap. All concealed, blending in. It's like what I said about Edna: merging so well with routine as to become imperceptible."

"I am sorry to sound skeptical, Nora. Especially when I see you so . . . pleased. But it makes no sense that a 'malevolent person' trying to *sabotage* Cheryl's surgery would also knuckle into her sternum, trying to *arouse* her. That seems contrary." She grimaced and continued, "I am worried about you. Did you ever get examined after your TBI?"

Acutely embarrassed, Nora shook her head.

"Well, you should get evaluated. I say this as your friend, and as someone who owes you."

Awash in self-doubt, Nora said, "You're right. I should get a head CT and . . ."

"And?"

"And I'm sorry, Ro. I shouldn't be spinning theories out of whole cloth and upsetting you."

"I am okay, really. Besides, you just called me 'Ro.' No one but my little brother ever called me that."

Nora blushed, pleased to stumble upon a tender connection with "Ro."

Rosalie said, "Still, it is not just because of this conversation about little bruises and invisible people in the OR. I also think you should be checked out because . . . well, you have been different for a while; not as sharp as you used to be. And your teaching . . . we have already talked about that. But you are also acting out of character with patients and families, with even the residents. So, I am worried about you." Her eyes reddened.

Nora turned away, her self-doubt amplified. "Look, it's time for me to leave. I have work tomorrow."

Rosalie grabbed Nora's hand. "Please, do not go. We were thinking *together* so well! You said it was helpful." Nora appeared hesitant, so Rosalie persisted: "Let us return to your theory. So . . . there is someone savvy enough to sneak, unnoticed, in and out of the OR and switch the stent. And, for some reason, at the same time, this person tries to rouse Cheryl and sabotage her surgery. Right?"

"It's . . . just a theory," Nora said.

"So, let me ask: why just one person? Why not two? Or several? And why must it be someone who had to *sneak* in and out of the OR? I mean, why not an insider job, by someone—or, some *ones*—who normally work in the OR? A nurse or doctor or OR tech who just slipped that AccuStent onto the table?"

Nora paused to double-check her own thought process before responding, "Yes, that's all possible." And she realized, given Rosalie's demonstrated insight and critical inquisitiveness, that she should accept her offer of help in Cheryl's case. Besides, it felt good to discover how her own thinking sharpened against Rosalie's incisive questioning. She could think of no good reason to decline further intellectual comradery with her.

"Another thing," Rosalie said. "I do not know about this person, or persons, being malevolent. You assume the AccuStent was sneaked into the OR and placed on the prep table. But maybe it was there just because of some dumb mistake? I mean, how often do you find things misplaced in supply rooms and cabinets? The wrong drugs go in patients' IVs, even. Hospital errors kill tens of thousands of patients every year."

But a gleam showed in Nora's eyes, and she confidently asserted, "It was no mistake. It was malevolent because it was *intentional*. And it was intentional because that AccuStent was *stolen*."

Rosalie's jaw dropped. "How can you say that?" She followed apologetically with, "Sorry! There I go again, questioning everything you say."

"No. I'm glad you're forcing me to think things through, Ro. Besides, I've felt so alone with it."

"Well, you are no longer alone. Still, you think the stent was stolen because . . . ?"

Emboldened by the comradery, Nora said, "*Because* it existed in a single location: a *secured* storage site in Cheryl's research office, a block away from the hospital. Well, obviously, *not* that secured. But, clearly, someone had to go through hoops to obtain that stent. It couldn't have appeared in the OR by error or happenstance."

Dismayed, Rosalie said, "Now I am afraid for you for a different reason. If any of what you say is true, then getting involved could be risky. Maybe you should stop."

"Don't worry about me," Nora said. "Besides, it actually feels riskier to *not* be involved. I mean, I've been feeling so useless and stupid lately. Anxious, too—thinking about Lydia, my aging brain, and my declining expertise. So, being forced to think again and to use my old diagnostic mind makes me feel more alive—as painful and humiliating a process as that's proving to be."

"You should take a break, at least. You just had a head injury, and a friend has died—"

"I'll be safe, Ro. And, anyway, my involvement in Cheryl's case will likely be brief."

"Why do you say that?"

Nora whispered, "Again, this is highly confidential, but Fred told me that Edna claims to have found a clue in Cheryl's office today. Something that could identify the person who broke into the box to steal the AccuStent."

"What is this clue?"

"I don't know. I expect to find out during tomorrow's SMART meeting. Anyhow, if Edna is correct, the investigation should move fast." Then, recalling Rosalie's earlier wish, she proposed a final toast: "So . . . to finding meaning and making sense of things. I pray that happens for you, Ro."

"Yes," Rosalie said. "I pray that happens for *us*."

FEBRUARY 15

Fred cleared his throat, pointed to his battered face, and opened the SMART committee meeting with, "So, let's just get this out of the way: you should've seen the other guy."

Guarded laughter ensued, affording him a momentary defense against the sorrows crashing down on him: Lydia's death, Cheryl's catastrophic surgery, and Vickie kicking him out of the house. Then he said, with no real conviction, "Good morning." After introducing Nora and Fergie as new members, he somberly remarked, "I can't recall when so much has been asked of this committee. It's been a trying time, and it's bound to get rougher."

Indeed, he knew that the egregious surgical error involving Cheryl was going to trigger another round of state and federal investigations of the hospital and its staff. Bureaucrats wielding arcane regulation manuals were going to poke their administrative sticks into every facet of Oakland City's surgical services: policies and procedures, operative mortality and complications stats, the surgical residency programs, and device research. And, because of Lydia's damning tox report, years of her path department's work were going to be mercilessly reviewed and critiqued. Patients and families were going to initiate lawsuits against the hospital, alleging Lydia's drugged incompetence to capably analyze pathology specimens. There'd be amped up scrutiny of narcotics dispensation within the hospital, further inhibiting physicians' opiate-prescribing practices, and making it even more difficult for deserving patients to obtain sufficient pain relief. News of these castigatory investigations was going to spread like wildfire through the media, rekindling damaging PR that still lingered from Jack's high-profile imprisonment for "mercy killing." Patients could lose all faith in Oakland City Hospital—if there remained any to lose. And yet, those who came here had nowhere else to go.

Fred stole a private moment to armor himself against the committee's probing looks and reminded himself: *Just stick to the facts, and limit information to a need-to-know basis.* He said, "So, we have two situations on today's agenda—"

The conference room door swung open, and the two pony-tailed lawyers entered. "Sorry we're late," said one. "Crazy bridge traffic," said the other.

Fred nodded and said, "All right now, I believe we all know each other."

The gray-haired lawyer said, "I would hope so, after a CFO's suicide, a doctor's drug-related fatality, and now this serious hospital error—all within one week!"

The dark-haired lawyer said, "But we shouldn't go on meeting like this."

Several committee members laughed, if somewhat awkwardly, while Fred fell into an increasingly anxious state. He blurted out, "Counsel, proceed."

Jarred by the abrupt directive, the gray-haired lawyer said, "Okay . . . well then. Dr. Chandler's death and Dr. Kluft's surgical catastrophe are creating serious problems for the hospital. Dr. Chandler had a blood alcohol level that registered at 0.09—just a hair above the legal limit."

"See?" said Fergie. "Like we told you—she didn't drink all that much the night of Pulaski's service. Not for her, anyway."

"But, if I may continue?" he countered. "Her drug screen? Now, there you got a major problem. Evidence of a veritable pharmacy: oxy, benzos, and even barbs."

The dark-haired lawyer emphasized, "*Lots* of them."

Hearing this, Fred felt unexpected comfort. He could hope that Lydia might not have suffered wretchedly at the end.

From across the table, Nora was unnerved to see relief in Fred's expression and perhaps, even, a faint smile. It brought to mind Lydia's claims about him acting paranoid and argumentative, insinuating she'd been trying to undermine his marriage. *Is it possible that Fred pursued Lydia home that night, on a road he knew by heart, with careless, crazy, even malicious intent?* Nora shuddered at this speculation. Still, she knew she had to consider the possibility—malevolence was certainly operative in Cheryl's case. And besides, *Lydia was always careful about her 'vitamins' and alcohol. She was the world's foremost expert on self-intoxication. She'd never ingest a lethal dose of drugs, and certainly not before driving home on that damn road.* Nora closed her eyes and wondered what Lydia's final thoughts—

"Dr. Kelly!" someone called out.

Nora opened her eyes to find everyone looking expectantly at her. "Sorry," she said. "I was just . . . thinking."

It was Edna who sternly addressed her. "As I was saying, Dr. Kelly, the assistant, Joel Plawecki, saw a woman in Dr. Kluft's office on Sunday night."

Sensing Nora's muddle, Fergie supportively offered, "And an AccuStent *was* missing from the sealed box inside her office."

Nora smiled shamefacedly. Then, hoping to contribute something worthwhile, she eagerly offered, "VivoZeel has records of the unique barcodes for each AccuStent, so it should be easy to prove that the one used in Cheryl's surgery was taken from that box in her office."

The gray-haired lawyer said, "Uh, yes, Dr. Kelly. Like I said earlier, her surgeon, Peter Yuen, initiated that inquiry. The barcoding confirms that the implanted stent is, indeed, the stent missing from that box."

Fred gritted his teeth upon hearing again about Peter's continued meddling. He complained, "There are too many amateur detectives in this case, conducting uncoordinated investigations—"

"Wait," Nora interrupted. "Did I hear that someone saw a woman in Cheryl's office on Sunday?"

Edna rolled her eyes dismissively and addressed the group, "We're surely dealing with a brazen, sick mind. Not only did someone commit this horrific crime against Dr. Kluft—and under our noses—but they also left behind a blatant clue. They're taunting us."

Nora asked, "What clue?"

"Good Lord!" Edna said. "Have you heard nothing I've said about the caduceus?"

Cheryl's Room, ICU

Oakland City Hospital

8:00 A.M.

Suddenly, Carl was aware of Rosalie standing beside him at Cheryl's bedside. He then noticed the maintenance worker and nursing assistant in the room, triggered by Rosalie greeting them. He was finally drawn out from his thickset isolation when Rosalie said, "I am sorry, Carl."

"Thank you," he said, slightly disoriented from his abrupt shift of consciousness. During the prior two days, he'd been living in timeless space, staring at his wife's body and wondering about its claim to life. Looking at her body now in the vivid present, he thought it otherworldly. Unconvincingly human, it was a Play-Doh mass, animated by machines.

"Such a tragedy," Rosalie said. She placed a hand on Cheryl's cold mottled arm and looked for the sternal bruise that Nora described last night.

Carl said, "The doctors all say she's brain-dead from massive CNS anoxia and multiple strokes, complications of stent surgery."

Rosalie sighed. "I never know what to say at times like this."

"I do. There are several standard options, but they don't change a thing. So, never mind." He looked away and said, "I don't know what I'm going to do."

"That will take time to figure out. You have been together so long, you cannot possibly know how your life—"

"No. I mean, I don't know what to do *now*. They want my approval for organ donation. They keep telling me she is *dead* but, at the same time, they say that she wouldn't want to be kept *alive* like this. You see how that makes no sense. It's an oxymoron."

"Well, yes, but—"

"Of course, Cheryl wouldn't want to 'stay alive like this.' But she also wouldn't want to 'stay dead like this.' So, what exactly is *this*? Which *this* is this?"

"Carl, please calm—"

"*Stay alive* can't be the correct term here if she's actually dead, which they insist she is. But then, if she is dead, why do they have her on 'life-sustaining' machines that they're asking me to discontinue? That's an oxymoron, too." He swept out his arm to indicate the plethora of so-called life-sustaining paraphernalia and asked, "If she is dead, which they say she is, then these things are actually *death-sustaining* treatments. Now, how can that be rational? And how can something be called a *treatment* if it's being given to someone who no longer exists? Still, they keep pressuring me to make decisions about these so-called 'treatments' and Cheryl's organs. I'm supposed to make these critical decisions based on what? Because none of this makes sense. And I'm a *doctor*."

Rosalie said, "Let me help you."

"You cannot. Because we're in alien territory here, ruled by an alien sensibility that no rational person can decode."

"Carl, let us think this through together. You are aware of the controversies concerning brain death. I remember your case discussion at grand rounds a couple of years ago. It was about your brain-dead pregnant patient, and how you struggled to keep her body—what?—'going' to keep her fetus viable. So, you have deeply thought about this brain death issue before. And like before, now you must be involved in making these tough decisions for Cheryl—even if they are not completely rational to you."

"It's different now. I'm not Cheryl's doctor. I'm her husband. And if she is so unambiguously dead, why are the doctors still treating her? Why should I be the one forced to take responsibility for stopping everything? If medicine and law and ethics are so clear about what should be done now, why isn't that just *being done*?"

Rosalie sat down, exhausted by Carl's intensity. She was also sleep deprived, having stayed awake all night wondering about the purported clue Edna was revealing during this morning's SMART meeting. Later today, after delivering the noon lecture to the residents, she would track Edna down to find out. Now, refocusing on Carl, she said, "When Cheryl made you her healthcare agent, she trusted you to make medical decisions for her in situations like this, where she cannot speak for herself. So, remember: you are making those impossible decisions with her *blessing*."

Carl said, "Often, when we conducted device research in the ICU, she'd comment about never wanting to be kept alive 'like all the vegetables here.'"

"Okay. Then you know the right decision to make for her now."

"No," he said flatly. "That was just a stock offhand comment that mostly healthy people make. No one knows what it's like to exist as a cucumber or tomato. You can't equate a casual speculative quip about existing as a vegetable with a healthcare decision grounded in thoughtful deliberation about your life as a human being." *And besides,* he thought, *being put in any position to speak for my wife is another alien concept. Just how am I supposed to make life-and-death decisions for someone who's never sought my counsel on anything—her hairstyle, her career, her investments, or her lunch order?*

Rosalie struggled to conceal her irritation. But Carl had this opportunity now to speak up and do the right thing, enabling others to live with Cheryl's transplanted organs. Still, he seemed so *willfully* incompetent and spineless. This, despite the fact that, unlike most people on the autism spectrum, he had been privileged with every opportunity to overcome the attendant challenges. With all of his advantages—his wealth, intelligence, education—he could have learned to be more adaptive and skillful in dealing with life's many trials. *But how inept he is proving to be! And so morally deficient, refusing to assent to organ donation because his logic is more precious than peoples' lives!* "Carl," she said, impatience infusing her tone, "donating Cheryl's organs could save many lives."

Carl estimated how often he had conducted similar conversations with his patients about end-of-life decisions related to organ transplantation (approximately 94). He recalled the pertinent communication templates he used for those discussions, and his "learnings" from role-plays while portraying "the physician bearing sad/bad news" to Huan Kim who was "the distraught family member." But it all seemed irrelevant now, considered from this other side of the conversation. He said, "The night before Cheryl's surgery, I got angry with her at work. And afterwards, she refused to speak with me during the drive home."

Rosalie said, "I am aware of your fight in the ER. I was there, remember? But, my god, you must forgive yourself."

"Traumatizing patients before they undergo surgery can be harmful. I traumatized Cheryl."

"You did not kill your wife, Carl!"

"How can you be certain?" His question was an academic inquiry.

Riffing off Nora's words last night, she replied, "Well, if arguing with Cheryl was lethal, then *many* people are responsible for killing her."

"But you were nice to her that night. I saw that. So, you can be at peace." He glanced at Cheryl's inert body and said, "People didn't understand her. They didn't know how hard she worked, trying to make me feel normal. But I was like a puppet, and she spent lots of energy trying to pull the right strings for me. I know that was hard on her."

"Yes, well, we are all so unique," Rosalie said. "Still, despite our differences, we have to speak up for one another and for what is right."

Rosalie's judgmental attitude stymied Carl. He didn't know whether he'd experienced this aspect of her before. Then again, he reasoned, a person's character or psychology was too nebulous a notion to get any handle on. Certainly, he had noted—and, therefore, remembered—the characteristics of her physical being: how her hands generally nested inside the pockets of her white coat and, when she withdrew them, how her polished, red nails gleamed. He knew how a third of her face was generally obscured until she tossed back her long, black hair while she spoke, revealing deep hollows in her cheeks and small, pearl-studded earrings.

Still, being stymied by Rosalie's attitude—being perplexed by *anyone*, really—was the most normal and grounding experience he had had for days. It was a blessing, and he wondered whether to thank Rosalie for it.

Cellblock 47, San Sebastian State Prison

Marin County

NOON

Jack paced, waiting for the operator to connect him to Nora. Other inmates impatiently waited turns on the phone. One told Jack, "Hey, sissy! You better clean that mouthpiece when you're done."

But the operator's response was the same as it had always been: "Sorry. Your party's unavailable." *Dial tone.*

Jack whispered into the receiver, "Talk to me, Nora. Visit me tomorrow, please."

Someone in line yelled, "We can hear the fuckin' dial tone, moron! Hang up!"

Jack wiped the mouthpiece against his shirt and hung up. As he turned away, he heard someone call him "loser." But that didn't bother him. *In fact*, he thought, *that sounds about right.*

Jack London Square

Oakland Estuary

NOON

Sitting on her favorite bench outside the Last Chance Saloon, Nora looked out at the Oakland Estuary. Ferryboats were disembarking from Jack London Square and heading toward San Francisco's Embarcadero. Her thoughts consistently drifted toward Lydia.

Que será, será . . .

By now, Carrie, Lydia's once-estranged twin, should have finalized travel plans to come help settle the estate.

But how weird to imagine Carrie in Lydia's home, using her dishes, her coffee mug, her linens, her fireplace . . .

Nine days had passed since her therapist left. Nineteen more before she would return from her month-long vacation.

Month-long. Long month.

Within the hour, Lydia would be cremated, reduced to a tiny bag of ashes and ready for pick-up. *Here you go, ma'am! Friend in a bag, just like you ordered!*

. . . Whatever will be, will be . . .

Right now, Rosalie was delivering a lecture to the residents, probably high-fiving with them all.

. . . The future's not ours to see . . .

Nora's cellphone rang, and she declined the call. *Jack, again. And this time, on my cell. Too much pressure . . .*

"Sorry I'm late," Fergie said, handing a sandwich to her. "And all they had left was this pastrami. They say it's a meat 'product,' whatever the hell that means."

"Thanks," Nora said. "It seems appropriate to chew on mystery meat, given all the actual mystery we're chewing on."

Fergie bit into her falafel. "It's good to hear you joke. I know it doesn't come easy now."

Nora grimaced. "Yeah, well . . . you saw how distracted I was at the meeting this morning."

Attempting Edna's Irish brogue, Fergie said, "Good Lord! Have you heard nothing I've said about the caduceus?"

Nora laughed. "You sound more like that cereal box leprechaun, with a hint of Chicago."

"Good. That's what I was going for."

Examining her sandwich, Nora asked, "Pastrami's actual meat, right? Wait, I don't really want to know where this comes from."

"For me, it's *knowing* where meat comes from that makes me want to avoid it. And besides, there's tons of data linking red meat consumption to cancer mortality, cardiovascular disease—"

"Hey! Hit the pause button on your public health announcement while I'm eating this . . . this sandwich."

"Okay," Fergie said. "But back to that SMART meeting? What did you make of Edna's report? She seemed kinda overwrought. And she made her discovery of that caduceus sound so . . . creepy, so theatrical."

"Agreed. And I don't understand how she can be so certain that someone left it behind intentionally, as a 'taunt.' I mean, why couldn't it be just a classic clue—something the stent thief left behind accidentally? What do you think about the caduceus?"

"I think it's an aesthetically disturbing symbol. Those snakes!" Fergie shuddered.

"Funny. But, really?"

Fergie shrugged. "Well, I didn't think you docs wore them anymore. I might've occasionally seen one on . . . well, a *senior* doc. But it's gone the way of the nursing cap in my profession—except for Edna's, of course."

Nora fell silent. Fergie asked, "What are you thinking?"

"I'm just remembering Lydia wanting to sell Edna's cap as an antiquity on eBay."

"Yeah, god," Fergie said. "I loved Lydia's humor." Following another silent interlude, she said, "You two were so close, Nora. I'm so sorry."

Unable to speak, Nora tried to anchor herself in the mundane act of eating. When able, she said, "I promised Carl I'd keep him apprised of any news about Cheryl's case. So, after the SMART meeting, I stopped by the ICU to tell him about the AccuStent being definitively traced to Cheryl's office. But when I got there, he and Rosalie appeared to be having a *very* animated discussion. So, I just snuck away. But now I have to find another time to talk with him today. Time I don't have."

"Yeah. And aren't you also picking up Lydia's ashes tonight?"

"Yep. And I'm scattering them tomorrow morning. Thank god, I have the next two days off."

"Sure you don't want me to come along? I'm not working AM shift tomorrow."

Nora smiled. "Thanks. I'd like your company, but Lydia asked in her will that I do this solo. To have a certain kind of experience she hoped to bequeath me."

"I get that."

"And I can't think much more about that right now. Not if I hope to get through the rest of my shift today." She tossed a pastrami morsel to a solicitous seagull, but it rejected the offering and flew away.

"That gull's got good taste," Fergie said.

Nora groaned. "Maybe I can get away with just phoning Carl this afternoon. Still, I'm not sure what to say about that caduceus."

"Well, you promised him you'd be wingman on the case. So, I'd tell him soon, before he hears about it from someone else. It's a trust issue."

"You're right," said Nora. "And, who knows? Maybe he can even shed light on it. A thing or a fact that's been on his radar, versus a feeling or emotion, is something he'd register instantly and remember forever. Maybe that caduceus even belonged to him or Cheryl. Maybe it just fell off one of them while they were packing the box or taking inventory."

"Regardless; Edna sure seems troubled by it. Before today's meeting, she even asked me to photograph it with my *personal* cell—*not* my work phone."

"Why?"

"She said, 'For safekeeping.' When I asked from what, she only insisted, 'Just do it.' She promised to explain later. She was so wound up, I just went ahead with it. But, after the meeting and now that I know the caduceus is being handed over to the police? I'm freakin' uncomfortable holding onto a photo of it."

"Of course," Nora said. "Still, I don't blame Edna for being a little paranoid. Too many horrible and unexplained things are happening at the hospital. And, with our laughable security systems? Don't get me started!"

"I'm with you there. Frankly, when I'm working ER, my only real sense of security comes from knowing that coworkers like you have my back."

Considering Edna's strange behavior and recalling Rosalie's inquiry last night, Nora asked, "Say, why is Edna leaving SMART?"

Fergie said, "All she told me was she wanted to start off-loading responsibilities."

"But it seems premature; her retirement is still about a year away, right?"

"Yeah, well, she's been acting strangely. I mean, she's always been prickly, but now she's downright irritable. Erratic, too. She suddenly disappears from the ER, and then she's suddenly back!"

"It must be disorienting to imagine yourself as a retiree, especially if you're leaving such a big identity like hers."

"Hmm. Might you be projecting about your own retirement, Nora?"

"Okay," said Nora, "time to switch the topic. Besides, I'd like to discuss something with you. But I need your promise to keep it confidential."

Fergie rolled her eyes. "You need to ask me that?"

Nora threw her hands up in apology. "Sorry! I'm just anxious. I can't stop thinking about all the shit happening at the hospital. And, okay . . . well, I think Cheryl's case is linked to Lydia's death. And I think they connect to Richard's, as well."

"Whoa," said Fergie, choking on a carrot. "I serve you pastrami; you serve me a bombshell?"

Nora patted Fergie's back. "Sorry, that was a lot to swallow. You okay?"

Fergie nodded and Nora said, "So . . . want to try to connect the dots with me?"

"You know I'm always up for a game," Fergie said. "I assume the usual prizes are at stake? Because someday I'm going to collect all the beers you owe me."

"You can't count that high."

Fergie smiled. "So, let's see. We got three deaths—and we're agreed Cheryl is dead, right?"

Nora nodded.

"Okay. Three deaths occurring close together within a week. And each of the deceased was working at the same hospital. I dunno . . . Beyond those two links, I'm not seeing much. As far as I know, there weren't strong personal ties among them . . . And we got one suicide, one drug-related MVA, and one surgical catastrophe . . . they're so very *different*, Nora."

Nora smiled broadly. "That's *exactly* what I was hoping you'd say! Because I think that's the key—the deaths *looking* so different."

"You lost me."

"Well, I keep thinking . . . each death *looks* so different . . . while each death also *looks* so *false*."

"Still lost."

"Okay, let's take Richard, the first death. You know my reasons for thinking he didn't commit suicide. But his death was certainly *made* to look like one."

"Nora, you have no evidence to support that. Factual evidence, I mean."

"I disagree. In evidence is the fact that Richard was a devout Catholic. We also have his demonstrated character and behavior in the world, and his love and commitment to Jack."

Fergie looked dubious. "And, so . . . Lydia?"

"Same thing. Her death was *made* to look like a drug-related accident. But I have no doubt it was a setup. Lydia, I've known forever. And I'd stake my life on . . ." She took a moment to regroup. "Lydia *never* transported drugs in her car. And she'd never ingest all the drugs they found in her system. She'd never risk her life or anyone else's by driving so impaired."

Fergie removed her bifocals and rubbed her eyes. "Then, Cheryl . . . you'd say her death was *made* to look like a surgical error?"

"Yes. And here we have hard evidence—'factual evidence,' as you'd say—that someone tried to create the *appearance* of a surgical mistake. Someone had to break into a highly secured office to steal that stent in the first place. Clearly, that was intentional—no error."

Packing her leftovers, Fergie said, "I'm losing my appetite."

"But see? None of those deaths is what it *appears* to be. What connects them is illusion."

Fergie looked probingly at Nora. "You're saying the deaths were disguised. But, if that's true, you're also saying . . . Damn! You're also saying they were *murders!*"

"I am. And the killer or killers tried to make it appear as though the deaths were *not* murders."

"That's so freakin' twisted!"

"But, see? *That* is the MO," Nora said. "Not only camouflaging the murders as everyday deaths, but also *making* them look *different* from one another. Each is being *staged* in a very particular way."

Nora and Fergie locked eyes. Fergie thought: *Another staring contest between us! But Nora isn't flinching this time.* Nora thought: *Fergie isn't expecting me to back down. What a relief that she believes me. I don't feel so insane and alone with my thoughts.*

Finally, Fergie said, "If what you're proposing is true, on what basis do you think the killer or killers select victims? Or choose the 'staging' for each one? Is it—I don't know—to make a statement about the victim, or something the victim represents?"

"I have no idea. But now you understand why I asked to keep this conversation confidential? Besides, too many people are already questioning my cognitive capacity—*me* included."

"Then maybe you should eat this carrot. Here; it's supposed to be good for your brain."

Nora grabbed the pack and said, "I need the whole bag."

"*Staging,*" Fergie said. "That word makes me think about cancer."

"But staging in the *theater*? That makes me think about a person standing behind the curtain who manages the performance on stage. Someone who is shaping audience perception of a story."

"Hmm. With our three 'staged' deaths, what stories do you think are being conveyed?"

"You'll think I'm nuts," Nora said. "But it's been hard not think about them literally. Like, Richard 'dying by the numbers'? Judgment about Lydia and drug abuse. And, yes, Cheryl dying by her own devices. You do have to wonder."

Fergie absorbed Nora's speculations with escalating anxiety— anxiety that fueled her mounting curiosity. She said, "Let's see if I can play this out further. Clearly, the AccuStent didn't accidentally appear in the OR. And Edna reported finding a caduceus in the AccuStent's storage box inside Cheryl's office. So ... if we can establish that the caduceus isn't Cheryl's or Carl's, then we can probably assume it belongs to the person who broke into the box to steal the stent— whether it was left accidentally or, as Edna insists, intentionally. So, if we identify the owner of the caduceus, we identify who's responsible for staging Cheryl's death."

"And if my theory about a unifying MO is correct, we simultaneously establish who's responsible for 'staging' Lydia and Richard's deaths as well."

Fergie took back her carrot sticks from Nora. "I'm cutting you off, because your brain's on fire."

Nora smiled appreciatively and said, "Speaking about being fired up. You mentioned earlier that you and Winston were here the night before Richard's service and saw ..."

"Yes, Fred and Lydia—they were definitely arguing."

Nora hesitated. "I don't know whether to say this ..."

"Really, Nora? Again? We can talk *murder* but not—"

"Sorry, *again*. I've just been feeling so hyper-protective of Lydia."

"Okay, but, before you start, everyone at the hospital knew about her and Fred. Certainly, all the nurses did."

Nora grimaced. "Yeah, well ... even Fred's wife knew."

"You're kidding?"

"Nope. Vickie knew all along, even before she married Fred. But the three of them worked things out. And then, for reasons even I'm not privy to, Fred and Lydia broke it off a couple years ago."

"Wow, that's . . . stunning," said Fergie. "And very 70s and 80s of them."

"It was a different era; different sensibilities."

"Still, I gotta say, for two people who ended things between them, they were arguing very passionately last Friday."

"It's complicated," Nora said. "Someone started calling Fred's home at night and hanging up. Then, a week ago, Vickie found an envelope on the doorstep that contained Fred's tavern receipt, and *Happy Anniversary* was written across it. Well, that made Vickie suspect Lydia."

"Whoa! Not Lydia's style! But . . . no . . . don't tell me that Fred believed Vickie's suspicions? Is that why he was confronting Lydia that night?" Nora nodded and Fergie responded, "God, he must've been pushed to the *edge*."

"It gets worse. Yesterday, Vickie kicked him out of the house. And then, hours later, she found *another* envelope on the doorstep. *That* one contained an old Polaroid of Fred and Lydia—naked."

"That's freakin' awful," Fergie said, "and disturbing. Who'd do such a thing?" She popped a peppermint to quell her stomach. "Well, at least Vickie must've realized that Lydia couldn't have left that Polaroid—not after she died. So, she must've also realized that those calls and the first envelope weren't from Lydia either."

Nora fell silent.

"Hey," Fergie said. "So, even Fred now."

"Sorry?"

"I'm just thinking. Fred's isn't a *literal* death, but, still."

"Still . . . ?"

"Well, he hasn't literally died. But his life seems kind of over. I mean, he loses his wife and family, and his home. Professionally, he's become captain of a sinking ship plagued by scandals. And, importantly, he loses Lydia."

Nora's heart knotted, and her stomach churned. "You're right," she managed. "It's another death, but a different kind. And the calls, the tavern receipt, the Polaroid—someone planted them. Someone staged Fred's—"

"Nora, I'm scared now. If that Polaroid was left just yesterday, who-ever's doing this shit is still very active." Fergie stood up and said, "Let's go. This stuff is giving me the deep creeps. And it's almost time to clock back into work."

Walking hurriedly back toward the hospital, Fergie said, "Last night, Win regaled me with fantasies linking each of us to Cheryl's demise."

"I don't think that required too much literary imagination," said Nora. "But I would've had a hard time falling asleep if I'd been you. I mean, made to imagine your colleagues as potential murderers!"

"Agreed. There can be risk (other than financial) in being married to a writer. Win likes to scare me with his creepy stories sometimes. I only put up with it because he gets such a kick out of doing that."

"So, how did he script my story?"

Fergie laughed. "He imagined you killing Cheryl in your quest to restore medicine's reputation. To wrench it from greedy corporate phy-sicians like her who'd taken over."

"Was I wearing a cape?"

"Not sure. But I could ask Win to include that in any final draft."

"It'd be great if he could also make my cape teal."

Teaching Conference Room

Oakland City Hospital

12:45 P.M.

Fifteen minutes left, Rosalie thought wearily, desirous for her teaching rounds to end. Throughout, she'd been contending with her resent-ment—teaching the residents now on her own time for free, meanwhile denied opportunities to earn income from ER backup. *The unfairness!*

And the irony. Because today she was teaching them about the ICD-10—the updated coding system expected to generate more money for the hospital. If they mastered the ICD-10, they could strategically code and bill for *everything* they did in the name of patient care. More codes—especially those associated with the most lucrative health insurance reimbursements—meant more income for the hospital.

Even more galling, the residents looked bored.

"Look," she said, exasperated. "I know this topic is not so exciting. But the more money the hospital receives, the more it can spend on our patients."

Lena said, "There's no guarantee that enhanced revenue from our more artful or aggressive coding will *actually* be spent on patient care. For all we know, it'll be used to buy new carpets for the C-suites. Or *another* mega-slicer CT scanner that nobody needs."

Darique said, "I'd get on board if it meant better lunches for us."

Stemming group laughter, Rosalie said, "This coding system is a reality of modern healthcare. You have to learn it if you expect to practice medicine."

"Dr. Karlov," Quincy said. "Learning how to tweak billing codes is not what doctors *should* be doing. This ICD system should be the concern of people in the business offices. I mean, the codes were designed for hospital billing purposes—not patient care."

"Besides," Lena said, "it's morally distressing to monetize the care of our patients. It creates ethical conflicts when we're being *pressured* to claim more and better-paying codes. That only gives us an incentive to provide unnecessary care. And then that drives up healthcare costs even more."

"Complain all you want," Rosalie said, "but—"

Darique interrupted, "It's pound foolish to ask docs to spend time picking billing codes for everything we do. We're already working overtime as clerks and secretaries. We type our own notes into the EHR. We have to enter our medical orders and prescriptions into the system. We even schedule our patient appointments! And now, we're supposed to take on medical billing?"

The residents applauded.

"It's very troubling," Aditya said. "While they keep making us do more computer work, they also keep telling us to spend more time with patients."

"What we really need is a healthcare revolution—not more draconian coding systems," Lena said. "We need a single payer system—universal healthcare."

Most everyone cheered. Someone shouted, "Medicare for everyone!"

Meanwhile, Rosalie thought: *What disrespect they are showing me!* She put aside her lecture notes, smiled perfunctorily, and just waited for the session to end.

Nora's Office

Oakland City Hospital

12:55 P.M.

With minutes to spare before her shift resumed, Nora decided to phone Carl and update him about Cheryl's case.

He answered on the first ring. "Hello, Nora. I recognized your number."

"Wow!" she replied, vaguely recalling having phoned him only once—years ago—from her personal cell. "That photographic memory of yours! I sometimes forget."

"Oh. A joke. I get it."

Nora took a moment to divine the joke she purportedly made.

He flatly asked, "Why are you calling?"

In person, it had always been problematic to interpret Carl's blunt, affectless tone. But now, over the phone and without attendant visual cues, Nora felt even more uncertain about his emotional state. Still, as cold and off-putting as he may have sounded, she knew that he likely intended to signal otherwise. She asked, "So, how is Cheryl?"

"I don't know," he said. "It's not known whether someone in her state feels anything at all." Then, remembering proper etiquette, he reciprocated, "How are you, Nora?"

"Oh ... well ... good enough, all things considered. But I'm calling to update you, as promised. I thought you'd want to know they traced the AccuStent to the box in Cheryl's office through its barcode."

"Yes, I'd want to know that. And Peter Yuen informed me of that this morning."

Nora winced. "Okay. Also, Edna reported that she found a clue in Cheryl's office."

Following prolonged silence, Nora asked, "Carl, are you there?"

"Yes. I was waiting for you to tell me what Edna found."

"Uh, well, it was a silver caduceus—a brooch or lapel pin—inside the box that had contained the stolen AccuStent. I think it's in possession of the police now."

"So, it's being assumed the caduceus belongs to the person who stole the stent to harm Cheryl."

"Yes, Carl. That seems to be the operative theory."

Another odd silence ensued, finally prompting Nora's realization that he was waiting on her to speak. She said, "Unless, by chance, you or Cheryl owned a caduceus pin that might've accidentally dropped into that stent box during your inventory or—?"

"There is no chance, because neither of us owned one."

"Okay. I just wanted to make sure the caduceus wasn't a red herring." Instantly, she regretted her word selection and said, "I mean—"

"Don't worry, Nora. I know you're not actually confused about the caduceus being a fish. You're simply using a literary device."

"Of course," Nora said, surprised to learn what she had purportedly done.

Then he surprised her again when he said, "Two people at the hospital wear a caduceus. It's a symbol of the medical profession, but also an ancient astrological symbol of commerce—"

"I'm sorry to interrupt, Carl; but, forgive me, I'm needed in the ER. So maybe you could just tell me who?"

"I acknowledge your stress, understand it, and forgive you."

"Yes, well, thanks. And . . . those two people?"

"Drs. Syd Fein and Rosalie Karlov."

Nora's brain rattled upon hearing Rosalie's name mentioned in such an unsettling context. She managed, "Well, that's certainly two ends of the age spectrum."

"Yes. Seventy-four and 36 years of age, respectively."

It's jarring, Nora thought, *how literal he can be.* And it seemed to her that the "Carl phenomenon," as Lydia used to call it, had become more pronounced without Cheryl serving as its mitigating filter. "Carl," she said, "there's that keen memory of yours again. I don't recall noticing a caduceus on either of them."

"Syd wears his as a tie clip. Rosalie wears one underneath the left lapel of her white coat—you see it when she raises her collar. But don't feel bad, Nora. It's common not to notice such details. For example, we often can't recall the eye color of the people we frequently see."

"I suppose you're right," Nora said, trying to remember her therapist's eye color.

Silence.

More silence.

"Actually," Nora said, finally picking up the beat. "If you'd like, I could ask Fergie to text you a photo of the caduceus. Edna had her take one this morning."

"I'd like to see it, because the caduceus is artistically rendered in many unique variations."

"So," Nora said, "I'll ask her to forward it to you. And when I'm back to work on Saturday, I'll stop by to visit you and Cheryl."

"What time?"

"Oh . . . would noon be okay?"

"I will see you in three days—Saturday at noon, February 18, here in Cheryl's room."

"Until then, I'll be holding out for the best for you both."

Carl blurted out, "Yes. We hope for the best, but plan for the worst."

Nora recognized Carl's comment—a familiar refrain from standardized communication templates used by physicians to deliver bad or sad news. And though imprecisely applied to the current context, it seemed to convey Carl's genuine attempt to connect with her. Using borrowed phrases and communication blueprints for social constructions he would never understand, by sheer force of his will and desire, he had struggled to build a bridge of words to her now. Nora smiled, surprised to discover this bridge between them, and surprised by her sudden and tender affection for Carl Kluft.

St. Catherine's Cemetery

West Oakland

AFTERNOON

Edna placed a rose on her husband's grave. "It's your favorite, Benny—a Peace rose from our garden."

Still wearing her nurse's uniform, she apologized, "Sorry, love. I had no time to dress for you today."

Using tissues from her pocket, she wiped Benny's headstone free of cypress needles, grass cuttings, and a bird feather. She considered laying her sweater on the lawn to protect her uniform before sitting at the graveside, but instead decided on its greater value for warmth. "Besides," she said, "this old uniform getting dirty doesn't much matter anymore."

She leaned against his headstone, stared at the sky, and reviewed her complex plans for tomorrow. She reassessed all possible contingencies should something go wrong. Ultimately, what counsel she derived from Benny's spirit seemed to support her finalized strategy. "Yes, love," she said. "It appears to be the least-worst alternative left to me now." Then, realizing he'd be concerned about the dogs, she added, "I dropped off Galway and Kinsale at Riter's K9 Kennel an hour ago. I'm sure they'll find good homes soon."

A young woman with a child in tow passed by. Her head down and dabbing her eyes, she didn't notice Edna who was watching her in hopes for an exchange that acknowledged one another's grief. The experience left Edna feeling even more bereft.

She sighed deeply and whispered, "Benny, I've made a mess of everything, haven't I?"

Nearby church bells announced afternoon mass. After their beckoning echoes silenced, she said, "I had a meltdown during a meeting this morning. I was so unprofessional." She yanked several weeds from the ground and anguished, "I'm losing it, Benny. Every time I think I'm doing proper penance for my sins, I only make matters worse."

Her voice shifted into a confessional tone. "Benny, I should've been straight with you about all of it from the beginning. But I really believed I could handle it myself and spare you. I never imagined things getting so out of hand. Such terrible things at work, and now the police involved *again*. And I'm so scared! It's just a matter of time before they uncover what I've done. So, you see, I've got to go. And before I do, I've got to make things as right as I can."

After a few calming breaths, she said, "Your chapel service on Monday was lovely. It was just me and a few of the old neighbors. And the church ladies and chaplain, of course."

But her calm instantly dissipated when her hand alighted on the reserved space of their shared tombstone. Her eyes welling with tears, she said, "You and I were supposed to retire to the islands next year. Limp off into the sunset together. Oh, Benny . . ."

Looking at her wedding ring, she recalled the day he slipped it onto her finger—a month after they eloped in Dublin to avoid predictable troubles with his unionist family in Belfast over wedding plans. "Thank you for choosing me," she said. "I just hope you felt well-loved by me. And that I came through in the end."

She kissed his tombstone and said, "Until we meet again."

Hallway, ER Admin Suite

Oakland City Hospital

AFTERNOON

Rosalie knocked on Edna's office door but got no response. Frustrated, she used her cellphone to call Edna's number, but only heard the landline ringing inside. And when she called Edna's work cell number, she heard silence.

"Hey!" someone called out.

Rosalie gasped and said, "You scared me, Fergie!"

"Sorry! I didn't expect to see you here. Looking for Edna?"

"Yes," Rosalie said. "I had drinks with Nora last night. She got me more interested in being on the SMART committee."

Unlocking the supply room across from Edna's office, Fergie said, "But, as a doc, shouldn't you discuss that with the medical side? With Dr. Williams, the MD cochair?" Scanning the supply room shelves, she grumbled, "Typical. Nothing where it should be."

"But I cannot ask Fred. He does not want me more involved in hospital activity. Did you know he even removed me from ER backup after our incident with Cheryl last Wednesday?"

Fergie grimaced. "Sorry. That was my fault. I shouldn't have called you in."

"No, you did the right thing. But that experience made me realize how meaningful it would be to work with the committee on medical errors. Real change will not occur by individuals independently confronting doctors like Cheryl."

"Look, I owe you. So, you're hoping to bypass medicine's approval and go through nursing instead? Hoping Edna will put in a good word?" Rosalie nodded and Fergie said, "So, I'll talk to her when I see her."

"When will that be?"

"Maybe this afternoon—*if* she returns from *wherever* she is. She's been . . . kinda erratic. But, if not, you could ask her yourself tomorrow. She's scheduled to work AM shift."

"I assumed she would be around now, because she was at the SMART meeting this morning, right?"

"Yeah, but she's on fuzzy 'admin time' today," Fergie said. She withdrew a yellowed packet of 4×4s from a shelf and complained, "Look at this: stored in the ACE wraps spot! Last week, I ran here looking for a wrist splint and found adult diapers in the bin instead. I suppose I should've just been grateful they hadn't been used."

Rosalie smiled politely. "Well, how was your first SMART meeting today? Any news in Cheryl's case?"

Fergie, still focused on locating an ACE wrap, said, "Well, Edna reported on her visit to Cheryl's office. She *maybe* found a clue there. She thinks it was left there by—" She stopped herself. "Well, listen to me! Miss Privacy and Confidentiality! Sorry, Rosalie. I shouldn't be discussing this stuff outside the committee." Then her face lit up and, pointing to a shelf, she exclaimed, "So *that's* where the crackers have been hiding!"

Rosalie said, "Well, thanks for offering to put in a good word with Edna. But I should probably talk to her in person instead."

"No problem."

"So, maybe I could ask for a different favor? Instead, maybe you could just text me as soon as you see her today?"

"I promise," Fergie said. But when she turned to say goodbye, all she saw was Edna's office across the hallway—looking atypically dark in the middle of an afternoon.

Rosalie was already headed for the elevator that would deliver her to her third-floor office where patients awaited. A tempest swirled in her mind. Wild mental storms kicked up suspicions about Edna's treason. But at least it was beginning to make sense—Edna's cold glares, her sudden and unexplained absences. *"Erratic" may be how Fergie describes Edna. But "treacherous" is the term I choose.*

Nora's Home

Oakland

EVENING

Nora kept shifting her plate, trying to shield her tuna sandwich from Bix's hungry mouth and quick paws. Conceding defeat, she placed a dollop of fish on the floor and watched him lap it up.

"You know, I had a very hard day," she said. "And I had to pick up your Aunt Lydia's ashes after work. *Hello?* I'm talking to you."

Bix meowed for more tuna.

"No," she said. "Not until you listen to me tell you about my day."

He curled around her feet. "Okay," she said, slumping against the sofa. "I've been so distracted. Lydia's gone, but now I see her everywhere. This morning . . . I was so unfocused . . . a real idiot at my first SMART meeting." She glanced at the two photos—of Lydia and their old residents' group—still propped against the armrest. "And my poor patients all day . . . I was so unavailable to them."

Bix stealthily extended a paw toward the sandwich, but she dodged its reach and said, "I'm not done talking. And I'm really freaked out by all the creepy stuff happening at work." She tried to calm herself by looking through the glass doors that opened to her deck and a view of the city, recalling times spent taking in this same view . . . sitting here with Michael . . . lying here for weeks, pregnant and waiting for the prescribed bedrest to end . . . holding Caitlin in her lap.

Her cellphone chimed, and Bix predictably sprinted away. A text from Fred: *Going 2 C Jack 2morrow. Come. I know U have day off.*

Nora's immediate inclination was to decline. *Scattering Lydia's ashes tomorrow is more than enough activity for the day.* Since picking up the small box at the crematorium mere hours ago, she'd been suffering the reality of Lydia's death in new and unexpected ways. It boggled her mind to see Lydia reduced to such a tiny, ashy mass. It had been surreal during the drive home, debating whether to strap a seatbelt around the box. Then, when she needed to free a hand to open her front door, it was strange to place that box inside the Safeway bag filled with bib lettuce and chicken thighs. It was odd to unpack the groceries in the kitchen, placing Lydia's box on the countertop alongside apples and avocados.

She couldn't imagine possessing sufficient psychic bandwidth to visit Jack after the cemetery tomorrow. And yet . . . spending time with Fred on a drive to the prison might provide needed comfort. Besides, she could use his counsel about her burgeoning theory of staged mayhem and murder.

She texted back: *Not sure. Check in 2morrow? Want 2 see how I feel after the cemetery.*

Fred: *OK. But please come*

Nora: *U OK?*

Fred: *Don't ask*

Nora: *Where did U decide 2 stay?*

Fred: *Paradox Hotel*

Nora: *Again, can stay with me.*

Fred: *Thx. But enjoying hotel. Hope 2 prickle U up 2morrow around noon*

Fred: ** 2 pick U up*

Nora set aside her phone and stared at Timmy who rested on the mantel. Fragments of today's conversation with Fergie darted chaotically through her mind. All the while, her anxiety quickened around her solidifying theory. *Someone is actually staging all the carnage. Going to great trouble to make each attack look so different. There must be meaning attached to the differences, but what? Lydia—maybe a morality tale about drugs? Cheryl—about corporate greed? Infidelity with Fred? Bean-counting with Richard—*

She shuddered and stopped herself cold, hearing the critical voice inside her head posing these justifications in such a cool, rational tone. How effortlessly, it seemed, she had adopted a perpetrator's dark vindictive mindset to seek out moral flaws in her colleagues as reasons for their fates.

Mortified, she looked at the photos propped against the armrest and apologized, "I was trying to reason why someone would hurt you based on who you are! I was blaming you for being victims!"

Consumed with shame, she returned to the kitchen in search of distraction. She resumed unpacking the groceries, this time able to work around Lydia's box of ashes without paralyzing sorrow. Once finished, she stood at the sink, drinking a glass of water and reviewing her plans for the morning. Increasingly, it seemed like a good idea to join Fred on the drive to prison after scattering Lydia's ashes. She could wait on making the decision about visiting Jack—

Jack!

She dropped her glass. It shattered on the tile floor.

"Shit!" she cried out, returning to the living room, picking up the group photo and fixing on Jack. "How could I have been so blind?"

Your crimes, Jack—they were staged, too! You were wrongfully convicted, as you've always claimed.

She paced, trying to discharge her escalating guilt and panic. And, for the first time in years, a mental space opened in which Jack appeared, untethered to the traumatic memory of losing her husband and daughter on the beach.

Jack, I see you now! And I see that you've been framed. You've been vic-timized like the others.

She stopped, now violently frozen in fear. Glancing at "the others" in the gang-of-six photo, she realized she was the odd one out, the only one not yet thrown onto a stage.

Part IV

Day of Reckoning

FEBRUARY 16

Bedroom, Fergie and Winston's Apartment

East Oakland

EARLY MORNING

FERGIE'S CELLPHONE rang again.

Winston asked, "Aren't you going to answer?"

"No," she said. "My *one* day off?"

"It could be your sister—about your mom."

Fergie rolled her eyes. "Well, thanks for that! Who could go back to sleep now?"

He pulled her closer. "I could help you relax."

"Yeah? And all the while, me thinking of my mom. How's that sound?"

"No comment."

"You're a jerk," she said, rolling on top of him, pinning his arms to the bed, and teasing him with her mouth.

The phone rang again. She smiled mischievously and whispered, "You're right. I should answer that." Despite Winston's moaning protestation, she peeled herself off his body and sauntered to the dresser.

"Come back!" he pleaded.

But she put on her bifocals and lifted the phone from its charger. "Damn!" she said. "It's work."

"Don't talk to them, Fergs! It's never anything good!" He desperately hummed "My Funny Valentine."

"Too late, pal," she said.

He overheard her questioning the caller, "But why? Is Edna sick? . . . Did you try calling her at home? . . . Wow. Well, maybe that old car of hers broke down on the way to ER? . . . No. I've never known her to have a personal cell, but she always carries her work cell. . . . Really? That, too? . . . I'm positive. I've worked with her for years. She always shows for work. . . . Uh, sure. I could come in. No worries."

Fergie ended the call and told Winston, "I gotta cover for Edna."

He groaned and tried pulling her back to bed. But she wrestled free and headed for the shower.

"Hey," he yelled after her. "What about our romantic morning in Sausalito?"

"There's trouble in my paradise," she yelled back, turning on the hot water.

Nora's Home

Oakland

EARLY MORNING

The alarm sounded at 7:00 a.m., but Nora had been awake for hours, worrying about her friends and colleagues.

She started the coffee, took a quick shower, and dressed in jeans and a long-sleeved shirt. She filled a backpack with a thermos, a bagel, a blanket, and Lydia's ashes.

Noting the ample time remaining before the cemetery even opened, she decided to follow through on an idea that had occurred to her in the middle of the night. She would make a copy of the old group photo to give to Jack when she visited him today and asked for his forgiveness. It might help them relocate to the emotional ground they once shared.

She scanned the photo into her laptop, watching the image constellate on screen, imagining Richard's original viewing of it from behind the camera. She recalled her hesitation that day about being photographed by him—a stranger at the time—especially while she was steeped in sadness over losing her last patient. But there was Jack beside her, acutely smitten with Richard, encouraging him to take the picture. And then their friends there, too, having come to the ER to drag her away to celebrate—

Like lightning, it struck her. *This photo . . . this photo is what links Richard's death to the other victims!*

Her hands trembled, compromising her ability to edit the photo. *A basic crop-and-print will have to suffice for Jack.*

But when she simply cropped the photo to center on their group of six, another lightning bolt struck: cutting out Edna in the background transformed the photo into a radically different picture.

She reversed the cropping and reinserted Edna—Edna in profile, looking down, standing in the background in the photo's periphery. And now she saw it. Edna's presence in the photo was not incidental—as she and Lydia had presumed. It was, in fact, essential to the wholeness of the picture; to the emotional truth about that last day of their residency. Indeed, when she zoomed in on Edna's face, she saw something other than Edna's usual pinched expression—alarm, perhaps. Or pain.

Edna is decidedly in this picture. Our gang-of-six photo is actually a photo of eight, with Edna and Richard included.

Cheryl's Room, ICU

Oakland City Hospital

7:45 A.M.

Carl was mesmerized by the ongoing physical changes in his wife's body. Small puckered craters formed on her arms and thighs, and the skin under her elbows reddened. Hair dropped off her scalp. Colors fluctuated in her lips. Her eyes sank into ever-deepening sockets. Her body—whether or not she was a living occupant of it—proceeded to change as if it were a living entity, independent of her existence.

"How we doing today?" asked Peter Yuen.

Carl was glad to see "the surgeon of record" for Cheryl's botched surgery who, unlike everyone else on staff, had visited every day. "The same," he answered.

"Sorry," said Peter, handing over another bag of supplies. "Look: I want you to use the razor today. You're beginning to look scary, buddy."

It was a kindness, Carl thought, to be so noticed. And that someone called him "buddy." "Thank you," he said. "I enjoyed the ham and Swiss you brought yesterday."

"Good," Peter said. He squeezed Carl's shoulder and left.

Carl told Cheryl, "I know, I know. But I think he's being honest about whatever happened." He withdrew a muffin from the bag and, while he ate, restarted his internal conversation with Cheryl.

In fact, let's begin with that premise—that Peter is telling the truth. Besides, no evidence contradicts him.

That being our premise, let's accept that (A), conditions in the OR that morning were, as Peter claims, unremarkable and routine, including his team's disregard for surgical checklists; and, (B), Peter did lay out the correct stent during OR table prep.

Then we must conclude that someone swapped his stent with the AccuStent. And, obviously, that had to have occurred within a very narrow time frame: after he prepped the table, yet before stent insertion was initiated. So, I think—

A woman attired in a nurse's uniform rushed in, apologizing, "Sorry to intrude! I'm *not* here!" She hurriedly turned Cheryl onto her side.

Given his surreal experience of this place and its governance by alien logic, he took her comment in stride. Still, he reasoned, he need not remain complicit. He said, "But I *do* see you here."

"No, you don't!" she insisted. "Please? I'm officially clocked out for a mandatory break." She checked Cheryl's ventilator settings. "If they catch me working, they'll accuse me of pulling for overtime pay, or sabotaging union rules."

"You're sneaking out of a break in order to complete your work?"

"Don't tell," she pleaded, adjusting the oximeter. "Seriously, they just fired a gal for working during her lunch breaks. But, god—they give us so many sick patients and then expect us to drop everything for official teatime?" She pushed Cheryl's hair away from her eyes and repeated, "I'm *not* here. You *never* saw me, okay?"

"I understand," he said, grateful that someone *finally* said something that acknowledged the surreal culture here. He replied conspiratorially, "I don't see you. You were never here."

She smiled and scurried out. But when the door closed, a disturbing thought entered Carl's mind: *I don't know the name or actual identity of the person who just left. I don't know who just transacted so intimately with my wife's body and so-called life.*

He said to Cheryl, "It would've been so easy for someone dressed in scrubs to slip unnoticed into your OR room that morning."

Mountain View Cemetery

Oakland

8:30 A.M.

Nora spread a blanket on the dewy lawn atop a high hill in Mountain View Cemetery. She sat down and watched the morning sun bring stone angels to life. English sparrows and scrub jays flecked the sky. A breeze rustled the trees. *How amazing to experience so much life in a place like this.*

She turned off her phone and lay down, allowing her body to yield to its commanding fatigue. In this place vacant of manufactured noise, she could hear the insistent stirrings of nature; of life and death. Her spine uncoiled, her muscles unclenched, and, soon, her exhaustion laid a consummate claim to the deep peace of the earth.

Her mind wandered freely, and she gently drifted into an excruciating stillness in which she became unattuned to her physical existence. Now she could be air, sky, sea, dream ... It was so wholly peaceful. Peaceful and still, like the ocean's quiet center ...

A violent surprise shook her—she was envisioning Michael and Caitlin here, staring back at her through an impenetrable wall of water through which she could not reach and pull them back into her life. She bolted upright, her heart racing and tears flowing freely.

After gathering herself, Nora opened her thermos and poured coffee. Delicate vestiges of steam escaped, spiraling upward and dispersing in air. *Lydia . . .*

So here we are, pal. I'm about to scatter your ashes, and I've got nothing profound or spiritual to say. Nothing sentimental even. I'm just . . . just so fuckin' sad you're gone.

Addressing the box of ashes, she said, "I'm doing this because you asked me to. But I'm asking a favor of you in return: come back to me, Lydia."

But nothing happened. The box didn't burst open against a backdrop of celestial music while Lydia rose from the ashes. No "sign" was revealed, as intensely and imaginatively as Nora searched the sky and graveyard. Finally, she said, "God, Lydia—you're still so contrary!"

Loud footsteps drew her attention to a nearby walkway. She saw a silver-haired man jogging by, his heels thudding on the path, his athletic shorts billowing around his flagpole thighs. His ultra-sleek body, all tendon and bone, moved between the gravesites as fast as it possibly could. Nora whispered to Lydia, "We know what he's hoping to outrun. Good luck with that, right?"

She reached for the ashes but hesitated. *Too soon; too soon.*

Besides, I want a final conversation with you before all physical traces of you are gone.

I want you to tell you how sorry I am for not being more available when you've needed me. I've been so out of it these last couple of years . . . I don't need to tell you that. But sometimes I couldn't see what was happening in broad daylight. And too often, that included not seeing you.

And I regret . . . I should've tried to intervene in your drug use. And I'm so fuckin' forever sorry I didn't drag you home with me that night at the Tavern.

She stood up and paced, literalizing her need to move through her grief.

Another thing, Lydia? Last night, I was looking at that gang-of-six photo you resurrected last week. I should've agreed with you before—you did look a lot like Amy Schumer back in the day.

A lumbering shadow rolled across the cemetery grounds, clouds clustering overhead. Out loud, Nora said, "It's time," and she unlatched the box. "Besides, it's probably killing you, not being able to talk back to me. I know that's killing me."

Nora opened the baggie inside, realizing this previously unthinkable moment was, nonetheless, unfolding and becoming real. "I guess this is just how this happens, Lydia."

She claimed a palmful of ashes for herself. "Love you, pal," she said, swinging the bag through the air, and watching streams of Lydia's ashes enter into her place of deep solace.

Cafeteria

Oakland City Hospital

8:35 A.M.

Fergie stared blankly at the hospital cafeteria's menu. It was hard to imagine consuming anything it offered. *There's a serious conflict of interest here*, she thought. *The cafeteria makes people sick, and then the hospital profits from treating them.*

A worker appeared behind the counter and announced, "We're out of shepherd's pie."

"Thank god," Fergie muttered.

"Sorry?"

"I mean, do you have anything fresh? Meatless? Something unprocessed?"

Hands on hips, the worker suggested, "And maybe without gluten?"

"That would be great!"

The worker cocked her head. "Well, we don't have things like that here. We're not San Francisco—at least, not yet."

"Okay, never mind," Fergie said, heading for the refrigerated items. She grabbed a fruit salad, and then jumped as a voice broke the silence.

"I am surprised to see you here."

Fergie turned to find Rosalie who said, "Sorry to startle you. I went looking for Edna in the ER, but the clerk said she did not show up today. When I asked why, he told me I should speak with you. I almost did not believe him when he told me you were in the *cafeteria*. You always say everything here is poison!"

"It is! But I'm starving. They called me in this morning to sub for Edna, and I didn't have time to bring real food from home."

Rosalie said, "And, so . . . about Edna?"

"Hey, I didn't forget my promise yesterday to contact you when I saw her. But, thing is, she never returned to the ER. Then, this morning, well . . . she didn't even show for her scheduled shift or call in ahead of time."

"Oh? Is she sick?" asked Rosalie, a worried look on her face.

Fergie scoffed. "Edna *sick*? She's *never* sick, even when she actually is." She grabbed an apple and headed toward the cash register.

"Then where is she?"

"Wish I knew. She's not answering her phones."

"Do you think she is all right?"

"I hope so. But she's been unpredictable lately, and under a lot of stress."

"Why do you say that?"

Fergie paid the cashier. "Look, I need to get back to the ER because I'm acting head nurse. Want to walk back with me while we talk?" She headed down the hallway, Rosalie following.

"This 'stress?'" Rosalie asked.

"Yeah, well, Edna's always tight-lipped about her private life. So, if something personal is upsetting her, I wouldn't know. But she's definitely been more tense and distracted at work lately. She's been coming and going without notice. At yesterday's SMART meeting, she worked herself into a lather over that—" Fergie silenced, then said, "There I go *again*! What's wrong with me? I shouldn't be blabbing about confidential committee matters."

"Look, I am very worried about Edna. You said she is never sick. But it . . . it *is* a medical problem, actually. That is the real reason I stopped by her office yesterday—to check on her and give her a prescription. So now, if we cannot get hold of her, I am even more worried. She could be having a seizure or worse. Please, can you tell me anything so I can help her?"

Fergie's jaw dropped. "I feel terrible! I never once considered it could be anything neurological, let alone medical. But maybe that explains some of Edna's strange behavior, her unpredictability, and her short—*shorter*—temper. Maybe the paranoia, too?"

Rosalie looked pointedly at Fergie. "Paranoia? About what?"

After momentary deliberation, Fergie decided that Edna's welfare trumped confidentiality of the committee's discussion. "Well, at the SMART meeting, Edna kept insisting she found a clue that should identify the person responsible for Cheryl's botched surgery; for her death. For her *murder*, actually. And she said that person was taunting us."

Rosalie looked incredulous. "I agree, that *does* sound overly dramatic. Or 'paranoid,' as you say. But what was this big clue of hers?"

"A piece of jewelry—a pin or brooch. Edna said it was inside the box that had contained the stolen stent."

"Oh? Did you see this piece of jewelry?"

Fergie nodded. "A silver caduceus."

Rosalie's face blanched, her brow furrowed.

"Hey, are *you* okay?" Fergie asked. "You suddenly don't look well."

"I am fine. I am just convinced now that Edna is sick and in trouble. And it concerns me that a common piece of jewelry is upsetting her when she needs to stay calm for her health."

Shaking her head in dismay, Fergie said, "I don't like the sound of things. I'll notify admin to get the police out to Edna's house for a safety check."

"Wait; I am sure I can locate her by phone."

"Well, we've tried her landline and work cell dozens—"

"No. She has a separate cell for personal use."

"Really? That's great. After all these years, I didn't know." Fergie whipped out her cell and said, "So let's call the number now."

"Actually, her private number is written down in my office. So, I will go there now and call her before my clinic begins."

"Okay, but you'll text me immediately after, even if you can't get hold of her?"

Rosalie nodded. "Of course. Just give me 10, 15 minutes." She waved goodbye and hurried toward the elevator, thinking, *That cannot be my brooch!*

She mentally retraced her steps on the Sunday evening she had visited Cheryl's research office. She remembered stumbling upon Cheryl, alone in the ER hallway and distraught by Carl's unprecedented contrariness. She recalled placing an arm around her and accompanying her to her office and waiting for Cheryl to put her records in order.

Entering the elevator, she recalled her caduceus being pinned, as usual, on the underside of her coat's left lapel while in Cheryl's office. Indeed, she clearly remembered removing her white coat and tossing it on Cheryl's desk, hearing the brooch scrape along its surface. She recalled feeling relieved at the time that Cheryl had been away in the restroom, and how easy it had been to dismiss the squinty-eyed boy who leered at her from the hallway. And later, when she retrieved her coat from the desk before exiting the office with Cheryl, she had slipped a hand under the caduceus to protect the desk. *I am sure of it! My caduceus was still on my coat when I left! The one Edna found cannot be mine.*

ER

Oakland City Hospital

9:00 A.M.

Per routine, Lizbeth reported at 9:00 a.m. to the nurses station. Today, however, she did not expect to find Edna there. Still, she dutifully waited, holding onto Edna's cap and a slim hope that her intuition was wrong.

Minutes passed. Nurses, doctors, and patients swarmed around her. So many sounds, human and mechanical, none of them Edna's commanding bark.

Finally, Fergie arrived, calling out to the LVNs, the orderlies, the residents, and perhaps an imagined savior. "*Get cardio in 8—now!* . . . *The chaplain, room 3* . . . *No, I said two bags of O-neg* . . ." Upon noticing

Lizbeth, she said, "Sorry, but Edna's not here. And it's a bad day for me to be teaching anyone."

"Will she be coming in?"

"Don't know," Fergie said, erasing two names from the whiteboard.

Lizbeth placed Edna's cap on the countertop between them. "I found this in my locker."

The world stopped spinning a moment; long enough for the same troubling thought to cross the two women's minds. They looked knowingly at each other. Lizbeth said, "I think this means that Edna's not returning."

Sadness and regret flooded Fergie's heart. "I've been worrying that something bad has happened to her. But, I suppose, if she's left her cap in your locker . . . well, she must've *planned* on not coming back. There's a little relief in knowing her absence was premeditated." Still, given what Rosalie told her minutes ago, she wondered if Edna's departure was triggered by a serious illness. Perhaps, even, a terminal illness that Edna chose to suffer privately, one severe enough to make a year's wait to retirement unfathomable. *I'm so ashamed about my obliviousness to Edna's predicament. I should've asked her directly about the troubling changes I noticed in her, instead of commenting sideways about them to everyone else. I could've been supporting her.*

"Fergie?" said Lizbeth. "I've been concerned about Edna, too. I've wanted to tell you things about her, but it's felt like a betrayal."

The desk clerk shouted, "MVA arriving in five!"

"Thanks," Fergie shouted back. Returning her frayed attention to Lizbeth, she said, "You were saying?"

"Well, Edna . . . she made me vow to speak up whenever I saw something wrong or suspicious, even if it implicated someone in power—*especially* if it implicated someone in power. But I never imagined that could mean me speaking up with concerns about *her*."

"Edna?"

Lizbeth nodded and steadied her voice. "I've watched her like a hawk and never had cause to doubt her before. And still . . . I don't know. Maybe I just don't understand what she was actually trying to do."

"Don't be afraid, Lizbeth. It's hard to speak up, especially when it involves your mentor. But if she did or said something that troubled you, it might help us understand what's troubling her." An orderly tossed a chart that landed on Edna's cap. "Hey! Manners, please!" Fergie reprimanded.

Lizbeth straightened the cap and said, "Edna's been different. Like, she's been leaving work or canceling meetings without warning or explanation. The other day, in the parking lot, I saw her sitting alone in her car, crying and—"

"Excuse me," Fergie interrupted. "See that patient there? He's scouting for syringes and drugs." She yelled, "Back to your room, Parker!" He smiled impishly and walked away. She returned to Lizbeth and asked, "Did you suspect Edna was sick? Maybe sneaking off to doctors appointments?"

"No! I mean . . . Omigod, is Edna sick?"

An LVN tapped Fergie's shoulder and said, "I can't find any 4×4s in the stockroom, if you can believe that."

"Regrettably, I can. Look on the top shelf, in the *Thumb Splints* bin."

Lizbeth continued, "On Tuesday, on our way to the research center, Edna was very sentimental and intense. And how she talked to me—well, it sounded like she was never going to see me again. Like she was passing on words of wisdom and making me vow to remember them. When I found her cap in my locker this morning, I knew for certain that was exactly what she'd been doing then. And that day, inside Dr. Kluft's office, she did something strange that's been bothering me since. I planned to ask her about it the next day, but she wasn't around. I saw her sneak—"

Aditya appeared. "Excuse me. Is Dr. Kelly around?"

"She's off today," Fergie said. "Quick—what d'ya need?"

"Nothing! I only wanted to tell her about the pericardial rub I just found on my exam of the patient in 16."

Lizbeth said, "I've never heard one. Mind if I listen?"

"Yes!" said Aditya, smiling. "I mean, no, I don't mind. Come. I will teach you how to identify it."

"First ambulance is here," the clerk shouted.

Fergie signaled the clerk and said to Lizbeth, "Sorry, but I'm needed in triage. Hang around, though. We really need to talk."

But as Fergie headed toward triage, her anxiety escalated. She was worried about Edna's health and whereabouts, and Lizbeth's disturbing comments about her. She was troubled that Rosalie had not called back after trying Edna's personal cell.

And when she saw Lizbeth disappear with Aditya into room 16, a disquieting question seized her: *Why is Lizbeth always so solidly present at the center of whatever's happening with Edna? Lizbeth finds Edna's cap and presents it as evidence suggesting Edna's premeditated departure. Now she is shaping perceptions about Edna's state of mind. Lizbeth seems to be driving a narrative about Edna to which she stakes a unique claim through her privileged witnessing.*

Suddenly, Lizbeth loomed large in Fergie's mind, no longer the naive, rather two-dimensional character that Fergie had subconsciously (perhaps, foolishly) supposed her to be.

Rosalie's Office

3rd Floor, Oakland City Hospital

9:00 A.M.

Rosalie headed straight to the office closet where her five white coats hung like flaccid ghosts. Certainly, she would find her caduceus pinned to one of them, concealed under her lapel, as always. Such an inexpensive piece of jewelry—though made with a solid, reliable clasp—could be of no value to anyone but her. And to her mother, of course—God rest her soul—who pinned the dream of becoming a doctor onto her one precious daughter: a doctor who would never allow the tragedy that had befallen their family to happen to other poor patients.

But after rifling through the coats, fingering their lapels, she couldn't find her caduceus. Hoping it may have fallen off, she searched the floor—in vain. Then she gasped when, reaching into the pockets, she found the cartoon that Nora had given to her. *This* coat, she knew, was the one she had worn in Cheryl's office on Sunday night.

Yet, no matter how often she inspected it, she couldn't find her caduceus.

"God, help me!" she cried, tossing the coat onto her desk. "This cannot be happening!" She paced the office, frantically wondering about the caduceus Edna reportedly discovered. *It cannot possibly be mine, because I clearly remember wearing mine when I left Cheryl's office. And yet, why is it missing now?*

She counseled herself to calm down and think. She must reconstruct her every move since her last certain possession of the caduceus.

I am wearing it when I leave the building with Cheryl. We cross Broadway, and head for the hospital. We arrive at the doctors' parking lot. Carl is there, standing outside his car, and waiting for Cheryl. I say goodnight to them, then I return to the ER and crash in the on-call room—

"Betrayal!" she shouted, having a painful epiphany. Only one person would have—and could have—taken her brooch. It was the only other person who understood its value.

ER Supplies Closet

Oakland City Hospital

10:20 A.M.

With nine minutes of mandatory break time remaining on the clock, Fergie secluded herself inside the storage closet across the hall from Edna's office, taking refuge from ceaseless interruptions in the ER. She attempted—again, unsuccessfully—to contact Nora. *How long does ash-scattering normally take?*

Perusing the usual disarray here, she considered reorganizing the storage bins. But then she realized how much she'd adapted to the current disorder. Any rearrangement would only create new confusion. Instead, she worried. *Where's Edna? How is she? Why hasn't Rosalie phoned yet? Why do I have these suspicions about Lizbeth? Did we get to the GSW in time? Did they remember to call the family of the patient who—?*

Her cell rang, and she brusquely answered, "What's up, Win?"

Winston said, "Hey, how you doing?"

"C'mon! I don't have time. And you know I don't like talking while I'm working."

"But I miss you. You left me hanging this morning."

"Ugh! Disgusting. Goodbye—"

"No! Look, I'm calling because you're worrying me. Your stress is showing."

"We can talk about that at home." She peered out of the closet and stared at Edna's unlit office. "The ER's crazy-times-ten and I'm super busy." She whispered, "And things aren't right around here. Edna has *literally* disappeared. She even handed her cap over to Lizbeth."

"Her student? You don't think she's actually gonna wear it, do you?"

"Damn it, Win! Not funny."

"Okay! Don't hang up! Tell me about Edna."

Fergie sighed. "Yeah, okay. Yesterday, Edna was hyper-anxious over a brooch she found in Cheryl's office—"

"A *brooch*? Now there's an archaic term."

"Again, not the point! You make one more knucklehead comment, and I swear—"

"Reading you loud and clear. The brooch?"

Fergie decided to try one last time for an agreeable conversation. "Edna believed it belonged to whoever stole the stent to sabotage Cheryl's surgery. And she made me photograph it before it was handed over to the police. She said my photo was for 'safekeeping'—from what, I don't know. And now . . . now we can't locate Edna."

"Hon, you guys gotta call the cops."

"We just did. They're on their way to conduct a home safety check."

"Well, good. Because when I drove by Edna's house about 15 minutes ago—"

"You *what*?"

"Hey, I'm a curious journalist who loves you. So, when you were called in to work for Edna and worried about her being unreachable? Well, that was a call to me, too."

"God, I have no freakin' idea about what's right anymore."

"So, Edna's car—her old blue Acura?—it was in her driveway. And when I knocked on the door and rang her bell, she didn't answer. I think the house lights were off, but all the shades were drawn. This morning's *East Bay Times* was still on her porch. And, you told me she had two dogs? Well, there was no barking—not even when I knocked on the windows or rang the landline. And now you say she surrendered her legendary cap to a *student*? In my book, Edna has gone missing. And it's clear she carefully planned ahead for it."

"But Rosalie told me Edna was sick. Maybe Edna's inside the house, collapsed or unconscious?"

"Again, the dogs didn't bark, even with all the commotion I created. Besides, you always say that Edna never gets sick. And if she did, wouldn't that hawk-eyed student of hers have noticed any evidence of that? Did you talk with her?"

"Yeah ... well, a little. We kept getting interrupted. We're supposed to catch up this afternoon." Fergie checked the time. She had two more minutes before she must clock in or risk disciplinary action. "Rosalie was supposed to call me after making contact with Edna through some private number she had."

"Did you call Rosalie to see if she got hold of Edna?"

"Twice; but she didn't answer. I'm afraid ..."

"Of what?"

"Quiet!" Fergie whispered. "I hear something." She muted her cell and peered out of the closet. Someone was at Edna's door, irritably tugging the knob. Fergie's heart drummed a panicky cadence as she stealthily looked out to see who was trying so desperately to get into Edna's office.

Only after she could no longer hear departing footsteps in the hallway did Fergie let down and exhale. "Win," she shakily managed, "that was Rosalie."

Chapel of the Chimes

Oakland

10:30 A.M.

Nora exited the cemetery and parked on Piedmont in front of the Chapel of the Chimes. Lydia's instructions requested that she take "15 minutes, minimum" to explore the chapel in which she'd meditated whenever rain precluded a walk in the cemetery.

When Nora entered the chapel, she felt as if she were stepping into a memory that Lydia had lovingly prepared for her. The interior was as Lydia described—elegant, haunting, otherworldly—only unspeakably more so, now that Nora was here herself.

She walked the labyrinthine columbarium, stepping into dozens of uniquely designed rooms with ubiquitous Moorish and Gothic influences. Some rooms contained gardens, pools, fountains, and even caged birds. Some had vaulted ceilings or clerestory light. The tile, the mosaics, the stained glass, the stoneware and statues . . . everywhere, art transcended time to companion with the dead who were interred here.

She sat on a bench and gazed into a reflecting pool, thinking about Lydia. The brass and chrome urns that were shelved in glass cabinets along the walls were reflected on the water. A breeze stole through an open skylight and ruffled the pool's surface. She thought, *Lydia carried by wind; my family by water.* She dipped her finger into the pool.

"Are you all right?"

A man—50ish, balding, casually suited—stood in the chamber entryway. Immediately realizing his imposition, he apologized, "Sorry to startle you. I work here and—"

"No need to apologize," Nora said, though feeling otherwise. *Why should someone act so officiously curious about a person exhibiting distress inside a columbarium?* She recalled Lydia's complaint about Carl's intrusion on her solitude during Richard's service, and she understood it in a new light. "I was about to leave anyway," she said. "And, actually, I'm not sure how to get out of here."

He smiled and said, "Happy to help! Even I still get lost in here sometimes." He led her down narrow stairways and through a majestic walkway adorned with ribbed vaulting. Finally at the exit, he asked, "I assume this is your first visit?"

"Yes. But my friend, she always talked about this place."

"Your friend . . . Did she pass recently?"

But feeling raw and porous, Nora couldn't absorb his sympathy—the additional influx of anyone's feelings was unbearable. "I can't talk about her now."

The attendant handed her a tissue which, Nora appreciatively noted, was not flimsy hospital quality. He waited for her to dry her eyes and said, "I understand. But please do come back. And take this brochure. It tells the history of our Chapel, which is a Julia Morgan building, but you probably knew that. It also describes the remembrance programs we offer. And it contains a map of the interior to help with your next visit."

"Thanks. I'll be back. And this map will help."

"Oh, also check out our events calendar. See here? We have community services, holiday events, and even jazz recitals."

Nora politely glanced at the calendar while he spoke, but did a double take when she saw an entry for February 13. Pointing to it, she said, "I think . . . actually, this has to be . . . a service for the husband of one of my coworkers."

The attendant replied, "Ah, for Bernard Atkinson on Monday morning. Yes, it was a beautiful annual sunrise 'service of remembrance.' Much like last year's."

"I had no idea," Nora said, wondering if Edna had intended to keep it private at work.

"Oh, don't worry. Enough people attended, mostly from their old neighborhood; and, of course, our 'chapel ladies' and myself. Bernard's widow, Edna, gave a lovely reading with poems from Eavan Boland and Seamus Heaney. And she offered refreshments in the lobby afterward— pastries from La Farine, no less."

"Well, good then," Nora said, shaking his hand. "Thank you for all the information, and for helping me out."

Visiting Room, San Sebastian State Prison

Marin County

11:00 A.M.

Baldwin told Jack, "It's a *lady*. Maybe not *your* type of lady, but . . ."

Jack cast a withering look at Baldwin and followed him to the visiting room. When he saw Edna waiting, he smiled and picked up the receiver. "What a nice surprise."

Edna weakly returned his smile. "I wanted to see you before I left. I'm leaving . . . leaving nursing for good."

"What?" he said, his jaw dropping. "Don't you have another year before you can collect pension and benefits?"

She looked away. "That won't be happening after all."

"What's going on?"

"That's what I'm here to tell." Her chin twitched. "You know, I'll always remain grateful to you."

He fumbled a reply. "Well, I'm grateful, too—for most of it, anyway. You practically taught me hospital medicine when I was an intern—"

"Please stop."

"Um, okay. But now I'm just confused."

"I haven't been straight with you, Jack. And I need to tell you about Benny."

"No, please! At the end of the day, I have no real regrets about that."

"But I do; and quite a few."

Jack sighed. "We've been through this so often." He leaned toward her and placed his palm against the glass. "And didn't we agree? There was no point in you taking blame as well. What good would that have done anyone? Besides, my having had the option to take the blame spared me from alternatives that were much worse."

"Please let me finish what I need to say."

Jack guardedly nodded, and Edna continued: "That night you showed up for Benny and me? Well, truth is . . . Benny *had* been receiving narcotic prescriptions all the while he'd been in hospice. He didn't need them, but I always filled them anyway."

Jack scoffed. "But you called me in the middle of the night and said he was in terrible pain. You told me he had no pain meds, and his doctor was out of the country. You begged me to help, Edna."

She pressed the receiver against her chest and took a moment to steady her nerves. "Benny *was* in terrible pain then—you saw that. But he hadn't had pain for weeks before."

"I don't understand. And you just said that you'd been filling his narcotics scripts regardless. So why didn't you just give him what you had stored up?"

"Because . . . because I had taken the drugs."

"Now I know you're joking! You don't do drugs."

"That's true; I don't. All the same, I took Benny's and . . . I sold them."

Jack scrutinized Edna's face, hoping for a hint of a ruse. Finding none, he searched her eyes, looking for the person he thought he'd known—an exemplary nurse who'd never peddle narcotics, an honorable human being who'd never risk her husband dying in pain. Finally, he asked, incredulous, "You *sold* Benny's meds and left him to die in pain?"

Edna cried, "I never intended him to suffer! Look, I'm not excusing my actions. But Benny . . . they had discharged him from hospice six days earlier. They said he was doing 'too well' to remain in the program. But then, the *first* day he's kicked out and sent home . . . well, he began to drift away and sleep all the time. He stayed unconscious the next *five* days. God knows, I didn't expect him to rally at that point and return to consciousness with terrible pain!" She steeled herself. "That night, when I called you, I was so shaken when Benny came to, with his eyes and mouth wide open with pain! And I've seen his face like that every night since!"

Jack's barely controlled anger rattled his voice. "The narcotics I prescribed that night—I prescribed them for Benny's pain, and *only* his pain. But I'm in this prison because he *allegedly* overdosed on them. Because, *allegedly*, I carelessly prescribed scheduled drugs to a person who wasn't an official patient of mine. But we both know about those allegations, don't we? So now, I'm looking at you, and it's dawning on me . . ."

"Go ahead, Jack. Say it."

"That it's not even true that Benny voluntarily overdosed. Now I'm thinking . . . that you might've used those drugs to *euthanize* him."

Edna nodded.

Jack forcefully pointed at her. "You! You *killed* your husband?"

"Yes," she whispered.

"My god . . ."

"Jack, please understand. Benny had been in hospice twice before, and he was kicked out each time because he survived longer than the six months certified for his care. This third time, his last chemo must've kicked in some, because he started to eat a little and gain some weight. And they discharged him for doing 'so well.' But then, on his first day home, when he started losing consciousness; well, I told nobody. I just prayed he'd go peacefully, like he wanted."

Jack stared back in disbelief. "Still, you could've called *his* doctor instead of me!"

"No. When Benny came to at the end, his regular doctor was away on vacation—that part of the story is true. But the horrid locum tenens MD who was hired to substitute? When I called, he refused to prescribe pain meds for Benny. He said he'd reviewed Benny's chart and couldn't fathom why someone who'd been doing 'so well' recently would have terrible pain suddenly. He told me to take Benny to the ER for an evaluation because he couldn't diagnose his pain over the phone! Can you believe that? The inhumanity!"

"But why didn't you just medicate Benny's pain with what I gave you? You didn't have to fucking kill him with it!"

"But I did. Benny and I . . . we were so tired after years preparing for him to die. He was so worn down and ready to go. It was mercy killing, Jack—genuine, loving mercy. And truth be told, in that same situation with Benny, I'd do the same thing."

"But the fucking point is, *you* would do that! Not *me!* And yet, *I'm* in prison when it should be self-righteous *you* taking responsibility for what *you* did!"

"And that's precisely what I'm trying to do now."

"All this time . . ." he said, banging his forehead with his hand as if pounding these extraordinary revelations into his mind. "Ever since my trial, whenever you mentioned 'owing me,' I always thought that meant payback for me showing up that night and risking my license by prescribing narcotics for Benny. Not once did I imagine you feeling obligated for my providing you with a *cover* for *killing* your husband!"

Baldwin yelled, "Griffin, keep it down!"

Jack lowered his voice. "And you did all that for *money?* You sold Benny's meds for, what, a few hundred bucks? You couldn't have just . . . sold your old jewelry on eBay, like everyone else? Worked extra shifts like Fergie? Thrown a goddamn bake sale?"

"Jack, please limit the sarcasm. I have more to tell."

"More? Impossible!"

"It wasn't just Benny's meds I sold."

Jack glared contemptuously at her, waiting.

"Benny had lingered so long with his cancer. And he'd been out of work since the recession. Our house sunk in the subprime mess. We were broke."

"Cut to the fucking chase, Edna!"

She nodded. "A few years ago, when he was first diagnosed, I began hoarding pills for him. I thought he might need them someday—his bones were riddled with prostate cancer, and his fascist doctor kept refusing to prescribe anything effective for his pain. In fact, that's why Benny entered hospice the first time—to obtain proper pain relief. Then later, it occurred to me that our patients or their families returned narcotics to us for disposal. So, I started hoarding them, too. And when patients died, I routinely 'volunteered' to unburden families of leftover drugs. Over time, I accumulated a lot of oxy and hydrocodone; codeine and sedatives, too. So, when we were desperately broke, I started selling them—mostly to other nurses or doctors. Lydia was a regular, especially these last two years."

"This isn't happening," said Jack, shaking his head. "I must be stuck in a Twilight Zone episode. Because I'm looking at you, and you look exactly like someone I've known for decades. But if what you're saying is true, I'm actually looking at an alien now—an alien who killed her husband and blamed it on me. An alien who sold drugs to doctors and nurses, facilitating addiction and death." He laughed. "Wait! This isn't real, because I just spotted a gaping hole in your alien logic! If you possessed so many narcotics, why would you have needed to call me that night?"

"Because I had sold the last of my supply that morning. At least, the supply I kept at home."

"Excuse me? You had *stashes?*"

"Two. I kept one outside the house in a storage locker in Richmond. But I couldn't drive the distance that night within any reasonable time. Not with Benny so desperate."

"This still makes no sense. Even if that were all true, why did Benny's death draw so much attention? Why would anyone question an elderly cancer patient dying peacefully at his home? In other words, how did I fucking get here?"

"Well, you know it's routine for the coroner to be notified of a death at home. And, as you'd expect, her office had no interest in pursuing an inquiry into Benny's death. At least, not until that horrid locum tenens refused to sign Benny's death certificate. He said he wouldn't put his John Hancock on a stranger's death certificate, especially when the death made no sense to him."

"I still don't fucking understand how that pointed the finger at me!"

Edna braced herself and continued, "That spiteful locum tenens . . . he raised his previous concerns about Benny with the coroner, and I got scared. I knew if they investigated, they'd find drugs in Benny's system that hadn't been officially prescribed. I panicked! I told everyone that Benny's overdose was . . . I said I had summoned you to the house that night, and that I should've known better, but I was beside myself with grief, and I knew you supported physician-assisted suicide—"

"My god, Edna! What *you* did to Benny was *not* PAS! You know PAS is *not* the same as euthanasia! And the big fucking point is that I had no hand in prescribing for Benny's death or suicide. I only pre-scribed for palliative intent—to treat his pain!"

"I know. You were only medicating his pain. No suicide and no death intended."

"How could you do this to me, Edna?"

Shifting uncomfortably in her chair, she said, "I abused your kindness."

"That's the understatement of the year," he fumed. "You better get yourself a damn good lawyer; a team of them! Because I'm coming after you—"

"Wait!" Edna said, fearing Jack was about to exit the conversation. "It's only half of what I need to tell you."

Jack hissed. "Half? Math is supposed to be a universal language. But clearly, in your alien world, things add up differently. Because you've already revealed *multiple halves* of a shitstorm!"

Edna stifled an urge to cry. "If I can't finish now, you'll never know the whole of it."

Jack stared murderously back, gripping the receiver.

She said, "The other cases against you? The ones dropped by the prosecution in exchange for you taking responsibility for Benny's death? Well, those were cases of my making."

"No . . ."

Edna said, "Also, when you and I worked hospice together, I skimmed narcotics from the program. I forged your prescriptions and doctored others that you wrote."

Speechless, Jack slammed a fist against the glass partition.

"Days after Benny died, someone—I don't know who—used that anonymous reporting system to tip off the state about discrepancies in our hospice pharmacy records. I knew, of course, that the pharmacy logs wouldn't match your medical orders and records, and I was already panicking about the coroner's inquiry. So, when they asked me—I'm so sorry, Jack—I told them the discrepancies were due to you providing PAS under the table to other patients."

Jack clutched his stomach.

"I'm so ashamed, Jack. But they promised I wouldn't have to testify against you in exchange for giving them evidence of other cases—cases they'd drop if you took the plea bargain and accepted charges for Benny's death."

"Unbelievable! You doctored cases to make it look like I was playing Kevorkian. And then you forced my hand to accept responsibility for Benny's so-called overdose in exchange for those bogus cases against me being dropped?"

"I gave them what evidence they wanted. It was during the time all those ObamaScare crazies were shouting about 'death panels.'"

"*You* should be sitting here on this side of the window! *You* had *me* imprisoned for *your* drug crimes and *your* narcotics fraud! For killing your husband! And my Richard? My beautiful, innocent, loving Richard who died a lonely death without me because of you!"

Tears streamed down Edna's face.

Jack raged, "Do you even care about the damage you did to our hospice program after all the damning PR about me and to the patients dying in pain who *you* scared away? You did more to ruin their trust in hospice than any ObamaScare crazy could ever hope to!"

Edna's expression suddenly assumed wooden resolve. She said, "But I'm here now, pledging to make things as right as I can."

"Oh? Just how the fuck do you propose to do that?"

"I can never make up for everything I did to you. Please believe how sorry I—"

"Fuck you, Edna! I don't believe a goddamn thing you say!"

Edna checked her watch, noting what limited time remained before she had to depart. "I'm mailing an envelope right after I leave here. It contains my signed confession and evidence of everything I did; everything I told you. It will exonerate you, Jack."

"You're joking! In the *mail?* It could take *days* before anyone . . ." He stopped himself. "Of course. Fucking brilliant, Edna. The delay gives you time to escape before anyone can see your evidence."

Edna whispered, "I'll regret what I've done 'til the day I die. You were a good friend."

"Don't you ever fucking call us friends!"

"All right," she said, looking at him one final time for any sign of forgiveness. But seeing none, she hung up the phone.

"Fuck you, Edna!" Jack yelled repeatedly while she walked away.

Minutes later, Edna stood outside in the prison's parking lot. She took one long moment to center herself in preparation for her flight from her past.

She walked toward the cab she had commissioned to wait, feeling a small disburdening of guilt with each step away from the prison.

The driver opened the door and said, "See? Your suitcases have been safe with me!" After assisting her into the back seat, he asked, "On to the airport now?"

"Yes," Edna said, withdrawing a thick envelope from one of her suitcases. "And we need to make a brief stop along the way so I can mail this."

Outside the Chapel of the Chimes

Oakland

11:00 A.M.

Nora stood under the Chapel of the Chimes' gabled entry, collecting herself. She looked up the busy street—so many cars on Piedmont, construction workers swarming around new condo developments, stylish joggers whizzing by. So many people with direction, plans, and places to go.

She decided to order takeout at Little Shin Shin's to fortify herself before visiting Jack. But when consulting her cell for its phone number, she was surprised to discover numerous texts from Fergie. Rather than reading through them all, she unmuted her phone and phoned Fergie directly.

But Lizbeth answered, against a clamorous backdrop of voices. "Fergie's in a code," she explained. "She asked me to hold on to her cell and pick up if it was you." She turned to Fergie who was performing chest compressions on a patient, and she silently mouthed, "Nora."

Fergie shook her head. *What rotten timing for Nora to finally call!*

"Wait," Nora said. "I thought Fergie had the day off."

"She did," Lizbeth said. "But then Edna didn't show up this morning. And we can't get hold of her. The police didn't find her at home, and she left her cap in my locker."

"I'm ... stunned," said Nora. "And worried."

"Yeah. Fergie *really* wants to talk with you about all this."

"Any idea when she'll be freed up?"

"It could be a while. She's in charge today, and just minutes into this code. We also received an MVA a couple hours ago."

Regretting her inaccessibility all morning and hoping that Fergie remembered the reason for it, Nora said, "Will you please tell Fergie my cellphone's back on? And that I'll soon be heading to the prison to visit Jack."

After signing off with Lizbeth, Nora scrolled through Fergie's texts. They lacked explicit content, but all brimmed with urgency: *CALL ME ... PLEASE ... ASAP ... STAT ...*

Fergie's amped-up texts and Lizbeth's troubling news instantly ejected Nora from any serenity she'd harvested from her morning experiences. Now she felt as anxious and fearful as she'd felt last night. And hearing that Edna may have gone missing, she was further convinced of her burgeoning theory, and more unnervingly certain that Edna was an integral part of the big picture.

Pacing the Chapel lot, she waited to hear from Fergie. But the unrelenting auditory assaults only aggravated her more—the zooming cars, barking dogs, muffler-deficient motorcycles, constant jet noise. She sought refuge inside her car and turned on the news. But hysterical squawking political pundits just made everything worse. Finally, her phone rang and she automatically picked up. "Fergie?"

"Uh, no. Just me. Fred."

"Oh. Sorry. I'm a little wound up."

"Yeah," he said. "I imagine your morning was hard. I wish I could've accompanied you."

"You know what Lydia's wishes were."

"I do, Nora. But that doesn't mean I have to like them."

"So, you're calling about our road trip today?" She searched the glove compartment for Little Shin Shin's takeout menu.

"Yeah. But I also wanted to know how you were doing after the cemetery. And whether you decided to see Jack. I put you on his visitors list in case."

"Good. So, yeah, let's see him together. But I don't want to talk with you about scattering Lydia's ashes. Not until I'm ready. Would you be okay with that during the drive?"

Fred hesitated. "Can't say I'd be okay with it, but I can accept it."

"Deal. Besides, there are lots of things—upsetting ones—I'd like to talk about with you."

"I'm in. And, look, I know it's earlier than 'noonish' like we planned, but could we leave now? I'd like to get ahead of bridge traffic. Things have come up at the hospital that I need to contend with this afternoon. So how 'bout I swing by your house and pick you up in 15?"

Nora looked longingly up Piedmont Avenue. "Sure," she said, returning Little Shin Shin's menu to the glove compartment. "I'll be waiting outside the house."

"Great," he said, "and I'm starving. I'll pick us up a couple of quarter-pounders at the drive-through. We can eat in the car."

Fred's Car

Westbound, Richmond Bridge

11:45 A.M.

Midway across the Richmond Bridge, en route to San Sebastian Prison, Fred noted Nora's untouched hamburger and asked, "You going to eat that?"

"It's yours," Nora said, positioning it within his reach. "I lost my appetite."

"Sorry, but thanks all the same. I've been fast-fooding meals since Vickie kicked me out."

"I told you that you could stay with me. Use the kitchen; make proper meals."

He shook his head. "It's a nice break, actually—staying in a hotel. Someone cleans up after you, no surly kids staring you down at dinner while your wife looks at you sideways. And besides; lately, you're even tenser than me. Can't be around that."

"Yeah, well. So many upsetting things are happening."

"All right now, a little tough love? You took on some of that *voluntarily*. I warned you not to get involved in Cheryl's case, Miz Nancy Drew. Miz Jessica Fletcher."

"DCI Jane Tennison, please. And besides, it's the other way around—Cheryl's case involved me."

"What's that supposed to mean?"

Nora fidgeted, wondering how to communicate her evolving theory. There were so many pieces to the puzzle, each one still shape-shifting. How could she configure a cohesive picture for Fred? "I mean, it not only captures my interest. It also *actually* involves me. And you. And Lydia, Richard, and Jack. And now with Edna gone missing—"

Fred nearly choked. "Edna . . . missing?"

Nora waited for him to stop coughing, meanwhile studying his profile—his face bruised, its wounds just beginning to heal. "I just learned that from Lizbeth, Edna's student. Remember her?"

He nodded, and she said, "I spoke with her minutes before you picked me up. Apparently, Edna didn't show up for work. And she gave no notice."

"Is Edna all right?" He gestured for some fries.

Nora dumped fries into a paper cup and placed it in the console cupholder. "I'm doubtful, because the police didn't find her at home, and Lizbeth found Edna's cap in her locker this morning."

Fred's eyes widened. "Hell, no! Edna's gone AWOL? This news is giving me a heart attack."

"Maybe it's all this vascular-clogging food you're eating."

He returned the fries and said, "Now I'm losing my appetite. And tell me, why the hell would Edna just disappear?"

"Don't know. But she finds that caduceus and . . . then she disappears."

"You're suggesting she was scared off?"

"Fred, you saw how riled up she was after finding it. And, remember: now knowing that the AccuStent was stolen, Cheryl's case becomes an official *murder* investigation once she's pronounced dead."

"Hell. So . . . someone threatened Edna? Or retaliated against her for finding it?"

"I don't know. The puzzle keeps getting bigger, with new pieces falling from the sky. And I'd like to discuss all of that with you, but I don't know where to start."

"Well, then, start from where we were—on Cheryl's case."

She looked apprehensively at him. "But I'm also concerned about your ability to drive. I hear your asthma kicking up already."

"Just hand me my inhaler from the glove compartment."

After Fred took a puff from his bronchodilator, Nora said, "So, I had a weird phone conversation with Carl yesterday. It was like talking with someone through spastic cell towers, except the disconnects felt . . . so human. Anyhow, when I told him about Edna finding that caduceus—"

"You told him? What is this, Amateur Detective Week? Really, this free-for-all is going to be the death of me."

"Don't worry. You're traveling with an ER doc. I'll do CPR if you're nice to me."

After a dramatic sigh, Fred said, "For health reasons, I'm going to remain calm, no matter what you say. But that won't last long, so hurry up."

"As I was saying," Nora continued. "Carl said he'd seen only two docs wearing a caduceus at the hospital. One is Syd Fein who would've keeled over and died if he'd lost his."

"It's pinned to his aorta," Fred said.

Smiling, Nora said, "Yeah, but the second is Rosalie Karlov."

Fred cleared his throat. "Now that's definitely fishy. And isn't Rosalie awfully young to wear one? Besides, this *alleged* clue of Edna's is possibly a red herring. I mean, didn't every doctor receive one of those cad— Oh hell, is it *cadu-cee-i* or *cadu-ce-us-ses*? What's the plural? Anyway, we all got one from some drug company when we graduated from med school. There must be millions of those . . . caduceus pins floating around."

"Yeah, but they stopped giving those out ages ago. I gave my caduceus to Lydia's niece a couple of decades back. And, by the way, the plural is *caducei*." She peered out the window, wondering how to contain their mutually mounting anxiety. She decided to wait until they were off the road before revealing her theory about their gang-of-six photo and the ominous bigger picture she saw developing.

But then Fred asked, "How are you putting things together?" And the longer he waited for her response, the antsier he became. His car even veered into an adjacent lane. After she released her white-knuckled grip on the dashboard, he pleaded, "Just tell me what you're thinking."

"I'd rather wait until you're not driving! Besides, I'd like to be calm—and *alive*—when I visit Jack."

"You're right," he said, patting her hand. Finding it sticky with ketchup, he feigned a look of revulsion that made her smile.

Nora took hold of his hand, and they proceeded silently across the bridge. All the while, Fred imagined Lydia's ashes floating forever away from him. He surprised himself when he blurted out, "I wish I hadn't confronted Lydia about those damn phone calls and that envelope."

"Don't go there now," Nora said, feeling more certain about his inability to tolerate the discussion she wished to share. And yet, there he was, suffering an atrocity that someone else had so artfully staged with intention to destroy his life. "Fred," she said, "there's so much we need to talk about. But I'm afraid to do that while you're driving, *and* thinking of Lydia, *and* struggling with asthma."

"Should I take another puff?" he said half-jokingly.

"No. You're already overusing your inhaler, and that's only making you more jittery."

"Please give me some idea about this 'puzzle' and how you're working it."

Nora sighed. "Okay. The missing puzzle piece is that 1990 photograph of our old gang of six, but with Richard and Edna included. I have a theory about what's happening to everyone. But my theory's going to upset you."

Fred gripped the steering wheel. "I can take it. Besides, it'll be worse if you don't talk."

This time, Nora decided to begin the conversation where Fred's attention had already alighted—on his guilt about Lydia. "So," she began, "that sick bastard behind the calls and deliveries to your home? I think it's the same person who is responsible for *all* the other tragedies."

Fred glanced at her. She was looking at him with that sad and certain expression that he intimately knew. She was going to tell him something difficult that she both knew and felt to be true, and she was going to be right. "That look on your face," he said, all bravado gone. "I know that look, and it's freaking me out. So, just give me the damn inhaler and start talking."

Curbside

Oakland International Airport

12:20 P.M.

The cab driver set down Edna's suitcases and said, "Have a safe trip, Mrs. Johnson."

Handing him the fare, Edna said, "Thanks for accommodating me today."

"My pleasure," he said. "I'm happy you had a good visit with your nephew in prison. And you got your important envelope in the mail! Now, I hope you will have a blessed visit with your grandchildren in Boise."

Edna entered the airport terminal and waited for the cab to disappear. Then she exited the building and walked to the taxi stand.

"Where you going, ma'am?" the driver asked.

"San Jose, please."

"Great! A good fare for me."

Minutes later, they were driving south on 880. The driver asked, "So, your flight only took you to Oakland? You could not connect through San Jose?"

"Unfortunately."

He nodded. "Are you visiting family in San Jose? Friends?"

"Both."

The driver looked at her through the rearview. "It's going to be a long ride. My name is Ezra."

"Mine is Florence," she said.

The driver smiled. "Oh, Florence. Like in Italy. Or like that nurse, Nightingale."

"Yes," Edna said. "Something like that."

Parking Lot, San Sebastian State Prison

Marin County

12:20 P.M.

After clearing the security gate to San Sebastian State Prison, Fred parked his car in the visitors' lot and slumped into his seat. "Well, that was a helluva ride, Nora. I'm wiped out. And it's a helluva theory you're proposing. It scares me to think about it."

"Do you think I might be right?" asked Nora.

"That's what's so scary," he said. "It makes sense in a dark, creepy-crawly way."

Pointing to the prison, she said, "Then, Jack being in there? We failed him, Fred. We missed something. Something we couldn't—or wouldn't—see when he was being set up."

"Hold on. Just because your theory makes sense, doesn't make it true. I mean, maybe it is. Or maybe only parts of it are. But you have no proof of Jack's troubles being—what's the word you're using?—*staged*. And remember: many smart people worked on his case. His own lawyers plea-bargained on his behalf and, well, the alternative allegations against him were even worse."

"But it was a Sophie's choice, I think. Jack was forced to make a pain-ful and impossible choice between two untenable options."

Fred sighed and patted Nora's sticky hand. "After all we've been through today and this entire week, we shouldn't be guilt-tripping ourselves—*and each other*—over Jack's situation right now. And we shouldn't be getting hotter under the collar just before visiting him. C'mon. We'll talk more about everything on the drive back. And P.S., wipe your hands before you go inside, or the guards will think you've got blood on them."

Wiping ketchup off her fingers, Nora asked, "You scheduled our visit for 12:30?"

Fred smiled affectionately and said, "Yeah. But how about you and Jack take some private time first?"

"I don't think so. I'm nervous enough."

"C'mon. It'll be good for you both. It's way overdue, and I just visited him last Thursday. Besides, today is a special day. It's Let-Everything-Happen-All-at-Once Day!"

Nora smiled faintly. "And Amateur Detective Week, too?"

"That's right. Wasn't sure you'd been listening to me."

Nora didn't budge.

Fred begged, "Do it for me? Seriously, I could use a moment to myself right now."

When Nora looked contrarily back, he returned a familiar expression that always won her over. His endearing grin and kind eyes pierced her resistance.

"Thanks," he said, recognizing her surrender. "Hey, maybe you two could start off talking about that photo you printed out for him. Reminisce together a little. Find a way back into your friendship."

"Stop nagging, Fred! You won." Nora pocketed her ID but stuffed her phone into the glove compartment to avoid its confiscation by prison security. "But 15 minutes, *tops*. Promise?"

"Yes. Look, it's near 12:25. So go on in and register. I'll be at your side in 15."

Fred watched Nora walk toward the visitors' entrance. He noted that she'd lost a little height over time, but her stride remained strong and graceful. It reminded him of a day long ago when he and Jack marched behind Nora and Lydia to the state capitol, protesting inadequate funding for AIDS patients. *Was that 1988? Maybe '89?*

He reclined the car seat, sank into it, and finally let down. And when he closed his eyes, he envisioned Lydia. She was so timelessly present inside him, so excruciatingly alive.

Rosalie's Office

Carl Kluft—childhood prodigy, endowed with a photographic memory, the guy with perfect SAT and MCAT scores—could effortlessly recall the names and dosages of every medication his wife received in the ICU. He knew her every recorded temperature and weight throughout her hospitalization. He could recite her serial oxygen sats to the first decimal point. He remembered results for each blood test, x-ray, MRI, and CAT scan that she'd undergone.

But presently, as he strode through the hospital corridors, those data dropped out of mind as he zealously pursued a single-minded mission: to contribute whatever he could to make any legitimate sense of his wife's baffling predicament. Damn the unsolvable mysteries of life and death beyond his—or anyone's—knowing. Damn the impossible and illogical decisions he was supposed to make on Cheryl's so-called behalf. Damn the irrational terrain of the ICU.

He'd wasted so much precious time trying to decipher the philosophical and biological underpinnings of Cheryl's condition, and that had taken a toll on his ability to further abide the surreal and illogical. However, having just received Fergie's texted photo of the caduceus, he now knew that he was able to answer at least one earthbound question to shed real light on his wife's predicament. He would determine with certainty to whom the caduceus belonged. And, using logic, he'd decipher the meaning—and the likely problem—of that determination.

Alone in the elevator, he saw his haggard reflection in the sliding chrome doors. He watched his visage pull apart like taffy when they slid open to deliver him to the third floor.

Upon entering the hallway, he ran into Stuey Holgren, a colleague from Ortho, who was rushing in the opposite direction, a broad grin on his cherubic face. In passing, he slapped Carl on the back and said, "Kluft! Did you see that third-quarter blitz last night? Warriors 109, Kings 86!"

Carl had no idea what Holgren meant to convey. By the time he turned around to inquire, Holgren was already bounding up a stairwell.

Finally at his destination, Carl scanned the interior of Rosalie's office. Its every detail was immediately imprinted on his memory. The desk drawers were opened haphazardly, exposing chaotic arrangements of office supplies. The books were shelved in no discernible order. The closet was in upheaval . . .

But only one detail genuinely concerned him. And for that, he needed to examine Rosalie's five white coats—the five, standard-issue hospital coats each doctor received with their name emblazoned above the hospital's logo.

He noted the coat that lay rumpled on her desk and examined it first. On top of it rested a yellowed *New Yorker* cartoon that he picked up and read. Unable to divine its humor, he turned his attention to the coat, immediately detecting the scent of his wife's perfume. *This coat*, he confidently deduced, *was the coat Rosalie was wearing on Sunday night when she accompanied Cheryl to her research office.* Indeed, when he flipped over the coat's left lapel, there was no caduceus—just as he'd predicted after viewing Fergie's photo.

Although he knew it provided only superfluous confirmation, he checked Rosalie's four other coats hanging inside the closet. And, as expected, none was pinned with her caduceus.

Holding the coat fragranced with Cheryl's perfume, Carl felt happy for the first time in days. Now he'd found a way to speak up for Cheryl in pursuit of clarity and justice in her case. Now he could help to anchor whatever had happened to her in concrete fact.

He wished he could tell Cheryl directly: *The caduceus discovered in your office belongs to Rosalie. But the problem that obviously creates—*

"Excuse me?" someone said. A pinch-faced woman in floral scrubs stood in the doorway. "You can't be here!"

"But I'm actually here," Carl countered. He would no longer abide the hospital's customary charade.

The woman's eyes widened. "Dr. Kluft, is that *you?*"

"Yes."

"I'm sorry. I didn't recognize you. That beard and—"

"Where is Dr. Rosalie Karlov?"

"Believe me, we all wish we knew."

"Thank you, but I'm not seeking anyone's belief or wish concerning a *fact*." He relaunched his questioning from Step Three of the "Being Clear" communication template, slowly enunciating each word: "Do . . . you . . . *know* . . . where . . . Dr. Karlov . . . is?"

"Well, no . . ."

"Thank you for answering my actual question," he said, discharging her. Then he phoned Nora. She'd want to know what he discovered so that sensible conclusions would be drawn about the caduceus. But an automated greeting instructed him to leave a voicemail. He said, "Nora, this is Carl Kluft calling from the hospital. Call me back when you receive this." He remembered to add, "Please. And thank you."

ER

Oakland City Hospital

ABOUT NOON

As usual, there were too many patients and too few nurses. So many alarms and buzzers were sounding at once that it was hard to tease them apart and prioritize. Fergie's wrists ached from performing CPR, and the face of her patient—who was surely already dead on arrival—haunted her with his wide-eyed stare into the afterlife the entire time she compressed his chest.

Now, while struggling to insert an IV into a septic patient's foot, she was approached by a piqued surgical resident. He said, "The coffee pot's empty."

Fergie spent her last nerve on maintaining a civil tone. She said, "Then make a new pot." The resident rolled his eyes and left.

"Wow," said Lizbeth, impressed in equal measure by Fergie's deft handling of the resident and her skill in threading a needle into a patient's miniscule toe vein.

"Well, I'm not conflicted about who I'm serving," said Fergie. "A patient needing an IV, or some able-bodied doc who wants coffee—no contest."

The patient—a 60ish-year-old woman who injected heroin—said, "Amen, sister!"

Using a copious amount of tape to secure the IV, Fergie said, "Okay, 'sister,' don't mess with this. You lose this IV, and we'll have to go through your neck vein like last time."

The patient told Lizbeth, "I always ask for Nurse Fergie when I come here. She can get an IV into a flea!"

"One of her many talents," Lizbeth said. "The fleas are grateful, too."

Lizbeth and Fergie headed back to the nurses station. It was 12:20 and, finally, ER chaos had dropped to a crazy-times-five level. Fergie was surprised by the amount of pain she felt throughout her body after all the lifting and standing and bending; after the rushing and reaching and turning of patients in beds. She asked Lizbeth, "Can you give me a minute to try to reach Nora before we pick up our conversation about Edna?"

"Of course," said Lizbeth, though anxious to convey her concerns. Then, watching Fergie turn more frustrated while getting no response from Nora, she offered, "From what she said earlier, Nora might be visiting at the prison now. And they don't allow visitors to hold onto their phones."

"You're probably right," Fergie said. "But of all freakin' days . . ."

And before Lizbeth could restart their conversation, Fergie abruptly turned to her and said, "You sure you never saw anything to suggest Edna was sick?"

"You asked me that before! I missed seeing something, right? She's sick?"

The immediacy and purity of Lizbeth's concern vanquished Fergie's fresh doubts about her. She replied, "No. It's just that Rosalie told me she was treating Edna for some serious illness. So, I've been worrying that might have something to do with Edna disappearing."

Flabbergasted, Lizbeth said, "That's funny! I mean, as in funny unbelievable. I'm sorry, Fergie, but there's *no way* Edna would be a patient of hers!"

Struck by the force of Lizbeth's conviction, Fergie said, "How can you be so sure?"

"Really?" said Lizbeth, surprised that Fergie seemed so oblivious. Because anyone who had paid the slightest attention to Edna and

Rosalie would've known. "I just mean, well . . . to be blunt? They *really* don't like each other. Edna can't stand to be around her." She grimaced. "I'm reluctant to use the word *hate*, but . . ."

Fergie searched her own recollections about Edna and Rosalie's relationship, but came up blank. "I guess I haven't been around them much when they've been together, or paid them any attention. So, help me understand. When you say they don't like each other—"

"Fergie, I don't like gossip. And I want to respect Edna and her privacy."

"Sure. But current circumstances are disturbing."

After brief deliberation, Lizbeth said, "I'm not as naïve as everyone here might think. It's just that I get flustered whenever I'm around Edna. And that only worsens whenever someone comes along to upset her, like Dr. Karlov always does—at lunches, patients' bedsides, meetings. Even at codes—remember Mr. Pulaski's last week?" She took a breath and continued, "But now I'm going to speak up, as I promised Edna I'd do the other day. I'm just going to say it: Dr. Karlov *has* to be lying about Edna being her patient. And if that's the case, then she's probably also lying about Edna being sick."

Lizbeth's shrewd remarks struck Fergie's mind like precision hammer blows. They nailed down a firm connection between Edna's abrupt disappearance and Rosalie's evident desperation to locate her. And they suggested why Rosalie had not called back.

"Lizbeth," Fergie said, "can you do me a favor *STAT*?"

"Yes."

"Can you run up to the third floor and see if Rosalie's in her clinic? Then phone me immediately when you know?"

"On it," Lizbeth said, heading to the stairwell.

Fergie leaned against the wall, imagining how radically different her day would've been had she listened to Winston this morning and not answered the phone. Yet her wistful contemplation proved brief. A text arrived, and it had to be Nora's.

But it wasn't. Instead, it came from Carl: *Thank you for forwarding the photo. That caduceus belongs to Rosalie Karlov.*

Fergie shuddered, and her brain spun. Now her cellphone rang, and Lizbeth reported, "Dr. Karlov is gone. They say she just walked out of her clinic without a word to anyone."

Visiting Room, San Sebastian State Prison

Marin County

12:30 P.M.

"Nora?" said Jack, feeling happy and tentative at once. "Fred said you might not come."

Nora's guilt acutely expanded when she looked through the glass partition and saw his sallow face and swollen eyes. He'd lost at least 20 pounds since she last saw him. "I'm sorry," she said.

"Sorry for . . .?"

Looking directly at him, Nora was reminded how much she had always loved to be held in his gaze. Her therapist's words rushed to mind: *You're afraid to see Jack because he reminds you of losing your family. And you can't face him until you can see him apart from that tragedy.* She said, "I'm sorry for not seeing you. Literally, as well as . . ."

"I know," he said. "Take a deep breath. I'm just glad you're here."

Though the anguish in his eyes was excruciating to bear, Nora held his gaze. She silently held it until she saw only him and no fatal fist of water hovering above his shoulder, snatching away her family. Finally, she smiled and said, "I'm glad, too. But you don't look well. Are you all right?"

So much had happened since he last spoke with Nora: Richard's death and Lydia's, his trial and ongoing appeals, and Edna's shocking revelation of her treachery just an hour ago. He said, "I'm not all right, Nora. But I don't know where to start."

"Then I will," she said. "I was wrong to abandon you and our friendship. I knew it made no sense—no *logical* sense. But on some twisted level, I blamed you for being there that day and for suggesting we take that walk on the beach, separating me from my family when they . . . they were taken from me."

"I understand," he said, wishing they could hold one another now. He waited for her to calm before tenderly suggesting, "And maybe for you not dying with them?"

Nora nodded, unable to speak.

Jack whispered, "Just so you know, I'm maintaining hope that someday you'll be grateful for surviving."

Nora vigorously shook her head.

"Well, *I'm* grateful for it," he said. "And as we both know, I'm always ahead of you on the learning curve."

Nora laughed, "Not!" After wiping her tears, she reentered his gaze and said, "So, anything new with you?"

Her question ignited a barrage of laughter—guarded for a nanosecond, unrestrained the next.

Parking Lot, San Sebastian State Prison

Marin County

12:30 P.M.

Fred's opportunity for solitude proved brief. Thinking about Lydia had only released a powerful flood of feelings and memories. And Nora's disturbing theory increasingly filled him with dread. He prayed that, by the time he joined Nora and Jack, they would have worked through any emotional upheaval in their reconnecting. *I can't accommodate any more drama today.*

To aggravate matters, Nora's hyperactive cell was ringing *repeatedly*. "It's her goddamn day off, people!" he yelled, grabbing her phone to mute its ringer.

But then he noted multiple unanswered texts from Fergie and a voicemail message from Carl. "What's so damn important?" he asked.

And yet, he knew that, on a day like today, the correct answer was, "A helluva lot."

So, he decided to text Fergie before Nora's phone time-locked off: *Fred here. Holding Nora's phone while she's in prison.* He amended that to: *while she visits Jack in prison. Do I need 2 get her 4 U now?*

A pause. Then Fergie texted: *No, but ASAP.* A second text immediately followed: *U should both know Carl ID'd caduceus. Belongs 2 Rosalie. Who is also gone missing. Thx*

"What the hell?" Fred exclaimed, reaching for his inhaler.

Cheryl's Room, ICU

Oakland City Hospital

12:40 P.M.

Carl returned from Rosalie's office, sat at Cheryl's bedside, and waited for Nora's call. He felt so good about contributing information that would guide everyone closer to the truth of Cheryl's predicament. And how pleasing it felt to be collaborating again with his old friend Nora!

He stared at Cheryl—now on day four of her unalive yet undead state—and guiltily recounted the prior evening. It was mistake—he knew that now—to stop at home with Peter's urging, to check the mail, shower and shave, and get a restorative night's sleep away from the ICU.

In fact, none of those things transpired during his brief 10-minute stopover.

Instead, the moment he had walked into the house, he tasted life without Cheryl in it. And its shocking sweetness terrified him. He felt wrong—perhaps even evil—to savor it, but his experience was automatic and unbidden. *Still, a normal person who'd lost his spouse should have experienced bitterness and sorrow.*

And, then ... discovering *all that room to breathe*! He took in the 4,236 square feet of living space inside their home that was suddenly released to him alone!

Overwhelmed and disturbed, within 10 minutes he was fleeing back to the ICU.

A nurse approached him now and said, "Dr. Yuen just left this bag for you. You were out when he stopped by."

"Thanks," Carl said, regretting that his excursion to Rosalie's office had cost him the feel of Peter's comforting hand on his shoulder. Opening the bag, he found a note, coffee, and the Tony Soprano special from Ike's Place that was stacked with provolone, ham, turkey, and salami.

The note read, "Carl, don't forget to eat."

Peter is right, he thought. *I should program reminders to eat into my daily calendar.*

He removed the coffee lid and watched steamy tendrils coil around the cup.

He thought about *The Five Stages of Grief* and realized he had unevenly skipped over them.

He studied his wife's body, hoping she was agreeably freed of it. And he apologized for having all the living space he discovered last night, while she no longer had any.

Parking Lot, San Sebastian State Prison

Marin County

12:40 P.M.

Fred stepped out of the car on his way to join Nora and Jack, but he was surprised to see Nora sprinting toward him with a vexed expression on her face. "Get back into the car!" she shouted. Before he could say anything, she took the passenger's seat and commanded, "Let's go!"

"What?"

"Fred, just drive!"

"Did Jack upset you?"

Nora scoffed. "Yeah, but for reasons you'd never imagine in a million years."

"So, I'm not visiting Jack? But I promised him—"

"Damn it, Fred! Jack doesn't *need* your visit now. We need to get back to the hospital!"

Fred switched on the ignition. "This is fishy. I don't like it one bit. And, by the way, you received some interesting texts while you were gone. I've got things to tell *you!*"

"I don't like this either. But we can't do anything here! And I can't think freely in a *prison* lot, with all these guards and guns."

"All right now," Fred obliged. But once they drove past the security gate, he demanded, "What the hell's going on?"

Nora cupped her hands around her head as if trying to keep information in mind. "Please, give me a minute. I need to concentrate . . . to remember everything Jack just told me. There was so much to take in."

"Hell," Fred grumbled, his angst mounting as he headed the car toward Oakland. After minutes transpired and they had comfortably entered a moving stream of bridge traffic, he said, "C'mon now. You've had *minutes* to remember and think. What happened, Nora?"

"Too much," she said, worried that Jack's reports of Edna's treachery would flip him out and risk their safe return. Hoping to stall the discussion, she reprised an increasingly topical refrain: "I don't even know where to start."

Fred blurted out, "Okay, then, here's a start! One: Rosalie just walked out of clinic. Two: nobody knows where she went. Three: Carl identified the caduceus as belonging to Rosalie."

But his rapid-fire reports whizzed by—*whoosh, whoosh, whoosh*—like bullets. "Slow down," Nora said. "Say again?"

"It was *Rosalie's* brooch, Nora! And now Rosalie's gone missing, too! So there has to be some connection with Edna."

Nora thought, *This—whatever this is—is getting way out of hand. And what could Rosalie possibly have to do with Edna?* She checked her memory but couldn't recall Jack mentioning Rosalie even once while recounting Edna's confessions.

Fred said, "Hello?"

"Sorry," she said. "Yes, there seems to be some connection between Edna and Rosalie."

"And that connection is circling around that caduceus and Cheryl's murder."

Nora said, baffled, "I've known Rosalie since her residency. I can't believe she'd be involved in anything . . . 'fishy,' as you'd say."

Fred hissed. "Listen: your Rosalie is no saint. She's troubled, if you ask me; scary troubled. She actually freaked me out in my office on Sunday. She's been acting . . . imperious. Self-righteous. Angry."

Nora felt the blood drain from her face as she looked out to the choppy Bay waters coursing toward the bridge. She could partly concede Fred's point—Rosalie may have been acting more confrontational and judgmental recently. But everyone at work had been stressed by the deaths, the drug and financial scandals, and the hospital's damning publicity. "Maybe you're right," she replied. "But *you* may be judging *her* harshly now. Work's been rough, and Rosalie is struggling financially. And, well, she could act a little high-and-mighty, but maybe from a moral battleground that neither of us fully appreciates."

"Well, that's mighty empathic of you. Maybe too much so. Still, I'm telling you, you should've seen her in my office. And you don't just walk out on your patients. Is she out tracking Edna down, or maybe fleeing to her family?"

"Her entire family's gone, Fred."

"Oh. Where were they from?"

"I'm not sure. She can only ever go so far in talking about them. It's too painful for her."

"Well, whatever. Just so you know, while you were visiting Jack, I called admin and legal after getting Fergie's text. *They* can start connecting the dots between Edna and Rosalie before we get back. With all the chaos at the hospital, we can use any help we can get." He cleared his throat. "Yes, I'll admit I'm even grateful for yours."

But now Nora realized that the longer she withheld Jack's news, the greater the risk of Fred first learning it from police or admin. She said, "Look, Jack had a lot to say. But I'm afraid to excite you while you're driving—"

"We've already been through this today—excited about what?"

Nora cringed. "About what Edna confessed to Jack this afternoon."

"What?! Edna contacted him today?"

"Yes."

"Does Jack know where she is?"

"No."

"Don't make me play 20 questions, Nora!"

"All right. Edna had been visiting Jack just minutes before we arrived."

Fred's wheezing revved up.

Nora said, "He's contacted his lawyer, hoping they can catch Edna before she—"

"Wait! He's hoping they'll 'catch Edna'?"

Nora nodded.

"Hand me my inhaler," Fred said, his foot pressing the accelerator, "and start talking, Nora."

Nurses' Locker Room, ER

Oakland City Hospital

AFTERNOON

"Thanks," Lizbeth said, handing Edna's cap to Fergie. "Holding onto this just makes me sad."

"No problem," Fergie said as they entered the nurses' locker room. "I can't even remember the last time I used my locker."

But when they walked past Edna's locker, Lizbeth stopped and said, "That's weird. I'm sure Edna's locker was closed this morning; locked, in fact." She pointed to her own, several feet away, and said, "That one's mine, and when I found Edna's cap inside it today, well . . . I just hoped that she'd misplaced it, given her distress. But when I tried to return it to her locker, like I said, it was *locked*."

"That is weird," Fergie said, examining Edna's opened locker. "And these dents along the door—it looks like someone might've pried it open."

"But you're head nurse today. Wouldn't admin or police have to inform you before they did something like that?"

"That would be protocol. But maybe it wasn't them. Or maybe this went straight through the higher-ups." But as Fergie closed the locker, her suspicions about Lizbeth boomeranged back. Because, yet again, here was Lizbeth "happening upon" ostensible evidence in the volcanic center of Edna's evolving story. In a spasm of paranoia, Fergie wondered whether Lizbeth had tricked her into leaving fingerprints on Edna's locker. Testing the waters, she said, "If this break-in is illicit, I'm an idiot for leaving my fingerprints all over this door."

But then Lizbeth surprised her by planting her own prints all over the locker. "It's not CSI," she said. "But it's evidence supporting that we took a look-see together, if needed."

Fergie smiled uneasily. "Well, I'll call security and report on Edna's locker after we store her cap in mine."

But when they arrived at Fergie's old locker, Lizbeth was discomforted to note the absence of a padlock. "Maybe this isn't such a great place for safekeeping?"

"Don't worry," Fergie said. "We'll add a padlock. There's a bunch of them in the supply room, though you'll never guess what they're filed under." Opening her old locker, she said, "I can't remember what's inside here. You interested in nursing journals from the last century?"

"No, thanks. I'm—"

"What the fuck?" Fergie said, withdrawing a thick envelope on which was written: "*To S. J. Ferguson. Confidential. Edna Atkinson.*"

"Hey, Edna left something for you, too," Lizbeth said. "But is that her handwriting?"

"Don't know. I've forgotten what that looks like. It's been so long since she—anyone—gave me something handwritten." She unclasped the envelope and withdrew three stacks of documents that she placed on a nearby bench. After inspecting them a while, Lizbeth said, "Look: this stack contains duplicated documents—all doctors' orders and narcotics prescriptions. The originals are paired with altered copies."

"Holy shit," Fergie said. "And they've got Jack Griffin's signature on them, with Edna cosigning. This stack I'm holding contains hospice records and Medicare billings—originals paired with doctored copies, too."

They examined the third stack together; spreadsheets containing numbers, many highlighted or circled in red. Lizbeth pointed to a reference key and said, "It looks like they're tracking money. It's hundreds of thousands, no, *millions* of dollars."

Slack-jawed, Fergie said, "Why would Edna give me these documents? And why would she possess them in the first place?"

Lizbeth shuddered. "They seem to be shouting 'dishonesty' about narcotics and hospice. Hospital billing, too."

"And they're shouting out a connection between Edna and Jack," Fergie said.

Lizbeth took deep breath. "And maybe Mr. Pulaski's death, too. These manipulated hospice and Medicare billings ... maybe he didn't even know about them. Maybe he was being blamed for someone else's dishonesty."

Fred's Car

Eastbound, Richmond Bridge

AFTERNOON

"You're right," Fred said. "I would've never guessed that Edna was selling drugs in a million years ... *two* million years. And, my god—what she did to Jack."

"You really should let me drive," Nora said. His asthma was flaring, and they'd already slowed to 50 miles per hour, risky during rush hour traffic on the bridge.

"No. We're more than halfway there." He glanced sideways at Nora and said, "Things feel dangerous. There are too many bodies: in the grave, prison, missing. . . . And now I'm also worrying that you might've put Fergie and Carl in danger. You shouldn't be pulling people into this scary mess if you can't protect them."

Nora was shocked to consider that possibility. Her heart reflexively clenched around her guilt over not protecting Lydia.

He continued, "You should give your amateur detectives a heads-up about Edna and Rosalie. Fergie's tried to contact you a dozen times."

"But if I call her now, you'll probably overhear even more asthma-baiting news."

He waited expectantly until she relented and phoned Fergie.

"Well, it's about time," Fergie answered.

"Sorry," Nora said. "My phone was off at the cemetery and chapel. Then, while I was at the prison. And I've been trying to keep Fred calm while he's driving."

"Nora, it's been crazy-times-infinity here."

"Same here; I can't wait to *really* talk. Where are you?"

"The nurses' locker room, with Lizbeth. And it seems Edna left something behind, other than her cap: an envelope in my locker, addressed to me. It contains confidential documents that scream whistleblowing."

"Shit! I'll bet they're about . . ." Then, baffled, Nora said, "Wait. Edna wouldn't leave something for you in your locker. She would know you never used yours."

"That's right. We even kept it unlocked so the rotating per diems could use it."

Nora said, "If anyone placed documents in your locker, it must've been someone who doesn't know 'normal' for you and the nursing per diems."

Fergie glanced at Lizbeth, her suspicions rekindling. "Nora, I wish you were here. It's hard to know who to trust." She turned her back to Lizbeth and whispered into the phone, "I kinda felt like I was being lead to those documents, and they're so radioactive. They're all cooked—prescription drug and hospice data, Medicare billings, and patients' records. And Jack and Edna's signatures are all over them."

Nora stifled a gasp and said, "Look, Edna was visiting Jack just minutes before we arrived. She confessed to him that she'd been selling prescription drugs—mostly narcotics. But she got them by forging his prescriptions, doctoring his orders, and manipulating patient records. She diverted narcotics from the hospice program, too. And when someone turned the heat on her, she blamed everything on Jack. She lied when she secretly informed authorities he was sidelining narcotics so he could provide PAS to patients. He took a plea bargain, accepting responsibility for Benny's death in exchange for getting most of the charges dropped."

An overlong silence followed. Nora said, "Fergie . . . are you there?"

"Yeah, I'm just trying to wrap my mind around what you said about Edna."

"I'll fill you in when we get back," Nora said, anxiously watching Fred reach yet again for his emptied inhaler. "But we *literally* need to take a breather over here. I shouldn't say much more, but I can listen."

"Got it," Fergie said. "But I mostly have questions. Like, why would Edna be confessing now, after so much time *and* so close to her retirement?"

"Agreed—odd. Something, or someone, must be forcing her hand."

"You got my text about Carl identifying the caduceus as Rosalie's, right? And then Rosalie disappearing, too?"

"Yes," Nora said. "Fred told me. And, for the life of me . . ." She paused, chilled, regretting her choice of words. "I don't know how that links to Edna. But it must."

"Do we know where Edna was heading after visiting Jack? My knucklehead husband went to her house this morning and said it was shut down—like Edna had planned to leave."

Now also worried about having put Winston in harm's way, Nora said, "Winston should stay out of this."

Overhearing Nora's comment, Fred groaned. "*Another* amateur detective?"

Fergie said, "Yeah, well, I was alone all day with this shit, Nora! *And* in charge of ER. Win called me while I was in the freakin' supply room and couldn't get hold of you."

"Sorry!"

"And I never *asked* Win to go there."

"Again, sorry. Please?"

Fergie sighed and said, "Okay. So, how do we put this together? Edna flees after finding Rosalie's caduceus in Cheryl's office, and she comes clean with Jack. Then Rosalie goes missing. Do you think—what?— Rosalie is trying to track Edna down, hoping to get her caduceus back? Maybe she even broke into Edna's locker, looking for it?"

"I suppose that's possible," Nora said, dismayed by Fred's increasingly labored breathing.

"It would explain why Rosalie's been trying so hard to locate Edna. She even lied about Edna's health and being her doctor."

Trying to contain her shock, Nora said, "I didn't know about that. And, look, we've got lots of information to share, but Fred's breathing is worsening. We should be at the hospital in about 15 minutes. I promise to text you the moment we arrive so we can really talk."

"Can't wait," Fergie said. "I think you'll be particularly interested to hear about the bad blood between Edna and Rosalie. I got an earful from Lizbeth today." She was distracted by Lizbeth waving at her but held up a finger to indicate "Wait." She whispered to Nora, "And I think Rosalie freaked out when she heard about Edna finding the brooch, thanks to my loose lips. It points the finger at Rosalie for the theft of that stent and—"

"Fergie, please!" Lizbeth called out.

Nora asked, "Did I overhear Lizbeth?"

"Yeah, she's still here," Fergie said, and turning to Lizbeth she discovered Rosalie standing nearby, glaring furiously at her.

"Fergie? You there?" Nora asked.

"Fuck," Fergie said, exchanging nervous looks with Lizbeth.

Lizbeth said, "Sorry! I was trying to get your attention."

Fergie told Nora, "I gotta go. Bye."

Nora's phone disconnected.

"Well, that was odd," Nora told Fred.

Fred grimaced and said, "Tell me something that *isn't* odd today."

Cellblock 47, San Sebastian State Prison

Marin County

AFTERNOON

Jack lay restless on his bunk, his mind weaving unstable thought patterns from numerous loose threads. He was livid about Edna and anxious for his lawyer to call back. He was grateful for Nora's visit, but disturbed by her theory of lurking menace. While staring at his outdated chart of the periodic table hanging on the wall, he reenvisioned the gang-of-six photo that Nora showed him today.

The guards could've allowed her to leave it with me.

Neon, sodium, magnesium . . .

In the moment, there was nothing he could do about Edna's treachery, or about an appeal, or about getting out of this damn prison and reclaiming his life.

. . . sulfur, chlorine, argon . . .

Nora's visit shifted to the forefront of his mind. He could hear her voice again, clear and conversant with his own.

He tried to recall her interpretation of the photo. But her words were often lost to his overwhelming emotions during their hurried visit. Now he began to unpack them from their urgent presentation . . .

She connected my imprisonment to the deaths of Richard, Lydia, and Cheryl, and to the troubles inflicted on Fred and Carl.

. . . titanium, vanadium . . .

He tried hard to reconstruct the photo itself.

Nora thinks someone is victimizing everyone associated with this photo. If she's right . . .

"No!" he shouted. "Impossible!" *If Nora is right, then even Edna is a victim, too.* "But that can't be true, because I only want to strangle her!"

He paced his cell, trying to discharge his outrage.

But if I trust Nora . . . trust her theory . . .

He recalled the day the photo was taken. They were six colleagues, gathered in the ER on their last day of residency, waiting on Nora to disengage from her final patient. He was trying to coax Nora away from that patient. Lydia and Fred were struggling to herd everyone out to a celebration at Trader Vic's. The Klufts were being the Klufts. Edna was, as always, in the background. And Richard—the future love of his life—miraculously appeared.

What am I missing in this picture?

. . . iridium, platinum, gold . . .

He stared again at the periodic table, wondering how everyone associated with the photo could fit into some unified field of endangerment.

. . . silver, cadmium, indium . . .

He tried to recall the names of the four new elements that had been added to the periodic table last December. Even the TV science reporter had trouble pronouncing—

A bolt of insight struck him, and he cried out, "Of course!" Suddenly, it was so obvious; *so elementary*.

He rattled his cell door and shouted, "I need to make a call!"

Nurses' Locker Room, ER

Oakland City Hospital

AFTERNOON

"So," Rosalie said, her glare burning holes through Fergie's customary self-confidence. "You think I killed Cheryl? You think I was *stupid* enough to leave a piece of jewelry behind while I stole something from her office?"

"Wait. That's not—"

"I overheard you!" Rosalie fumed. "You should be ashamed! And believe me, I no longer care what you or Nora think about me. But you should know that I was looking for Edna because I knew *she stole* my pin and was using it to *frame* me!"

Lizbeth said, "Fergie, I was trying to tell you about Edna earlier! But things got so hectic. And we were supposed to talk about her later; now, actually. But not like this. And then her locker, and these documents . . ."

Rosalie turned ghostly pale and leaned against the wall for support.

"Lizbeth, what've you been trying to say?" Fergie asked.

"Dr. Karlov might be right about the caduceus and . . ." Her voice faltered.

"Take your time," Rosalie said.

Lizbeth finally managed, "Fergie, it was one of Edna's odd behaviors that I was wanting to tell. You know that day she and I went to Dr. Kluft's office? Well, I watched her reach into her pocket and take out a pair of gloves before she opened the stent box. But I also saw something small and shiny in her hand—it had to be that caduceus. And then she reached into the box and acted surprised, as if she found the caduceus inside it."

Rosalie appeared to almost faint, and Lizbeth said, "I'm so sorry! I thought it was strange! But I also trusted Edna had a good reason for whatever she was doing. We were each headed home afterward, so I planned to ask her about it the next morning. But then she wasn't around after the SMART meeting. And, honestly, Dr. Karlov, I had no idea the caduceus was so important. I didn't even know it was yours until you just said so."

Deeply ashamed, Fergie said, "Rosalie, I apologize—"

"Edna was framing me because I knew about her narcotics schemes and hospice fraud!" Rosalie yelled into Fergie's face, "I knew she was stealing drugs! I knew the lies she told to protect herself that put Jack in prison."

Fergie felt violently ill. She glanced at the confidential documents that, in retrospect, seemed to back Rosalie's claims. She stammered, "I . . . feel . . . terrible."

Jabbing her finger into Fergie's chest, Rosalie hammered, "I discovered Edna's drug scheme during my hospice rotation with her and Jack. I saw how she fudged prescriptions and medical records! And now she is trying to frame me—just like she framed Jack!"

Nurse Sarah June Ferguson was as unflappable as they come. Blood, gore, chaos, codes blue or black or red—nothing fazed her. But now she felt completely undone. Her solid self-assurance instantly dissolved, and her clear eyes clouded with doubt. She said, "I don't know how I could've been so oblivious. And stupid."

Lizbeth watched the unfolding drama, trying to hang onto her faith in Edna. But how could she do that now, as she was forced to consider Rosalie's claims?

Rosalie said, "Edna knows they are going to scrutinize the hospital's narcotic records because of Lydia. So she is afraid—as she should be!— that they will discover the truth about her *this* time. And she *knows* I am ready to tell them that truth!"

Rosalie took Lizbeth's hand and said, "Thank you for speaking up for *me*." Then she pivoted to Fergie and said, "But you? You were so eager to believe Edna's lies. You chose to condemn me; to disrespect me."

With evident humility, Fergie said, "I'm so freakin' sorry, Rosalie. I wish I'd known what Lizbeth had seen." She looked inquiringly at

Lizbeth, thinking, *She could have been more insistent in telling me about Edna's handling of the caduceus. She could have prevented this fiasco!*

Feeling responsible for the fallout, Lizbeth tried to create a distraction to defuse the tension. Remembering how Carl Kluft often succeeded in this endeavor by tossing a sideways comment or question into the minefield, she said, "Dr. Karlov, how could Edna have gotten hold of your brooch in the first place?"

Rosalie's reply was immediate; she had figured that out in her office earlier. "Edna removed it from my white coat on Sunday night while I slept in the on-call room. My coat was hanging on the door. I am sure she was not happy to find me there, especially after getting Fred to take me off ER call that very day."

Fergie haltingly said, "I don't know how to ask this without sounding inflammatory, and I don't want to cause more hard feelings. But, I don't understand how Edna framing you for Cheryl's *murder* would silence you about her *fraud*. How does that make sense?"

"I will not speak for Edna or her motives!" yelled Rosalie. "Edna is evil! You have all this evidence of that! I do not even want to *imagine* being inside her sick mind." She paced, calming a little, and said, "But she was one of the few people around who valued professional symbols. She knew I cared about mine. It should be obvious that Edna wanted to destroy me because I knew of her unethical behavior. Because I *did* have values. I *lived* my principles. She could not even stand to *see* me! Banning me from ER backup . . ." She turned to Lizbeth and said, "Thank you. The truth is important. It is all we have, really." She walked out of the locker room, taking Lizbeth with her.

Fergie felt thoroughly foolish and morally bankrupt; suddenly unmoored from her self-identity. In a single day, she had managed to misjudge so many people and to destroy her relationship with Rosalie. Most upsetting, she realized she'd lost sight of Edna, literally and figuratively. *How did I not notice Edna's huge dark world spinning so out of control?*

And why has Nora been so inaccessible throughout this day's many crises? And then, when we finally talk, our discussion prods me into disaster with Rosalie? She removed her bifocals and rubbed her eyes, her blurred vision symbolizing her sensation of internal distortion.

She increased the volume of her cell's ringer so as not to miss Nora's text upon her imminent arrival to the ER. It was critical to inform her of

Lizbeth's revelation about Edna planting Rosalie's caduceus, in addition to Rosalie's damning claims against Edna.

When Fergie replaced her glasses, she was surprised to see a woman standing before her with a sickly child in her arms. The woman said, "Excuse me, pero, are you a nurse?"

The inquiry jolted Fergie, externalizing the question that was emerging from her acute self-doubt. "Yes, I am," she finally said.

"Mi hija is sick," said the woman. "We have been waiting so long for help."

Fergie escorted them to an exam room. And upon entering it, she firmly reentered her old identity. Her self-doubt vanished when the relieved mother and child smiled at her, and she dropped into her old nursing groove with quiet, fierce delight. She realized that she belonged here at the bedside, not in the head nurse's office, and not on powerful hospital committees. And any lingering doubt about that was vanquished when the child looked wide-eyed at her while pointing to the tattoos on her arms—a V and an E on one, a half-heart on the other. With unfiltered glee, the child exclaimed, "See, Mama? I *can* still be a nurse if you let me get my tattoos!"

Cellblock 47, San Sebastian State Prison

Marin County

AFTERNOON

"Seriously, Griffin," Baldwin warned. "Shut the fuck up."

But Jack felt newly freed from the mental imprisonment to which he'd become inured. He repeated, "I need to make a call."

"You deaf now?"

"It's a life-and-death situation!"

"Look, Griffin, you already phoned your lawyer today, and you had *two* visitors. This isn't a spa, and I'm *not* your social secretary."

Jack's eyes constricted around his rage. "Allow me this call, and I'll tell you why you have that rash on your neck."

Baldwin reflexively scratched above his collar.

"And why your left eyelid droops."

Baldwin deliberated.

"Let me make the call, and I'll tell you why you're a set-up for a heart attack."

"My wife," Baldwin whispered. "She and my doc want me to take a statin because I got high cholesterol. What do you think?"

"I think you and I don't need to be enemies. And yes, I can help you with that."

"I don't know . . ."

Jack sighed. "Look, I *am* getting out of this prison soon enough. And after I do, you're still going to see me around, because I'm going to reclaim my license and come back here—as a *doctor*. I've seen the terrible care inmates get in this prison's so-called health system. So, mark my word: I'm coming back to make things better. And that may as well start now."

"You seem awfully confident about getting out."

"I am."

Baldwin looked away, thinking.

"All right then," said Jack. "A few months ago, do you remember that Legionnaires' outbreak because of the contaminated cooling towers here? When everyone got so sick? That wouldn't happen if I—"

"Okay!" Baldwin relented. "I'll get you one fucking minute on the phone tonight. But that's it. I'll clear it with my partner and take you after dinner."

Nora's Office

Oakland City Hospital

LATE AFTERNOON

Nora and Fred snuck through the ER's back entrance, hoping to steal into her office. But Aditya spotted them and called out, "Hello!" He was eager to tell Nora about the pericardial rub he detected today.

Nora pulled Aditya into her office and said, "Please keep this quiet! I don't want *anyone* knowing we're here."

Aditya looked apprehensively at the chief of the medical staff who was laboring for breath. He asked, "Dr. Kelly, what is going on please?"

"Just bring us a nebulizer, spirometer, oxygen, albuterol, and steroids," she said.

Aditya said to Fred, "But, sir; isn't it safer to treat you in an equipped room?"

Fred marshaled sufficient strength to reply, "Son, just do what Dr. Kelly asks."

"Of course," Aditya said. He nodded to Nora and left.

Nora's tensely knotted muscles loosened so abruptly that she felt she might collapse. Finally, she was off perilous roads with an imperiled driver, and they had alighted in a safe place that could shield them from the turbulence being generated by Edna and Rosalie. Most importantly, she had delivered Fred to the hospital in a timely manner. After Aditya returned and Fred's treatment began, she would notify Fergie of her arrival and resume their ruptured conversation. Fred would improve and then obtain updates from police and lawyers. Together, they would figure things out.

Nora asked Fred, "Sure you don't want me to call Vickie?"

"You that worried about me?"

"Don't be silly. The nebs will help within minutes, and the steroids will kick in soon enough. You're going to be fine."

Fred smiled, but Nora sensed little conviction behind it. Then her office door swung open and Aditya appeared, pushing a wheelchair piled with supplies. And right behind him followed Rosalie.

"Sorry," said Aditya, setting up equipment. "I was not as invisible as I tried to be." He smiled, pointed to Rosalie and said, "But good news, see? We have more help."

Rosalie stared coldly at Nora. In an injured tone, she said, "So, Nora, you suspect me?"

"What are you talking about?" Nora lamely replied, hoping to stall long enough to figure out what was happening now, because *something was definitely happening now*. Even Aditya was alerted by the odd strain, and he fumbled while inserting Fred's IV.

"I overheard Fergie talking with you on the phone," Rosalie said. "And I learned Edna 'found' my caduceus in Cheryl's office. I *know* what you suspect of me." She walked to Fred's side, and the awful tension pressed against his chest. He looked beseechingly at Nora.

Watching Fred struggle and, realizing there no longer existed a reason to treat him privately, Nora said, "Aditya, you can move the chief to a treatment room now."

But Rosalie demurred. "Why? It is so cozy here." Unbidden, she adjusted Fred's IV drip. Then she frowned at Nora and said, "Oh, of course—because you think I am a *murderer*."

It chilled Nora to hear Rosalie articulate a speculation she had raised privately with Fergie. And, worryingly, that speculation remained plausible, given the recovery of Rosalie's brooch in Cheryl's office, and Rosalie's aggressive and deceitful pursuit of Edna. She stared intensely at Rosalie, trying to decide whether she saw genuine injury or contempt—perhaps both—in her expression.

Aditya said, "Excuse me. But, this upsetting talk is not good for my patient—"

The door swung open. Carl entered. He rapidly scanned the room and said, "Nora, I've been looking for you. Why didn't you return my call?"

"Please, Carl," she said. "As you can see, we're busy."

Carl auscultated Fred's chest, checked his oximeter, and inspected the IV drip. He said, "Fred will be safe within one hour."

The room fell silent but for Fred's wheezing and the oxygen tank's *whooshing*. Meanwhile, Nora felt her reality bending and twisting into bizarre new shapes while Carl looked expectantly at her. Finally, she blurted out, "I *did* get your message, Carl! But then I heard from Fergie that you identified the brooch. So, I wasn't aware I *still* needed to call you."

Her reply stymied Carl. He said, "Nora, I responded to Fergie's text *to Fergie*. I believe that was the normal thing to do. I called *you*, but *you* did not call *me* back. They are two separate events. I don't understand your confusion."

Aditya intervened, "So, Dr. Kluft, perhaps now you can tell Dr. Kelly why you called her?"

"Yes, that's sensible," Carl said. He turned to Nora, explaining, "I called you because you were helping me with Cheryl's case. And it occurred to me, after I conclusively identified Rosalie's caduceus, that people would presume the wrong thing about that. They would erroneously assume it had slipped off her coat while she was breaking into the stent box."

Rosalie moaned, and sat down.

Trying not to sound defensive, Nora replied, "But, Carl, don't you agree that raises suspicions?"

Carl looked surprised. "No. Just the contrary. That's what I wanted to talk with you about. That's why I called you."

Nora and Fred exchanged muddled glances, and Rosalie looked probingly at Carl while everyone waited for his explanation. Then, it dawned on Nora that he required prompting. She said, "Carl, please tell us."

"Of course," he said. "Everyone appears confused, as I'd predicted." After straightening journals on Nora's desk, he said, "I fought with Cheryl in the ER and left her alone in the hallway the night before her surgery. I will always regret that. But when I turned back to apologize, she and Rosalie were exiting the ER together. I was relieved to see someone comforting Cheryl when I failed to." He paused to smile at Rosalie. "They went to Cheryl's research office—that's how Rosalie passed undetected through security—and they put Cheryl's paperwork in order. Cheryl phoned me from the restroom there, asking me to drive her home. Twenty-one minutes later, I was standing outside my car in the doctors' parking lot, waiting. It was a cool night, and when Cheryl and Rosalie arrived, I noticed Rosalie had her coat buttoned, with its lapels raised up against her neck. So, I saw her caduceus, under the left lapel, as usual."

Rosalie broke down, sobbing.

"So," Carl continued, "it's basic logic. Rosalie couldn't have left her caduceus in Cheryl's office Sunday night. Because, (A), Rosalie was still wearing it after she left that office, and (B), security logs show that no one else entered the office *after* their departure and *before* Cheryl's surgery the next morning."

Rosalie cried out, "Thank you, Carl!"

Carl said, "No thanks required. It is mere logic and factual observation. But that is what I have to offer."

Rosalie wailed, "But Nora and Fergie . . . they think I stole the stent! They accuse me of . . . of *murdering* Cheryl." She wept so hard that she couldn't speak.

Nora was beyond mortified and struggling to configure a worthy apology to Rosalie when Carl added: "Today, when Fergie texted her photo of the caduceus to me, I knew it belonged to Rosalie. I expected people to jump to a conclusion—*erroneously*—that Rosalie left it in Cheryl's office while stealing the stent." He said to Rosalie, "So I went looking for you. I wanted to warn you about that landmine so you could protect yourself." He said to Nora, "I'm using *landmine* as a metaphor."

Rosalie, looking alternatively wounded and wrathful, said, "Nora, of all people! How could *you* have suspected *me*?"

A quick rap on the door preceded Fergie's hapless entry into Nora's office. She was shocked to discover so many people inside—so many distraught-looking people. She was immediately flooded with dread while absorbing Rosalie's livid expression, Nora's evident misery, and Fred's frailty. She stammered, "Aditya . . . I . . . got your text about needing a cannula. Why is everybody here?"

Rosalie shouted, "You were all ready to hang me!"

Nora apologized to Fergie, "This is my fault. Carl phoned me earlier and tried to tell me how Rosalie couldn't have left her caduceus in Cheryl's office. But I never called him back."

Fergie cast a disapproving look at Nora whose unavailability—*this* time, for Carl's call—continued to fuel flames. "Just great," she said, her face reddening. "Because Lizbeth also reported that she saw Edna plant the caduceus in Cheryl's office."

"Well," Carl said, "that offers surplus confirmatory evidence for what I said. Still, it uniquely explains how the brooch arrived in Cheryl's office two days after her surgery—Edna brought it there."

"She knew what that brooch meant to me!" said Rosalie. "And then she tried to frame me for murder with it!"

Vexed about her unwitting inclusion in yet another trauma involving Rosalie today, Fergie reproached Nora. "If you'd texted me as soon as you arrived at the hospital, like you *promised*, I could've told you about Lizbeth's news. We wouldn't all be here like this now."

Nora said, "Fergie, I had to get Fred taken care of first."

"I am so devastated," Rosalie bemoaned. Pointing to Fred, Fergie, and Nora she said, "You needed so much proof from Carl and Lizbeth to believe my innocence."

Fred set aside his oxygen mask and said, "Can't talk much now. But, Rosalie, I'm very sorry, and very ashamed."

Nodding her concurrence with Fred, Nora was dumbfounded by the enormity of her idiocy and her stupendous misreading of Rosalie. *How can I ask for forgiveness?*

Carl's phone chimed. He said, "Excuse me—it's my reminder to eat." He left the office, and Aditya followed him out, finally transferring Fred to the ER proper.

Nora looked shamefacedly at Fergie and said, "Please understand; Fred was having a severe asthma attack on the drive back. He had used up his inhalers. We got here as quickly as we could and snuck into the ER—"

"*Because*," Rosalie charged, "you were afraid of me. You suspected me of murdering Cheryl and going after Edna! And then—what? Stalking you and Fred, too? Do you hear how crazy and paranoid you sound, Nora?"

Overcome with guilt, Fergie said, "Rosalie, I can only hope you'll forgive me someday." She didn't even look at Nora when she exited, leaving her and Rosalie alone in the office.

Rosalie paced before Nora who, with eyes averted, stood demoralized. Finally, Rosalie said, "So here you are again, making another colossal misdiagnosis, Nora!" She slammed her fist on Nora's desk and demanded, "Look at me!"

The startling intensity of Rosalie's fury shook Nora free of any hope for redemption and reconciliation. Privately conceding her incompetence, she felt like a foolish old doctor who had exceeded her expiration date. When she did look at Rosalie, she no longer saw even a vague reflection of herself now. Fumbling for an apology, she said, "I feel so . . . stupid."

"Do not expect my pity, Nora!"

Tears welled in Nora's eyes, but she managed to say, "I'm floundering here. Look, I've made a huge mistake. I really hurt you. And I was wrong, wrong, wrong."

Rosalie swept an arm across Nora's desk, sending her calendar and notebooks to the floor. She seethed, "I told you not to ask for my pity!"

"I . . . I didn't mean to. Clearly, I can't do anything right. And I don't know what to say. I feel horrible."

"I do not care how you feel. And I do not care what you think. That is a waste of my time."

Nora thought: *I have lost all sense of control, of reason, and of judgment. But here's Rosalie standing in front of me, raging against my stupidity, and looking expectantly at me.* Flailing and desperate, she said, "Please, let's talk. We need to talk. Why not come over tonight so we can do that? I'm begging you. Look, I've already placed an order with Delmonico's for a delivery tonight."

Rosalie looked stunned. Outrage soon followed. She said, "*Pizza*? You are offering me *pizza*?"

Nora stammered, "God . . . I'm just making things worse by the minute. Please, Rosalie? Just give me a chance. You . . . you were like a daughter to me and—"

"Oh, do not go there, Nora! No. You just *used* me to plug in the dark hole that was left in your life after your *real* daughter died. Is that not true? And tell me—I am curious—did you never hug your *real* daughter, too? Were you as repulsed hugging her as you were with me?"

Nora placed her hands over her ears and pleaded, "Please, stop!"

Rosalie persisted. "Then you not only refuse to defend me when people suspect me of murder—my god, *murder!*—but you join in their witch hunt!"

"I wasn't thinking clearly—"

"What a massive understatement! You were *wrong*. Dead wrong. And you have been so wrong for so long about so many things, that your 'friends'—people like *me*—are suffering or dying right under your nose. And you keep proving yourself incompetent to do anything about that. Some *mother* you are. Some *friend*. Some *diagnostician*."

Nora fell silent while she dropped into the nothingness that Rosalie clearly saw inside her.

In a calm voice, Rosalie said, "Everyone here laughs at you, Nora: the residents, the students, the staff. *Everyone.*" With a pained expression on her face, she added, "I wish I could laugh at you, too, like the others. But my disappointment in you ... it is too depressing." She walked out of Nora's office, slamming the door.

Driveway, Nora's Home

Oakland

EVENING

"Thanks for driving me home, Fergie. Want to come in for a beer? I owe you, what, a billion from today alone."

"No thanks," Fergie said.

"Okay. And, again, I'm sorry for being so unavailable today. And for any part I played in you having to suffer two traumas with Rosalie."

"Enough with the apologies," Fergie said, turning her bright red Subaru into Nora's driveway. "I understand our disconnects today. I'm just ... just broken for the day. There's too much to take in. Especially what you told me about Edna, and the things she did to Jack. I never saw any of that coming or going, and I need to think hard about why I didn't."

"Yeah, well, there's going to be a lot of soul-searching all around."

"And PTSD, too! God, that was freakin' rough walking into your office! My *second* Hurricane Rosalie of the day."

Nora grimaced. "And, after you left, Rosalie *really* lit into me. No one has ever taken me down so low in my entire life."

Fergie sighed. "You should get an award for surviving today, Nora. Let's not forget, you also scattered Lydia's ashes. And you visited Jack. And you saved Fred's life. So, let's just agree it was a crazy-times-a-million difficult day and try to be a little compassionate with ourselves, okay?"

Nora smiled. "Fred christened today, Let-Everything-Happen-All-at-Once Day. And, at the time, the day wasn't even half over!"

"Hey, you think he's going to be all right? His asthma was pretty severe."

"Yeah, though I don't like that he's heading back to his hotel room alone. I wish he'd stay with me tonight."

"It's incredible," Fergie said. "You two must've been sneaking into ER at the same time Rosalie was storming out of the locker room. You and I *just* missed a check-in with each other that would've prevented *Nightmare with Rosalie: the Sequel.*"

"Ugh! Yeah, that horror film's going to replay inside my head forever. So much mistimed communication today! And not just between *us*. I mean, *if only* I had called Carl back and heard what he wanted to convey."

"And *if only* I'd taken time to hear what Lizbeth wanted to say about Edna planting that caduceus."

"True. In either case, we'd have known earlier that Rosalie didn't leave it behind in Cheryl's office. And we'd have avoided one—if not both—calamities with her."

"I'm still feeling shockwaves," Fergie said. "And during the first one, in the locker room, she kept screaming about Edna 'framing' her. And about you and me being cruel to suspect her. Her howling expression is stuck so deep inside my eyeballs."

Looking sympathetically at Fergie, Nora said, "Still, as brutal as the second confrontation was, I'm grateful for the clarity it produced. And for Carl correcting misperceptions."

"Agreed. Because, frankly, if Rosalie's innocence depended solely on Lizbeth's report of Edna's behavior . . . I dunno."

"You're doubting Lizbeth?"

"I still can't understand how she happens to appear at the epicenter of every big-tent event involving Edna. She's definitely not the country bumpkin in nurses' clothing, as I may have subconsciously assumed."

Gathering her purse and unbuckling her seatbelt, Nora said, "Speaking of purported coincidence. Isn't it odd that *Dr.* Rosalie just happened to be in the *nurses'* locker room—and right after you discovered those documents?"

"Definitely freakin' odd. I can't imagine what business she'd have being there. *Legitimate* business, anyway."

"Especially after she'd been missing all day. God, it's like she ambushed you."

"Okay, now I'm getting nauseous. Now I'm wondering if Lizbeth even led me into that ambush. But I dunno. My judgment about people . . . Edna, Rosalie, Lizbeth . . . it's been so out of whack."

"Don't be so hard on yourself. You're tired. I can hear Chicago in your voice."

"Wait!" Fergie said. "You were right about what you said earlier. Edna would never leave 'evidence' for me in my locker."

Nora hesitated, one foot out the door. "And if she *was* mailing documents to exonerate Jack, why would she place redundant proof in your locker? Besides, that could've risked her chance to get away if someone found them before her mailed documents were received."

Fergie coaxed Nora back into the car. "Whoever put those documents in my locker wasn't aware that I never used it, or that it functioned as a public locker for other nurses. Someone like . . ."

They said it in unison: "Rosalie!"

"Whoa," Nora laughed. "We'd better be careful! I'm afraid of being struck by lightning again."

Fergie turned off the ignition. "I'm texting Win to tell him I'll be a few minutes late."

"But . . . sure you don't want to come in? You could invite Winston, too? I've already placed an order for pizza, and it should be delivered soon. You can pick off the sausage."

Fergie shook her head. "Can't. Win's got something other than pizza on his mind tonight." After sending her text, she exclaimed, "But can you believe Edna planted that caduceus to frame Rosalie for Cheryl's murder?"

"It does sound wild; unbelievable. And yet, planting evidence like that caduceus . . . it's certainly aligned with the 'staging' we've talked about. And, according to Jack, Edna herself admitted to staging crimes involving him."

Fergie winced. "But *murder*? Murdering Cheryl and trying to frame Rosalie for it?"

"Maybe Cheryl knew about Edna's drug scheme, too."

"It's possible. She's probably scoured every patient record at the hospital during her research—"

"Wait!" Nora said. "I'm an idiot! Edna couldn't have murdered Cheryl! So, she wasn't trying to shift the blame to Rosalie!"

"Because . . . ?"

"Because Edna was at a memorial service for her husband all Monday morning—*with God as her witness* (and a chaplain and church ladies, as well). There's no way she could've snuck out of the chapel and into the OR with that killer AccuStent."

Teary relief welled in Fergie's eyes.

Nora continued, "Besides, security logs show that Edna's first-ever visit to the research center was on Tuesday—one day *after* Cheryl's stent had been inserted."

"Then why would Edna plant Rosalie's brooch in Cheryl's office?"

Nora shrugged.

Fergie said, "Man, this is giving me such a freakin' headache. I wish I had a doobie."

Nora reached into her purse and withdrew a pack of cigarettes. "I confiscated these from Fred. They're old and may not be as much fun, but . . . ?"

"I'm in."

Nora lit up and took the first puff. She handed the cigarette to Fergie and whispered, "Please don't tell Fred we smoked this."

Fergie took a drag. "Deal," she said. "But back to Rosalie in the locker room, revealing all that shit about Edna skimming narcotics and selling them. At the same time, Rosalie's letting on that she's known about it for years; since her hospice rotation with Jack and Edna. So why does our upright citizen and drama queen sit silent on that information until now?"

With a triumphant look on her face, Nora said, "Hand me that cigarette! I just earned a toke! *Because* . . . because Rosalie wasn't actually *sitting* on the information. She was *holding it over Edna's head*. Rosalie was *blackmailing* Edna."

"Freakin' brilliant! It makes sense. Those incriminating documents in my locker belonged to Rosalie! She'd been hanging onto them. She put them in my locker, and that's why she 'happened' to be in the locker room at the time."

They high-fived one another, and Fergie claimed, "My turn now for the smoke."

Nora smiled and passed the cigarette. Fergie took a toke and said, "And the blackmailing—that's why Edna despised Rosalie."

"Okay, that's excellent! But, sorry; my turn again."

"Oh?" said Fergie, passing the cigarette. "Nora, this stuff seems better for your brain than all those carrots the other day."

Nora said, "Tuesday night, Rosalie freaked when I told her about Edna leaving the SMART committee. I was unconsciously vague about it. But she became suddenly unnerved, anxious about Edna leaving *everything* for good. I think that's why she was so desperate to hunt Edna down over the next couple days. She suspected Edna of bailing out of their blackmail arrangement."

"You earned another toke for that," Fergie said. "Man, that also explains why Rosalie got paranoid when I told her about Edna finding a caduceus in Cheryl's office. She must've suspected Edna's motive for retribution or—" She laughed too hard to continue.

"What's so funny?" Nora asked, laughing companionably.

After collecting herself, Fergie said, "Well, it's just . . . First, let's be clear: none of this is *funny*, but I gotta hand it to Edna. She won! She trounced Rosalie! It looks like Edna fled their blackmail arrangement, escaped town, and left Rosalie holding the bag."

They high-fived again. Nora said, "And double funny, because, as it turned out, Rosalie's paranoia *was* warranted! Edna actually planted her caduceus at a crime scene!"

They laughed hard. "Karma," Fergie said. "Karma," Nora agreed.

Then Fergie took another toke, while Nora cleared steam from the windshield to look out for the pizza delivery.

"Nora, I think this cigarette has marijuana in it."

"It might," Nora said. "It's really old, but in good shape. Fred always did the best roll-ups."

"Well, it was good of you to commandeer this and save Fred from himself."

"I hope he agrees," Nora said, pausing and wondering about his health.

"It just occurred to me," Fergie said, revisiting today's ugly ambush in the locker room. "Rosalie spilled her guts about Edna's crimes *before* Lizbeth, or Carl, publicly cleared her about the caduceus. She jumped the gun and self-incriminated. But if she had just waited until one of them revealed what they knew, she might've gotten away, too, or at least bought some time. In fact, come to think of it, I don't remember seeing her name even mentioned in those documents."

"And she wasn't aware when she spilled her guts that Edna had just confessed her crimes to Jack—without implicating her, according to what I heard."

"Talk about fucked up timing today!" Fergie said, handing the cigarette over. "Rosalie's *really* going to freak when she finds out she incriminated herself for no good reason."

Nora flicked ashes through the window and said, "But you're absolutely right—Edna won big. God, she was clever, planting that so-called 'clue' she 'found.' It bought her enough time to set things in motion against Rosalie without tipping her off prematurely and ruining her exit strategy."

"Yeah. And for me, knowing that Edna used some of that time to come clean with Jack beforehand . . . Well, that's more like the Edna I knew."

Returning the cigarette stub to Fergie, Nora said, "After what Rosalie's put us through, it's chilling to imagine what her ultimate undoing will look like. But when she discovers that Edna confessed, she'll realize she no longer has any power over Edna. Poof! Gone! And then, when she finds out that Edna *escaped* and left her holding the bag for whatever they were involved in . . ."

"Man! I'd love to be a fly on the wall and see what desperate things Rosalie does then. After her terrorizing performances today . . . God, what was all that?"

"Theater," Nora said. "Very bad, but very effective, theater."

Fergie had a coughing fit. Nora confiscated the cigarette and asked, "You okay?"

"Yeah," Fergie managed. "It's just that an idea dropped into my head . . . but, at the same time, it was leaving my mouth in words." She laughed. "It came out as a cough!"

Grinning, Nora said, "So, what's your idea, if it doesn't kill you to say?"

"Well, Edna must've been paying a price in exchange for Rosalie's silence about her crimes, right? So, wouldn't you like to know what Rosalie was getting out of Edna?"

A white sedan parked across the street. A skinny young man holding a Delmonico's pizza box got out and headed toward Nora's house. Fergie said, "Well, pizza's here. Time for me to go."

They hugged, and Nora said, "Goodnight. I really appreciate you thinking through this mess with me."

"More to come," Fergie said. "See ya."

Nora bounded up the walkway toward her porch. Fergie checked the time and, realizing she was more than a "few minutes" late for Winston, drove away.

The young man with the pizza joined Nora while she unlocked the door. He said, "Great timing!"

"Yes," she said, "and I'm starving." She ushered him into the foyer and foraged through her purse for cash. He knowingly said, "The munchies?"

Nora's Home

Oakland

EVENING

"Hey, Bix," Nora called from the foyer. She dialed up the thermostat and carried the pizza to the living room. She said "Hello" to everyone in the two photographs, which were still propped up against the sofa armrest. After retrieving a bottle of merlot from the kitchen, she called out again for Bix and plopped down on the sofa.

Immediately, her day began flashing by like snapshots blown out of a cannon. Lydia's ashes: in a bag, in the air, inside her palm . . . the prison gate opening . . . Jack's piercing gaze . . . Fred gasping for air . . . Fergie's varied expressions and her laugh . . . Rosalie's aggrieved looks and her extremely angry face . . .

Glancing at Lydia's photo, she said, "Where the hell to start, pal? There's no discrete beginning to this day—it began so many years ago."

She kicked off her shoes and opened the Delmonico's box. "Damn," she muttered, discovering onions and peppers slathered over the pizza. "They delivered the wrong one again!" She considered phoning Delmonico's to complain but, given the time required for a new order and delivery, she decided otherwise. Besides, she knew she didn't possess the most judicious frame of mind for any further conflict.

Picking off the peppers and onions, she told Lydia, "Fergie and I were just talking. (Maybe you know that.) And something she said about Edna coming clean has me wondering . . . If Edna is suddenly clearing her conscience—about Jack, the fraud, Benny's death, the drugs—and she's surrendered her cap (sorry you missed your chance to sell it on eBay), it appears to be an epic time for her reckoning with truth. So, if that's the case, Edna must be conveying another truth by planting Rosalie's caduceus. But what?"

Grabbing another slice, Nora tried to ward off intrusive memories of Rosalie's debasing attacks.

Lydia, you were right to be cautious about Rosalie. She's in thick with Edna, somehow. Still, no one—not even Rosalie—deserves to be framed for murder, and I was wrong to suspect her before the facts came out. Thank god for Carl and—

She gasped and said, "Wait! Just because Rosalie didn't leave her brooch behind in Cheryl's office doesn't mean she didn't steal the stent."

Lydia, suppose Edna planted that brooch because she was planting a truth bomb about Rosalie! A bomb that would explode only after she skipped town. She relied on others to detonate it: me, Fergie, Lizbeth . . .

She shuddered, now forced to consider the possibility that Rosalie could have murdered Cheryl. She picked up her cell to call Fergie, but then remembered Fergie's overdue evening with Winston.

She downed more merlot and reasoned with Lydia: *Okay, if Rosalie killed Cheryl, and if my theory is correct, then Rosalie also staged your accident and Richard's death, too. And the calls and deliveries to Fred's—*

Fred. It occurred to Nora that only she and Lydia purportedly knew about the existence of the Polaroid that was slipped to Vickie. Clearly, however, its provenance was not so narrow, and someone else had had access to it—or, perhaps, a copy of it. She decided to call Fred to explore what he might know about that. Perhaps, too, he'd reconsider her offer to stay the night for her well-being as much as his.

Fred answered the call and reassured Nora about his recovery. "In fact," he said, "I'm on my way to pick up a few things in my office before I leave the hospital. It's been one helluva day."

"Well, if you're up for it, I've got a warm pizza here. Half of it has your name on it; no anchovies."

Fred declined. "After today, I just want to grab a drink, collapse on fresh white hotel sheets, and sleep a long night." The hospital elevator opened and he stepped inside, heading for the C-suite.

"I understand. But, I have one burning question for you. That Polaroid of you and Lydia—is it possible someone sent Vickie a *copy* of it, or was it the original?"

"Please! You're triggering my asthma again! Christ, a *copy*? I can't imagine who'd be sick enough—"

"Wait. Let me ask my who-mighta-dunnit question differently. Here goes: can you imagine how *Rosalie* mighta-dunnit?"

Fred scoffed. "Rosalie? Really? You're still burning her at the stake? After all we put her through this afternoon? God, it was awful watching her being tortured."

"Deep breath, Fred. Just humor me."

He sighed. "Fine. All right now. Let's see . . . I went into Lydia's office the day she died. I was just looking to protect her. I wanted to remove any evidence of . . . hell, I know it was wrong." A clang signaled the elevator's arrival at the 10th floor, and he headed toward his office. "I wasn't exactly shocked to find that Polaroid in her desk. Lydia promised me she had destroyed it, but, as I'd suspected, she didn't." He unlocked his office door and went inside.

"Well, what did you do with it then?"

While collecting items for his briefcase, he tried to remember. "Well, I came here to the office afterwards. And between you and me, I took a little private time to break down. Anyway, then I had to get home in time for Sunday supper. Things were already tense between Vickie and me, and it was already such . . . such a horrific day."

"And the Polaroid? It's hard to imagine you taking it home with you that night—especially under the circumstances."

"You crazy? Of course not! No. I put it here in my . . . desk . . . drawer."

"Fred?"

"Yeah, uh . . . I'm sure it was here."

"And . . . now it's not?"

"And . . . now it's not."

"Fred?"

He cleared his throat. "It's just dawning on me. That day, just before I left for supper, I had an appointment here with Rosalie."

"That's right; just before my shift ended, I remember her saying she was going to meet with you, and feeling relieved at the time that she had somewhere else to go."

Continuing to search his desk, he said, "She'd been at the hospital all day, like us. So, I figured I might as well take care of some business while we were both here. Besides, I was looking for ways to distract myself from Lydia's death."

"What 'business' did you have with Rosalie?"

"I had to inform her that I was removing her from ER backup. Edna had complained again and . . ."

"Fred? You still there?"

"Hell! I'm so stupid!"

"Don't tell me—you left Rosalie alone in your office that day?" She heard Fred's wheezing renew.

"Yes; alone. It was just for a few damn minutes, and . . ."

"*And* . . . your Polaroid is missing?"

"And my Polaroid is missing."

Exit Stairwell

Oakland City Hospital

EVENING

Lizbeth sat on the stairwell outside the hospital's back exit, which led to a small landscaped lot where the "No Smoking" signs had been creatively re-messaged by local taggers. Several stalwart lamps shone, casting a lonely glow along the perimeter of the dark yard.

She stared at a weakly illuminated rosebush and thought about Edna, who often displayed her garden roses throughout the nurses station. How to understand her abrupt disappearance today, and under such damning allegations about her character?

The signs of Edna's mounting distress had been obvious for weeks. Physically, even, it showed in the dimming of her emerald eyes, the letting-go of her red highlights, and the slackness in her face. But Lizbeth had felt shy about inquiring into Edna's well-being. How imprudent it had seemed to question her feelings and behavior. And yet, she knew of several classmates who had formed personal relationships with their mentors. Perhaps, had she been more like them—more self-confident and poised—perhaps she might've been capable of befriending Edna and helping her through her troubles.

And yet . . .

It suddenly occurred to Lizbeth that the contrary might be true. That, perhaps, she may have been helping Edna all along. In fact, Edna had depended on her watchful eye and respectful observance, and her unwavering loyalty and good faith. *So much so that, minutes before obviously planting that caduceus in front of me, she made me promise to speak up whenever something didn't look right—no matter the power of the person involved. So, now it fits: Edna knew she could rely on me to do exactly that! And today I did right by her by revealing what she'd done with that caduceus, as she had trusted me to do.*

"Lizbeth?" someone called out. It was Fred, descending the stairs. "Are you all right?"

"Oh, Dr. Williams," she said, drying her eyes. "I'm okay. But, how are you? I heard you were in the ER with an asthma attack."

Fred sat beside her. "I'm much better, thanks. But isn't it a little chilly to be sitting out here, especially on this cold cement?"

"I prefer the cold. Besides, it's quiet here."

Wondering what Lizbeth knew about the allegations against her mentor, he offered, "I'm sorry about Edna."

"Yeah, thanks. But do you know where she is?"

"No, the police are still out looking for her. They tracked down a cab driver who drove her from San Sebastian to the Oakland airport. But there's no evidence of her taking any flights out." He scoffed, "With all the airport security these days, you'd think it'd be easy to trace her."

"From what Dr. Karlov said in the locker room today, it sounds like Edna's in serious trouble. Is that true?"

Her open and inquiring gaze penetrated his reluctance about sharing information. "All right now," he said. "I know Edna is very important to you. But we need to be cautious about what's being said. No loose lips."

She nodded.

"Okay. I can say that it *appears* bad for Edna. It looks like she may have gotten involved—"

"Dr. Williams? Just so you know, I saw documents this afternoon that Edna *supposedly* left in Fergie's locker. But I don't believe Edna did that. Besides, the handwriting on the envelope didn't look like hers at all. Anyhow, I read those documents, so I know Edna's possibly involved with prescription drug fraud and data tampering. Also, that she was doctoring—oops, sorry, Dr. Williams—*manipulating* hospice records and billing."

Fred couldn't believe that Lizbeth was so far ahead of him on the information curve. "Where are those documents?"

"Fergie handed them over to admin, like she's supposed to. She also reported Edna's locker being broken into."

My god, Fred privately lamented. *She's viewed critical evidence that I can't even retrieve from admin at this late hour. Amateur Detective Week, indeed! And I'm its knucklehead poster child!* He cleared his throat. "Well, those documents will be examined carefully and—"

"Sorry again, Dr. Williams. But if you don't mind, I'd like to say more about them?"

Surprised by Lizbeth's assertiveness, he said, "Have at it."

"I think Dr. Karlov planted them in Fergie's locker."

"Oh?"

"Yes, sir. You see, she'd been *missing* all day. She even walked out on her clinic patients, if you can believe a doctor would do such a thing."

Fred thought, *Oh, you've no idea the things I've known my colleagues to be capable of doing.* He replied, "So I heard. And her department chief will be pursuing disciplinary action—"

"But then—abracadabra!—she's suddenly in the *nurses'* locker room. *And* those documents just appear in Fergie's locker. And Edna's locker is pried open."

"Wait," Fred said. "You're suggesting that Rosalie was in the locker room to break into Edna's locker?"

Lizbeth nodded. "I think she was looking for her caduceus, because she didn't know at the time that it'd been turned over to authorities, *or* that I'd seen Edna plant it in Dr. Kluft's office. And I think she also wanted to sneak those documents into Fergie's locker."

Fred shook his head in amazement.

"Fergie and I must've interrupted her," Lizbeth continued. "Because, I mean, she was *right there.* And you should've seen how angry and tense she *already* was."

"Excuse me," Fred said, taking a puff from his inhaler.

"And another weird thing . . . when I told about Edna planting the caduceus—wow! Dr. Karlov got so pale and weak, it looked like she was about to faint. And I just don't think that's how a truly innocent person would react."

"But Carl Kluft provided independent confirmation that Rosalie couldn't have—"

"Forgive me for interrupting *again.* But none of this means that Dr. Karlov didn't steal the stent. It only means that, if she stole the stent, she didn't leave her caduceus behind."

Fred wondered how he had missed making this clear distinction. And yet, today, on Let-Everything-Happen-All-at-Once Day, sorting through so many complex events had proven impossible. He looked admiringly at Lizbeth and said, "I see why Edna thought so highly of you."

Blushing, but emboldened by his tribute, Lizbeth said, "Today, after Dr. Karlov went ballistic on Fergie, she dragged me out of the locker room and kept thanking me for 'speaking up' about the caduceus on her behalf. But, truthfully, I was speaking up for Edna. Because I think Edna was trying to tell us that it *was* Dr. Karlov who stole the stent that harmed Dr. Kluft."

Stunned by her bold suggestion, Fred remarked, "But Edna was never shy about saying anything. So why wouldn't she just say that explicitly?"

"But thing is: she wasn't herself lately. And she was pretty secretive about her mysterious comings and goings. I think that's because she was planning to leave, and she didn't want anyone to suspect that. But that also meant she couldn't say anything explicit about Dr. Karlov because, oh my god, as we've seen, she would've gone after Edna and busted her immediately! Edna would've lost her chance to get away."

"I'll be damned," Fred said, his head spinning. "Clearly, you've been thinking deeply about Edna. It must be hard . . . very painful, for you."

"Yeah, well, I'm still holding onto lots of good things about Edna. She was a great clinical teacher. She empowered me to speak up—that's such a gift. And I understand now that she wanted me to see her plant the caduceus and trusted me to speak up about it at the right time."

Fred fell speechless while Lizbeth's analysis struck chords of plausibility that harmonized with his own experience of Edna's character. "Good god," is all he finally said.

"Well," Lizbeth said, "I don't know about that—I'm agnostic. But I have faith in Edna. And I know that good people, like Edna, sometimes do . . . not such good things. Whatever bad she's done, I'll bet she feels terrible about it. And that she'll try whatever she can to make amends."

Fred marveled at what he'd learned about Edna and Jack today, and how naïve he'd been about them. How *very wrong*. He looked appraisingly at Lizbeth whose clear eyes emanated earnestness and resolve. He recalled, in contrast, Rosalie's cold and aggressive stare. How imperious she had looked sitting behind his desk, having stolen—he now knew—his Polaroid. Hers was a look disconnected from propriety—from law. A look reflected from a dark interior mirror.

Nora's Home

Oakland

7:00 P.M.

Nora searched the bedroom for Bix, but he wasn't in his usual hideaways: behind the desk, under the nightstand, inside the laundry hamper.

The landline rang, and she looked for signs of his reactionary movement. Sadly, detecting none, she walked to the living room, expecting a phone apology from Delmonico's.

But the call originated from San Sebastian. Though wishing she were not so influenced—by wine and, perhaps, Fred's cigarette—she accepted the call.

"Nora?" Jack said.

"Jack?" she answered.

He was surprised to feel such comfort in hearing her speak his name.

Baldwin barked in the background, "One minute, Griffin!"

"It was good to see you today," Nora said. "Even under the circumstances—"

"Nora," Jack interrupted. "I can't tell you how much your visit meant to me. But *only* because *they* won't give me time to do that. We need to triage this conversation."

"Got it," Nora said. Her cell chimed a text from Fred: *In bed w Carl. Don't ask. We can trace all 'staging' to RK. Call me. STAT.*

"Was that your cell?" Jack asked. "Because, look, we only have a minute to talk."

Baldwin barked, "Forty-five seconds."

Nora put aside her cell and walked to the glass doors leading to her deck. "Sorry," she said, pulling the landline's curlicue cord as far as she could. "It's Fred, and I'll call him back."

Jack said, "That photograph you showed me today of our old gang of six? Well, I kept thinking about it and your theory. And your suggestion about there actually being *eight* people in the picture, including Richard behind the camera, and Edna in the background."

"Yeah?"

Baldwin: "Thirty seconds."

"Well, here's the kick, Nora. I think you were right *and* wrong. There are actually *nine* people in the bigger picture."

Nora picked up the photo and sat on the sofa. "But I'm looking at it now, Jack. Maybe you're not remembering it correctly?"

"Look at Edna!"

Baldwin: "Fifteen seconds."

"Still, all I see is Edna at the periphery. She's looking sideways; down."

"But that's it! Edna is looking *down* at someone outside the photo's margin. A *ninth* person cropped out by Richard's framing. Someone must be there—sitting? Or, someone really short? A child, perhaps? And look at the troubled expression on Edna's face."

Nora's heart pounded. "So, there's a *ninth* person in the picture."

"Yes, and—"

Baldwin: "Call's over." *Click.*

The dial tone sounded. Nora put down the receiver. Suddenly, her house was so profoundly quiet that she heard only her body's internal machinations—blood whooshing through her neck arteries, her gut churning.

She reexamined the photo, focusing on Edna. It was obvious now. Jack was right. Edna's troubled look was directed toward someone outside the frame, someone whose returning gaze would have also witnessed the chaos and trauma inside the room. Indeed, Edna's visage alone carried the emotional weight of the photograph. *That's why I couldn't crop her out without destroying the essence of this image. But who is she looking at, and why—?*

"My god," Nora said out loud, dread consuming her. "My god. Of course. Edna was looking at Rosalie."

"Well, *finally!*"

Nora flinched and stood up, the photograph dropped from her hand. She turned to find Rosalie standing in the kitchen entry.

Lobby Bar, Paradox Hotel

Berkeley Marina

EVENING

"Hello, Fred," said Carl, settling on an adjacent barstool.

Fred, lost in thought, nearly aspirated his Manhattan. "Carl?"

"Well, yes. It's me. Carl."

"I just meant . . . well, I didn't expect to see you here."

A quizzical expression on his face, Carl said, "But you told me to stop by some time."

Fred downed his drink and signaled the bartender. "I did, didn't I?"

"I just reminded you of doing that."

The bartender acknowledged Fred's request for another Manhattan and asked Carl, "What'll you be having?"

"A light ale, please. A Larson's if you have it; but only if it's still in the can or bottle. Unopened."

The bartender delicately raised his brow and said, "Coming up."

Carl withdrew a sani-wipe from his trouser pocket and cleaned the countertop. "This is a nice hotel you're staying in, Fred. I've been inside its conference rooms many times."

"I know," Fred said, relinquishing hopes for a restful evening.

"You could stay with me until you resettle. There's extra room in my house, especially with Cheryl gone."

"That's very generous, Carl. But I don't—"

"My house has 4,236 square feet of living space. Even if you took half—2,118 square feet—it leaves me with more than adequate room."

Trying to change the subject and curb Carl's obsessiveness, Fred said, "Again, thanks. But you'll need that space when you bring Cheryl home. The hospital bed, all that equipment—"

Carl raised his voice: "Are you having trouble hearing, Fred? I said Cheryl is *gone*."

Mortified, Fred apologized, "Forgive me! I—"

"No, your misunderstanding is my fault. I used a euphemism for death when I should've stated explicitly that Cheryl was *dead*. I've heard that from many of the communication seminars you've sent me to. Euphemisms like *gone, passed, crossed over, no longer with us* . . ."

"I'm so sorry, Carl. When did she die?"

"It's impossible to say precisely. You know that, right? Because there are different perspectives concerning the specific moment that life ends and death begins. So, Cheryl may have died as early as Monday, during her surgery, or as late as an hour ago when we extubated her. Or at any point in-between."

"I'm . . . just sorry."

"It wasn't your fault, Fred."

Fred was about to clarify his intention to offer condolences when the bartender arrived with the drinks. Carl popped open his beer with a keyring and wiped the bottle's neck. Fred held up his glass and somberly toasted, "To Cheryl."

"She's not here," Carl said, a concerned expression on his face. "But maybe you believe that people linger for a while? Or maybe you're in denial? I'll repeat it for you, simply and without euphemism: Cheryl *died.*"

Fred nodded and decided against further attempts to explain himself.

Carl said, "When I left the hospital tonight, it felt strange to step into a life that no longer included Cheryl. I thought: where could I go where I won't be a stranger? That's when I decided to accept your invitation to drop by some time."

They sat together companionably, sipping their drinks. Meanwhile, Fred thought about the daunting tasks awaiting him tomorrow: overseeing so many investigations, dealing with police, legal, admin, PR, distraught staff . . . And now, with Cheryl's death proclaimed, her "situation" transitioned into a bona fide murder case. Then, Rosalie's egregious theft of his Polaroid—

"What are you thinking?" Carl asked.

Fred hesitated, uncertain how to converse efficiently with Carl. Then he remembered how Nora had streamlined her inquiry about the Polaroid—not asking how "someone" might've gotten hold of it, but, rather, how *Rosalie* may have done so. He took a chance with Nora's strategy and began, "You're a logical man, Carl."

"It's good logic to think so!" Carl replied, smiling broadly. "Cheryl always told me that line was clever."

"Yes. All right then, I'd like to pose some logic puzzles to you—not formal logic, but practical logic."

Silence ensued, unsettling Fred. He finally said, "Hell—of course. Sorry. It's tone deaf of me to talk about puzzles after you tell me about Cheryl's death."

"I was waiting for you to start a puzzle."

"Uh, okay," Fred said, taking a hefty swig of Manhattan. "So, tell me: you think it's possible that, let's say . . . Rosalie? Is it possible she could have stolen the stent from Cheryl's office and snuck it into the OR the next morning?"

"Of course."

Fred choked. "All right. But you also have to explain your practical reasoning."

Carl shrugged. "Sure. I know Rosalie accompanied Cheryl to her office on Sunday night, ostensibly to comfort her. So, she entered the office, and subsequently left the office under Cheryl's security clearance. But while they were in the office, Cheryl had excused herself to the restroom—that's when she phoned and asked me to pick her up later. But during that brief absence, Rosalie was alone in the office."

"Alone in the office?" Fred gasped, unsettled by this phrase a second time tonight.

"The other half of what you asked concerns how she could have snuck the AccuStent into the OR the next morning."

His asthma beginning to flare, Fred said, "So, can you—no, *will you*—address that now?"

"Yes. Rosalie was wearing blue scrubs under her white coat when she arrived with Cheryl in the parking lot that night. That's when I saw the caduceus still on her lapel and why I knew she hadn't left it behind in Cheryl's office. Then, when we all said goodnight, Rosalie told us she was going to crash—meaning *sleep*, Fred—in the ER on-call room. She had clinic in the morning—the day of Cheryl's surgery. So, it would've been easy for her to (A), enter Cheryl's OR the next morning and (B), remain unnoticed. Anonymous figures pop in and out of hospital rooms all the time, Fred."

Experiencing Carl's quick mind made Fred feel dim-witted. But then he self-reassuringly pointed to a potential flaw in Carl's reasoning. "Wait—Rosalie couldn't have been *planning* to steal the stent and then use it against Cheryl the next day. It was mere happenstance that she was in Cheryl's office in the first place."

"Isn't it obvious, Fred? Rosalie's plan could've been inspired while she was inside Cheryl's office. A crime of opportunity." Carl's tone turned somber. "And if that's true, I blame myself, because if I hadn't fought with Cheryl, Rosalie wouldn't have had an opportunistic opening to offer Cheryl 'support' and accompany her to the office."

Fred pushed aside his drink. "What about the caduceus? Lizbeth said Edna planted it in the stent box on Tuesday. But wouldn't Rosalie have been aware of Edna taking it off her?"

"Of course, Fred . . . *if* Rosalie were aware at the time. But Edna could've removed it from Rosalie's coat while Rosalie was asleep or not wearing her coat, or both. And both likely prevailed on Sunday night. We know (A), Rosalie slept in the ER on-call room that night and (B), Edna was in the ER at the same time."

"Hell," Fred muttered, disturbed by the alarming reasonableness of this dreadful narrative.

"The timing also fits. Because, obviously, the caduceus had to be taken from Rosalie's coat sometime between Sunday evening when *I saw it* on Rosalie's lapel, and Tuesday afternoon when *Lizbeth saw it* in Edna's hand."

"Well, there *was* bad blood between them. And earlier that day, I removed Rosalie from ER backup at Edna's request—her *demand*, actually."

"So, it probably infuriated Edna to find Rosalie in the on-call room that same night. I once attended a communication seminar, 'Reasoning Emotions Using Your Senses—'"

"Okay," Fred interjected. "So, Edna finds Rosalie asleep in the call room, and she rips the caduceus off her coat?"

"I just said that."

Fred blurted out, "Well, why the hell would Edna do that?"

Carl's eyes widened. "Clearly, because she reveres symbols like that. She's the only nurse at the hospital who still wears a cap!" He sani-wiped the hand he'd used to push aside the complimentary snack bowl. "Edna expressed judgment in confiscating Rosalie's caduceus. But only later did she realize how she could use the caduceus against Rosalie *personally*."

"What you're saying . . . it's difficult to digest."

"Then maybe we should stop playing your practical logic puzzles. Or play puzzles that are easier on you."

Fred wished Nora and Lydia were with him now, sharing this encounter with Carl. How maddening, but how carefully and creatively he thought. How interesting to spend time with him on his own terms. "No, let's keep on," he said, thinking now about Nora debunking Richard's suicide. "Remember Richard Pulaski's ... Wait, let me rephrase. Can you imagine a logical scenario to explain how Rosalie could've killed Richard?"

"I can."

Surprised by the unequivocal response, Fred waited eagerly. Finally, he grasped what must happen next and said, "Please tell me."

"That puzzle's easy. Rosalie's at the hospital most Sundays, catching up in her office. She probably visited Richard in his office the Sunday he died. We know she helped to set up his chemo infusions, so it would've been easy to inject him with potassium during that visit. And then we know that the next day, she was first responder on the scene, and alone with Richard's body for some time before she called the code. She could have put her prints over everything, as a cover. And, according to what Lizbeth told me tonight about the hostility between Edna and Rosalie—"

"Edna's student? You talked with her?"

"Fred, I just said so."

"All right now," Fred said, wondering whether to order a third drink. "Didn't know you knew Lizbeth is all."

"I often saw her in the ER with Edna. And tonight, after extubating Cheryl, I ran into her on the back stairwell when I left the hospital. I find her interesting, Fred. She sees things and intuitively registers their emotional significance. I see things and just remember their physical properties."

Acid pooled in Fred's stomach. "But Rosalie couldn't have ... I mean, she seemed so devastated when I arrived second at Richard's code."

Carl wagged a finger at him and said, "You! *You* should take some of those role-play workshops you mandate for me! First, you'd learn some acting skills, like, how to adjust your voice and body language so patients believe you're thinking and feeling what's required to grade you higher on those physician surveys you're so focused on. My point is, you'd learn that people—physicians included—don't always communicate their true thoughts and authentic emotions through their words or outward behaviors."

Fred sighed and said, "All right now. Just give me a minute to think." He couldn't stomach the notion that, under his nose and paternal watch, one of his staff *could* commit two murders. And then, if Nora's misgivings about Lydia's "accident" . . .

"Fred? It's been longer than a minute. And I'm reasoning that, because your puzzles have concerned the deaths of two colleagues, you're probably thinking about Lydia's."

Fred looked away.

"You're crying," Carl said. "So, I must be correct. And if you like, I'll address that puzzle, maintaining your baseline premise concerning Rosalie's culpability."

Fred nodded, and Carl continued: "Okay. We know that Rosalie, Nora, and Fergie were at the Tavern with Lydia the night she died. And police reports note Rosalie and Fergie leaving the table for a 15-minute break. During that break, purportedly, Fergie took refuge texting at the bar while Rosalie was in the restroom. But during her unwitnessed leave, Rosalie would've had opportunity to sneak out to the parking lot, plant drugs in Lydia's car, return to the bar, and spike Lydia's drink—the drink *she* carried back to the table."

Tears streamed down Fred's face.

Carl said, "Rosalie would've needed to sneak Lydia's car keys from her purse and return them later. Not too difficult to do, I imagine, under the table, with Lydia intoxicated and everyone distracted by alcohol and disagreement. I assume the final piece of this puzzle is obvious: Rosalie could have followed Lydia home in her car and forced her off the road."

Sweat beaded on Fred's forehead, and his face turned ashen. Carl's horrifying proposition wedged deeper into the realm of probability. *Is Rosalie responsible for all the sorrow and tragedy? For "staging" everyone's fate, as Nora would say?* "Carl," he urgently said, "can you—*will* you tell me how Rosalie could be responsible for Jack's imprisonment?"

"I need a minute."

Fred reached for his inhaler when, seconds later, Carl exclaimed, "Yes!"

Fred startled, and Carl said, "Sorry, I didn't mean a literal minute. But the only logical explanation is that Rosalie coerced Edna into framing Jack. It was framing by proxy that sent Jack to prison."

"What?!"

"Okay, I'll speak slower for you: (A), Edna committed crimes. (B), Rosalie discovered them. (C), in exchange for keeping silent about those crimes, Rosalie demanded that Edna frame Jack. So (hopefully I'm making this clear) Edna became Rosalie's proxy for framing Jack and putting him in prison."

"No, no, no."

"But yes, Fred. Lizbeth told me tonight that Rosalie claimed to know for years about Edna's drug schemes. So, why would Rosalie wait until today to reveal that? The only logical conclusion is that she had been blackmailing Edna with the information she possessed. And a blackmail arrangement like that would also shed light on Lizbeth's observations regarding Edna's animosity toward Rosalie."

I'm such a dolt, Fred privately rued. *How do I miss so much happening around me? That damn admin ladder I've climbed . . . I can't see what's happening on the ground anymore.*

"Fred? You're looking glum, and your asthma is worsening. Let's play a game that's safer for you."

"Please," Fred implored. "Why in god's name would Edna and Rosalie hurt Jack like that? How did they even . . .?"

Carl signaled the bartender for another beer and said, "According to Lizbeth, Jack's name was all over the falsified records and evidentiary documents. So, it couldn't have been that difficult to implicate him in the fraud. We suspect—well, it was Lizbeth's idea, actually—that Edna initially refused Rosalie's demand that she frame Jack. Lizbeth firmly believes that Edna wouldn't betray him unless she had a gun to her head—*metaphorically* speaking, Fred. So, Rosalie 'pulled the trigger' and intimidated Edna by tipping off the state and DEA to drug discrepancies in the hospice records."

While Carl sanitized his second beer, Fred tried to suppress overwhelming dread, thinking: *I have to remember that these logical scenarios aren't factual proof of Rosalie stealing the stent or sneaking into the OR. They're not proof she injected potassium into Richard's vein, or that she drugged Lydia and forced her off the road, or that she framed Jack by proxy.* He waited for Carl to complete his cleaning ritual and said, "We need to be clear: this discussion is just speculation about Rosalie."

"I thought that *was* clear. Solving a puzzle with logical proposition is inherently speculative."

"You're right," Fred conceded, thoroughly spent. He told the bartender, "Charge everything to my room, please—and 20 percent for you."

"You look unwell," Carl said. "Your game was unhealthy for you."

"Probably so. And I should get some sleep."

"I'll escort you to your room."

"No, I'm fine."

Carl smiled artfully and said, "This is a moment in which my 'learnings' might help. Because I sense *disconnect* between what you say, and what your body language is conveying." He held out an arm to Fred.

Fred rotated on his barstool to face Carl. He said, "One last thing. Let's take it all a step further and suppose . . . suppose that all the scenarios you speculated were actually true?"

After an unwieldy silence, Fred said, "Carl?"

"I was supposing, like you asked."

Fred longed for his old marijuana-laced cigarettes that Nora recently confiscated. "All right then. Supposing they're all true, is there a logical explanation as to *why* Rosalie would do all those terrible things?"

"I can't answer that from fact and neutral observation. You're asking me to speculate about human behavior and psychology—a realm in which I don't converse well."

The alcohol, the anxiety, the stress from the day—they all weighed oppressively on Fred's mind. And when he stood up, that weight dropped precipitously to his feet. He suddenly felt emptyheaded, and about to topple over. His ears hissed. The dim lights in the bar dimmed further. He was about to vomit; to faint. And, while passing out in the hotel lobby, his memory flashed on the old group photo.

When Fred awoke in his room, Carl was lying beside him in bed. It took a moment to wrap his mind around that fact. He said, "Did we . . . ? Wait. We were at the bar, right?"

Carl nodded. "You drank too much, too fast. Your asthma flared. You overused your inhaler. You got upset playing your logic puzzles. Finally, you passed out."

"How long have I been out?"

"Well, it's 6:55 p.m., so, 13 minutes. And you talked a lot while you were out."

"Oh, hell; about what?"

"You weren't always coherent, Fred, but you kept repeating Nora's name. And you kept saying words like *stage* and *staging*. You said something about a 'morality play.' Here, drink some water."

Fred sat up and leaned against the headboard, shocked to see Carl and himself reflected in the bureau mirror. It brought to mind their old group photo and he said, "Carl, do you remember that photograph of our gang of six, from our last day of residency in 1990? It's been on my mind—and Nora's—a lot lately."

"No."

"I'm surprised. You have such a powerful photographic memory."

"But having a photographic memory doesn't mean remembering photographs, Fred. You know that, right?"

"Yes."

"Besides, I can't remember something I never saw."

"Come again?"

"Jack promised to distribute copies of that photo to everyone, but that didn't include Cheryl or me."

"I'm sorry," Fred said, guiltily reminded of the group's gradual distancing from the Klufts. He withdrew his copy from his wallet and handed it to Carl.

"It's nice to see this finally," Carl said, smiling. "And look at Cheryl . . . Would you mind making a copy for me?"

"You keep this one."

"Thanks, Fred. And are you showing this to me because it relates to our earlier discussions?"

"Yes. I'm very interested in how you see things. You're a unique and talented observer. No wonder your patients always remark on how attentive you are."

Carl's smile widened.

Fred said, "So, Nora keeps looking at this photo, insisting there's something about it that links all the bad things happening to everyone. But I just can't see it, Carl."

"Well, even though I couldn't remember this photo—having not seen it before—I do remember the day it was taken. I remember Cheryl and me, you and Lydia, and Jack—all of us waiting in that patient's room for Nora to finish so we could celebrate at Trader Vic's. I remember the conversations we had. I remember Richard taking the photo and what the ER room looked like—the smells, the colors of the walls . . ."

Fred pointed at the photo and said, "And that's what I'm counting on, Carl. I want you to tell me what your mind's eye saw that day. Tell me everything you remember about the moment captured in this photo."

Fergie and Winston's Apartment

East Oakland

7:15 P.M.

The candles glowed, and the bedding Winston had arranged in front of the fireplace felt warm and luxurious with Fergie beside him. The curry aroma from takeout created an alluring, spicy atmosphere. In the background, Nina Simone sang "For All We Know." Still, Fergie seemed distracted. And now she turned away to answer her phone.

He watched Fergie's soft-lit expression alternate between upset and very upset. He overheard her say, "Well, I drove Nora home. Then we talked a while in her driveway. I left maybe 6:15?" She whispered to Winston, "It's Fred; he can't get hold of Nora."

"Nora was on her porch when I left," she told Fred. "The Delmonico pizza guy was right behind her. . . . No, I didn't see him enter or leave her house. . . . His car? Yeah, it was a white sedan. . . . I texted her, too, less than an hour ago, but just to wish her a good night's rest. I didn't expect to hear back on that. . . . Well, we talked about different things. Mostly about what happened today with Edna and Rosalie. . . . It's odd you ask, because we also started out feeling guilty about suspecting

Rosalie. But after we talked a while, we ended up feeling the complete opposite about her."

Winston heard the trepidation in her voice when she then told Fred, "I'm positive—it was a *guy* delivering the pizza. No way could it have been Rosalie." Seconds later she said goodbye and hung up. She looked fretfully at Winston and said, "I should've waited for that guy to leave Nora's house! I was just trying to get home to you."

Winston gathered her clothes and car keys. "C'mon, Fergs—we're going to Nora's. That's where you've been all night anyway."

Nora's Home

Oakland

EVENING

"So, you see me *now*, Nora?" Rosalie's long black hair was swept back, a steely expression on her face.

Nora's heart jackhammered inside her chest. Her brain instantly absorbed a potent cocktail of wine, adrenaline, and maybe marijuana. Recalling Fred's worrying text, she stammered, "What are you doing here?" But she knew. She knew that this moment was, finally, her moment on the stage under Rosalie's dark direction. She'd been ambushed by the fate she had failed to foresee, conscripting her into a narrative that was going to leave her dead or grievously ruined.

Rosalie cocked her head and looked probingly at Nora. "Well, I am hiding. And why? Because I do not feel safe at home or work, thanks to you and Edna." Holding out Nora's cellphone, she stepped closer. "I volunteered to hold onto this because you were so busy. Looking for your cat . . . staring at pictures of old friends . . . talking with Jack." She scoffed, "Even talking to your *dead* friend Lydia."

Nora reached for her cell, but Rosalie yanked it away and said, "And you are so popular! All these texts and calls coming in from Fergie and

Fred. I imagine it comes with privilege—having the chief of staff as a friend? Well, tell me your PIN so we can see what all the fuss is about."

Nora shook her head.

Rosalie shrugged, slipped Nora's cell into her back pocket, and looked disparagingly at the Delmonico's box. "*This* is your so-called peace offering to me? And how rude—starting without me. What kind of host are you?"

"How did you get into my house?"

"Really? Is that the most pressing question you have? Under the circumstances, there are more interesting ones to ask." She stepped closer. "But, then again, you have not been at the top of your game for a while. I have noticed—*everyone* has—how difficult it has been for you to think clearly. To make diagnoses. To teach. I can hear your old brain cells *creaking* and *grinding* right now, trying to figure out what is happening." Pointing to Nora's wine glass, she asked, "Does that help lubricate your ancient neurons?"

Nora lunged toward the landline phone. But Rosalie easily snatched it and pitched it against the floor where it broke into pieces. Rosalie chided, "And how slow you are physically, as well."

"I don't know what you think you're doing here."

Rosalie laughed. "That just underscores my point."

Nora tried to ward off the humiliating intimidation and create a mental clearing in which to think. *If I can figure out the morality play she's staging for me, I'll have a fighting chance to get ahead of her plot.*

"And after all the clues I have given you, Nora! Still, you do not understand. What a shame—your mind has become so soft."

Dread coursed through Nora's marrow. *She's right. If Fred and Carl were able to figure out her role in the disasters . . . If she's given me clues . . . Why can't I see what she's enacting with me now?* She stared at Rosalie, searching for any remnant of the person she'd previously known. But all she saw was a menacing stranger emerging from a beautiful façade.

Rosalie picked up the gang-of-six photo and stared at it, her expression alternating between rage and grief. But when she finally turned back to Nora, she had a dull, faraway look in her eyes.

Her faraway look to the past was so potent and magnetic, it pulled Nora back to the day the photo was taken. She could feel Rosalie there now. She could envision her standing with her mother and brother a few feet away, the child looking back at Edna.

"Rosalie," Nora beckoned, trying to wrench her away from the pain. "Please, Rosalie," she said, trying to loosen her from her fixation on the past.

But Rosalie just stared blankly back, her annihilating expression unwavering.

She keeps looking at me as if I were an object.

And as Rosalie approached now, the more chillingly evident that became. Her darkly appraising gaze reflected no felt recognition of Nora's being.

The experience felt dreadfully familiar. It reminded Nora of standing within view of the scamera's nerveless eye that remained unaffected by what it saw.

Rosalie, looking out through those dead eyes, is capable of committing murder. And, my god . . . I'm standing in her crosshairs.

Nora glanced at family portraits on the mantle—*one last look*. She furtively scanned the room for Bix and chose a happy memory of him to hold onto while waiting on her demise.

But then Rosalie yawned—a loud, operatic yawn smacking of aggression—and Nora flinched. Pleased with the effect, Rosalie grinned and said, "You look like you have seen a ghost."

Infused with adrenaline, Nora dashed toward the foyer. But Rosalie easily outran her and blocked the front door. She dragged Nora back to the living room, shoved her onto the couch, hovered over her and threatened, "Do not test my patience!" She tossed the photo at Nora and kicked her shin—"A reminder not to try that again."

Nora's leg throbbed so intensely, she feared she might faint. With feigned sympathy, Rosalie said, "Sorry about that." Then she sat down in an adjoining chair and added, "But you must be used to worse pain, falling from high pedestals."

Nora privately conceded that she'd lost all control to Rosalie. *Does it even matter anymore to try to figure out her plans?* Her only hope, whittled down to the current reality, was to see Bix. But she was afraid to reveal any evidence of that and place him at risk of Rosalie's spitefulness. She willed herself to feel something other than this consummate despair during her final moments. So, she closed her eyes and envisioned her family . . . her hand in the Chapel's reflecting pool today . . . her morning spent in Lydia's sanctuary . . . visiting Jack . . . talking with Fred and Fergie . . . her newfound connection with Carl. But when she opened her eyes, they alighted on the photo in her lap, and she saw her old friends looking back at her through time—a Greek chorus, reminding her of who she was.

I can think this through . . .

She looked again at the photo, drawing further encouragement.

Why is Rosalie taking her time to inflict her punishment on me? Given all the damning revelations about her today, she should be fleeing; trying to stay ahead of the hounds who have surely picked up her scent.

But then Rosalie nudged her into more conversation. "Well, Nora, at least you *finally* figured out I was a ninth person in your photo. No, wait, Jack had to tell you that."

It was another grueling provocation to stay in the torturous game that Rosalie was playing according to her insular logic and rules. Nora was afraid to move, and afraid not to move. She knew she couldn't outrun Rosalie, but if she positioned herself optimally, she might gain tactical advantage and make it through the glass doors to jump over the deck. The drop down to the hillside was treacherous, but, still . . .

As if having sensed Nora's strategy, Rosalie suddenly stood before her, obstructing any path to the deck.

"Who are you?" Nora despondently asked.

Rosalie leaned close, her face mere inches away from Nora's, and she pointed to the photo. "I am the nine-year-old girl Edna is looking at in this precious photo of yours. And I am watching you and your friends pose for this happy photo while you kill my father and treat us like garbage."

Horrified by Rosalie's depiction, Nora gasped. But now the stage was clearly lighting up for the dark epiphany. Nora stammered, "My last patient in residency . . . he was your father."

Shoving the photo in Nora's face, Rosalie seethed, "He was a *10th* person in this picture, Nora! *Another* person you did not see! While all of you were smiling and posing for this, my father was dying like a dog in the background." She held out the photo and pointed to his body, barely visible on the gurney behind them. Her eyes burned furiously, their voltage stunning Nora to silence. She yelled, "Do you see him now?"

"Yes," Nora tensely answered. "I can't imagine . . . how it all looked through your eyes."

"You never *tried*," Rosalie charged, slamming a wineglass against the coffee table and holding its jagged remains like a dagger. "I was there in the ER with my mother and little brother. We stood between those blue curtains and watched everything. To this day, I thank God they did not understand English then. I thank God that, unlike me, their lives were not haunted forever by the inhumane things you all said and did that day."

"I'm sorry, Rosalie! But what was *really* happening was that I was trying to *save* your father. And I *kept* trying to save him! That's why everyone was in the ER. I was late meeting up with them, so they came to drag me away!"

"How fucking sad! My father's dying was so untimely for you and your friends."

"That's not what I meant. I'm asking . . . asking you to understand. I wasn't comfortable just handing over your father's care to some new intern, a kid right out of med school. Your father's condition was critical. And still, I know . . . still, he died."

"Yes, Nora. He died. And *not* with your undivided attention! You were so preoccupied. You had so many friends to attend to. There was some place you all had to go, and already so late. Then . . . then having to take this happy picture, too."

Nora attempted to sound calm. "I did everything I could for him. And, yes, maybe it was stupid or arrogant for me to keep trying. To think I'd be better than that new doctor. And, yes, it was insensitive for everyone to be there—I see that. But, my god, Rosalie! It was just one foolish moment for some sappy photograph."

Rosalie's face flushed with rage. She crumpled the photo and tossed it to the floor. "If you had been looking beyond your enormous ego, you might have seen me and my family. Instead of focusing on that camera, you might have noticed us staring at my father while you posed for your picture. If you had paid attention to people other than your whiny friends, you might have heard my brother and mother crying."

Nora hung her head, forced to imagine the horrors Rosalie recounted.

Rosalie continued, "My father worked *all* the time, at *any* job he could find. We lived in our car. One day, he came 'home' to our car and looked very sick—pale and sweaty. We were so scared. But he said everything was fine, and we should take a little drive to calm down. I was surprised we would waste our gas money on a 'little drive.' And I was *shocked* when that drive took us to Oakland City ER. Imagine: my father driving to the hospital during a heart attack."

"His MI was massive, Rosalie. Nothing could've saved him—"

"Shut up! I am not done! You did not hear us then, and you did not see us then! So, you are going to listen and see us now. Do you understand me?"

Nora nodded, her hands trembled.

Rosalie brusquely lifted Nora's chin to force eye-level contact and continued. "So, we are watching through those blue curtains, and I am trying to explain to my mother what is going on. But what do I know really? I am a child! I know that something dangerous is happening to my father, and he cannot understand what you are all *saying* and *doing* to him. No one even tries to understand what he is saying. He is so alone! And then, after he stops moving and becomes totally silent, do you know what I hear?"

Nora shook her head.

"I hear you arguing over who is in 'charge of the case' with the new intern! Over who should be 'calling the shots.' And then? Then, your happy friends come in. Jack complains that you are holding up the party and *wasting time* on my father. Lydia tells you to let my father 'go'—that he is just 'some homeless guy,' maybe an 'addict off the street' looking for pain meds. Fred says you should 'hand off' my father to the new intern—like he was a thing, a football—so you will not be 'stuck' having to 'deal with any family' later. And Cheryl? She bullies that new intern into practicing intubation on my dead father! To *practice stuffing tubes* down his throat! Spineless Carl doesn't speak up, though I see how uncomfortable he looks. And Richard—Mister Moneyman—barges in, demanding you not waste any more of the hospital's *money* on my father."

Nora said to herself as much as to Rosalie, "It sounds barbaric and cruel . . ."

"And *you*, Nora? You completely miss the big picture."

New lights flickered on in dark corners of Nora's mind—the stage continued to illuminate.

"You, the great Dr. Nora Kelly. You preside over my father's death—a miserable and lonely and undignified death! You are in charge, 'calling the shots,' setting the stage for my family's ruin. And you remain blind to every transgression on display. Blind to the torture you put my father through; blind to my family's witness of it all."

"Please understand—"

"And then . . ." Rosalie glanced at the broken wineglass in her hand. "At the height of my family's suffering, Richard says, 'Smile, everyone.' And you do. You all smile. You pose to immortalize your last precious moment together in a photograph. Well, Nora, that moment was immortalized for my family, too. But the way we have pictured it over the years is very different. And it is not a happy picture."

Nora faltered, "I can't think . . . of any right words to say. Words to explain . . . apologize for you having to carry that awful burden."

Rosalie sneered, "How empathic of you, Nora."

It was evident to Nora that she was hopelessly stuck inside an inescapable nightmare that she had unwittingly helped to conceive. She resignedly said, "I'm ready."

"Oh?" scoffed Rosalie. "You think I am going to follow your timetable and change my plans? Sorry, but you are no longer 'in charge of the case.' You no longer 'call the shots.'"

"But it just keeps getting later, Rosalie. And people are onto you. Clearly, you've been planning this elaborate revenge for so long. You might as well finish me—"

Rosalie shouted, "This is not 'revenge'! There is a huge difference between *avenging* an injustice and getting revenge. I am *avenging* my father's death and the suffering you caused! I am keeping a vow to my mother to make things right."

Feeling she had nothing to lose, Nora made a Hail Mary appeal to their old relationship. "This violence—it's not like you."

"Wrong again! And you have been given so many clues! What do I have to do to make you see?"

Rosalie's abrupt change of tone stymied Nora. *She's not only deriding me for not figuring her out. Now she's also gloating over my failure to do that.*

"You failed to see what you were doing to my father and family. You failed to diagnose what was happening to your friends right under your nose. Your ineptitude allowed so much death and destruction, Nora. So many people suffered because of your phenomenal incompetence."

Rosalie's cutting accusations struck like knives to Nora's heart. And that, of course, was their aim. Nora struggled to not fall apart, forced to consider Rosalie's claim that she could have prevented her friends' fates, if only she'd been sufficiently perceptive and smart.

"Everyone is disappointed with you, Nora; or dead, because of you."

She's right, Nora anguished. *I've been oblivious to the terror she's been inflicting. And how did I not see this capacity for evil in her?*

Rosalie menacingly waved the jagged wineglass near Nora's eyes and said, "Can you see what is happening right now?"

All Nora could do was wait for her last moment to arrive. She sought some comfort in imagining a reunion with her husband and daughter in an afterlife—even though she'd never believed in one.

But then Rosalie sat down, put her feet up on the coffee table and provoked Nora again: "You can choose to find out, like Cheryl, at your last minute. Or you can go like my father, not understanding what is killing you."

Nora's Street

Oakland

EVENING

Fergie turned her Subaru onto Nora's hillside street, a thin black ribbon of tar-topped road. Winston said, "Man, you'd never catch me living up here. I can barely see the roads. And they're so narrow—our car barely gets through! In a fire or an earthquake, how would people escape?"

"Win, I'm freakin' nervous enough if you don't mind!" Fergie said. "You always bring up the scariest scenarios when I need calm."

"Sorry, Fergs."

After negotiating another bend in the road, Fergie exhaled and said, "I'm sorry, too. I'm just wound up. What a shit day this has been. God, I hope Nora's okay. That she's just . . . passed out on the couch, asleep."

A moment of silence ensued. Winston said, "Remember that movie, *The Bad Seed*?"

"Aw, c'mon, Win!"

"I'm not trying to upset you."

"Really? Psychopath scenes starring Rosalie are playing in my mind, and you're reminding me about a creepy homicidal child?"

"Please listen. Because I've been thinking about Edna and Rosalie, you know, whatever story they're in? And that keeps reminding me about that old film and the relationship between the mother and her evil daughter."

Fergie swerved, ostensibly to avoid another pothole. Winston grabbed the dashboard and, eyeing her suspiciously, said, "Are you using road therapy to discharge your irritation with me?"

"No." Sigh. "Yes. Sorry. It won't happen again."

They sat in silence until Fergie relented, "All right. Go on."

"Thanks," Winston said. "Okay. So . . . Edna skipping town today? It's like the mom in that movie trying to put a stop to everything her daughter's doing, even if that includes major self-sacrifice. But she can no longer witness or be complicit with what her *murderous* daughter keeps doing—you know, *murdering people!*"

"Stop with the theatricality!"

"My bad," he apologized. "Rewind? But mom is stuck with her killer daughter because, well, because she's the mom. Likewise, Edna's stuck with evil Rosalie in a blackmail relationship—"

"Win—fair warning. I don't want to hear anything about the drowning boy or the handyman."

"Okay, sure. But, like the mom forced to witness her daughter's murders, Edna's forced to witness—maybe even facilitate?—some badass stuff Rosalie keeps doing. That escalates—gets out of control—and at some point, Rosalie crosses a line for Edna. And because Edna has a conscience—if even a flawed one—she knows she has to stop Rosalie. So, she confesses her own involvement and exposes Rosalie, essentially ending the lives they each had. And—spoiler alert!—like the mom, Edna actually survives."

"We're not in some freakin' movie, Win."

"Yeah, but maybe in life that's imitating art. I even wonder if, like in the movie, there might've been a maternal component in Edna's protecting Rosalie. Something stronger than fear of being blackmailed that allowed Edna to endure the blackmail so long. Or maybe it was more explicitly maternal—like Edna feeling that she'd somehow helped to create the monster in Rosalie."

"Why must you always put such disturbing stories and images in my head at night? And by the way, now I'm sure: we're never going to have children."

"You don't mean that."

Fergie swerved and pulled to the side of the road, a short distance from Nora's house. Winston braced himself against the dashboard and protested, "You said you weren't gonna do that—"

"Shush!" Fergie said, switching off the ignition. She pointed up the unlit road, her heart thumping in her throat. "That white car—see it? Across the street from Nora's? It's still here. It's the pizza guy's car."

Nora's Living Room

Oakland

EVENING

Rosalie saw Nora glance at family photographs on the mantle. She said, "*Your* family was destroyed by an ocean wave—a force of nature, an act of God. Mine was not. Mine suffered a man-made tragedy of *your* making."

Nora's cell rang. Rosalie withdrew it from her pocket and demanded, "Give me your PIN number! Let us see why your friends keep trying to contact you."

But Nora froze, thinking she might've heard the familiar thump of Bix leaping onto the deck. It rekindled hope that he was still alive, that she might see him one final time. Afraid to show relief, she looked stonily away, her eyes alighting on Lydia's photo against the armrest. *Can you fucking believe this, Lydia? All those miles I jogged around the lake . . . the therapy sessions with 'Frenchie' . . . all the mindfulness meditation! And it's just leaving me on my knees in this pathetic moment in my own living room!*

Despite Nora's goal to appear nonreactive, Rosalie detected a shift in her expression—a subtle but definite flicker of disburdening and release. It was sufficiently grievous to reanimate her need to restore Nora's fear and diminishment. She said, "Nora, I keep wondering why you allowed Lydia to drive home that night, when she could barely stand. And why you had remained silent for years, watching her kill herself with those drugs in broad daylight! And still, you . . ."

Those punishing words trailed off. Nora heard nothing after Rosalie said "in broad daylight"—a jarring phrase, striking a vital nerve. She stared at Rosalie, who was gesticulating, saying *something, something, something,* while she returned to the moment in which she stood in the ER, wondering the point of the security camera that observed her with such programmed indifference. She remembered the unheeded alarms and alerts. She recalled thinking then: *Someone could commit murder here in broad daylight, and no one would even notice.*

But those conditions of peril and indifference . . . *They're not confined to that moment in the hallway. I've allowed them to condition my life. Horrific things that Rosalie has been putting into play have skimmed across my radar, barely penetrating my consciousness. I didn't see her plotting vengeance. I didn't notice it destroying my friends and colleagues.*

Rosalie bemusedly said, "Hello? I can hear your creaky old neurons trying to work again. How can you even think with all that background noise?"

The mounting triumph in Rosalie's demeanor was blatant. *Some winning transition must be transpiring for her—but what is it? And what does she still wait for? Something . . . something I still can't see that must . . .*

. . . Of course!

Nora looked to Lydia's photo, feeling stupid and brilliant at once. *My god, Lydia, that's her point. She's seeking vengeance against me for not seeing what I should've seen. While her father was dying . . . Throughout all the havoc she staged in broad daylight . . . That's the morality play she's plotting for me now. That's the stage on which I'll be killed or ruined.*

But still, she waits.

"So quiet," Rosalie said. "Having trouble with your words now?"

She's taunting me, Lydia. What clue is she dangling before me? I blindly followed her stage directions, self-destructing according to her plan. I accepted my degradation and diminishment at her hands—handiwork I didn't foresee. I suffered incompetence and self-doubt that made me feel responsible for the fates of others: your death, the tragedy of Rosalie's family. I was ready to cede my reputation as a doctor. Tonight, I was prepared to cede my life. What more does she want to extract from me before her kill?

"I asked you a question, Nora. But your silence answers it."

Nora urgently reasoned: *If Rosalie is setting the stage for me to capitulate and self-destruct because of what I don't see . . . then what I don't see is actually killing me.* She desperately steeled herself and tried to adopt a dispassionate stance—a shift that resurrected the kinship she had felt with the unfeeling yet all-seeing scamera. She fixed her eyes on Rosalie with a clinical stare, and they scanned her with cool analytic detachment. They channeled observations through internal circuitry, which looped through networks of thought and reasoning, generating insight within her reawakening mind. She felt the good fire enter her again, burning away the fog in her brain, rekindling her intellect.

It infuriated Rosalie to see Nora looking at her with a steady, defiant gaze that was free of fear and defeat. *I will not allow Nora to turn the tables on our dynamic now! Not after I have so masterfully executed my moves against her. Not when I am so close to calling checkmate.* She pointed the jagged wineglass at Nora and said, "You seem to have trouble seeing the predicament you are in."

But Nora didn't flinch. She was thoroughly preoccupied, finally making connections among telling clues, and diagnosing the malignant pathology behind it all.

Lobby, Paradox Hotel

Berkeley Marina

EVENING

"Fred, you're not coming," Carl repeated. "From what you told me and what Fergie told you, there could be trouble."

Fred protested, "You're not going to Nora's alone."

Carl looked quizzically at him. "Well, without you, I *would* be going alone."

"Damn it, Carl! You can't stop me. I'll call a cab!"

Carl sighed. "I phoned Vickie. She's coming here to sit with you."

"You did *what*?"

"You really should get your hearing checked, Fred. I said—"

"Oh, hell."

"Look. I had to make a 'sensible' decision about taking Cheryl off senseless machines today. So, I'm sorry, but right now, I have no tolerance for you not even trying to be sensible about less confounding quandaries. Fred, today you were in the ER with an asthma attack that hasn't fully resolved. And tonight, you had a syncopal attack in the bar."

The lobby door opened and Vickie approached. She looked appraisingly at Fred.

Carl said, "Thanks for coming, Vickie." He nodded and exited.

Fred said, "Didn't know Carl was going to call you. If I did, I would've—"

"You look like hell," she said.

Fred stared uncertainly at her. "Well, yeah. That's where I've been."

Meanwhile, outside the hotel, Carl reasoned that, having never been to Nora's house, it made better sense to be driven there by someone familiar with the cryptic hill streets. He hailed a cab and provided Nora's address to the driver. The driver said, "No problem."

"But there is," Carl said.

"What? Sorry?"

"A problem. There is a problem."

The driver looked at Carl through the rearview mirror. "Do you want to talk about it?"

"Yes."

They proceeded onto the freeway. The driver, after waiting respectfully, said, "Sir? Your problem?"

"My friend—actually, I'm not sure I can call her that... But her name is Nora, and we think she's in trouble. We couldn't get hold of her. Another friend—well, maybe not a friend, either... Her name is Fergie, and she drove to Nora's house. She told us that the house lights were on, and a white sedan has been parked across the street all evening."

The driver sounded untroubled but curious. "Well, maybe your friend is just wanting privacy because she—"

"I want to be clear. I don't know whether she considers me a friend."

"Yeah, okay. But maybe she just has a... you know, a 'visitor' and so she is not answering calls."

"Of course, that is a possibility. But we don't want that visitor to be a murderer."

Smiling appreciatively, the driver said, "I like you, pal. Yes, you are right. A murderer would be an undesirable visitor."

"Precisely."

"So, then, what do we do if we drive to this Nora's house and find a murderer visiting her? I carry a metal bat that comes in handy often." He withdrew the bat from under his seat and held it up for Carl's view.

Carl said, "No. We will appeal to reason."

The driver laughed. "Now that's an interesting strategy to decrease Oakland's murder rate! You should propose it to the mayor—and the police chief."

"Thank you. It's refreshing to talk with another sensible human being today. My name is Carl, Carl Kluft."

"Pleased to meet you, Carl. I'm Ahmed. And no one has ever accused me of being sensible."

"I don't understand. What do you mean, *accused*?"

The driver slapped the dashboard in glee. "You, friend, are my favorite customer of the day! Of the entire week!"

"Thank you," Carl replied, smiling shyly back.

Nora's Living Room

Oakland

EVENING

In a voice so calm that it unsettled Rosalie, Nora finally replied, "Actually, I see my predicament clearly now. And you've lost."

Rosalie bolted out of the chair, slapped Nora's face and yelled, "I could kill you right *now*!"

Keeping a cool dead eye on her, Nora said, "But that would only be my physical death. In the end, you would *not* have destroyed me, though I admit you came close. You almost had me believing I was so worthless and incompetent that I deserved to die. You almost convinced me I was responsible for all the horrific things happening to people that *you* were responsible for."

"You sound so cocky," Rosalie scoffed. "Bad move."

"No. Because I finally see what you're doing. It may be under the wire, but I see now. And that means I've redeemed myself. Your vengeance has no standing target anymore. In fact, I just heard the tables turning."

"That is only your old neurons groaning while they die off."

"You tried hard to annihilate me by destroying my reputation. By taking me down at work; criticizing my teaching and patient care. Making me doubt myself so much that I felt responsible for Lydia dying. So, you think you're so smart? So smart, you could do all that to me? So smart, that you could get away with murders?"

"Your belabored point, Nora?"

"You really don't know! Then it's *you* who doesn't see and can't figure—"

Rosalie slapped Nora again, causing blood to trickle from her lip. But Nora proceeded undeterred: "I won, because I saved myself from your sick plot. I figured out how to neutralize your plan to destroy me. And, a bonus: I proved I'm smarter than you. That must really hurt."

Rosalie picked up the broken wineglass. "You are pathetic! Using Psych 101 is child's play."

Nora bulldozed through, "This is what I see now. You decided it was karma for Richard to suffer Edna's financial fraud—for him to drop dead on a stack of spreadsheets. It was your vengeful payback for him complaining about wasting hospital resources on your father. And you possessed the means and opportunity to inject him with potassium."

Rosalie laughed derisively. "No way are you getting credit for figuring that one out! It is too easy. I even kept *telling* you I killed Richard! So, it is hilarious, really, if you think that makes you smart."

"All right then: Cheryl."

"Go ahead," Rosalie said spiritedly.

Nora's face ached from Rosalie's attacks, but she was resolute about concealing the pain. She matter-of-factly replied, "Because Cheryl encouraged a new intern to practice intubation on your father—"

"No, to *shove* tubes down his throat!"

"Okay, 'to shove tubes down his throat.' So you made Cheryl suffer a procedure—one that even killed her."

Rosalie grinned. "She, how do you say it ... she 'died of her own devices.'"

Nora refused to react to the crass remark. She focused instead on steadying her nerves while absorbing Rosalie's explicit confession.

"Now, Cheryl's case was *gratifying* for me," said Rosalie. "Just before she went under anesthesia, I made sure she heard my voice. I made sure that she saw one of her precious stents and had a moment to fear it being shoved into her. And, such a shame—just like my father, she could not give consent."

Now Nora realized it was Rosalie who created the bruise on Cheryl's sternum while forcing her to experience a tortured last-minute awareness of sheer dread. But this expanding clarity also revealed greater depths of Rosalie's dissoluteness, making it harder for Nora to tame her escalating fear. She counseled herself: *Think scamera. Do not show that you're affected by what you see in her.*

Rosalie continued, "It was easy to enter and leave Cheryl's OR. I had the advantage of being invisible—and not just to you, Nora."

But you're increasingly visible to me now, Nora thought as the false images she'd held of Rosalie instantly dissolved—*Rosalie my daughter, Rosalie my protégé, Rosalie my friend, Rosalie the virtuous physician.* And through this recalibrated view, she boldly asserted, "You tried to sabotage Fred's marriage and family so he'd have no family to 'deal with.'"

"Good guess, Nora. You surprise me."

"It's no guess. I figured out how you staged that. I discovered how you stole the Polaroid from Fred's desk. And those calls to his home; they began that night at the Tavern, after you saw Fred and Lydia together. I noticed your curiosity about them. And then you somehow got hold of Fred's tavern receipt from that night, and the next day you made sure Vickie saw it."

Rosalie laughed. "*Somehow?* That is insufficient. You must explain *how* I obtained Fred's receipt."

Nora desperately searched her memory for clues . . .

"The clock is ticking, Nora. You have 10 more seconds."

It was so quiet during the standoff that Nora heard the kitchen clock tick off the seconds. Just under the deadline, she blurted out, "From the table server! That man from the kitchen! You befriended him—I saw that. He brought you wine once and . . . yes, he must've given you the receipt."

"Ah, no. You must tell me his name."

"I . . . I don't know his name."

"His *name*, Nora!"

Nora shook her head.

"You have been going to the Tavern for—what?—hundreds of years? And this man *hobbles* to your table every night to serve bread and water to you and your friends. Still, you do not know his name?"

Silence.

"Victor!" Rosalie shouted. "The man's name is Victor!"

Nora tried to regather her wits and, at least, reset the combat to match point. She risked, "Then, Jack, because he said time was being wasted on your father, now his time—his entire life—is being wasted in prison. And you . . . you blackmailed Edna into giving him up to make that happen."

Rosalie turned restless, walked to the mantle and knocked over Nora's family portraits. "It is getting late," she said. "Still, you have some time. Want to try someone else? Carl, maybe?"

Nora conjured up Lydia's chutzpah and said, "That's too easy."

But her bravura merely reignited Rosalie's rage. Rosalie picked up the fireplace poker and swung it at Nora, barely missing her head. She seethed, "I told you: do not test my patience!"

But Nora stood up to her and said, "You knew it was killing Carl—his inability to logically interpret Cheryl's brain death. Still, you badgered him into giving away her organs. You diminished him when he couldn't speak up for someone who never once in her life allowed him to speak for her."

Grinning smugly, Rosalie said, "I am curious why we did not first discuss your friend, Lydia. Such a tragedy that she died. Such a horrible *accident*. I wonder what happened."

Rosalie's malevolent insincerity destabilized Nora's fragile equilibrium. Nora acutely feared that she'd break down and lose control if she tried to speak.

After a brittle silence, Rosalie shrugged and said, "Of course, that one is difficult for you. But me? I think Lydia died as one might expect of a worthless addict." She shoved Nora back onto the sofa, returned to her chair, picked up a slice of pizza, and complained, "Not enough peppers."

Nora froze in fear of Rosalie's arctic nonchalance and brutality. She doubted her stamina to continue the intensifying battle that Rosalie continued to wage. It was proving impossible to mount an exit strategy, given the constantly shifting battlefield and the treacherous terrain of Rosalie's unstable mindset. Every tactic had ultimately failed to win redemption and release: truth, apology, supplication, empathy, explanation, surrender, saving intellect. *It's come to this end . . . a brilliant young doctor with immortal wounds that can never be healed, and which everyone must suffer.* She stared at Rosalie and wondered: *Did I actually make things worse by solving her clues and injuring her pride? Was it a mistake to try to claw out of the grave she had prepared for me, making myself vulnerable to her brutal improvisations?*

Rosalie whispered, "Creak! Creak!"

Still, she is fucking waiting for something. Something that remains in play and at stake. Then there's a chance for me yet!

"I am sorry I broke your wineglass, Nora. Your mind could use some lubrication."

When Nora looked down at her bruising shin, blood dropped from her lip and onto her lap. She reflexively determined the suture material and number of stitches her lip would require. She instinctively reviewed the standardized assessment of traumatic wounds in the ER ... *location, severity, vascularity, hygiene ... last tetanus booster ... the extent of internal and external bleeding ... if a GSW or projectile injury, searching for an exit wound ...*

"Search for an exit wound."

To make the truly saving diagnosis and survive the acute peril, Nora realized she had to look more deeply to find the exit wound.

"Nora, I am getting tired of our game."

Nora lamely said, "You're throwing away everything you've accomplished—for yourself, and in your mother's name. You could still do great things in the world. And you could balance your scale of justice in more defensible ways."

Sounding bored, Rosalie replied, "Well, I once believed that, too. When I first came to Oakland City—the scene of the crime, yes?—I was going to do many 'great things' as a doctor. And I was going to right a wrong by making sure that my patients—regardless of their skin color, poverty, language—they would never suffer what happened to my father and family. They would get the best care, regardless."

"But that's how I felt when I took care of your father!"

Rosalie shouted, "*You* are not entitled to appropriate *my* feelings!"

Anxiously watching Rosalie pace, Nora gambled, "But then, every day at the hospital, you kept seeing the people who were in your father's room that day." She pointed to her old group photo. "Every day, you saw us working there, getting on with our lives, seeming unaffected by what you and your family went through."

Rosalie leaned close and said, "The only way I could get by ..." She took a deep breath. "I would create scenarios in my mind to punish each of you for what you did—little morality plays. I would make them up in the middle of the night. And, during the day at work, I imagined enacting them whenever I saw one of your smiling faces."

Nora's heart pounded so rapidly it felt like one long contiguous beat. But now she knew she was getting closer to the exit wound.

"My execution was not always perfect," Rosalie said. "Obstacles kept popping up. Situations changed. Sometimes new opportunities arose out of nowhere. So, I had to improvise sometimes. Fortunately, I had prefigured so many backup scenarios in my mind during all those years. I think you call that a 'prepared mind.'"

It's appalling, Nora thought, *to feel anything other than loathing toward this monster!* Still, she couldn't deny the revolting sympathy she was feeling toward Rosalie now. Rosalie, who was destroying herself with the same vengeance-seeking hands that she'd used to destroy others. With disgust toward herself and, in equal measure, with Rosalie, she blurted out: "But you *staged* murders and *actually killed people!* You *intentionally* destroyed lives! Your father's death was never anyone's *intention*; never anyone's *desire!*"

Rosalie swiped the broken wineglass perilously close to Nora's eyes and shouted, "Well, I had to move my *theory* of justice to a *real* stage! Because I did not have your same privileges! I did not have the same access to justice as you! I did not have powerful friends in powerful positions who even cared about people like me!"

Nora was afraid to breathe, move, tremble. She watched Rosalie walk to the lamp and turn it off. Sepia-tinged light lingered and dimly illuminated the room. Rosalie said, "Now the final act, Nora."

Outside Nora's Home

Oakland

EVENING

A bat-wielding man appeared at the windshield and Fergie screamed. A split second later, Carl appeared, a finger to his lips urging silence.

"Holy shit!" said Winston, embracing Fergie, calming her down. "It's just Carl and . . . I don't know. Someone."

Fergie got out of the car and complained, "You scared the hell out of me, Carl!"

Carl replied, "But I heard Fred telling you over the phone that we were coming. *And* that we needed to be quiet. You can't scream, Fergie."

Winston whispered to her, "Please, don't start with him. Not now." He nodded to the stranger and asked, "Who's your friend, Carl?"

Ahmed preempted a complex response from Carl with, "I'm Ahmed, the taxi driver, and I have this bat."

Fergie pointed up the road and said, "That white sedan belongs to the pizza delivery guy."

Tapping his bat against his boot, Ahmed asked, "Did you see his face? See him enter or leave the house?"

Fergie looked shamefaced. "No. When I drove away, Nora was on the porch, and the guy was coming up behind her."

"Look," Winston said, "Fergs feels bad enough. She said she saw some guy with a pizza box. Someone as tall as Nora. Slim. It was hard to see, right, Fergs?"

Fergie nodded. "Still, I should've waited and watched him leave before I drove away. I feel sick."

Carl said, "Fergie, I'm sorry you don't feel well. There is a norovirus going around. But let's talk about that later, please. Right now, we should focus on Nora's safety." His three companions exchanged knowing looks, and Fergie just said, "Sure."

Ahmed said to Carl, "My friend, you are making very good sense again."

Carl smiled and said, "Ahmed and I are going to check out the white sedan. You two stay here. And Fergie, make sure your cellphone is charged and prepared to call Nora and Rosalie."

Part V

Final Acts

FEBRUARY 16

Nora's Home

Oakland

EVENING

ROSALIE CHECKED THE TIME. "It will not be much longer for you, Nora."

Nora racked her brain, recalling the day with Rosalie's father, searching for the penultimate clue to the fatal finale of this morality play. *Rosalie has been taunting me all along, claiming she's given me the clues. She's punished me for guessing them, and punished me for not. I've postponed my annihilation, yet still not won redemption.*

She stared dully at the mantle, the lamp, the crumpled group photo, and the broken phone on the floor. They were fast becoming remote and otherworldly as she mentally prepared for her exile from life. To allay the expected agony, she visualized being taken out by the same ocean wave that had claimed her daughter and husband. *With them is where I want to be located forever—not inside some urn or grave.* Experiencing this internal momentum transporting her to an afterlife, Nora finally moved free of that awful moment on the beach with Jack—

Jack.

Nora gasped, and that saving breath delivered her solidly back to her life. She had located the exit wound. Looking clear-eyed at Rosalie, she said, "Jack had a visit from Edna today."

Visibly rankled, Rosalie said, "What did you say?"

"And Edna confessed *everything* to him."

Grabbing the fireplace poker like a shiv, Rosalie yelled, "You are lying!"

"No. Edna admitted to pharmacy and medical records fraud, and to selling prescription narcotics. To framing Jack."

A sneer skimmed across Rosalie's face.

Nora took another reviving breath. "She confessed to everything you've been blackmailing her with."

Rosalie's body stiffened.

"What's especially intriguing: Edna never mentioned you, Rosalie. She incriminated only herself. She didn't give you up."

Rosalie whacked Nora's arm with the poker. And though the pain was swift and excruciating, Nora knew she was close to the grim central truth of Rosalie's mindset. She struggled to say, "You almost got away with murder . . . in broad daylight. But then you publicly revealed that you knew about Edna's crimes . . . that you were even holding onto evidence. You only incriminated yourself."

"Where the fuck is Edna?"

"I don't know."

Rosalie slammed the poker against Nora's leg and yelled, "Liar!"

Nora moaned. "But it's true. Edna fled after visiting Jack. The police are out looking for her."

Rosalie stood rigid before Nora, storms brewing behind her eyes. "She planted my brooch in Cheryl's office, Nora. So, do *not* pretend she intended to *protect* me."

Silence.

"Say something, Nora!"

Nora pressed her leg against the sofa to staunch the bleeding. "Edna may have planted your caduceus, but as evidence against herself, as well as you. That's why she brought Lizbeth with her—to witness it. She trusted Lizbeth to speak up."

Rosalie kicked the remnants of the phone across the living room.

"And it's doubly funny," Nora said, "because, knowing Edna, I think she was also providing you a chance to escape. You could have fled, too, once you heard that your caduceus was 'found.' Instead, you chose to stay and try to ruin Edna."

"You make no sense! I told you to have your TBI checked out!"

Nora defended against Rosalie's enduring intimidation, thinking: *It does seem more logical that Edna would retaliate against Rosalie, given the blackmail and hostilities between them. And yet, I'm shocked by my own feelings of sympathy toward Rosalie tonight. Depending on your frame of view . . .*

Of course!

Edna's view of Rosalie . . .

Nora steeled herself and said, "Edna was the only one who really noticed you when your father was dying. And when she discovered you watching, you saw her pained expression mirroring yours."

Rosalie's jaw clenched, and her grasp tightened on the poker.

Nora stood up, despite severe pain in her leg. She locked eyes with Rosalie and continued: "So years later, when you began residency at the hospital and stumbled upon Edna's drug schemes, you gave her a pass. You reminded her about that day in the ER, and how she'd been the only person to notice you suffering. You promised her, in gratitude, that you wouldn't report her."

"Everyone will appreciate and understand that when they hear what I—"

"No," Nora interrupted. "Because then you lorded your silence over Edna. You made her pay for it, and you kept raising the price. You coerced her into helping you bring your so-called theory of justice to a 'real stage.' *That's* why your vengeance began with Jack and Richard—it was convenient to stage their fates as extensions of Edna's drug and financial crimes."

Rosalie scoffed. "Me and Edna: Bonnie and Clyde."

"Well, Edna may have helped you set Richard up on financial fraud. And she may have helped you frame Jack with the documents she tampered with. But, when she began to wonder whether you could have *murdered* Richard, and when she realized Lydia's death involved drugs that you'd forced her to supply, you crossed the line, and Edna couldn't tolerate your blackmail any longer. She couldn't tolerate knowing how complicit she'd been in creating the monster in you."

Rosalie shoved Nora back onto the sofa and said, "You are boring me."

"But you haven't heard the punchline, Rosalie. For Edna, it was worth confessing her crimes and abandoning her career and pension to be freed of your power over her. So, see: it's not just that she figured you out and didn't give you up. She also stayed steps ahead of you and *escaped*. *You* blew it, Rosalie. *You* became a major victim of your own grand morality tale!"

"Fuck you," Rosalie said. "And time is up." She opened the doors to the deck and said, "Come in." A shadowy figure entered the room.

Outside Nora's house, Winston and Fergie waited for Carl's and Ahmed's return. Winston said, "I wish we could think of some compelling reason to get the cops out here now."

Fergie said, "They don't come to the hills unless you're feeding them live video of your murder."

He grimaced. "Now who's creating scary scenarios?"

She aimed to plant a kiss on his cheek, but instead was startled to see two figures approaching behind him.

Reflexively shielding Fergie, Winston turned to find Fred and Vickie. "Fergs," he said, "it's only hospital people."

"Hi," Vickie said. "I couldn't keep Fred settled down at the hotel. He told me what's going on. And he didn't think it right for you two and Carl to be out here alone."

Fred, huffing and wheezing, said, "Had to leave our car down the road, behind some taxi blocking the street."

Fergie, still shaken, explained, "That's the taxi Carl came in, and it's blocking the road on purpose."

Winston pointed up the road. "The other end is a cul-de-sac. We're trying to barricade that white sedan."

"Is that the pizza delivery car you mentioned over the phone?" asked Fred.

"Yeah," Fergie replied. "Carl's there now, checking it out with Ahmed, the taxi driver."

"Have you seen any sign of Nora?" Vickie asked.

"No," Fergie said. "We haven't tried to go in because . . . we don't know anything about this guy."

Carl and Ahmed returned. Carl said disapprovingly to Fred, "Obviously, I wasted time arguing against you coming here." He smiled at Vickie and said, "Hello." He then reported to the group: "In the back seat of the white sedan are (A), two suitcases (B), 12 bottles of water, and (C), three shopping bags filled with food. The car doors are locked."

"And," said Ahmed, nodding amiably to Carl, "I and my friend here observed no pizza boxes or delivery items inside the car. And the outside of the car has no pizza advertising!"

Carl returned a companionable nod and said, "So *we* think—"

"Look!" Fred exclaimed, pointing toward Nora's house. "Someone's on Nora's deck."

Vickie whispered, "And he's going inside the house."

"My god," Fergie said, straining to see. "I think ... no, I'm sure! That's the pizza guy!"

"Time to act," Carl said. He thumbs-upped to Ahmed, who dutifully stole toward Nora's front door, bat in hand. Carl turned to Winston and Fergie and said, "Remember: our base camp is under Nora's deck. Fergie, make sure your cellphone is ready. And wait until I get to the kitchen window and give you the signal to call."

Fred asked, "What about Vickie and me?"

Carl said, "But you seem to have trouble following directions, Fred."

"Damn it, now—"

"Okay," Carl said. "Immediately after Fergie makes her two calls, one of you phones Nora while the other phones Rosalie at the same time."

Fred asked, "At exactly the same time?"

Trying to remain patient, Carl said, "Fred, the 'same' time and 'exactly the same' time are the *same*." He sprinted toward Nora's kitchen window.

"He's right, Fred," Vickie said, heading toward the deck to join Fergie and Winston.

Nora froze when a wiry young man entered the living room in response to Rosalie's invitation. She stammered, "But you ... you're the guy who delivered the pizza."

He rolled his eyes and complained, "It was getting cold out there, Ro. What took you so long to decide?" He headed for the pizza and wine on the coffee table. All the while he ate, sitting on the floor, he dispassionately eyed Nora. Finally, he asked Rosalie, "So, this is *her*?"

Rosalie affectionately stroked his back. "Yes. She is our *last* one. The big one." She handed him a napkin and said, "I will get you a fresh bottle of wine."

"Thanks," he said, and Rosalie headed to the kitchen.

Nora's despair violently resurrected. This man, whoever he was, was not in the picture a moment ago. Everything was overturned again.

Grinning mischievously, he told Nora, "When I picked up this pie at Delmonico's for you, I told them to add lots of peppers and onions. Hope you like my taste."

Rosalie returned with a bottle and two glasses, in time to overhear Nora say, "You're . . . you're no delivery man."

He and Rosalie laughed. Then Rosalie said, "Ah, Nora. See? You did not win after all!"

Stunned, Nora thought: *I'm such an idiot! He must've unlocked my door or wedged it open on his way out the foyer. That's how they snuck in later.*

Rosalie said, "Nora? You are so quiet suddenly. Maybe you feel self-conscious in front of this fine young man?"

The only thing on Nora's mind: singing with Lydia, *Que será, será* . . .

Rosalie tapped the man's shoulder and said, "Show her your arms."

"Don't want to."

"Show her your tracks! Show her what she and her friends did to you!"

Nora's mind reeled back to the horrifying present while the man pulled up his shirtsleeves, revealing knotted roadmaps of old track marks and fresh injection sites covering his arms. "No," she whispered, "it can't be." But she knew otherwise. It was obvious now—the resemblance to Rosalie was telling; the intimacy between them palpable.

"And show her your legs, and your feet," Rosalie said.

Nora said, "But . . . I thought your brother was dead."

Rosalie and her brother stared incredulously at Nora. "Ro," he said, "you sure this is the know-it-all who was in charge of dad's care? Because, wow . . . she's pretty thick."

Rosalie shrugged. "I told you, Ricky. She misses the important stuff. You have to explain everything to her." She said to Nora, "I told you I *lost* my family. After our father died in your hands, surrounded by all your happy friends . . . every night, our mother had nightmares of what she saw. And she worked herself to death, trying to take care of us alone. So, Nora, what chance at life do you think my little brother had after you took our parents from us?" Getting no response, she kicked Nora's injured leg and said, "I cannot hear you!"

Fearing additional attacks, Nora said, "It must've been hard. Extremely hard."

Ricky sneered, and Rosalie said, "You don't know 'hard,' Nora. Apparently, I must explain again. The day our father died, after you and your friends left for your party, well, when *we* left the ER, we could not even get our car out of the hospital parking lot. Our mother did not drive, and the two of us were too young. But that car was our only home. And a couple of days later, they towed it away somewhere. We could not get it back."

Ricky stood up and said, "Come on, Ro. You gave this woman her chance. God knows, you took long enough for it. But we should go. It's getting late. I don't want to miss our train."

Nora's cellphone rang. Rosalie withdrew it from her back pocket and held up a hand, signaling her brother to wait. "Nora," she said, "it's Fergie again." But the call abruptly ended in a hang-up. "Fuck this," Rosalie said, tossing Nora's cell to the floor.

Ricky raised a foot, ready to stomp on Nora's cell. But now Rosalie's phone rang. "That's weird," he said, "both your phones ringing."

Rosalie's eyes widened. "Mine is from Fergie, too." It also abruptly ended.

"Who the fuck is Fergie?" Ricky demanded.

"A nurse. A friend of Nora's from the hospital."

"That's too weird, Ro! Does this Fergie person know you're both here?"

"No!"

Nora was equally perplexed by Fergie's paired calls. And given the day's grueling events, why would Fergie initiate any contact with Rosalie, especially at this late hour when she is supposed to be with Winston?

"Well, is this Fergie a friend of yours, too?" Ricky asked.

Rosalie shook her head. "It is probably nothing. A dialing mistake."

But then a muffled voice sounded nearby. Ricky pointed to the kitchen and whispered, "There!" But when Rosalie ran into the kitchen, she found no one. She returned to the living room and demanded of Nora, "Who was that?"

Nora wasn't even sure that the vocalization was human. And, as indistinct as it was, on a human scale it most sounded like Carl Kluft's. And that was improbable. So improbable, she thought: *If it's insane to hear voices, it's got to be doubly insane to hear them sounding like Carl.* Nora responded, "I didn't hear anything."

"Well, I heard something, Ro! I mean . . . well, it could've been an animal. There's lots of them up here." He looked sympathetically at his sister and said, "Come on—you're almost done with what you needed to do." He handed his wineglass to her and said, "Take a few sips—you're getting jumpy. But let's just finish what we came here to—"

But now, Nora's cell rang simultaneously with Rosalie's. Ricky grabbed Nora's from the floor and handed it to Rosalie who stared dumbfounded at the two phones. Vickie Williams was calling on Nora's, and Fred was calling on hers.

"Who the fuck are *they?*" Ricky panicked.

Frantic, Rosalie turned to Nora and said, "Why are Fred and his wife calling like this?"

"I don't know," Nora said. *In fact*, she thought, *it's hard to imagine those two coordinating any kind of communication.*

"Something's up, Ro," Ricky said. "That's four weird calls to the two of you!"

Nora tried to silence the apocalyptic demons screaming inside her head while Rosalie and her brother argued. She thought, *Those four calls, so coordinated and regimented, signal intention and strategy. Fergie calling serially on our two phones, connecting Rosalie and me. Then Fred and Vickie calling simultaneously. My friends must be together . . . signaling . . . they know I'm with Rosalie! They're looking for me! It is so . . . so logical. It is so . . . My god! It is so Carl Kluft!*

Carl moved swiftly from Nora's kitchen window to the hillside slope under the deck where Fergie, Winston, Vickie, and Fred huddled. He reported to Fergie, "I heard their phones sequentially ring in response to your calls. So, we know that Rosalie's inside with Nora." Turning to Fred, he said, "You and I were right about Rosalie."

"But I'm positive," Fergie said. "It was a *guy* who delivered the pizza! The *same* guy on the deck who went inside. And his car is still—"

"Fergie," Carl said, "you are correct as well." Nodding to Fred and Vickie, he continued, "Because I saw a second figure through the kitchen window, and I heard *him* curse when *your* calls rattled them." Turning back to Fergie, he said, "So, that must be your 'pizza guy,' though I seriously doubt he's a legitimate pizza worker."

"What about Nora?" Fred asked. "Did you see her? Hear her?"

"No," Carl said. "But now we have compelling reasons for the police to come quick."

Fergie said, "I'll call the detective who gave me her card last week."

"Good," Carl said. "And I'll signal Ahmed to leave his station at Nora's door and go back to man—oh, forgive me, ladies—*to take possession of his taxi.* He'll let the police pass when they arrive." He flashed his penlight three times, and Ahmed approached. The two men exchanged a thumbs-up, and Ahmed handed his bat to Carl before heading to his taxi.

Winston said, "But the police could take forever to respond. Maybe Nora's in danger now."

Everyone looked anxiously at one another.

Vickie said, "Wait. That sedan is packed with luggage and supplies, right? So, Rosalie and this man must be planning to go somewhere after doing . . . doing whatever they intend. So, they're still inside the house—"

"Let's barge in now, *before* they hurt her!" Fred insisted.

"No!" Vickie countered. "Just the opposite."

"She's right," Fergie said. "That psychopath Rosalie and that guy . . . we have no idea what they might do to Nora if they were ambushed."

Winston agreed, "Besides, they might have weapons. All we have is Ahmed's bat."

Carl calmly interjected, "And *reason.* We have reason on our side."

Among the group, a chain reaction of jaw-dropping ensued. Vickie said, "Carl, some people can't be reasoned with. And this is a pretty dangerous situation to be so idealistic—"

"Forgive me for interrupting," Carl whispered. "But I know where you're going with this. What I mean is that we"—he made a circle with his finger, including everyone—"*we* have reason on *our* side. And we must use it."

Not waiting for the customary pause, Fred asked, "Do you have a suggestion, Carl?"

"Yes."

"For god's sake, Carl! What is it?" Fred blurted out.

Carl admonished him, "Well, first, we must stay calm. And you are overusing your inhalers and getting jittery from that." Then, addressing the group, he said, "We don't know the man who is with Rosalie. But, clearly, they are working together as a *unit*. I know a lot about that." His memory flashed on scenes in Cheryl's room this afternoon: machines being disconnected, tubes withdrawn, monitors silenced, his hand resting on her motionless body. The same hand now holding a metal bat. He continued, "Rosalie and pizza man went inside together. They're clearly planning to escape together. They're up to no good together, and they're bound together in a singular mission. So, if we can separate and disrupt them, we destroy *who they are*—both as a unit and as individuals. In the process, we interrupt their mission and their plans for Nora. Under threat, they'll prioritize looking out for one another over any other pursuit."

Fergie worriedly said, "Well, how are we supposed to separate them?"

Fred and Carl turned to one another and smiled. Fred said, "Finally— an easy logic puzzle for me! You game, Carl?"

"Of course," Carl said.

Fred grabbed Ahmed's bat and ran down the hill toward the street, Carl following close behind.

Inside the house, Rosalie fumed, "Tell me, Nora! Why are these people calling?" She answered Nora's silence with a wicked slap to her face.

Nora moaned, the gash in her lip widened, the blood dripped freely. She fell against the armrest and saw Rosalie pick up the poker.

A car alarm blared.

Ricky rushed to a street-facing window and shouted, "Fuck! It's my car!" He returned to the living room and said, "Damn it, Ro! It's got all our stuff in it. Let's go!" He handed his hunting knife to her.

"Calm down!" she said. "Someone probably just bumped your car. The roads here are so damn narrow."

"Even so," he said, "I don't want neighbors calling the cops because of the alarm." He rushed toward the foyer, ignoring Rosalie's objections.

The front door slammed. Nora was alone with Rosalie.

Ricky arrived breathless at his car. After scanning the perimeter for lurking threats, he unlocked the door and disabled the alarm. The passenger's window had been shattered, and its glass was strewn across the front seat. "Fuck!" he cursed, taking in this added inconvenience to their getaway tonight. He circled the car, inspecting for further damages. And, suddenly, it hit him—their suitcases and shopping bags remained in the backseat. The glove compartment remained closed. Even the coin box wasn't—

"Hello, Ricky."

A woman's low, throaty greeting startled him. Before he could turn toward it, he heard it again: "Hands up!" Then, reflected in the car window, he saw people standing behind him. "Turn around slowly," the woman commanded. "You know the drill. And I got my gun out, okay?"

Ricky Karlov's hope to escape his tattered life vanished instantly. He glanced across the street, to the house in which his sister awaited his return, his assistance, his repayment for the million favors she'd granted him throughout his life. All the bailouts. The numerous rehab stints. The many nights spent on her couch. All the sacrifices she made for him after their parents died. And now, with guns aimed at him, he was being held back from delivering on the one thing he'd promised her in return: to help her attain the justice she sought in order to be free of their ruinous past.

He turned to face several officers with their handguns drawn. One approached with a set of cuffs. The policewoman said, "Remember me, Ricky?"

"Detective Johnson," he said.

"Looks like you got yourself into a whole new kind of mess," she said.

Her partner, Detective Burka, peered appraisingly into the sedan. "Going somewhere, Ricky? Got a little vacation coming up?"

But Ricky didn't hear them. He was completely focused on the terrible calculation he had to make before his fleeting opportunity passed. He knew that, no matter what he decided, the police would track his sister to the house. Still, if he could just delay them a little, he might provide her the time she needed to complete her mission. And if he caused sufficient commotion in the process, he might even alert her to escape! He lunged toward Detective Johnson, screaming.

With each passing second after the car alarm silenced, Rosalie's anxiety about her brother escalated. She could think of nothing other than his safety and whereabouts. *Why has he not returned?* She envisioned him as she always had: a frail young boy, looking to her for answers about their puzzling predicament. For a way out of their misery. For reasons why they had no food, no home, no parents, no place to sleep.

When the gunshot sounded, Rosalie instantaneously fell apart. Fragments of her mind and heart and soul dropped into a void.

A knock on the front door repeated before she consciously registered it. And then she heard her brother's voice: "Ro, help me."

That familiar refrain roused her back to awareness, to relief, to joy. And yanked back into life and purpose, she ran to the front door and flung it open. Ricky was there! But . . . his hands were cuffed, a bloodied bandage covered his arm, and he was surrounded by police who immediately encircled her. Ricky looked up to her in the old way and asked, "Ro, what are we going to do now?"

Carl ignored police orders to step away. He forged a path through the official commotion, insisting it made no sense to keep him from Nora. "You now have the culprits in custody," he asserted, "and the victim may need a doctor." He entered the house and saw Nora who sat trembling on the sofa. "Hello, Nora," he said.

Nora let down when she saw him. Tears of gratitude and release flooded her heart, blurred her vision, drenched her face. She stood up weakly and threw her arms around him. "Carl," she kept repeating.

Carl tried to reciprocate the embrace, which felt over-long from its inception. Intending to limit it with a polite but distracting comment, he said, "Your house looks nice. I've never seen it before." But that only made Nora cry harder, her embrace tighten.

An OakCity ambulance siren whirred. Police car lights pulsed through the doors to Nora's deck. And Nora, glancing over Carl's shoulder, saw Bix cowering under a deck chair, his face pressed against the glass.

Handcuffed and bookended by police, Rosalie was surprised to experience any solace in her capture. But as she stood in Nora's yard and watched her brother being ushered into a police van, she felt acutely disburdened. Suddenly, she was no longer responsible for her hapless brother; no longer the custodian of his perpetual needs. She was liberated from his painful and insoluble questions. And, it was a perverse relief—she understood that—but now she would also keep her vow to her mother, that neither she nor Ricky would live life inside a car.

And there were so many people here at Nora's, investigating and asking questions—the police, neighbors with cellphones, and TV crews and *reporters!* Yes! Her quest for justice might actually receive its due attention on a huge public stage, a scale not possible had she merely escaped with Ricky tonight to live a fugitive life on the road. And how wonderfully ironic that Nora survived her fate! *The media will descend upon Nora, and she will have to tell my story! Millions of people will hear it, and the righteous ones will support my views!*

Rosalie gasped when she saw Nora step onto the porch, holding Bix, surrounded by Fergie, Carl, and Fred. "Nora!" she reflexively called out, brimming with relief and anticipation.

But it was Fergie who walked up to her. And with a cold disparaging look, she declared, "Show's over, Rosalie." She told the attendant police, "The victim wants to talk with this woman."

The police refused, but Detective Johnson intervened and granted permission. Fergie nodded to Nora who handed Bix to Carl and began limping down the stairs.

Rosalie watched in awe as Nora walked slowly but steadily toward her. The closer Nora approached, the closer Rosalie felt to the moment when her story would be told.

Nora stopped mere inches away and stared unflinchingly at Rosalie. All her bright projections onto Rosalie dimmed, the shiny identities extinguished. Against an expanding darkness, Rosalie became excruciatingly visible.

Taking a deep breath, Nora thought: *It's not only that she's always felt invisible. She's also never really been seen.* Then, aiming a penetrating look at Rosalie, she said, "You were right. I didn't see you. Not when you were nine, between the blue curtains. Not for years, behind all your beautiful facades at the hospital. Not even while you were committing murder in broad daylight."

Pierced by Nora's penetrating gaze, Rosalie shuddered. It felt so intimate—Nora seeing what had never been seen inside her before. My god, how thrilling! The exhilaration was almost unbearable! And suffused with triumph, Rosalie's expression turned radiant. She smiled at Nora and began to—

"Seen," Nora said, turning away.

As Nora walked back to her house, she again saw her own internal demons, discovered through her epic struggles with Rosalie. But she could view them now in the sympathetic light that she'd extended earlier to Rosalie. Stepping onto the porch, into the arms of her anxiously watching friends, she felt she might be able to forgive herself one day.

Epilogue

FEBRUARY 17

Mountain View Cemetery

Oakland

AFTERNOON

"A LITTLE CLOUDINESS—perfect for a day like today," Fred said.

"Yep," Nora agreed. "Not too bright. Not too dark."

They continued their walk through Mountain View Cemetery, having just laid a winter bouquet on Richard's grave. The air was moist and cool, a salve for Nora's bruised lips and limbs. While passing the burial plot for Civil War veterans, she said, "So, speaking of civil wars?"

Fred put an arm around her and smiled. "Yeah. Vickie agreed to take me back in. But it'll be an upstairs-downstairs arrangement for now."

"Still, I'm glad to hear it," Nora said. "My god, last night I was as surprised to see you two together as I was by *anything* else!"

"Don't I know!" Fred laughed.

They proceeded on a gravel-strewn path that wound circuitously up a hillside. She said, "And, speaking of living arrangements. Last night, while we were all waiting for the police to leave, Fergie casually mentioned something about apartment-hunting. So, Carl said it just made sense that she and Winston move in with him. Or, to quote him precisely, into his extra '2,118 square feet of living space.'"

"Really? Now, that's an interesting trio. But I'd be the first to admit I may be the least qualified person to predict which relationships work."

"It's funny . . . these last few days, Carl didn't seem like the old Carl I'd known forever. Or, I guess, that I *incorrectly* knew forever. I actually like him, Fred. Not that I disliked him before, but—"

"Stop. I know what you mean. It's been different relating to him without . . . well, without Cheryl in-between, God rest her soul."

"He saved both of us, Fred."

"Big time."

Nora said, "I was also thinking how great it was to see how well we all worked together as a team, and under such terrifying conditions: you and me; Carl and his new bud, Ahmed; Fergie and Winston. Jack, even. The experience is reminding me of being in the trenches together when we were younger. Fighting the good fights. The important ones."

"I was thinking the same thing, Nora. Which reminds me, when you get a moment, could you make me a copy of your old gang-of-six photo? I gave mine to Carl."

Nora nodded and Fred asked, "I take it you're accepting Carl's and Ahmed's invitation to drinks at Rigby's tomorrow? Vickie and I will be going."

"How could I not go?" Nora answered, affectionately considering Carl's brave new foray into friendship. "It feels as right as anything does now to mark closing the book—or at least a chapter—on such a painful time in our lives." *And*, she thought, *I'll finally make it out to some restaurant on Piedmont Avenue.*

They continued up the stony walkway toward the hilltop where Nora scattered Lydia's ashes yesterday. The effort taxed Fred's lungs, and Nora slowed her pace to keep his company. She was finding it surreal to be reenacting such an inconceivable experience. And yet, circumstances were inviting her back to this place of repose and reflection, just as Lydia had wished for her. "Que será, será" began looping inside her head, and she made a mental note to consult finally with Google translator to determine its language of origin.

Fred said, "You've been quiet this last stretch. What are you thinking?"

Nora smiled and said, "Everything."

"Want to be more specific?"

"Okay. I was thinking about Lydia, my absentee therapist, my family, red wine all over my carpet, and never ordering from Delmonico's again. I'm thinking about Jack's prison release, and how great it will be to pal around with him again. And that it's going to be a tough year of holidays without Lydia . . ."

"You know, you're more than welcome to spend holidays with me and the family. I think Saint Pat's is up next."

Nora looked apprehensively at him.

He laughed. "You're right! I was probably hoping you'd run interference for me."

"Actually," she said, "I promised Carrie I'd spend Saint Pat's with her."

With a fearful expression on his face, he stammered, "Carrie Chandler? Lydia's twin?"

"Yes. A few weeks ago, she accepted Lydia's invitation to the annual party at her house. Carrie called this morning to tell me she was going forward with it, in honor of Lydia. In fact, it's likely she'll be moving soon into Lydia's house."

"No, no, no! Carrie coming to Oakland? This *cannot* be happening!"

"Calm down, Fred. Please don't have another asthma emergency—certainly not here, not in a cemetery."

"Nora," Fred grumbled, "she's Lydia's *identical* twin! And Carrie is like . . . like *two* Lydias put together! Her tongue's *twice* as sharp and—"

"Fred, I promise to protect you. Besides, you might need her services."

"I'm not even going to ask what you mean by that."

A smile illuminated Nora's face while she stared at her old friend. "I mean, Carrie *is* an oncologist. And she's been practicing hospice and palliative medicine for years. And, since Jack's decided to become a prison doc instead of returning to Oakland City . . . and our hospice program's in a mess . . ."

Fred shook his head. "Look, I know Carrie could whip things into shape in a millisecond. But . . . it just can't be right. I know that in my gut, Nora. And I can just imagine Vickie's face if she heard—"

"Okay," Nora said. "I shouldn't have brought it up right now. Besides, we're here. This is where I scattered Lydia's ashes yesterday. Well, most of them."

Fred held out his hand to receive the ashes that Nora withdrew from her pocket. They felt so weightless and so unbearably heavy at once. "I . . . I can't do this," he said.

"I know," Nora said. She held his trembling hand within hers, and they waited together.

CPSIA information can be obtained
at www.ICGtesting.com
Printed in the USA
FSHW01n1300011018
52659FS